STEVE HEUZINKVELD

TREADING ON ASHES

Treading On Ashes Series Book 1

Dedicated to Mel and Jarek.
Congratulations on getting engaged!

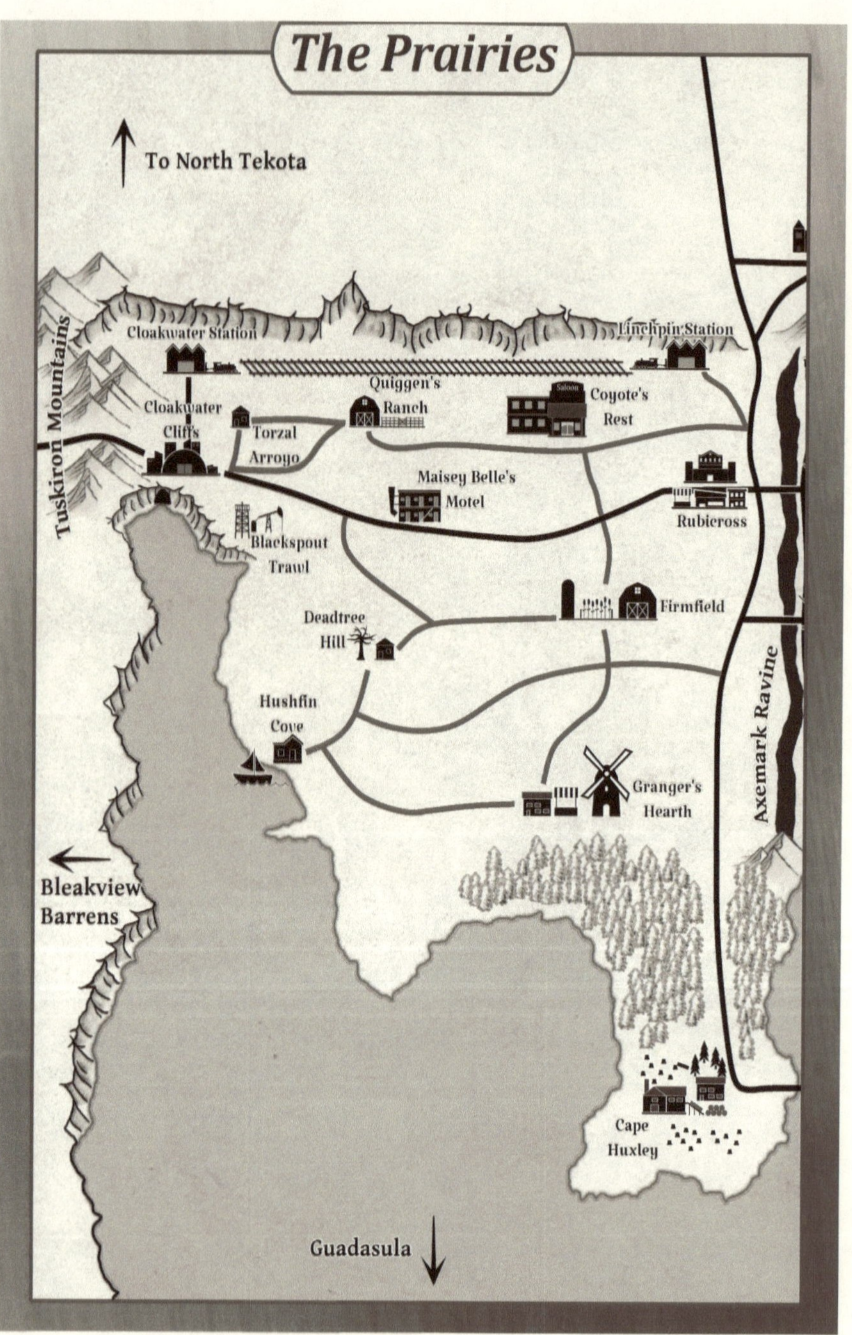

The Prairies
To North Tekota
Tuskiron Mountains
Cloakwater Station
Linchpin Station
Quiggen's Ranch
Saloon
Coyote's Rest
Cloakwater Cliffs
Torzal Arroyo
Maisey Belle's Motel
Rubicross
Blackspout Trawl
Firmfield
Deadtree Hill
Hushfin Cove
Axemark Ravine
Granger's Hearth
Bleakview Barrens
Cape Huxley
Guadasula

The Bay

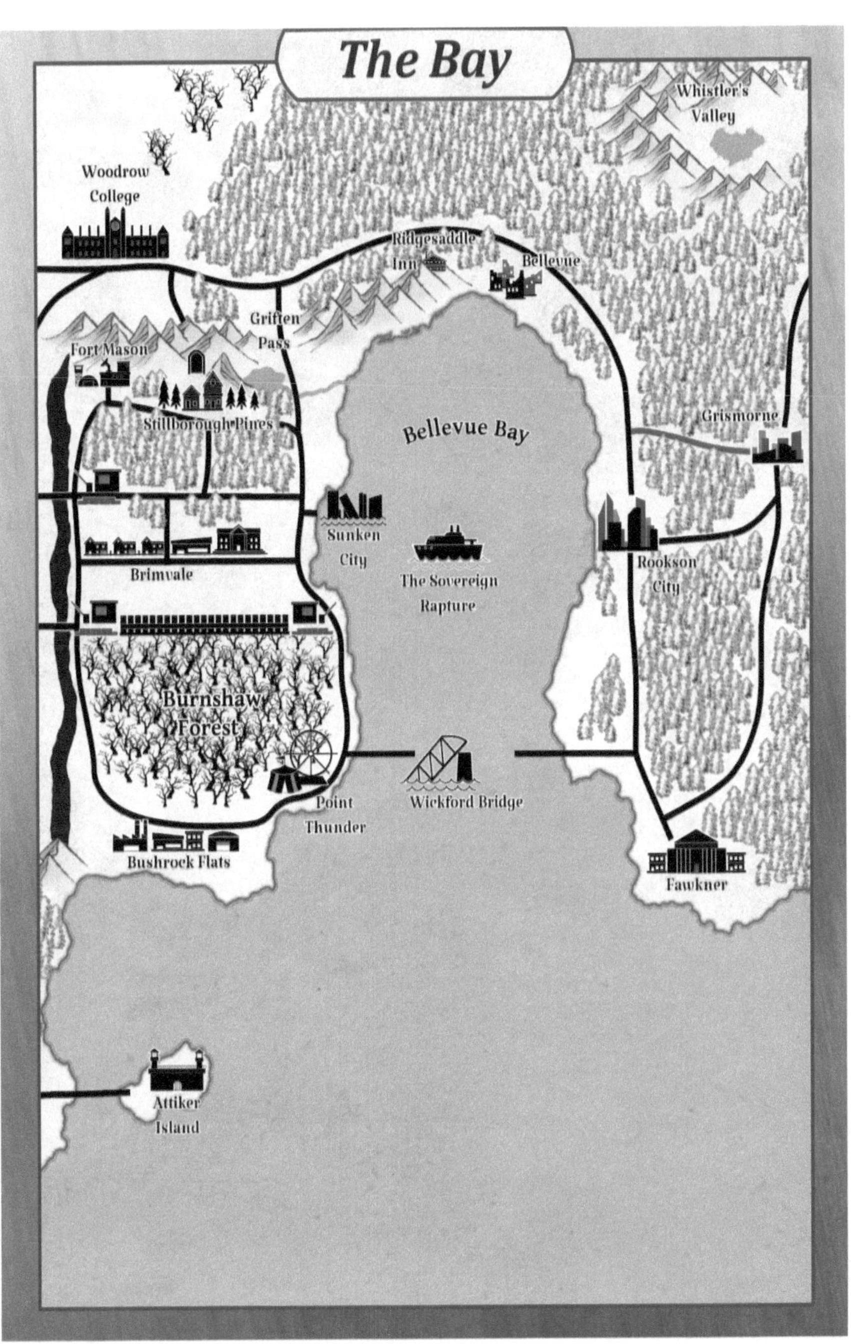

The Bay
Whistler's Valley
Woodrow College
Ridgesaddle Inn
Bellevue
Griffen Pass
Fort Mason
Grismorne
Stillborough Pines
Bellevue Bay
Sunken City
The Sovereign Rapture
Rookson City
Brimvale
Burnshaw Forest
Point Thunder
Wickford Bridge
Bushrock Flats
Fawkner
Attiker Island

PROLOGUE

Eben was hungover up to his eyeballs after another heavy night of drinking cheap vodka. Leaning against the dirt wall of the mining tunnel in his yellow hard hat and hi-vis orange overalls, he thought that he would have built up an immunity to Haydar's hooch by now, given that he had repeated the same routine every week for longer than he cared to remember.

A more sensible man would have been sitting down in the makeshift break area with the rest of the miners, telling the same old stories to the same old people while lining their stomachs with the same old greasy breakfasts; but that wasn't him, and it certainly wasn't the rest of his team, either.

They had just discovered something buried deep inside the Tuskiron Mountains. It wasn't the usual copper or iron ore veins that they normally came across though. It was something unnatural; a sheet of black metal, lined with bolts of purple that shifted and shimmered in the dim light, like a lightning storm on a moonless night. It was dense, too, whatever it was. Ken's pickaxe had struck a chunk of it hard enough for his tool's spike to bounce back and knock his hardhat to the ground.

"Oi, Eben, come give us a hand," Curt called over his shoulder in a low voice. "Before one of those fuckers up there sees what we're doin' and tries to stake a claim."

Ignoring the stomach bile bubbling in his digestive tract, Eben rejoined the team, scraping his shovel against the rock wall alongside Hal and Kristie. There were six of them in total, with Kara working farther up the tunnel, making sure that there was enough dust in the air to obscure their find.

"You think it's an asteroid?" Kristie asked through gritted teeth as they chipped at the wall.

"Either that, or a dud missile," Ken replied between grunts of exertion.

"If it was a missile, you would've lost more than your hat," Hal remarked out of the side of his mouth.

Eben dropped his shovel, his fingers scrabbling at the wall.

"Are you still fuckin' drunk?" Curt hissed at him, dust motes swirling. "Get yourself together, dickh–"

"If it's an asteroid, then explain this," said Eben, taking a step back.

The five miners huddled together, their headlamps all trained on the perfectly-cut vertical crack in the wall, their beams casting light into a shadowy chamber beyond. Kara's headlamp shone down at them from farther up the tunnel, but after a glowering glance from Curt, she quickly returned to maintaining their smokescreen.

"Ken, grab the pike," Kristie whispered, thrusting her shovel blade into the ground.

The others followed suit, taking up positions along the pike pole as Kristie guided the spike into the crevice. Ken checked that his hardhat was securely on his head this time. Using the pike as a lever, they braced and heaved to one side, almost falling over as the strange door glided open with ease. What remained of the rock wall crumbled as if a curtain had been dropped.

They waited for their eyes to adjust as the veil of dust from the tunnel swirled through the opening, but it was the smell that hit them first. With no time to react against the invisible surging cloud of stench, the festering fumes smacked them in the face like thick cold slabs of moist rancid meat. The sickly-sweet cocktail of fermented rotten eggs, diarrhoea and cheap nail polish flooded their senses.

Eben, Kristie and Ken projectile-vomited into the darkness, as if they had been gut-punched simultaneously. The pungent smell of decay filled the void as they gasped for air, forcing its way down their throats and pervading their lungs, permeating through their hi-vis overalls and clinging to their skin. Halfway up the tunnel behind them, Kara stifled a gag, dropped her shovel and fled out into the open air.

"Fuck this," Ken muttered, clapping a hand over his mouth and staggering up the passage in Kara's wake.

Pulling the neck of his soiled orange shirt over his nose, Hal ventured inside. Queasy, but curious, Curt followed. Kristie wiped her mouth and willed her legs to move. Eben leaned against the entrance, still panting and dry-heaving in moral support.

They stared around the dank gloom of the stark chamber, looking for any valuable treasures that they could pocket before the rest of the miners ventured down the shaft to investigate. Their shadows danced across the dark walls as their headlamps' beams swivelled like a light show, and a silhouette began to take form in the centre of the strange room.

Eben lifted his gaze from the inky floor to stare at the man-sized spire-like stalagmite, which he could only describe as a ribbed and veiny black tongue.

"Toss me a shovel, Eben," said Kristie, her voice echoing unnaturally, as if she was standing right next to him.

Eben plucked one of the shovels from the ground and tossed it over the threshold. She caught it, fixing her gaze on the spire as Curt and Hal stood warily on the other side of the room. Kristie prodded it with the shovel's blade. The spire turned. She gasped before choking on her sudden inhalation of the chamber's putrid gas.

"Keep turnin' it," Curt urged, his neck craning with curiosity, "There's somethin' here."

Kristie gave it another nudge, and the source of the pervading stench rotated into view. Eben retched again at the sight of it. Perched upon the obsidian skeletal throne was a rag-clad woman's emaciated shrivelled corpse. Rotten strips of slimy flesh, perhaps preserved within the sealed chamber, glistened as they hung from the decomposing carcass. The black pits of the skull's eyes seemed to stare out at them, its lower jaw suspended by a deteriorating pair of overstretched ligaments like frayed rubber bands.

"Died of a severe case of bad breath," Hal chuckled as Kristie lowered the shovel.

"This is either a tomb or a space ship," Eben said from the entrance, covering his mouth. Despite his nausea, he kept his headlamp trained on the carcass, his eyes drawn to it with a morbid fascination.

Curt snorted at the suggestion, but he didn't want to deny it either.

"No space suit," Kristie commented as she leaned on her shovel. "Hal, search the body. See if you can find something."

"Fuck that, I'm not going near that thing," he replied, taking a step back.

The sound of steel scraping leather was amplified in the strange chamber as Curt unsheathed his pocket knife, his headlamp's beam focused on a glinting green gem hanging from the corpse's necklace. As he neared the body, a console behind the throne flickered to life, a spider web of weak purple light feebly pulsing from the control panel.

Kristie bent over the console, trying to make sense of the controls to bring up an interface while Curt cut the necklace from the dead woman, standing back and holding the green gem aloft to admire it.

"It's a space ship, then," Hal concluded, striding towards the entrance. "I'm getting the fuck outta here before the doors close. Come on, Eben."

"Do you hear that?" Kristie asked no one in particular, her voice still echoing unnaturally.

"Let's go, let them figure it out," said Hal, putting an arm around Eben and guiding him back up the tunnel.

The moment their boots crunched across the dirt, Curt began yelling. They whirled around to see Kristie on top of him, pinning him to the chamber's black floor.

"Get the fuck off me, you crazy bitch!!" he managed to yell before she thrust her elbow into his windpipe, her face inches from his ear as she held his head in place with her other hand.

Curt's eyes went wide with panic and he instinctively plunged his knife into her shoulder, but she made no reaction, not even the slightest gasp of pain. Her hair obscured most of her face, but they could see her lips moving, smiling fanatically as she whispered something into his ear.

"Stop, you're gonna kill each other!!" Hal shoved Eben a few steps up the dirt passage before picking up his shovel and rushing headlong back inside the chamber. "Get off him, Kristie," he warned, giving her a few seconds to comply before he wound up for a baseball swing, arcing the flat metal blade into the small of her spine with a resounding clang.

She didn't budge.

Curt's face was turning blue, veins bulging from his forehead as he flailed his arms and arched his back in a frantically futile attempt to get out from underneath her. In a fit of desperation, he ripped his knife out from her shoulder, holding it in front of Kristie's unhinged face to show her the blade, but not even the sight of her own blood dripping from the knife's razor-sharp edge could bring her back to her senses.

Screwing his eyes shut, Curt sliced her throat open, spraying himself red.

Kristie's lips finally stopped moving, and she slid her arm from his neck.

"Fuck me..." Hal breathed, the shovel slipping out of his hands and falling to the inky floor with a hollow clatter. "Eben, get a medic down here! Now!!"

Frozen in place, Eben watched in horror as Curt and Kristie turned to face Hal, their pupils dilated, blue veins protruding from their faces. The pair shot off the floor and charged across the room before Hal had time to react, tackling him out of sight. Eben tottered back to the entrance, the sound of scuffling echoing near and far, the chamber's eerie acoustics distorting his ability to pinpoint them. His headlamp's beam darted around the room, and for a split-second, the ray of light came to rest on the corpse perched upon its black throne. The staring skull snapped its eyeless gaze at him.

Eben's feet were moving before he could think, carrying him out of the waking nightmare, knocking wheelbarrows over as he sprinted and scrambled up the shaft towards the surface, ignoring Hal's shouts for help.

Huffing and puffing, Eben staggered blindly out of the tunnel as the light of day exploded across his retina. His stomach was churning, threatening to jump out of his mouth again, but he forced himself to swallow his retches.

"What's down there?" asked Ken, waiting for him at the entrance, gearing up to brave the rotten stench again if there was something of value to be gleaned from it.

"Seal it," Eben wheezed as he stumbled towards the miners still eating underneath the canvas of the open-aired breakfast marquee, tripping over his own feet and falling to the ground. "SEAL THE TUNNEL!!"

Ken switched his headlamp back on and peered down into the tunnel's darkness, and some of the miners stood up in alarm, until a dry chuckle began to ripple through the crowd.

"Must be a hell of a hangover," Brody laughed, flecks of scrambled eggs flying from his mouth.

"I think he's still drunk!" Jarrod roared, elbowing Peggy beside him.

"Hurry, before it's too late!" Eben pleaded before hurling what remained of his stomach acid into the dirt, bringing on a fresh wave of laughter.

"There it is!" Harper called, smiling over her cup of coffee, "Let it all out."

Boots crunched towards Eben as his spit strung across the ground. Rough hands pulled him up to his feet, and suddenly he was staring into Pete's stony face.

"Listen up, asshole," Pete menaced, Eben turning away from the foreman's hot breath. "I don't care what you do in your spare time, but when you're on-site, you either focus or you fuck off. This is your last warning. Got me?"

"Hey, it's Hal, he's coming back up!" Ken shouted from the tunnel.

Eben shrank in Pete's grip as they both stared sidelong at the entrance.

"You wanna seal the shaft while we've still got people underground!?" Pete growled before clocking Eben across the jaw, sending him sprawling into the pool of his own vomit. "You're done. Get the fuck outta here."

Eben scrambled backwards as Hal burst out onto the surface, breathing hard. Everyone was on their feet now, staring at the blood smeared across his face and staining his hi-vis overalls crimson red.

"Dude," Ken took an uncertain step forward. "What the fuck happened? Where are –"

Hal snapped his gaze in Ken's direction at breakneck speed, and despite Ken being the larger of the two, Hal picked him up with ease, slamming him back against the cliff wall and leaning in close.

Without hesitation, Ken pummelled him with devastating hooks to the face and ribs, launching his fists with bone-crunching impacts, breaking himself free of Hal's grip. Several miners had rushed forward to help break up the fight, but Pete was the first on the scene, the big foreman holding Hal in a full nelson. Ken straightened out his overalls before winding up to sink an uppercut into Hal's gut for good measure.

Kara came up behind Eben with a cup of water. With trembling hands, he grasped it and slurped greedily, choking it down.

"Come on, we're ghosting," she whispered in his ear. "I don't wanna be around when Pete starts asking who else was down there."

"I have to warn them," Eben replied, gazing at the other miners.

"You tried," her lips tightened as she pulled him to his feet. "Whatever shit you guys saw down there, and whatever happens next, that's their problem. Unless you wanna stay?"

He shook his head, and they marched past the breakfast marquee towards the trucks as everyone crowded around Hal. Kara stopped next to an old blue pickup truck.

"This one's Peggy's. Keys should still be in the ignition," she muttered, more as a prayer than a prediction as they climbed into the truck's cabin.

Someone in the crowd screamed just as Eben was about to close the passenger door. He glanced up to see the unmistakable figure of Kristie emerging from the tunnel, the front of her hi-vis overalls soaked with her own blood. With a burst of unnatural speed, she lunged and latched onto the closest person standing beside the entrance, Ken, biting deep into his neck before he could so much as clench a fist.

Curt erupted from the shaft next, plunging into the crowd, knocking Jarrod off his feet and crouching over him. Hal, still locked in a full-nelson, managed to reach up over his shoulder and clutch the back of Pete's head, his face tinted blue as he whispered into the foreman's ear. The rest of the workers scrambled in every direction, madly searching for their tools. Some attempted to pull Kristie off Ken, only to become the next victim to her snapping jaws. Brody swung his pickaxe at her, embedding the spike deep in between her shoulder blades, but he only succeeded in drawing her attention.

The fight fled the group of miners the moment Ken, Pete and Jarrod recovered, only to join the attack, their eyes glazed over as they launched the frenzied assault against their former colleagues. Some of the workers ran towards the trucks, although most headed straight for the road back to Cloakwater.

Kara ripped her eyes away from the grisly scene, fumbling with the keys and gunning the engine just as Harper and Peggy reached the truck, jumping in through Eben's open door. He slammed it shut behind them as they piled in, the wheels churning up clouds of dust in their wake even as the other miners banged on the rear quarter panels, begging for them to slow down.

Eben stared at the side mirror as the pickup lurched uphill. Not all of the workers had been lucky enough to reach the vehicles in time, let alone find the keys. Pete and Hal tackled runners to the ground like a pair of professional footballers, while Ken gained ground on a third, Matt, who was lucky enough to grab hold of the truck's side railing and jump head-first into the tray before they could clear the dirt road's crest, rapidly picking up speed as Kara floored the accelerator downhill.

"What the hell's going on!?" Harper sobbed, Peggy holding her in the cramped space, their eyes wide and trembling.

"Eben, start talking!" Kara snapped out of the side of her mouth, clenching her teeth as she blared the truck's horn at the runners up ahead. "MOVE OR I WILL RUN YOU DOWN!!"

"I don't, I don't," he stammered as the forest whipped by on either side. "The dead woman. In the space ship. Curt killed her. And then, and then…" he dry-heaved, having nothing else in his stomach.

"You're not making any sense!" Harper screamed beside him.

"Breathe, both of you," Peggy cooed, taking her own advice, "Just breathe."

"I'm in my bed, I'm in my bed, I'm in my bed!" Eben repeated feverishly, screwing his eyes shut and opening them again only to find that he was – undeniably – not in his bed.

"We've got half a tank," Peggy glanced at the dials on the dash. "Where are we heading?"

"Hamilton's," Kara replied, her eyes keenly focused, honking as she swerved to avoid the other miners.

One man turned and stopped in the middle of the road with his hands held out wide in a desperate bid to hitch a ride. She tried to manoeuvre around him, but he anticipated the move, sidestepping back into their path. Eben shielded his face as Kara stomped the accelerator, his head splitting like a watermelon on the windscreen, cracking the glass in a spider web as his body somersaulted out of sight. Matt yelped as he was sprayed with blood in the back.

"Fucker," Kara muttered under her breath as she flipped the switch for the washer fluid, the twin jets spraying the splash of blood on the windscreen.

"You're gonna wanna slow down when we hit the main road," Peggy said hoarsely, a tear trickling down her cheek as the wipers smeared red streaks across the glass. "The turn's sharper than it looks."

The town's sirens were already blaring as Cloakwater began to materialise from behind the trees. One of the sentries must have spotted the flood of hi-vis overalls pouring down the mountain. The townspeople were running through the streets towards Hamilton's Lair, the underground shelter where they had all taken refuge five years ago.

Satisfied with the distance between themselves and their pursuers, Kara eased up on the accelerator, slowing down so that the pickup could comfortably take the upcoming right turn at the intersection, when a kid popped out from behind a parked car. Kara swerved left, narrowly avoiding the boy, but now they were heading straight towards a family of four. Peggy reached across the dash to grab the wheel and both women pulled to the right moments apart, overcorrecting and tipping the vehicle.

Time slowed down as they rode on two wheels, watching the inevitable unfold. The family ducked out of the way. Matt leapt from the tray. Harper instinctively reached over her shoulder for a seatbelt, punching Eben in the eye instead. He could barely curse before the moment passed, and they were barrelling sideways across the intersection.

* * *

"Worst hangover ever," Eben groaned into somebody's boot heel as he awoke to the sounds of Kara kicking the windscreen, their four bodies tangled together as the truck lay on its side.

"Geroff me," Peggy gasped feebly as she clawed at the crushed ceiling's upholstery, "Geroff!"

Eben hoisted himself up by the passenger seat's headrest, pulling himself free. He joined Kara in kicking at the glass, grimacing as he pinched a cluster of nerves in his lower back with each jolt.

Footsteps sounded on the asphalt outside, and a silhouette appeared behind the veil of the smoking engine just as they managed to dislodge the windscreen, breaking their only barrier to the outside world while the other three were still tangled together on what was left of the driver's side door.

A hand reached through the plume of smoke. It was Matt's.

Screams erupted from the outskirts of town as he pulled them one by one from the wreckage. Faces bleeding, bones broken and lungs wheezing, they limped towards Hamilton's together, soldiering on to salvation only a few buildings away.

The dome of the underground shelter was wide and oval-shaped, like a giant turtle's shell, with concrete walls two-feet thick, reinforced with a network of steel rebar. On top of the dome was a small outpost, with bulletproof windows facing all sides; the "Turtle's Head", as Mr Hamilton liked to call it, complete with a trapdoor to get back inside the shell. It was practically impenetrable, they would be safe.

"No… No, no, no, no, no!!" Matt broke away from the others and half-ran, half-limped towards the shelter's blast doors just as they closed, sealing off access to the staggering five. "Let us in! We'll die out here!!" he yelled as heavy bolts slid and locked into place behind the doors.

They knew that the blast doors wouldn't open for them. The sealing process took too long. A woman's shriek from a couple blocks away punctuated their despair.

"You and your fucking driving…" Peggy muttered out of the side of her mouth.

"What was that?" Kara asked in a menacing tone, shrugging Eben's arm from her shoulder.

"You heard," Peggy squared her chin. "I *told* you to take that corner slow."

"Shut up!!" yelled Harper, too loudly, her voice echoing in the silence that followed. "There has to be somewhere else we can go."

Eben stared up the street, past the smoking wreck of the pickup truck, towards the train station nestled beside the cliff wall at the northern end of town. There were a handful of guards hurriedly preparing the train for departure, but even as he and the others began limping towards the station, they saw the hi-vis uniforms of their frenzied ex-colleagues jumping off the top of the cliff, hurling themselves at the people on the platform below, despite their broken bones upon impact.

"Alright, we can either run or hide," said Kara, although she didn't seem like she was offering options on how they could live, but rather, how they would die.

"We'd have a better chance if we hide," Eben replied, pivoting on his good leg to lean on Kara's shoulder again. "I don't think we're in any condition to be running."

They began looking around at the surrounding buildings, searching for a place that they could barricade in a hurry, when the first of their pursuers rounded the corner, slavering with blood-tinged saliva before sprinting towards them.

CRACK!

The monster seemed to float on midair as a small fountain of blood erupted from its forehead. When its feet hit the ground again, it crumpled onto the asphalt, rolling and scraping to a stop.

"Oi!" a voice shouted down from above. They looked up to see Mr Hamilton, poking his head through an open window of the Turtle's Head, holding a smoking rifle.

"Mr Hamilton!" Matt yelled, elated, holding his hands skyward. "Throw us a rope, please!"

"I'll do you one better," the white-haired man smiled, keeping an eye on the street as he fumbled for something in his pocket. "I need you to do something for me. For all of us," he withdrew a set of keys, throwing it down at Matt's feet. "The garage across the street, take the van. Don't stop until you get to Rubicross. Find Nathan Royce. Tell him what's happened!"

"Which key for the garage?" asked Matt, puzzled as he held up the jangling shrapnel.

Mr Hamilton had already settled onto one knee at the window, taking aim at a few more of the overall-clad creatures hurtling down the road to buy them some time. He took three shots in quick succession, bringing down two of them, but missing the third.

"MOVE IT!!" Kara yelled, snatching the keys from Matt's hand and scampering across the street. She struggled with the keys, cursing under her breath after each failed attempt as the others crowded around her.

Eben glanced up at the monster rapidly closing the distance between them, moving too fast for Mr Hamilton to draw a bead on it. Peering closer at the ex-miner, Eben saw that it was Hal. His eyes were dilated, with bulging veins in his face and neck, but it was Hal.

"FUCK!!" Kara screamed as she dropped the keys.

Ignoring the pain in his leg and his lower back, Eben bounced on the balls of his feet, sucking in shallow breaths of air, before breaking into a headlong run at Hal. The spike of adrenaline negated his injuries from the crash, and he sprinted towards his old friend.

They collided hard enough to pop Eben's shoulder out of place, and Hal soon had Eben's cheek pressed into the sidewalk, whispering a crazed chant into his ear.

His skull flat against the concrete, Eben watched Kara fling the garage door open, urging the others inside as she ripped the keys from the handle. She took one fleeting glance back at Eben, mouthing "thank you" before slamming the door shut.

"I should have come back for you," Eben mumbled over the sounds of Hal's hisses, his remorseful gaze staring down the empty sidewalk, seconds before a well-placed bullet ripped through both their skulls.

CHAPTER 1 - HARLAN

Harlan Reid sipped his neat whiskey, listening to the rain hit the saloon's tin roof as he toyed with his last remaining golden bucks, having gone from a full case packed with the gilded plastic chips down to a mere pair in the space of two short years. He was lucky that they were a pair of fifties, otherwise he would have had to sleep outside, although considering the rate at which he was drinking, he would have to forgo the breakfast of his bed-and-breakfast accommodation at the boarding house.

What the hell, he thought to himself. It was his last night of having a roof over his head. *May as well enjoy it.*

Lorelei's Saloon was nothing special, and yet it had a certain magnetic pull on every dirt-faced cowboy and dolled-up whore in Coyote's Rest, constantly drawing them back in through the swinging batwing doors to make new memories that they would all forget by morning.

Tougher to shake were the old memories though, because they always came back. For many, those memories were of graduating high school, deciding whether they wanted to travel overseas or buy their first car, and not caring about which political party they voted for, as long as they didn't have to pay a fine. Simpler times.

But that was five years ago now, and everything had changed since then.

For instance, none of them would have ever envisioned a life without the internet, fast food, or modern medicine, nor would they have considered the practicality of wearing wide-brimmed hats and leather dusters while riding a horse, the most readily-available method of transportation across the rugged landscape of the apocalypse, yet here they all were, delighting in the fanciful facade of dressing up like a bunch of cowboys and cowgirls despite having been born and raised in the 21st Century, swigging spirits in the frontier-style saloon of an Old West re-enactment town.

Harlan, a slender brown-haired blue-eyed man in his mid-twenties, sat alone at his table opposite the bar, his umber brown cowboy hat pulled low over his eyes, as if the only thing that mattered in the world was the drink in his hand. He didn't have to see the place to remember what it looked like though; he knew the saloon like he knew the bottom of a glass.

A shoddy upright wooden piano squatted in the front corner in between the bar counter and a grime-covered window that looked out onto the veranda. Half a dozen tables topped with green felt occupied a third of the room, where drunken career gamblers slurred bets and insults at each other over cards and dice. On the other side of the bar were the kitchen's double doors and a small corridor that led out back, along with a bathroom that was only ever clean in the morning.

Roughly hewn tables, barrels and booths were spread throughout the rest of the saloon, with a staircase in the back corner that led up to a series of private rooms behind the second-storey's balustrade where the town's hastier harlots would compete with each other to see how many clients they could clear out in one night.

Taking another small sip of his whiskey, Harlan tipped back the brim of his hat and looked over at Millie Quiggens, a plump woman who had set up a booth in the corner of the saloon, hiring new guards for her ranch out in the prairies. Rampant rumours of the Rauders' raids returning had been spreading like a cheap whore's rash over the past week, with the entire population of Torzal Arroyo having seemingly vanished overnight.

Millie swore that she had seen clusters of shadows moving just beyond the reach of their ranch's spotlights only a few nights ago, but she had always been known to exaggerate. Torzal Arroyo was one of the many unremarkable small towns that had thrived and died during the railroad's construction. More than likely, everyone stubborn enough to stay after the work dried up had either died of boredom or simply picked up and left, and some traveller who had lost his way between settlements found the town abandoned.

All the same, a few of the cowboys signed their names on her list.

Harlan knocked his glass around the table, sliding it from one hand to the other. A short stint of guard duty at Quiggens' Ranch would solve his money problems while giving him a place to stay. He caught what was left of his whiskey and dug his boot heel into the floor, ready to kick his chair out, when a commotion erupted from the other side of the room.

"If I ever ran outta money, I'd join the raiders and just *take* what I want!" Big-Stack Billy, a burly boisterous redhead, called out from the dice tables.

"She'd be paying us with the same golden bucks," Dante added dryly.

"Where's the booth for the raiders at? I'm fixin' to sign me up now!" Elwood shouted, bringing on another round of laughter.

One by one, the men and women who had shown some interest slunk back to Millie's table and scratched out their names, her face twisting and contorting at every scribble, as if they were drawing lines through her skin. Finally, when her scowl couldn't get any worse, she scrunched up her piece of paper and stormed towards the front of the saloon, hips jiggling and chins quivering. The room exploded with a chorus of mocking jeers.

"I hope the raiders come here next!" she spat, pausing at the exit.

"I hope they do, too," Big-Stack yelled back. "I've been itchin' for a good fight. You're shit outta luck if they come for you first though!"

Millie Quiggens screeched internally before punching the batwing doors open, which swung back into her flanks as she shambled out into the rain.

Harlan sank back into his chair, slouching as he watched the evening unfold. Toby, the bashful black piano player, was setting up for the night, stealing furtive glances at Brandi Beckett, the barkeeper's curvy yet slender daughter. She had thick luscious lips, her caramel face framed by long mocha brown hair, with a voluptuous hour-glass figure that would tempt man and woman alike.

"Hey there, pretty lady," slurred Flem Wakefield, the piteously gaunt grave digger, calling Brandi over with his routine conversation starter. "I got a son your age, if'n you're interested."

"Flem!" Big-Stack hollered from across the room, also enraptured by her enticing figure as he watched her from his table. "How many times she gotta tell you? She ain't interested. You don't even know where that son of a bitch is."

Brandi quietly excused herself as Flem hid his gloomy face behind his glass. She smiled, approaching the dice tables with another round of drinks. Raking in his winnings, Billy tipped her generously, inviting her to stay a while, kicking his chair back and slapping his meaty thigh. The barkeeper's daughter blushed, toying with her hair.

"Brandi, honey," Lyle called from behind the bar, spilling a drink as he watched the exchange, "I need you in the kitchen."

"Maybe next time, darlin'," Big-Stack winked. He leaned out of his chair, wolf-whistling at her bulging mini shorts as she crossed over to the other side of the bar. Once she disappeared into the back, he glowered at Lyle before turning back to the dice game.

Lyle Beckett was one of the few decent folk in town, although considering he was running a watering hole in a town full of degenerates, his morals were less of an asset and more of a liability. The bespectacled widower had brought his daughter to Coyote's Rest with the ironic intention of keeping her safe, where he had restored, restocked and reopened the saloon, naming it after his late wife, Lorelei. She probably wasn't even dead yet, but Harlan would be willing to wager that she wished she was.

Lyle and Lorelei had worked on the railroad, along with countless others, until his wife was kidnapped during one of the Desert Marauders' frequent raids. The scavengers living in the remnants of the blast zone in North Tekota had often stolen women, food and supplies from the budding settlements in the prairies, striking at random and then disappearing into the night. It was anyone's guess as to what the Rauders did with their spoils, but they had a fair idea.

It rarely took much for the fringes of society to turn on each other, especially these days, Harlan mused to himself. One simple breakdown of the protections that civilisation had put in place, and the inner beasts of men would come back with a vengeance.

Many of the cowboys and cowgirls in Coyote's Rest had barely graduated high school when the missile dropped five years ago, turning the valedictorian's speech about hopes and dreams for a bright future into nothing more than a bright flash and ashes. They had endured twelve years of education to prepare them for a world that they would know nothing about. Meanwhile, basic survival skills like hunting, foraging and scavenging for food had never been a priority in their school curriculum.

Despite all that, they had successfully made it through the food shortages while the missile's fallout had plagued much of South Tekota, but after the residual radiation had settled and it became safe to venture outside the towns of Stillborough and Brimvale again, they found that much of the surrounding landscape had either been picked clean or depleted of its natural food sources. The only way that they would be able to survive was if they worked for their food.

To make matters worse, what was left of civilisation sorely needed diesel supplies from Cloakwater Cliffs to run their generators. However, all of the pre-existing highways had been damaged in the missile's rippling earthquake, and any trucks driving slow enough to wrestle with the broken terrain were more susceptible to raids from the Rauders.

With precious few jobs available for people with no practical work experience, the former students of the surviving towns had jumped at the opportunity to become unskilled labourers working on the proposed solution, a railroad, which now spanned the entire length of the prairies, from the diesel-rich town of Cloakwater to the diesel-poor town of Rubicross.

A butterball of a man named Wallace Pelletier had overseen the railroad's construction. The workers had caught the feeling that they were being underpaid, but at least they had been getting paid. Until, of course, Wallace decided to cut and run with the remaining golden bucks before the railroad was completed.

Together with the other workers, Harlan had hunted Wallace across the prairies, eventually catching up to him and taking back everything he had stolen, distributing the golden bucks among the others who had joined the pursuit. As it turned out, each of the workers had only been receiving a third of what Wallace had been instructed to pay them, plus Wallace's agreed profit margin for overseeing the project, so they shared a far greater prize than what they had initially thought before embarking on the manhunt.

Each member of the search party had received enough golden bucks to live a modest lifestyle for at least a decade, or a decadent lifestyle for a few years. Young and dumb, the vast majority of them opted for the latter.

Harlan finished his glass, bitterly reflecting on the fact that his greatest achievement since finishing high school was forming a lynch mob and chasing after a fat man until his heart gave out. And then he had drunk and fucked his way back into poverty. That sure wasn't in the valedictorian's speech.

Brandi pushed through the kitchen's double doors carrying a plate of minced beef and stewed vegetables, picking up a pint of beer along the way, serving Emmett Pearce in the back corner of the saloon. Harlan had no idea how long Emmett had been sitting there, but the man always seemed to appear and disappear at his own leisure. Considering that his hat lying on the table in front of him – a custom that he never tired of – was still wet from the rain outside, he couldn't have been there for very long. But it had been long enough to order dinner.

Emmett Pearce was a ropey wide-shouldered man in his thirties with broad cheekbones and a strong jaw. Quiet and reserved, but every word he spoke carried weight. Whatever he did, the others followed, although they always managed to bring their own impulsive behaviours along with them. Normally, Emmett would have chosen to sit next to Harlan, but the two men had been at odds for the past few weeks.

They hadn't spoken since Harlan had approached him about how some of the boys were complaining that their stacks of golden bucks were beginning to run low, and it wouldn't be too long before they all parted ways to do their own thing, legal or not.

"How much do you need?" Emmett had asked, somehow seeing straight through him.

"I don't want your money," Harlan replied, refusing to take a handout. "But I've been thinking. Maybe there's a way that we can earn more together, like, hiring out our services to the other settlements around South Tekota."

"And what would those 'services' be, exactly?" Emmett narrowed his eyes, already scrutinising the plan before hearing it out.

"Whatever doesn't involve breaking our backs in the hot sun for a third of the pay we should be getting," Harlan answered, more aggressively than he had intended. "We've got strength in numbers. We should use that to our advantage, while the numbers are still on our side."

"You wanna turn our boys into a bunch of mercenaries like those gangs across the bay?" asked Emmett, raising an eyebrow. "Let me tell you something. Chasing down Wallace was the easiest payday we'll ever get, because I can guarantee you, it'll never happen again. Nobody in their right mind is gonna be riding around with that amount of chips, and anyone willing to pay you to solve a problem could just as easily hire another crew for less to make sure you don't come around to collect. And in case you forgot, Wallace didn't even put up a fight."

Harlan caught his empty glass as it slid across the table. He wasn't sure how long he had been lost in the memory, but when he looked over at the back corner again, Emmett had already pushed aside his empty plate, drinking his golden dessert.

The saloon's batwing doors swung open, and a clean-shaven man with cold blue eyes and close-cropped copper red hair strode in, sizing up the place with a sneer before approaching the bar, taking a wide berth of the gambling tables, his dead stare locked on Lyle as he silently waited to be acknowledged.

"Welcome! What can I get you?" Lyle asked with a smile over the upbeat ragtime rhythms of Toby's piano chords.

"Two whiskeys, on the rocks," the newcomer said tersely. "Who's in charge?"

Lyle faltered as he reached for a bottle, looking back at the man, "I get the feeling you aren't looking for me," he supposed, despite being the owner of the saloon. The out-of-towner showed no reaction, he simply stared until he got an answer. Lyle leaned over the counter, pointing at Emmett in the back corner. "That's the guy you wanna speak to."

The man dropped a gilded plastic chip on the bar and thanked Lyle for the drinks; although it wasn't a "thanks" out of genuine gratitude or respect, but more as a part of the transaction, as if he was obligated to say the word. Almost mechanically, he walked over to Emmett's table, sat down opposite and slid the second glass towards him.

Harlan scraped the floorboards as he kicked his chair out. He marched towards the back corner and sat beside Emmett, taking the glass on his behalf and scooping out an ice cube, chewing it, to the out-of-towner's frowning displeasure.

Emmett raised an eyebrow at Harlan, who immediately remembered to take off his hat. Emmett nodded his approval before levelling his rugged gaze at the newcomer.

"I'm very impressed with all of the work you've done here," the self-satisfied son of a bitch said in an overly-nice tone, straining to maintain a friendly face, yet even now, he was sneering at them. He looked like a man preparing to shave his upper lip. "Building the railroad to supply us with enough diesel to keep the gears turning, making an example out of that thief, Wallace Pelletier, and all the while, managing to keep such a strong crew in line and out of trouble."

Emmett was unmoved by the forced flattery. It seemed the newcomer had met his match in only sparing words for the people who mattered. Harlan chewed another ice cube in the silence, crunching it with his mouth open.

"Forgive me," the man offered a handshake that was promptly ignored. "Quentin Davis, I'm a representative of the Mayor's Office in Brimvale."

"Here to extend Brimvale's jurisdiction into the prairies so you can start taxing us, huh?" Harlan goaded.

"Quite the opposite," Quentin replied, his cold blue eyes flicking towards Harlan for a moment. "We'd like to pay you." Harlan leaned forward, but Emmett just kept on staring deadpan. Quentin took it as a sign to continue, "Mayor Paxton wishes to keep the peace both inside and outside of Brimvale.

The return of the Rauders' raids on the outlying settlements has been some very troubling news, and, since the prairies are your territory, we thought *you* would be the most qualified to handle the situation."

"Handle the situation?" Emmett repeated, breaking his silence, to Quentin's delight.

"Eliminate the threat," he said coolly, as if handing out death sentences was the most mundane part of his job.

"How much?" asked Harlan, shrugging sidelong at Emmett.

"We'll pay you ten full cases of golden bucks," Quentin answered, loudly enough to be heard over the sounds of the piano in the background, causing the men drunkenly slurring at the nearby tables to drop their conversations, eavesdropping excitedly.

"You'll have your answer by morning," Emmett replied, stone-faced, not even giving him the slightest hint of a reaction.

Quentin nodded, his ears perking up at the sound of a woman's high-pitched laugh as the prostitutes of Coyote's Rest made their way into the saloon, wet from the rain outside, but fresh and ready to work the crowd of liquored-up cowboys. He promptly excused himself from the table, leaving his own glass of whiskey untouched.

"Looks like we're back to this conversation again," Harlan remarked, finishing the first glass and claiming the second.

"Answer was 'no' as soon as he walked in," Emmett said flatly, examining the dregs of his pint. "We're not hired killers, and the people he wants us to hunt will be shooting back this time."

"If you're so sure," Harlan shrugged and sipped, not wanting to flog a dead horse. "But why do you want him to wait until morning before he gets his answer?"

"I want to make sure he's on his way out when I turn him down," Emmett replied, squaring his jaw before looking directly at Harlan. "That way, nobody else can cut a deal. We've got some good men here. Stupid, but good. Be a damn shame to let them volunteer to get themselves killed."

"And what are you gonna do when you run outta money?" asked Harlan. Taking the moral high ground was all well and good while the wolves weren't at the door. "Ten full cases of chips… you'll wish you said yes."

"Well, unlike the rest of the boys," Emmett began before finishing his beer, "I haven't wasted all my reward money on whores and gambling."

"You might not wanna say that too loud," Harlan cautioned, glancing at the men seated at the nearby tables who were poorly pretending not to listen in. Like him, they sorely needed more golden bucks to continue their lifestyle of debauchery. None of them wanted to go back to long hard days of honest work.

"I've still got plenty left over to start up a business," Emmett replied in a low voice. "I'm just waiting for the opportunity to present itself. If you're looking for work, you'd be one of the few people I'd consider taking on. It won't be easy, but I can promise you this: you won't be breaking your back in the hot sun, and you'll be earning a decent-enough living to branch out on your own one day."

Harlan sipped his drink before sliding it from one hand to the other. Emmett had just removed his two biggest concerns from the last time they had argued.

"And what about the rest of the boys?" Harlan finally asked.

"I hear Quiggens' Ranch is hiring," he replied.

The men eavesdropping nearby shot death stares at Emmett.

CHAPTER 2 - LIAM

Liam Caldwell fidgeted with the top button of his light blue pinstriped business shirt as a drunken oaf staggered into his table.

Watch where you're fucking going, he rolled his eyes before wiping down the side of his glass of cola with a table napkin. *So this is what I've been* missing out *on,* he stared around at the saloon's sloshed swarm of simpletons before shaking his head in disgust.

Liam was in his early twenties. He had a slim build and short black hair, with shadows over his dark brown eyes after having seen too much too young, although anyone who had witnessed the horrors of The Long Summer Night, the haunting images eternally etched into their eyelids, were tainted by the same dour shadow.

He turned his gaze back to the pair of wannabe cowboys in the rear of the saloon as they muttered back and forth, one of them only a few years older than Liam, and the other well into his thirties. Apparently Liam hadn't been the only one paying attention to their conversation though. Several of the men seated at the nearby tables turned away from the muttered exchange with disgruntled expressions.

Having pushed through the batwing doors a few minutes after Quentin Davis, nobody had realised that Liam was the other half of Mayor Paxton's delegation; or, the more likely scenario, nobody cared. His job had been to watch whoever Quentin sat down with in order to gauge their level of interest in the deal he was offering, but it seemed that the gauge's interest level was hovering somewhere between indifferent and irritated. In fact, it seemed as though the pair of men had already changed the topic.

"Sleep in the car," Quentin said out of the side of his mouth as he stalked by, his cold blue eyes trained on the prostitutes at the other end of the saloon as they filtered out into the crowd of drunken men and women.

Liam nodded subtly, sipping his cola as he eyed the wedding ring on the man's finger. Quentin Davis was one of the Mayor's senior officers in Brimvale. He had been forced to bring Liam along with him on his diplomacy mission out into the prairies. If either of the two would have had any say in the matter, Liam would have been all too happy to spend the night in Brimvale.

The last place he had wanted to be was in a room full of drunken degenerates, and Coyote's Rest was notorious for being a town teeming with boozers. He pressed his lips together with distaste as he listened to the cowboys hurling slurred insults at each other, some in good nature, but some with troublesome undertones, as they argued over which women they would be bedding tonight.

These were the same types of men who had ended his world almost five years ago.

Plenty of people would have argued that it was the missile that had struck North Tekota, and countless other places around the globe if hearsay was a reliable source of news, that was responsible for the end of the world, but for Liam, the end of the world had started with the drug addicts. The missile didn't kill his family, the drug addicts did; desperate men and women from The Gutter who were looking to score their next high, and were willing to gun down anyone who got in their way. But for some of those depraved men and women, drugs weren't the only way to have fun.

Everyone who was old enough to remember The Long Summer Night wished that they had been young enough to forget. While the majority of Brimvale's upstanding citizens had been marching on the town hall, protesting against the tyrannical rule of the Army Reserves who had put themselves in charge, the suburbs had been left virtually defenceless against the flood of fiends who knew that the authorities would have their hands full.

And while the protesters, former police members and the Army Reserves were battling it out in the plaza, all of the suburban neighbourhoods, all of the close-knit communities, and all of the peaceful family homes, were served up on a platter. Medicine cabinets, wine cellars and carefully-rationed food stockpiles were all ripe for the taking. Even as the saloon's piano player tapped out a knee-bouncing boogie-woogie beat that had a few drunken fools clapping along, Liam could still hear the sounds of tyres screeching, windows breaking, shrill screams and maniacal laughter.

He screwed his eyes shut for a moment, the scenes of his home invasion flashing in grisly black-and-white snapshots; his father clutching his torso on the staircase in futility, bleeding from more bullet holes than he could staunch; his mother shoving him out of the second-storey window before they caught her from behind; himself slipping down the tiles as he lunged for the windowsill, landing hard on the ground and twisting his ankle, unable to do anything but listen to his mother's screams before one final gunshot silenced her forever; the sounds of slicing and stabbing and deranged giggling that still haunted him to this day.

Liam took a sip of his cola to bring himself back to the present.

A buxom brunette garbed in a loose and lacy see-through red dress – though not for long – was leading Quentin by the hand past Liam's table and upstairs to a private room. If the man was happy about at least one successful negotiation that night, he sure didn't show it. The boys in the office had dubbed him "Quentin the Unsmiling" – brazen enough to even say it to his face. Liam smirked sardonically as he recalled that Quentin had especially earned his nickname that day.

A big boisterous redheaded brute of a man sitting at the dice tables attempted to flirt with the curvy mocha-haired bargirl, despite the plethora of prostitutes milling about the gamblers, measuring their worth by the size of each man's stack of golden bucks. The piano's tune played off-key momentarily as the manic-handed musician in the front corner of the room eyed the pair enviously, his jaw set as he resolved to finish the song.

Liam was watching intently when a young blonde woman wearing a dainty white button-down shirt fell into his lap, spilling his drink.

"Oh, I'm sorry! I wasn't lookin' where I was goin'," she exclaimed, wrapping an arm around his shoulders, "Good thing you were here to catch me." She studied his face, her thin eyebrows furrowing slightly as she compared him against her long list of ex-clients. "You're new here, aren't'cha? What brings you 'round these parts?"

Liam sighed through his nose as he mopped up the spill with a napkin, more concerned with the cola stain spreading across his shirt's chest than making up some trivial answer for her to caw over.

"Oh, I can take care of that for ya," she offered, coyly pulling a frilly strip of linen from between her perky cleavage. "I mean, it's the least I can do…"

It was only then that Liam realised that she wasn't wearing a bra, her firm nipples forming tiny lumps in her white button-down shirt. She parted his knees to kneel in front of him in one fluid movement, tenderly placing one hand on his upper thigh with practised technique as she dabbed at his chest. He had the feeling that this wasn't the first time she had spilled someone's drink.

"So, you here for a good time?" she asked, getting to business, her hand creeping down his abdomen, leaving the stain as she worked towards his crotch.

Liam looked up at the balustrade of the second level, taking a deep breath and pinching the bridge of his nose as he felt himself stiffening at her touch. If this had happened back in Brimvale, people would have stopped and stared at them, but out here in Coyote's Rest, all of the other men in the saloon were too preoccupied with prostitutes of their own, and any other woman not working the crowd was already numb to the sight. He raised his eyebrows, looking back down at her as she licked the side of her mouth, eagerly awaiting his reply with a kittenish smirk.

"I was having a good time before you came along," he answered flatly.

She dropped her jaw in surprise, more shocked than offended, before stowing the dirty cloth back in her cleavage. Slightly, she dug her fingernails into his thighs as she stood up.

"Gee, you really oughta lighten up," she said. Then, leaning down far enough to give him a full view beneath her airy blouse, and what he would be missing out on, she murmured softly into his ear, "And to think, I would've given you a discount 'cause I thought you were cute."

She brushed his face with her breasts before strolling over to the bar with a pronounced sway in her hips, gazing back over her shoulder to see if he had begun to have second thoughts prior to ordering herself a drink.

Pulling himself closer to the table to hide his discomfort, Liam turned his attention back towards the two cowboys he was supposed to be watching. The big boisterous brute who had been flirting with the bargirl earlier had swaggered over to their corner table, leaning against a brass sign in the corridor that pointed the way towards the bathroom. Apparently, he had been on a winning streak at the dice tables, and he wanted to see how far he could push his luck.

"I got five hundreds that say I can beat you 'round Ramblin' Gulch with your own horse," the brute boasted, his beer spraying the floor as he made the wager.

"And why would Emmett give you his horse, Big-Stack?" asked the younger cowboy sitting at the table.

"Well, why the hell not?" Big-Stack growled through gritted teeth, "If he wants to prove he's a better rider'n me, then it don't matter which fuckin' horse he rides, does it? I'll let him ride mine if that makes him feel better."

"I've got nothing to prove to you," the man named Emmett replied quietly. "Besides, you're drunk and it's raining outside. Mighty fine night for an accident."

"Afraid to get wet, huh?" Big-Stack chuckled, raising his voice for others to hear. "Y'know, I always figured you for a pussy, but now I know for sure."

"You take that back," the third man snarled, moving to get out of his seat, but Emmett held him down firmly. He kicked the table instead, drawing the attention of the other men drinking nearby, temporarily averting their gazes from the women sitting in their laps.

"I'll take your money," Emmett decided with barely a shift in his expression, accepting the challenge, "Two thousand, you good for it?"

Big-Stack swallowed, his forehead perspiring now, feeling the weight of the stares in the room as more drunken revellers turned to face them.

"Make it three thousand, and your horse if I win," he replied, less boisterous than he had been a minute ago.

"You got yourself a deal, partner," said Emmett, donning his coal black hat and leather coat.

Big-Stack stood in dumbfounded disbelief for a moment as the rest of the cowboys and cowgirls rose to their feet, cheering them on. He downed the rest of his beer, slamming the empty glass on the table.

"About time you grew a pair, Emmett!" the big brute yelled, clenching his fists to disguise his shaky hands. He thrust his burly arms into the air, as if he was already victorious, bringing on another cheer from the crowd as they all hustled outside onto the veranda.

Only a handful of people remained in the saloon; mostly men who were too drunk to stand up straight, and women who were too preoccupied with making money of their own. The piano player stopped mid-tune with a downward cascade of the keys, ambling towards the bathroom corridor, relieved at the prospect of an unexpected break. The curvy bargirl hurriedly cleared the glasses from the empty tables, setting them down on the wooden bar counter before rushing over to watch from the grime-covered front window.

"Oh, I'm sorry! I wasn't lookin' where I was goin'," the braless blonde with the white button-down shirt recited her line as she fell into another man's lap.

Seeing that there was no longer anything worthwhile watching in the saloon, and hearing Quentin's buxom brunette prostitute shrieking in pleasure from one of the private rooms upstairs in the relative silence left behind, Liam headed outside onto the veranda to join the group of booze-breathed spectators, only to see mud fly from the hooves of the two men's horses as they disappeared behind a building in the distance.

Having no desire to follow them to the racing track on the dark wet evening, the crowd began to disperse, some pushing back through the saloon's batwing doors, and others rushing through the rain to the boarding house, eager to undress their companions for the night.

Liam ducked out from underneath the veranda's tin roof, splashing through the puddles in the town's dirt road as he ran towards the black SUV parked beside the feed store on the corner. He wasn't sure why he was so concerned about getting wet since his blue business shirt was already ruined by the cola stain, yet he ran all the same.

Fishing into his trouser pockets for the keys, he unlocked the SUV's doors with the remote before climbing into the driver's seat. Quentin the Unsmiling would just have to wear his default blank face of disapproval in the morning when he would discover that his car's pristine black leather interior had been sullied by Liam's wet ass.

He pondered why Mayor Paxton had seen fit to send him to accompany Quentin at all. He had missed half of the negotiation, could barely hear the other half, and he had nothing to report from his surveillance other than Quentin paying a prostitute with taxpayers' money, which was meant to have been allocated towards their mutual accommodation. He supposed it was due to Lora Purcell's recent promotion that he now had to step up to take over her old role of being the diplomat's bitch, and all of the trappings of success that came with it, like sleeping in the car.

Ten full cases of golden bucks, he had heard that part of the negotiation, at least. They had brought one of the cases along with them as a persuasive tool, but only if the situation called for it. Most people would have run away with that kind of money. Not Liam though. He despised thieves, just as much as he did drunks and drug addicts.

For two years after the world had ended, money theft had ceased to be an issue, for Brimvale at least. In the advent of the apocalypse, the internet had gone offline, along with everyone's bank balances in the former cashless society. The only measure of wealth had been in the form of goods and services which people could use to barter for their needs. But bartering was only feasible on a small scale. So, once trading partnerships had been formed between the re-emerging settlements, Victor MacDougall, the owner of the Golden Buck Casino in Rookson City, proposed a new monetary system: his casino's gilded plastic chips embossed with the antlers of a golden stag.

The leaders of each established settlement had agreed that the old currency could no longer be used as a viable financial system for trade between communities. Anyone could have stumbled upon a hoard of cash and retired without ever having contributed to the new world.

With the golden bucks however, Rookson City had the sole power to control and dictate the supply of the new currency. Once a mutual agreement had been reached with the governing bodies of the other settlements, Victor freely distributed large supplies of his casino's chips to every prominent political leader and business owner in South Tekota, to be paid to their people in wages.

After the golden bucks had been apportioned, no transactions without the casino chips as payment would be accepted, except in The Gutter. The criminals of Bushrock Flats were the only people who still placed any value on cash money, but only because their gang leaders had stockpiled so much of it.

The thought behind the free distribution of the new currency was that those who were too greedy to pass on the golden bucks would either be ousted by the masses who would be left without means to buy food and other essential items, or they would be robbed by people who would eventually put the currency back into the economy themselves, as in the case of Wallace Pelletier, the railroad's former foreman, thus restoring an easily divisible, portable and recognisable medium of exchange.

Liam's stomach grumbled, and he realised that he had forgotten to eat dinner at the saloon. He reached for his backpack on the floor of the passenger's seat, searching for the apples from Brimvale's orchards which he'd had the good sense to pack. While eating, he fiddled with the seat's height and angle, finding a comfortable position, ensuring Quentin's maximum displeasure in the morning.

This would be a nice town, if it wasn't for the people, he reflected, admiring the quaint and rustic architecture of the surrounding buildings for the first time since they had arrived. Coyote's Rest was a re-enactment town of The Wild West, for cultural preservation and tourist attraction purposes. It had been abandoned during the missile's fallout, but after a few years, when the level of residual radiation became mild enough to safely move out into the countryside again, the town was recolonised and refurbished, the old buildings serving an actual purpose, rather than just being there for show.

The rain came down harder as droplets tracked down the windows. Only a handful of stragglers were standing underneath the saloon's veranda now, peering out into the night. Another cowboy had turned to head back inside when one of the riders galloped back into town. He jumped off his black horse, throwing the reins to one of the spectators as he whooped and hollered in victory, the rest of the saloon cheering him on as he strode inside.

There was no sign of the other rider.

CHAPTER 3 - ODESSA

Spittle flew from his mouth with each laboured growl as he swung the axe, splitting firewood over the chopping block in the yard strewn with fallen leaves and pinecones, his scraggly beard and unkempt blonde hair stirring in the late afternoon's cool breeze. Dess watched him toiling from the veranda of her modest log cabin, her ropey arms aching from another long day's work.

Despite having slept on her living room's floor for the past two years, he was still a stranger to her. She had only heard stories about him from other people who recognised him in passing, as Fritz himself never talked. From the snippets of hearsay she had stitched together over the years, the man had lost his entire family during The Long Summer Night while he attended the protests in the plaza outside Brimvale's town hall. No one could say with certainty whether he had supported the Army Reserves in office or the angry protesters outside, but whichever side he had been on, he had lost everything he held dear.

Most remembered him as the human statue that had stood seething in Brimvale's plaza for days at a time, staring at the Mayor's Office long after the staff inside had drawn the curtains and exited through the rear of the building, ashamed of what they had brought on the poor man. Any offer of reparations for his loss had fallen on deaf ears, and food donated by the sympathetic townsfolk had often lain untouched, left in the rain to rot or in the sun to spoil.

Then one day, he disappeared, doggedly stalking off north until his feet bled, eventually drifting up into the small town of Stillborough Pines, full of anger and rage.

Dess remembered the day she had met him on the outskirts of town. The man had been rooted to the spot on the side of the road, smashing a fallen branch against a tree. Testing him, she put an axe in his hands instead. The widower's face had lit up with a crazed smile, and for a horrifying instant, she had thought that he was going to use the hatchet on her, but to her relief, he turned back to the tree, chopping in grunts of cathartic release until it fell, and he had been helping her cut down trees ever since.

Dess had tried on many occasions to bring him out of his spiky shell, but he never spoke a word. She had thought that perhaps he was a mute, but when she offered him something to write with, he snapped the pencil in half and ripped up the piece of paper; despite neither of which being easy to find nowadays. He simply had no interest in communicating, but he would listen to her commands. Guiltily, she admitted to herself that he made the perfect worker, and she took care of him as best as she could.

Fritz often scared the other residents of Stillborough though, but they couldn't be blamed; he had scared her on occasion, too. At night, he would have feverish dreams, foaming at the mouth as he clutched his hatchet to his chest, grappling with some phantom night terror in his sleep. And during his waking hours, the only thing that made him appear remotely sane was his reverence for routine.

Seeing the sun begin its descent over the treetops of the pine forest, Dess called him away from the chopping block, cracking open a pair of cold beers. Fritz's head jerked up at the sound, like a deer hearing a twig snap. His googly grey eyes fixated upon the frosty mist emanating from the brew's neck. Embedding the axe head into the stump with a conclusive *thock*, he loped across the yard and up the veranda's stairs two at a time.

The moment she pressed a perspiring bottle into his outstretched hand, he took a long pull, the beer trickling down into his beard until it was empty. Trading his empty bottle for the second beer, he hunched down upon the stairs and savoured small sips, gripping the wooden railing with his free hand, his callused fingers fitting perfectly into the grooves he had squeezed into the balustrade over the years.

A sad smile tugged at the corners of Dess's thin lips as she watched stray strands of his bird's nest blonde hair flap back and forth with each swig.

Dess surveyed the pile of firewood with one hand on her slender hip, her crow's feet crinkling as she decided that she would load up the wagon tomorrow. She tossed her thick brunette braid over her shoulder as she descended the stairs into the yard, covering up the woodpile with a blue tarp. Just as she finished tying the canvas down, she heard the sound of an old supermarket trolley trundling up her street, and a mailman stopped next to her letterbox, looking puzzled at the name on an envelope.

"You lost?" asked Dess, dusting her hands on her jeans as she approached the fence.

"Yeah, I'm looking for a uhh... Odessa Sheridan?" he said, peering at the envelope again and looking up at Fritz uncertainly.

"I don't imagine anyone else in their right mind would go by that name," she replied, holding her callused hand out.

Having been born and raised in Stillborough Pines, a small lumber town at the base of the Shield Mountains, her parents either had a lack of modern fashion or a queer sense of humour when they named her, sentencing her to a lifetime of displeasure any time someone called Dess by her full name.

The envelope was dated yesterday. She opened the letter inside and scanned over the words. She looked at the mailman, looked up at the overcast sky, and then looked down at the letter again.

"You can go now," she said quietly, her almond brown eyes staring at the page.

The mailman cleared his throat and held out his hand, expecting a tip. Fritz leapt up from the stairs and stalked across the yard, yanking his hatchet from the chopping block with a mad gleam in his eyes. The mailman wheeled around and took off down the street so fast that the rest of his parcels and envelopes threatened to bounce out of his trundling trolley.

The mailman was never in any danger though. Fritz simply had impeccably poor timing. He spat on the axe's blade and squatted beside the tree stump, pulling a whetstone from his pocket to hone the edge.

Dess hadn't received mail in the longest time, and now she regretted ever having opened the envelope. She sat down on the tree stump beside Fritz, her rough fingers trembling as she read the sloppy handwriting again.

Dear Dess,

It is with my deepest regrets to inform you that our friend, Emmett, fell to his death during a horse ride late last night.

A stubborn man, through and through, we owe him a great debt of gratitude for the lessons he taught us, and the values he fought to uphold.

Celebrate his life and honour him at the funeral service next Sunday at Coyote's Rest, so that he may pass in the presence of his friends who he often called family.

Sincerely yours,
Harlan Reid.

A brisk breeze stirred the fallen leaves in the yard, blowing a stray strand of hair across her face, and faintly, she could hear a voice calling her name. She looked up, half-expecting to see Emmett striding up the road, casting a long masculine shadow in the late afternoon. She had been waiting for him to walk back into her life for the past two years, but now, she could be certain that the day would never come.

"Why couldn't you just apologise?" she murmured, not sure whether she was asking Emmett, or herself.

"Dess!" the voice called again.

Instinctively, she stared sidelong at Fritz, the deranged-turned-docile labourer still happily sharpening his axe beside her. She looked around to see her older neighbour, Errol Chandler, leaning over the fence. Dess turned away for a moment, quickly brushing her cheek before getting to her feet.

"Must be important," he nodded at the page in her hand as she walked over. "I called your name a few times. Good or bad?"

She took another glance at the letter, hoping for the words to change, before holding it out to him. He read it in the blink of an eye, having been a history teacher for forty years. He was retired now, dabbling in home brewing to pass the time, but still in good shape for a man in his sixties, his grey beard casting a shadow over his broad chest.

"That's a shame," Errol's shoulders slumped as he shook his head and clucked his tongue. "That's a damn shame. He was a good man, one of the few who managed to keep his head straight through this whole mess." She caught him taking a fleeting glance at Fritz as he handed her back the letter. "My condolences, Dess. You're welcome to join me for dinner if you need to talk. Actually, I insist. I've left a shoulder of pork in the crock pot long enough to melt in your mouth. Mulled wine for dessert."

"I don't know, I kinda –" she looked around her yard for an excuse, only to see Fritz slavering at the invitation. Her thin lips curled into a weak smile, turning back to face Errol. "Okay, we'll be there. I won't be staying for dessert though. I need to start packing for the early bus."

"Why so soon?" he asked, his brows creasing slightly as he studied her. "The service isn't for another week."

"I'm not just going there for the funeral," she answered, her expression hardening as she flexed the slender muscles in her jaw. "If anyone else had fallen from their horse, I would've dismissed it as a tragic accident, but Emmett Pearce was the best damn rider I've ever known."

* * *

Breathing the early morning vapours in the shadow of Mount Fairstream, Dess waited for the bus to take her west. She couldn't remember the last time she had left Stillborough, and she was ready to see the world again – or what was left of it – but she knew that she had to remain focused.

She glanced at the small golden watch on her wrist, a gift to her from Emmett back when they had been together. She had found it while packing her duffel bag last night, lying among the few items she had kept to remember him by.

Errol and Fritz stood beside her, both with bleary red eyes from their overindulgence on dessert. Dess's eyes were red as well, but not from wine. She had fallen asleep cradling a picture frame of her thirtieth birthday. She wished that she had a more recent photo of herself and Emmett together, but after cell service and the internet became things of the past, people soon began to question why they were still using preciously-limited electricity to charge their smartphones. Like everyone else, only in hindsight had she realised that the device was also her calendar, compass, clock and camera.

Dess heard the bus's engine approaching from the south, like a strong wind blowing through the pine forest, and turned to see its faint outline steadily growing larger as it hurtled towards Stillborough's main intersection. Fritz stooped to pick up her duffel bag.

"I got it," she said, snatching up the straps and hoisting it over her shoulder. "You be good to Errol now, y'hear?"

Fritz nodded obediently, although she wondered how Errol would cope with the rabid snarling during his feverish dreams at night. She had at least warned her older neighbour about Fritz's sleeping companion, to which Errol had laughed nervously, before realising that he should probably lock his bedroom door, just in case his temporary guest was a sleepwalker.

"Be careful out there, Dess," Errol spoke over the bus's engine as it ground to a halt. "I've heard the Rauders are back."

"Wouldn't be the first time I've had to deal with them," she called over her shoulder, stepping aboard and rummaging in her bag's side pocket for her stack of golden bucks.

"Put that away, this ride's on me," the bus driver said in a familiar drawl.

"Archie!?" Dess exclaimed the moment she recognised the old war dog underneath his khaki-coloured trucker cap. He smiled back at her, sporting the beginnings of a rusty red beard speckled with grey bristles. "I didn't know you worked this route?"

"Not usually," he replied, readjusting his cap, "But after I got that letter yesterday, I knew you'd be on the first bus out, so I swapped routes with one of the guys."

Dess set her duffel bag down on the front passenger seat and settled in while other travellers climbed aboard the bus. She nodded at Fritz and Errol through the window as the door closed. For a moment, Fritz didn't seem to understand that she wouldn't be stepping back off the bus, and Errol had to guide him away. Fritz turned as the engine rumbled, remembering to wave – albeit with a bewildered frown – before the bus turned left at the intersection.

"How are the kids?" asked Dess, knowing that they weren't actually his children.

Many of the survivors of The Long Summer Night had chosen to live together after losing their loved ones, for safety or for company. Archie Callahan had lost his elderly mother over the contents of her medicine cabinet while he was at the town square. He wasn't one of the protesters though; he was a sergeant of the Army Reserves, and one of the first to abandon his post when they had been ordered to open fire upon the unarmed civilian protesters.

She had met him during the railroad's construction, along with countless other men and women, and he always had an entertaining story to tell. From sneaking alcohol on base, to his deployments overseas, as well as his countless after-hours encounters on the occasional late night trip to the Red Light District in Bushrock Flats. Archie had never settled down to start a family of his own, but the man had certainly lived a full life.

"They're fine," he smiled up at the big rearview mirror, his eyes warm yet sharp, "When I see them, at least. Liam's got a new promotion at the Mayor's Office, he's not too excited about it though. Camryn's Camryn."

"She'll open up eventually, don't worry," Dess said as she wondered how long it had been since she had seen Archie.

"I know," he replied solemnly before another smile began to play at his lips. "I'll bet you a fifty that I'll have a full conversation with her before your man says a word."

"That ain't a bet I'm willing to take," she laughed, the sound strange in her ears as the pine forest flashed past the windows.

"He still scaring half of Stillborough?" he chuckled, glancing up at the rearview mirror.

"Mailman almost shat himself last night," she laughed again, relaxing into her seat as she told him the story.

They reminisced for hours as the landscape rolled by. Eventually, the forest thinned out, and the suburbs of Brimvale came into view away on the left in the far distance. They passed the old Fort Mason on the right, abandoned and ransacked. The security checkpoint for Axemark Ravine's north bridge glinted in the midday sun as they turned south.

"That dirt road between Rubicross and Coyote's Rest still has more potholes than an unmarked minefield," Archie remarked as he brought the bus to a stop at the bridge's boom gate, "But I'll take you the whole way."

"Thanks," Dess replied, shaking her head at his dark humour, "But I've gotta make a stop at Rubicross anyway. I can grab a horse from there."

"Fair enough," he shifted the bus into gear again as the checkpoint guards waved them through. "Y'know, Emmett never had any intention to stay in Coyote's Rest forever. He didn't wanna lead those boys as much as they wanted to follow him around. He would've come back to you, eventually."

"I don't know," she stared out the window as they approached the trading town of Rubicross. "Like Harlan wrote, he was a stubborn man, through and through. Always putting the people first..."

Archie pulled up at the designated bus stop in Rubicross, in front of a row of commercial storefronts which collectively bore a single sign for Drew & Colin's Metalware. He waited for the other alighting passengers to disembark before turning around to face Dess.

"If you need a hand, now's the time to tell me," he eyed her solemnly. "Y'know I'm only a letter away, but that letter might not reach me in time."

"No, you've got your kids to take care of," Dess replied as she shouldered her duffel bag and descended the stairs. "You get home safe. I'll see you at the service next week."

He nodded, and she lost him behind the crowd as the bus was swarmed by a wave of new passengers.

Dess walked through the bustling streets of Rubicross, marvelling at how much it had all changed as street vendors plied their wares to the new arrivals from Stillborough. Buildings that had once been riddled with bullet holes and charred with flame now stood restored and ready for business. She supposed that after two years of silence from the Rauder raids combined with the amount of diesel and food from the farm belt that flowed through the town, the local traders had the time and money to renovate.

Her boots carried her to where she remembered Royce Manor had once stood, and she stopped to make sure that she had her bearings straight. She was staring up at a solid concrete wall, at least two storeys high, with an open wooden gate that was double the width of the bus she had just rode in on.

For the first time, Dess felt the weight of her duffel bag. Adjusting the strap, she headed inside, ready to see some more ghosts from the past.

CHAPTER 4 - NATHAN

Nathan Royce toured the grounds of the estate with Enrique Garrido, the portly fastidious event coordinator, making sure that everything was ready for tonight's celebration, with the career military man, Captain Karl Thornton, trailing along behind them like a shadow.

Technicians were busily testing the strings of coloured lights interwoven with the streamers swaying in the faint breeze as they hung overhead from every corner of the courtyard, from the gardening shed to the guard barracks, from the warehouse to the two-room bachelor pad, and from the gatehouse to the grand double-storey residence.

A crew of caterers were tying down white tablecloths and smoothing out the creases. The crockery and silverware would come later, as Nathan's wife, Evelyn, didn't want anything baking in the hot sun any longer than it needed to.

Most people had stopped keeping track of calendar dates ever since the apocalypse. In only a few short weeks following the missile that had struck North Tekota, and seemingly the rest of the world, they had become less concerned with what day it was and more concerned with whether they'd live to see tomorrow. Not Nathan though. He knew the importance of routine, not only in business, but also for maintaining the social aspects and occasions of their thriving community, and above all, the common courtesy it was to remember a significant date in someone else's life.

Today was his younger brother's thirty-ninth birthday, whether he knew it or not. Jeremy Royce always seemed to celebrate his birthday year-round, but at least today, everyone else in Rubicross would be celebrating along with him.

Besides, it made him happy to see Jeremy happy. Given the loss that his younger brother had suffered when the missile hit, it was all Nathan could do to lighten up his life wherever he could, and also, because he knew that his brother would have done the same for him.

"… if I may say so myself," he tuned into Enrique's high-pitched monologue, his clean-shaven double chin dancing as he chittered away. "Canapés will be served the moment the first guest arrives, with beer and wine to follow once they have lined their stomachs. We will be saving the liquor for later in the evening; however, exceptions will be made for the celebrant and any guests of honour. We will have room for eight hundred seated guests, but, as per usual, the chefs have been instructed to cater for a thousand. We will be serving an alternating menu, with entrees consisting of…"

He drifted back out of the conversation. Enrique was in his element. Nathan could rest assured that tonight's celebration would go smoothly, as ever. He simply enjoyed the company while getting a breath of fresh air. He had figured that he should probably have some form of exercise before ploughing into the feast of food that their small army of chefs were busy preparing.

They always catered for an extra two hundred guests. Taking a page out of his wife's book, Nathan would rather be over-prepared than under-prepared. Half the population of Rubicross was comprised of guards, a large proportion of which would no doubt be in attendance, with some of the wealthier businessmen numbering their security forces at over a hundred, including his own. He had lost count of the amount of staff in his employment, but if he ever cared to learn the number, he was certain that he could ask somebody who could ask somebody who would know.

Besides, he had known hunger. Looking at the broad-shouldered man's cheerful green eyes framed between deeply-crinkled laugh lines beneath his neatly-combed light brown hair, one would never have guessed that he and his entire family had been faced with the possibility of death by starvation on a daily basis throughout the food shortages that had plagued Brimvale. Having prospered on the other side of such troubled times, he made it a point to ensure that every single one of his guests – invited or otherwise – could leave at the end of the night after having eaten their fill.

Barrels of wine from the farm belt and kegs of beer from Stillborough drummed noisily on handcarts through the front gates, when Nathan laid eyes on an old friend. She walked falteringly amidst the crowd of deliverymen, peering around at the estate's walls and new buildings that had been erected in her absence.

"Dess!" Nathan called, moving to greet her.

Behind him, Enrique snapped his fingers at the catering crew, signalling them to bring out the canapés, immediately stressing over the event schedule.

Dess moved to the side once she was clear of the gate's foot traffic, thumbing the straps on the duffel bag slung over her shoulder as Nathan drew closer.

"It's great to see you again, you look well!" he exclaimed, offering his hand. She shook it firmly, her calluses rough against his smooth skin. She was a handsome woman, graceful yet gritty, although she was a few skin tones lighter than when he had last seen her, the result of residing in the shade of Stillborough for the past few years. "I can have a room set up for you in no time."

Dess had kept his family safe during a particularly brutal Rauder raid on Rubicross, back when they had no walls surrounding the residence, and their garrison of guards were thinly stretched between patrolling the railroad and the farm belt. He would never allow himself to forget what she had done for them.

"No, it's fine – I'm just passing through," she replied. Her slender face was lined with determination, yet her gaze kept straying to admire the decorations.

"It's Jeremy's birthday," Nathan explained, taking a moment to appreciate the splendour himself. "You picked a great day to drop in for a visit. We'll be having a feast later."

She smiled politely, but he could tell that she was troubled by something.

Suddenly, they were overwhelmed with platters stacked with spinach and mozzarella quiches, fresh salmon tartlets, and ham and tomato crepes, followed by a waiter whose tray bore a selection of sparkling wine flutes, glasses of dry red, heady brown lagers and crisp summer ales.

"Is there somewhere we can talk?" Dess asked, stepping out of the circle of servers.

"Of course," Nathan said as he munched on one of the bite-sized salmon pastries, leading her past the rows of trestle tables towards the gardens. Karl, the tall sharp-eyed guard captain, kept a respectful distance, but he followed them with his perpetual frown nonetheless.

The waiters and waitresses hovered around in their absence, looking for other guests to serve. Some of the technicians began sampling the food platters before Enrique chased the caterers back into the kitchens, happily unburdened by the false alarm.

"Will you be staying for the festivities?" Nathan asked as they strolled through the colourful floral array of bluebonnets and columbines. "We've got more than plenty to go around, and you're welcome to spend the night if it gets too late."

"I'd love to," she said in an apologetic tone, "But I'm afraid it'll have to wait until the journey home. I was hoping to ask you for a favour."

"Of course," Nathan replied immediately, eager to repay his debt to her. "Anything you need, it's yours. All you have to do is ask."

"The guy I signed up with," she began, squinting up at the sentries patrolling the walls before turning to face Nathan again, "Garrett Ridley. Is he still around?"

Nathan remembered that both Dess and Garrett had joined the garrison shortly after the railroad workers had chased Wallace Pelletier to his death. She had decided to part ways after Nathan completed the railroad's construction with what remained of his own funds, but Garrett had chosen to stay.

"I think so," he answered, turning to the guard captain. "Karl, you think you can track down the tracker?"

"There are a lot of new people in the estate today," Karl reminded him, trying hard not to pointedly stare at Dess, but not hard enough. "I can call for someone else to find him."

"Oh, I'll be fine," Nathan smiled, waving him off. "She was one of the good ones, remember?"

"Good ones stay," Karl murmured under his breath, but he left all the same.

Captain Thornton had been the Army Reserves' highest ranking officer remaining in Brimvale after the protests at the Mayor's Office during The Long Summer Night. When his superiors had issued the order to open fire on the unarmed civilians, he commanded his soldiers to stand down. Other companies soon defected to him, many of them having friends and family scattered among the crowd, standing aside to let the protesters administer their brief and bloody justice against the remaining perpetrators who had abused their power for too long.

He had led all of the soldiers back to Fort Mason, but as their stockpile of non-perishable foods ran dry, many of them became deserters. Karl had allowed them to leave, as it meant that there would be fewer mouths to feed, but also because he would have appeared a hypocrite if he admonished them after disobeying his own superiors. Approximately half of his original company remained loyal to him though, and Nathan was thankful for it, as Karl had been the first person he thought of when he needed to hire protection.

"Business must be good," Dess remarked as they waited, unshouldering her duffel bag and sitting down on a garden bench.

"As long as the diesel keeps flowing, we keep going," Nathan quipped, settling in beside her.

"I wish firewood was in as high demand as diesel," she replied, watching Imogen Hainsley, one of the gardeners, as she silently tended the plants nearby.

"Come wintertime, you'll have buyers lined up around the corner again," Nathan said reassuringly. He scratched his unshaven cheek as an idea occurred to him. Thinking on it for a moment, he clasped his hands together and turned to face her. "That is, unless, you'd be willing to do business here in Rubicross?"

Dess frowned, puzzled.

"I've been meaning to offer this opportunity to someone else," he began to explain, "But since you're here, I wouldn't feel right without offering it to you, first. We have almost everything we need here in Rubicross, but we don't have much in the way of medical care. We can ask other settlements for help when we need it, but if there's an emergency, we're out of luck. I need someone to open up trade relations with the survivors at Woodrow College."

"The mutants?" she asked in disbelief, eyeing him with an expression that was both wary and curious to know more.

The students and professors at the university campus on the other side of the Shield Mountains had been situated at the edge of the blast zone when the missile struck North Tekota, and had suffered the debilitating effects of the ensuing wave of radiation, disfiguring them. Many of the other established settlements considered them to be lepers with an untreatable and infectious disease, but apart from the superficial aspects, they were just another group of normal human beings trying to survive.

"Yes," Nathan answered, scratching his cheek again at the term. "My hope is that all of their medical equipment is still intact, and with luck, med students and professors who would be willing to lend their skills or share their knowledge with us. In return for brokering the deal, I'd bring you on as a business partner, and you would share in the proceeds of any food or diesel we supply to them. There's a big potential for ongoing income once this is set up, regardless of the time of year, but more importantly, we could be saving lives here. What do you say, Dess?"

"This is a little sudden," she admitted, looking at the ground as she gathered her thoughts before mustering a reply. "Thanks for thinking of me, but I can't give you an answer right now. There's something else I need to take care of first."

Boot heels scuffed the garden path as Karl and Garrett approached.

"Been a long time, Dess," said Garrett Ridley, standing at attention in the captain's presence.

"Too long," she agreed, looking him up and down. He was in his early twenties, but he looked much older with his shrewd blue-grey eyes and unshaven facial hair, along with the hints of grey growing through his unkempt shoulder-length brown hair. "You got the letter?"

"Yeah," he replied, his jaw clenching as he looked away. "I think it's bullshit. The way he died."

"That makes two of us," Dess said quietly, a shadow crossing her face.

"My condolences," Nathan offered in the silence that followed. "If you don't mind me asking, who died?"

"Old friend, by the name of Emmett," Garrett answered, before turning back to Dess. "Only planned on going for the funeral though. Ain't know him as much as you." He glanced at the small golden watch on her wrist.

"Have you filled out your application for leave?" asked Karl, his eyes piercing Garrett.

"Let him go," said Nathan. *Old habits die hard*, he supposed. "And give them anything else they might be needing; a truck, food for the road, some water... and an armed escort."

"Thank you, sir," Garrett replied before stroking his scruffy beard. "But a truck ain't gonna get us where we need to go. Too many potholes from here to Coyote's Rest. Horses would be better."

"Ah yes," Nathan remembered. It was a wonder how the farmers were able to navigate that dimpled dirt road without losing half their cargo. He turned to Karl, "Could you ask somebody to fetch a few of our horses from Mallory's Ranch?"

"*Bruce Mallory?*" Dess soured at the name, as if merely mentioning him had left a bad taste in her mouth.

"The same," Nathan answered, knowing the luckless businessman's reputation. "He's not a bad man, just has a habit of making bad friends."

"Birds of a feather," Dess replied with a sideways glance.

"Well," Nathan shrugged, moving the subject back on course. "A horse is a horse no matter where it's kept. You'll probably be needing a few tents and some proper provisions if you're going the old-fashioned way."

"Yeah, I guess it couldn't hurt," Dess admitted, smiling at the trouble he was going to. "I don't imagine we'll need the armed escort though. I don't wanna cause too much of a fuss."

"No, I insist," Nathan replied firmly, gesturing at the guards patrolling the walls. "We're well-protected here, but with all the rumours of the Rauders raiding out west again, I'd sleep much better knowing that you had a few more pairs of eyes to watch your back."

"About that," Garrett interjected, leaning back into the conversation. "Ain't a good idea to be bringing tents. If anyone tries sneaking up on us at night out in the prairies, we don't want anything blocking our view of the landscape."

"You gonna turn down the food and water next?" Karl asked, frowning at the guard. "Bring the damn tents. Use them as a decoy campsite if you're not gonna sleep in them."

"Thank you," said Dess, picking up her duffel bag and slinging the straps over her shoulder again. "Really, this is more than I was hoping for."

"Any time," Nathan smiled, getting to his feet. "A hundred favours couldn't repay the debt I owe you. But, if we're talking about the same Emmett from Coyote's Rest, then the loss couldn't have happened at a more tragic time."

"Why's that?" she and Garrett asked in unison.

"That opportunity that I've been saving for someone else," Nathan explained, the cheer fading from his eyes. "I was saving it for Emmett Pearce. He was supposed to be here tonight. I was looking forward to offering it to him. Emmett had been wanting to go into business with me for the longest time."

Dess's boots were pointing down the garden path when she stopped to exchange a curious glance with Garrett.

"Did Mallory know you were planning on working with Emmett?" she asked, turning back to face Nathan front-on.

He swallowed before nodding.

"I ran it past Bruce just to make sure there'd be no issues, given their history," Nathan scratched his cheek, searching for the right words. "He was a little shocked, but... He said that he was willing to leave the past where it belongs."

"He's not exactly famous for telling the truth," said Dess, putting a hand on her hip.

"Mallory can hide the truth as much as he likes," Karl chimed in, scanning her waist warily, "But when it boils down to it, he isn't the type of man who could take another man's life."

"With all due respect, sir," Garrett offered, his eyes flitting between Nathan and Karl. "If a man's got money, he ain't need to do anything himself."

Breaking the silence that followed Garrett's remark, Dess thanked Nathan again. He smiled politely, wishing them a safe journey before sitting back down on the garden bench, letting Karl see them off.

Leaning back in the chair, Nathan recalled Bruce's role during the railroad's construction. Wallace Pelletier had put the man in charge of managing payroll for the workers, where he was tasked with making up excuses as to why their wages weren't in line with what they had been expecting when they signed up. Naturally, he made the perfect scapegoat when Wallace decided to vanish with the stolen golden bucks.

On his knees before the lynch mob, Bruce confessed that they had all been underpaid from the very beginning, but only under instruction, or so he claimed. The workers hadn't even needed to ask him the question before he gave up the direction the former foreman had fled. Bruce Mallory was perhaps the happiest among the workers when Wallace had been found, otherwise Emmett and the others could have just as easily hunted Bruce down like an animal across the prairies.

A thought like that could not be forgotten so easily.

CHAPTER 5 – EVELYN

Throughout the day, Evelyn Royce had intermittently sat in the plush green armchair beside her bedroom window, watching the caterers and technicians setting up the courtyard below. It didn't matter how many parties they had thrown, watching all of the effort that was put into the preparations always seemed to enchant her. Even now, workers were scurrying in and out of the food and wine cellars. Warehouse clerks were inspecting last-minute deliveries and drearily signing their autographs, while apprentice chefs ran back and forth from the kitchens with their grocery lists.

Her husband, Nathan, always insisted on inviting the entire town of Rubicross twice over. Their family had come from such humble beginnings only a few years ago, so he made it a point of giving back to the community that had allowed them to prosper so much. And she, in turn, made it a point of ensuring that their food storehouses were always packed to capacity, refilling the shelves just as quickly as they were emptied, so that each event didn't reduce them to hungry beggars.

Prior to the missile strike, the Royces had lived a modest lifestyle in Brimvale, like any other family in the 21st Century. Work to pay off the mortgage, see the kids through school, and maybe go on a holiday at the end of the year. And, like any other family, they were nowhere near prepared for the apocalypse. No canned foods, no boxes full of jerky, no cartons of long-life milk. Ferguson's Supermarket had provided them with everything that they had ever needed on a week-to-week basis. That was, until Flynn Ferguson had decided to sneak a group of grocers and their families into the supermarket overnight, boarding up the windows and shooting at any approaching panic-buyers in the parking lot on sight.

It wasn't long before the Army Reserves stationed in Fort Mason had realised that without communication to the outside world, they had become the highest link in the chain of command, and their attention quickly focused on every usable resource in Brimvale. Within twenty minutes of arriving in the supermarket's concrete no-man's-land, they had successfully smoked out the grocers, executed Ferguson on his knees, along with anyone else who had been holding a weapon – regardless of whether they had already dropped it – and exiled the survivors to The Gutter.

Relieved by the swift justice and the initial distribution of goods, not even a few days had passed before everyone realised that the Army Reserves were just as bad at sharing. Further goods were only distributed on an "as needs" basis, which, by their definition, meant "visibly near starvation", unless the supplicants had something worthwhile to offer the soldiers.

It was only a few short weeks before one could distinguish the whores and hoarders from the beggars and scavengers. Rather than allowing herself or her two daughters to become playthings in exchange for soup cans, Evelyn and her family went for days at a time without food, watching each others' cheeks turn sallow, hair and nails become brittle, and bones protrude from their skin, until they would qualify for another half-empty hand-basket of rations.

They had lived through the worst of the food shortages following the end of the world, and despite her open-handed husband's best intentions to give away as much food as he possibly could, Evelyn did not mean to ever let her family go wanting again.

"Mum?" Sadie appeared at the bedroom door, biting her lip. Just like Evelyn had been at eighteen years old, her daughter was lithe and slender, with long light brown hair cascading down to the small of her back, although Evelyn had always preferred to tie her own hair back. "Do you think I look okay?"

She was beautiful, but Evelyn crossed the room and pretended to fuss over her eldest daughter's airy blue dress all the same, if only just to set her insecurities at ease.

"There, perfect," said Evelyn, taking one final glance at her own green off-shoulder gown in the full-length mirror before leaving the bedroom. "Come on, the guests should be arriving any minute now."

Sadie's shoulders slumped slightly, but she followed Evelyn dutifully all the same. Being the middle child, Sadie had always been a shy girl, yet even as she tried to avoid being the centre of attention, she rarely failed to impress her long list of suitors.

Aimee, on the other hand, the youngest of Evelyn's three children, was the polar opposite. They passed by her bedroom on their way downstairs, which was the quiet embodiment of her own appearance; a butchered wardrobe which spilled across the floor, an experimental rainbow of cosmetics on her dresser, and peeling posters of rock bands who had died long before the apocalypse.

The two boys standing in the glossy white-tiled hallway at the bottom of the flight of stairs already had drinks in their hands.

"Mum," they said in unison, raising their bottles of beer in salute before taking another swig.

Evelyn caught the staircase's handrail, fumbling a smile. She had never gotten used to Jeremy's son, Jordan, calling her "Mum", but she would never dream of correcting him. Having taken on the responsibility of raising the boy ever since the aftermath of the missile strike in North Tekota, Jordan was practically her own son anyway, except that he looked nothing like the rest of her children with his shoulder-length tousled black hair.

"Where's your sister?" she asked as they carefully descended the stairs in their heels, addressing her eldest, Ryan.

"Right next to you," he grinned, nodding at Sadie.

"Your *younger* sister," Evelyn sighed, yet again having set herself up for his time-honoured joke. Practically a clone of his father in his early twenties with his broad-shouldered frame, his light brown hair brushed and gelled with aloe vera, along with the beginnings of bristly stubble lining his chiselled chin, Ryan had also unfortunately inherited Nathan's cheesy sense of humour.

Even as she had asked the question, she knew that it was redundant. It was more of a habitual phrase than a pressing concern. Aimee was wherever she wanted to be, but they could at least rest assured that she wouldn't stray too far to risk missing her performance tonight.

"I'm sure Marv's chasing after her and Bianca somewhere," Shirley breathed, appearing beside the wide arch of the games room, apparently having given up on her fruitless search as she smoothed the form-fitting fabric of her black cocktail dress over her slender waistline.

The sparkling blue-eyed Shirley Beaumont, along with her daughter, Bianca, were two of the housekeepers, both possessing a natural beauty. At first, Evelyn had been apprehensive of Nathan's decision to hire them, especially given Shirley's note of refined elegance, although his reason had been to keep them from stooping to the shameful and humiliating alternatives for making ends meet in the post-apocalypse. There were far worse people to work for than the Royce Family.

At fifteen years old, Bianca was the same age as Aimee, and although Evelyn and Nathan had given their youngest daughter a partner-in-crime, at least they had taken some small comfort in knowing that she would no longer be wandering off by herself anymore. Forming a friendship seemingly overnight, the two teenagers had decided to start a band together, along with Jake Mallory, Bruce and Audrey's son.

"They might be rehearsing somewhere, I guess?" Ryan shrugged as he took another swig.

"*Hope* would be the word," Jordan chuckled, making Ryan snort and spit his drink.

"Behave, you two," Evelyn suppressed a smirk, "And pace yourselves with those beers, please. I don't want to hear about any trouble tonight."

Just last week, Ryan and Jordan had been involved in a fight with a group of cowboys at The Oxhouse, the bar across the road. She had given them a stern lecture, while Nathan was just happy to see that they had come out in one piece. Jeremy's only concern was whether they had won, and of course they had won; just about every off-duty guard in town had been on their side.

Forced to carry the burden of administering discipline, she had grounded the two boys, forbidding them from venturing outside the estate until she said otherwise, but with all of the guests who would be coming and going tonight, she would just have to hope that they could keep themselves in line.

"Yes, Mum," they said in unison, before racing each other to the bottom of the bottle.

Sighing, but not surprised, Evelyn looked out the front doors, which stood wide open, to see the first guests beginning to arrive through the gates in the early evening air. Enrique Garrido was hastily bustling about the tables as he pedantically checked the place settings while snapping his fingers at the caterers.

Evelyn thanked the fussing event coordinator for all of his hard work as she and Sadie crossed the grounds. Suddenly self-conscious, Enrique wiped the sheen of sweat glistening beneath his hurriedly-combed wavy black hair and forced a graceful smile in return, which soon disappeared the moment he discovered a spoon that was slightly out of place.

Nathan waved at them from the front door of Jeremy's bachelor pad, a two-room bungalow with its curtains constantly drawn, patiently waiting for the birthday celebrant to piece himself together and make an appearance at his own party.

Evelyn smiled back sympathetically, knowing that her husband would have his hands full trying to ensure that Jeremy wouldn't make a complete fool of himself, but she also knew that all of Nathan's effort would end in utter futility.

"Stand up straight," she reminded Sadie as they moved to greet the guests. She knew that her daughter always hated this part of the night, and the feeling was mutual, but they had to play the part of being the hospitable hosts.

They exchanged pleasantries with a few of the less-prominent families of Rubicross, along with a smattering of vagrants – who she only regarded as freeloaders – as they swarmed the platters of delectable pastries circling the crowd, the type of company that her brother-in-law would normally surround himself with.

Haydar, the short round and perpetually drunken potato farmer who had taken on the appearance of his own stock bumbled through the gates, holding his tall bodyguard's hand like a horribly-mismatched couple. He eyed the serving trays, scrutinising the perspiring pints of frothy lager and bubbling wine flutes before taking a finicky pull from one of his hip flasks. Evelyn saw that Omar, his bald and brawny goateed bodyguard, had been laden with extra flasks like a pack mule, the oblong shapes bulging from his black suit jacket's breast pockets and slacks.

At least he's not a freeloader, Evelyn thought to herself.

There was an air of mystery around Omar that she couldn't quite put her finger on. Such a disciplined and well-trained guard would have been a boon to anyone's security staff, but for some odd reason, he had chosen to become a bodyguard for Haydar, of all people.

Sadie straightened up at the sight of Kristian Mackenzie, the carefree aloe vera farmer from Firmfield. As far as Evelyn was aware, he hadn't been invited, yet he was more welcome than some of the other guests. Michelle Tan, the Royce Family's petite personal accountant turned inventory manager, greeted him warmly. Evelyn never knew the origin of their friendship, although they had both come from finance backgrounds in Sunken City, so there was a high chance that they had met sometime before an earthquake had put the city underwater.

Marvin Devereux, the head of the house staff, exasperatedly emerged from behind the barracks, clearly clueless as to where Aimee and Bianca were. Shaking his head, he swiped a wineglass from a serving tray and began flirting with one of the guests. With his penchant for Hawaiian shirts, Marv was one of the seldom few who made his job seem like a holiday.

Evelyn waved at Drew and Colin the moment she spotted them in the crowd, promptly extracting herself and Sadie from a conversation that was saturated with small talk. Unlike the many fair-weather friends the Royce Family had, Evelyn had formed a genuine friendship with the industrious pair of metalworkers from down the street.

Drew and Colin had abandoned the railroad's construction shortly after the first Desert Marauder raid, choosing instead to take over an old wood-fired pizza restaurant in the relative safety of Rubicross, converting its oven into a furnace while drawing inspiration and equipment from the disused blacksmith in Coyote's Rest.

At the time, nobody in the rustic re-enactment town had opposed the tools being removed, since their cobweb-covered workshop had already fallen into a state of disrepair. Although, after seeing the extent of the pair's success only a few weeks later, the cowboys of Coyote's Rest soon realised the value of what they had so thoughtlessly given away.

Drew and Colin had rapidly turned sizeable profits by making horse shoes for the riders and the ranchers in the prairies, decorative silverware for the wealthy in Rubicross, and various custom-made tools required throughout the farm belt, holding a monopoly over the metal-working trade.

They were also some of the only men in town who would compliment Sadie without the underlying tone of wanting to get into her pants; although their comments towards Ryan and Jordan were openly less above-board, but all in good humour.

"Evelyn, you look absolutely stunning in that dress!" Colin exclaimed, greeting her with a kiss on each cheek, brushing her with his scruffy ginger beard. "And Sadie, if Drew wasn't here, I swear, I would turn straight for the night."

"Fine by me," Drew smiled, the veins of one of his ropey forearms bulging beneath the weight of a large handsomely-wrapped gift. "I'd finally have the bed to myself."

"You'd miss me," Colin teased, draping an arm around Sadie's shoulders. "See how good we look together? You'd be jerking your jackhammer from afar."

"And you would miss his jackhammer," Sadie told Colin with a smirk.

Despite being nearly half their age, Sadie shared Evelyn's fondness for the two men. She was glad to see her daughter finally warming up to the party. Sadie had almost seemed like a smiling statue by her side for all of the other guests.

"Hello, you two," said Evelyn, happy to unwind after the parade of welcomes. She reached for a spinach and mozzarella quiche and was about to ask their thoughts on the rumoured return of the Rauder raids when somebody tut-tutted from behind.

"Those look terribly fattening," Laszlo Snyder commented, pointedly staring at the pastry in her hand, his deriding tone disguised underneath one of his patented charming yet sleazy smiles. The silver-sideburned snake had mastered the act of sneering with his cold and calculating blue eyes. "But I'm sure they're delicious."

He stood proudly between Janelle and Anton, his expressionless young wife and spoilt son, along with a retinue of fifty guards who immediately dispersed to swarm the food platters. They did this at every event, making sure that the caterers were overworked and the rest of the guests struggled to find a canapé.

"Let's get a drink," Anton suggested to Sadie with a smug grin, trying to draw her away before even acknowledging Evelyn's presence. Anton had inherited zero charm from his father; he had only managed to pick up the excessive sleaze.

Sadie's hazel eyes went wide as she looked to her mother in dismay. Laszlo raised his eyebrows, watching Evelyn's reaction as her lips tightened and shoulders stiffened, even as she knew that his eyes were upon her.

"We'll join you!" Drew decided cheerily. "I'll drop off this gift first and catch up. Colin, could you grab me a beer?"

"Yes sir!" Colin mocked him with a hand salute before draping his arm around Sadie's shoulders again. "You can find us wherever Ryan and Jordan have been hiding away their eye candy."

Evelyn breathed an inaudible sigh of relief as they left together, with Colin between Sadie and Anton, although now she was stuck alone with Laszlo and Janelle.

Evelyn despised him. Laszlo Snyder had once been the landlord of a strip of commercial stores in Brimvale. Nathan, who had been the owner of a modest electronics shop, had discovered that Laszlo was levying his annual rental increases based on the amount of customers seen entering their store on a given day. While the practice was perfectly legal, they could never shake the feeling of being discriminated against for running a successful business.

Now, Laszlo ran a nude gallery and a brothel in Rubicross Elementary, deplorably refurbishing and repurposing the old school; and again, merely providing a place for others to conduct their business, and taking his cut of the profits.

Evelyn had nothing to say to either of them. She glanced back at Sadie, and was pleased to see Colin leading the conversation, while Anton seethed to the side, grinding his teeth in jealousy for not being in her centre of attention.

"Always a pleasure, Evelyn," Laszlo lied, breaking the brief spell of awkward silence with another fake smile, "But we don't want to be selfish with your time. I'm sure you have plenty of other guests to entertain." Placing one hand on Janelle's lower back, they turned to leave, but he paused to deliver a parting barb. "I think we'll find the birthday celebrant. It would be bad for business not to give our well wishes to our best customer."

Evelyn popped the quiche into her mouth, chewing with her eyes narrowed as she watched them strut into the crowd. Bitterly, she doubted that Janelle would be allowed to enjoy more than a mouthful of any of the enticing food on display. Laszlo would want her to maintain her slim figure.

She remembered overhearing the guards spreading a rumour about his young wife, who wasn't actually his wife. Janelle had simply been the best-looking girl working in his nude gallery until she had the misfortune of catching Laszlo's interest. Supposedly, he had given her a choice; she could either become his companion or work in the brothel at one fifth of the regular price. Of course, whenever someone so young is given an ultimatum, they always assume that there are only two options.

Evelyn caught sight of Bruce Mallory's skinny physique as he joined Laszlo and Janelle on their way towards the small crowd clustering near

Nathan and Jeremy, who had finally emerged from his bachelor pad, and she looked around for Audrey.

After Wallace's death, the Mallory family had moved to Rubicross to start their own ranch, buying livestock in bulk from the farm belt and selling them fresh to the butcher shops in other settlements around South Tekota. They also tended to the horses of Rubicross; chiefly the Royce Family's, the beautiful animals now retired from the mounted patrols back when their guards had been assigned to keep watch over the prairies.

Ever since their name had been besmirched by the railroad workers' backlash, Bruce had tried to rebuild his family's reputation by currying favour with all of the major traders in Rubicross, using every celebratory event as a networking opportunity. Evelyn shuddered at the thought of how he could be friendly towards both Nathan and Laszlo, both men at polar opposites of the ethical business spectrum. Bruce always had a conflicted sense of morality, which was perhaps why his wife preferred to distance herself and their son from his business affairs.

"You look like you could use some company," a friendly woman's voice came from behind. Evelyn turned to see Audrey Mallory, holding a pair of sparkling wine flutes with a wry smile. "Don't make me drink alone, because you know I will."

"You are a sight for sore eyes," Evelyn beamed, kissing her on the cheek and wholeheartedly quenching the thirst she had been harbouring.

"Let's move to a table before someone else tries to steal you away," said Audrey, glancing over her shoulder at the next wave of guests flooding through the gates.

"Let's," Evelyn agreed, raising her glass. "Here's to another hopefully uneventful night."

Yet even as they clinked their wine flutes together, Evelyn could not shake the nagging feeling that something was missing.

CHAPTER 6 – ADRIAN

He had no idea how she had managed to get inside the crowded barracks, but here she was, interrupting everyone's early dinners of rice and minced beef stew. Adrian Wakefield had been preparing for the evening shift in the mess hall with all of the other guards when one of the Royce Family's guests had decided that the entire estate had an open-door policy.

At first, he and his four friends had thought that she was drunk, staggering in from the dusk and hurling herself at the first chair in sight, with a view to harass the men. But, leaning closer, he realised that it was Millie Quiggens, a pouty woman who he had known years ago, before he and his forsaken father had moved to Coyote's Rest. She was recruiting security for her ranch, rather unsuccessfully, fearing the recent return of the Rauder raids.

Adrian was happy to see that what little welcome she had was quickly wearing thin. Every single guard that she had approached had already turned her down irritatedly, not even giving her proposition a second thought. They were paid far better in Rubicross, and had far fewer threats to deal with than what she was trying to offer them.

"Here we go," said Todd Kingston, one of the senior guards seated at a nearby table. "Another Wallace Pelletier, promising long days for shitty pay while her fat ass gets fatter."

"One thing you can bet on," Darcy Foster remarked around her mouthful of stew, "Neither of those fuckers ever lived on food rations, much as they expected everyone else to."

"And how'd that work out for Wallace?" Adam Ryker asked rhetorically.

"Imagine the size of either of them back when fast food was still around," Terry Delaney grinned, although even as he said it, they all salivated at the nostalgic thought of an artery-clogging cheeseburger's sloppy water-injected meat patty raised on growth hormones and coated with enough preservatives to withstand a nuclear war.

Despite being one of the gardeners, Terry always ate in the barracks with the guards. The forty-something-year-old's childhood dream had been to join the army, although he paradoxically hated the idea of having a boss breathing down his neck all the time. Adrian had already been a cadet when he heard the man's outlook on life. It had been too late for Adrian to change his career, but it never stopped him from wondering what his days would have been like if "being off-duty" actually meant being off-duty.

For a tall and wide-shouldered eighteen year old, the world should have been full of opportunities for the black-haired and dark brown-eyed adolescent to learn a trade or start his own business. Even in the post-apocalyptic world, much of the fertile farm belt was still as yet unclaimed, and there were still plenty of unfulfilled needs to be met, yet Adrian had been hamstrung so many times throughout his teenage years that he had eventually accepted that a life of guard duty was all he would ever be cut out for.

"She must raise donkeys at Quiggens' Ranch," Reece Jensen observed beside Adrian, the slim cadet's protruding Adam's apple bobbing up and down as he watched Millie persistently plead and petition above the noise of the barracks. "She's as stubborn as a mule, with an ass for a face."

Flecks of food flew as a few of the men and women at the nearby tables laughed with their mouths full. Even some of the seasoned veterans choked on the joke, and they normally liked to pretend that the relatively new guards didn't exist.

Millie's ears pricked up, as if she had just been summoned. She weaved her way over to their table, squeezing through the crowded mess hall. Adrian suppressed his smirk at Reece's statement which became truer with each passing moment as Millie approached with her arms folded across her chest, her dirty blonde hair tied in a low ponytail which only accentuated her sagging jowls. She could have easily passed for a puffy red-cheeked colonial farm boy reluctantly readying himself to help birth his first calf.

Remembering that she was in their domain, her scowl soon morphed into a forced smile.

"Any of you fine young soldiers interested in an adventure?" she asked, hoping to at least coax some interest out of them first before being rejected. Like every other guard in the barracks, Adrian and his friends ignored the question, continuing to eat their meals and pretending that she wasn't there. Naturally, she took their silence as an invitation to continue, pulling up a chair and plopping herself between them, "Because I have something exciting for you!"

"Listen, lady," said Reece, levelling his fork at her. "I can guarantee anything that might seem exciting for you, probably wouldn't even give me the *mildest* of erections."

Adrian bit his cheeks to keep from chuckling. Simon Yu turned away, shaking silently. Devon Bailey hid her smirk behind another mouthful of stew, but Stacey Sherman laughed uproariously, food dribbling into his short beard as he choked and spat and pounded the table.

Millie Quiggens shifted in her seat uncomfortably, the chair creaking in protest.

Stacey looked around at them all incredulously before he began to explain the intricacies of the joke, as if they hadn't understood.

"'e means you don't turn 'im on!" he exclaimed, before laughing again.

"Thank you for the clarification," Millie replied with pursed lips, "But it's not that type of proposition."

"Why are you even approaching *us?*" asked Simon, wiping his chubby cheeks with a table napkin. "None of us have a license to carry."

"She likes 'em young," Stacey winked before elbowing Reece, causing him to drop his fork in annoyance.

"Joke's over, Sherman, drop it already," Devon chided as she gathered up her cutlery and excused herself, carrying her plate to another table, preferring to sit with Lexi and Nina on the other side of the cafeteria rather than endure any more of Stacey's nonsense, the big oaf still utterly dumbfounded as to what he had done wrong.

"Out on our ranch," Millie began to answer Simon's question as she spread herself into Devon's former space, "You wouldn't need a license to carry. You'd all have firearms on your first day."

"It's about time you got yourself some decent security," Adrian finally spoke, straight-faced. "You're only a few years too late."

Her mouth opened in silence, and then closed again, like a fish in an aquarium after realising who he was, and what he had lost.

"And do we have to bring our own bullets, or are they included in the pay cut?" Reece asked, feigning curiosity as he leaned across the table.

Millie sighed as she clambered to her feet, giving the entire room a stink-eye before storming out, her capacity for courtesy coming to a close as she shoved her way through the seated guards in the packed mess hall.

"I guess we'll never know," Simon grinned as he pushed his black-framed glasses up the bridge of his nose.

"You boys certainly 'ave a way with women!" Stacey roared, more stew dripping into his beard as he elbowed Reece in the ribs again.

Reece gave him an exaggerated smile as he slid his chair out of elbow-reach.

"I thought she'd never leave!" Javier Cortez piped up across the room.

"Is no one going with her?" Andy Baker called out, the barracks erupting in laughter.

The imposing figure of Captain Thornton appeared at the doorway, sizing up the mess hall with his sharp eyes before marching into the room.

"ATTENTION!!" Daniel Lennox yelled, killing the noise.

Seeing the guard captain at the entrance, they all stood up, chairs screeching backwards and cutlery clattering on plates. There were hundreds of guards in Rubicross, comprised of ex-soldiers from the Army Reserves, police officers, remnants of the railroad workers and those who had never gotten the chance to learn a trade. While Captain Thornton had been a senior officer in the Army Reserves prior to its disbandment, Adrian Wakefield had most certainly been from the bottom of that list.

Nodding his approval, the guard captain closed the door behind him.

"As usual, I want everyone's heads on a swivel tonight," he said sternly, his eyes sweeping across the room while simultaneously piercing each guard to their core. "We need to watch what's happening inside the walls, just as much as what's happening outside. I don't want anyone getting distracted. You are not guests. You are guards. Clear?"

"Sir, yes, sir!"

"Clear?"

"Sir, yes, sir!"

"Dismissed," he opened the door again and stood to one side, watching like a hawk whether anyone had the guts to finish their meals.

Adrian adjusted the baton on his waist and filed out with the others.

The senior guards received handguns and rifles from the gun cage, while the juniors carried either a holstered baton or a crossbow slung over their shoulder. Adrian, Reece, Simon and Stacey were still in their first year of service as guardsmen, so they were only licensed to carry batons. Unlike other settlements around South Tekota, Rubicross guards weren't given their firearms immediately, as there were relatively too few guns and ammunition to pass around to all of the guards in town.

In a few months' time though, Adrian would begin his crossbow training, and a year after that, if he was deemed ready, he would be licensed to carry a firearm while working a shift. After five years of service, any long-serving guards would be allowed to carry at all times, but no one had reached that level of tenure yet; although Captain Thornton and Lieutenant Grady were never seen without their weapons. But then again, the pair of officers never seemed to be off-duty.

They marched around the throng of guests in the courtyard who were happily chatting, sipping drinks and occasionally glancing at the way to the kitchens, hoping to catch the next wave of caterers carrying canapés. Adrian took up his usual guard position outside the warehouse. The irony had never been lost on him, given that prior to becoming a guard, he had been caught stealing food. It was a mediocre spot on most evenings, since deliveries were rarely made after hours, but at least he would have a decent view of the festivities.

Despite Captain Thornton's emphasis on not getting distracted, it was difficult to resist being fascinated by the colourful hanging lights and streamers rippling in the wind. Skimpily-dressed prostitutes from the Snyder Family's Backstage brothel were dispersed throughout the crowd. All of the guards knew that Mrs Royce held a deep hatred for seeing the hussies and whores so close to home, but that just meant that the women had to pay an "entry fee" to the men watching the gates.

Later in the evening, Adrian knew, the prostitutes would brazenly walk in and out of the estate, either arriving shortly after men wearing smug grins, or leaving with new clientele, Laszlo Snyder's eyes twinkling as his investments continued to produce profits while he enjoyed the party. With the amount of wealthy businessmen and well-paid working class men in attendance, the opportunity to make money was too good to pass up.

Many of the guests looked like a faceless blur of people adorned in fine clothing and jewellery, having persevered through the hard times after the apocalypse, and now they were comfortably enjoying their success. Perhaps the end of the world had been the best thing to have ever happened to them.

Adrian, on the other hand, hadn't been so lucky. Years ago – which may as well have been a lifetime ago – his family had spent a few months at Quiggens' Ranch during the railroad's construction. Despite numerous warnings of the savages who came down from the ruins of North Tekota, stealing supplies, killing men and kidnapping women, Ernie and Millie Quiggens had been far too relaxed when it came to the security of their late father's ranch. They refused to believe that anyone could have survived the lingering radiation in the badlands of the blast zone for so long, dismissing the rumours of the Rauder raids as wild stories being spread by the railroad workers who would rather get paid for sitting in the shade all day, diligently guarding against a threat that they knew would never come.

Then, one day, the ranch came under attack, and Adrian lost his mother and two sisters to the savages. His father had hidden in the stables during the raid, pinning Adrian to the ground with a hand over his mouth. Adrian resented him for it, and idly watched as his cowardly father spiralled into an alcoholic stupor once they moved to Coyote's Rest.

On one of his father's particularly boozy nights where he had fallen unconscious in a public outhouse behind the hovel that their dwindling finances had forced them to live in, Adrian had decided to take half of their food supply, choosing to roam the prairies to live off the land, hoping to track down the Rauders with a fool's fantasy that the rest of his family would still be alive.

Nearly three months later, the land that he had decided to live off turned out to be a string of private properties scattered throughout the farm belt, and a group of farmers had caught him sleeping in a barn. Having lost everything but his hunger, Adrian had welcomed the thought of death as punishment for being a thief, but the farmers, not wishing to kill a boy in his late teens who was simply stealing food to survive, brought him to the Royce Family, hoping to claim some sort of bounty for catching a criminal.

Nathan Royce had given Adrian the time to tell his entire story since the end of the world, and it was then that the man offered him a job, stating that his knowledge of how to survive in the prairies may someday prove useful. After months spent feeling like an outcast with nowhere to belong, Adrian was thankful that someone had finally accepted him and given him a home again. He would never forget Mr Royce's act of kindness.

Voices coming from behind the warehouse snapped him out of his recollection. He looked around. The sky had turned a deep purple hue as the day gave way to night. Moths and mosquitoes buzzed around the coloured hanging lights. Several of the guests had found their way to a table, finding it easier to drink and sit rather than drink and stand. Haydar, the infamous potato farmer, had already fallen asleep in his chair, his hands clasped over his rising and falling belly as his vigilant bodyguard kept watch.

Placing a precautionary hand on his baton, Adrian rounded the corner, heading down the alley towards the back of the warehouse to investigate the voices. The gardening shed stood closed on the right, the generator's access panel was away on the left between the warehouse and the outer wall, and he had been posted at the only entrance to the passage. Cautiously, he rounded the second corner.

The voices belonged to a group of young adults sitting in a circle, all of them ranging from their late teens to their early thirties. He was surprised that they had been able to sneak past him, or perhaps they had been there since the start of his shift. He recognised them all. They were the second generation of the Royce Family, along with their friends, children from other traders in Rubicross, and a few of the residence's staff who had been given the night off.

This is where I would be if things were different, Adrian thought to himself as Paige Spencer, one of the kitchenhands, spun an empty beer bottle on the ground.

"Oops, sorry," Sadie Royce was looking up at him, biting her lip as she clumsily hid her drink. "Are we allowed to be back here?"

He wasn't sure why she was so worried, since he worked for her father, and, by extension, he worked for her, but now everyone else had turned around to see him.

"Of course we're allowed to be back here," Anton Snyder scoffed. He was a smug-looking youth around Adrian's age, with slicked-back black hair and ice chip blue eyes. "We can go wherever we want. What's he gonna do anyway? He's only carrying a baton. It's probably his first day!"

"Dick…" Adrian muttered, turning to leave. *You should watch how you talk to people who get paid to make sure nothing bad happens to you.*

"What?" asked Anton, scrambling to his feet. "What was that? Did you say something?" Anton took two steps, grabbed Adrian and shoved him into the wall. "I can't hear you."

Adrian's shaky fingers fidgeted with the strap on his baton's holster.

"Say it again," Anton menaced into his ear. "I dare you."

Adrian wasn't quaking out of fear. He was simply torn with indecision. Whatever he did now, he would have to live with it. Whether that was whipping out the baton and caving in this rich kid's skull in front of his friends at a party, or letting himself get humiliated so that he could go back to his life of being a good little subservient guard. He squeezed his baton's grip with white knuckles.

"Let it go," Ryan Royce appeared behind them, pulling Anton away. "Just let him do his job in peace. You *were* being a dick."

"I was, wasn't I?" Anton agreed with a fake smile, shaking off Ryan's hands to reach up and check his greasy black hair. "At least he knows who's boss."

Adrian loosened his grip on the baton, taking deep breaths to calm his nerves. The relief was plastered across each of the onlookers' faces, too, but they all avoided making eye contact with the two troublemakers.

"Well, that was exciting!" Drew declared, the thirty-something-year-old blacksmith from down the street, "All this masculine energy, I'm working up quite the sweat."

"Oh yes," Colin agreed, grinning around at the rest of the group before looking up at Anton, "We were about to join you. We also like to play rough."

The others broke out into nervous laughter, soon sliding back into the party's ambience. Sadie cringed away from Anton as he swaggered towards her, having hoped to sit beside her in the circle.

"Should be dinnertime soon," said Jordan Royce, getting to his feet. "We'd best find some seats before there's none left."

"Sounds good to me, I'm starving," the spurned Anton replied, eyeing Sadie coldly. He kicked his beer glass over before smiling at Adrian, "Hey *dick*. Clean this mess up, would you?"

Drew shot Adrian a sympathetic glance before leading the way back to the courtyard, with the rest of them all too happy to follow him out of the alley.

"Go," Jordan nodded at Adrian, lagging behind as he took a swig of his beer. "I've got this. Don't want Terry and Imogen finding it in the morning."

Adrian knew that Mr Royce's nephew occasionally lent a hand to the estate's gardeners.

"Leave it for the servants," Anton's snide scoff came from around the corner. "That's what they're paid for."

"Have a bit of respect for the people who live with us," Ryan's voice followed as they faded out of earshot.

"Thanks," said Adrian, thumbing his baton's strap back into place, "To you, and Ryan. Thank you both."

"Don't mention it," Jordan replied, running a hand through his shoulder-length black hair before bending down to pick up the glasses left behind. "Nobody likes Anton anyway."

"I wonder why," Adrian snorted before turning the corner, marching back to his post beside the warehouse's entrance.

No distractions, he tardily reminded himself.

The evening wore on, a tide ebbing and flowing from the tables as the dedicated crew of caterers served and cleared dishes. Well-dressed traders talked business and off-duty guards pretended to be alert between drinks, which they swore were the same ones from the hour before.

Jeremy Royce slurred his way through his birthday speech, one gangly arm hanging around Jordan's shoulders to hold himself upright. Mrs Royce sat with her arms crossed, clearly unimpressed, waiting for her threadbare-clothed brother-in-law to wrap it up. Adrian was certain that the shabby man wouldn't even remember the party. He looked away for a moment, because even as Jeremy spoke, Adrian could see his own father spitting and staggering with the microphone.

"Cheers!" Jordan cut across his father's nonsensical rambling, ending everyone's polite suffering as he raised a glass to the crowd. He led Jeremy back to his seat, making way for his dark blonde cousin, Aimee Royce, along with her teen rock band as they set up for their performance.

"Cheers," Adrian muttered, idly wondering if his own father had ever made it out of the public outhouse back in Coyote's Rest.

Haydar had finally awoken from his hooch-induced slumber, and he wandered out onto the dancing square the moment Aimee began singing. The balding man swayed drunkenly, raising one of his hip flasks to the music and yelling broken English with a dazed grin as everyone cheered him on, despite sounding not even remotely similar to the lyrics of the song. Others began to file onto the dance floor with him, clapping in time to the music.

Seeing that Haydar had stolen the spotlight, his bodyguard ushered him back to their table, having saved his bumbling boss a plate of food. Haydar held his bodyguard's hand like a young boy being led across a street.

Aimee and Bianca took turns singing and strumming their electric guitars, with the Mallory kid on the drums, although Adrian had never bothered to learn the kid's name. As far as he was concerned, his only purpose was to protect the people who lived inside the estate's walls. He had only to think of the brief run-in with Anton Snyder if he ever had any doubts about his opinion.

Sadie stumbled up to him, spilling her wine.

"Are you okay?" Adrian's hand shot out to catch hold of her glass before she could spoil her airy blue dress. She was beautiful, despite having had a few too many drinks. Her light brown hair cascaded past her slender shoulders, and her hazel eyes twinkled beneath the soft hues of the coloured hanging lights.

"I'm fiiine," she mumbled before giggling. "I wanted to make s*hure you* were okay."

"Yeah, I'll be fine," he replied, setting her wine glass down next to the warehouse's entrance.

"I was watching you, from that table," she confessed, sweeping her hand at every single table in the courtyard, spinning herself off-balance in the effort and stumbling back to face him as if her impromptu twirl had been intentional. "And I jus*ht* thought it was s*ho* unfair. Everyone els*he* is having fun, but not *you*. S*ho*, I want you to join us*h*."

"I'd love to," he smiled. And he genuinely would have loved to enjoy the party with her, just to feel like a normal teenager without any responsibilities, even just for one night. "But, I'm working."

"Well then, maybe I'll jus*ht* have to fire you," she replied, giving him what she must have thought was a coy grin, regardless of how lopsided it was.

"If you fired me," Adrian paused for a moment, deciding whether he should really be flirting with Mr Royce's daughter. He supposed that after what had happened with Anton earlier, he might already be getting in trouble after his shift, so he may as well make the most of it. "I'd miss getting paid to watch you having fun."

Sadie blushed and swayed, hiccupping and giggling.

"I think you might need to take a break though," he suggested lightly, his time spent with his wretch of a father having given him plenty of experience on how to handle a drunk. "Maybe take a quick nap and come back strong?"

"Like Haydar!" she grinned, taking his arm and resting her head on his shoulder.

Adrian wished that he could have savoured the moment for longer, but sadly, he wasn't one of the guests. *No distractions*, he reminded himself again. Feeling the steadily-building weight of the crowd's stares upon them, both jesting and jealous, he escorted her back to the residence, where Shirley Beaumont, one of the house staff, stood by the entrance.

"I'll *shee* you *shoon*," Sadie mumbled as Shirley brought her inside.

Adrian was about to say something back to her when he caught a glimpse of Mr Royce and Captain Thornton – who was frowning more than usual – through the open doorway. Overwhelmed by curiosity, he advanced to the threshold, taking care not to be seen as he listened in.

"… informed about this earlier?" Captain Thornton demanded.

"We thought they were just running late," an unfortunate guard making his report replied, "And I – I didn't want to interrupt the party."

Adrian couldn't see them anymore, but he could imagine the daggers in Thornton's eyes.

"Relax, Karl," Mr Royce said cheerfully. "There's no harm done. It was nice to be able to enjoy the party, and we still have plenty of time to act. If the next delivery doesn't arrive on schedule, I'll travel to Cloakwater myself."

Hearing nothing else, Adrian started back towards the warehouse, until he heard boot heels crunching across the courtyard behind him, rapidly closing in. He turned around to see Captain Thornton's eyes piercing through him.

"You left your post," he growled sharply. "What did I say about not getting distracted?"

CHAPTER 7 – LIAM

Quentin Davis spoke very few words to Liam Caldwell throughout the entire bumpy drive back to Brimvale, as was the senior officer's custom with anyone he didn't feel the need to impress.

They drove with the windows down in the midday sun, despite the dust being kicked up by passing horses, bicycles and the occasional car as they bounced along the pothole-ridden dirt road that snaked its way through the farm belt. The black SUV's leather interior reeked of pungent sweat and soured apple juice stains. Liam had been living in the car since Monday with only one change of clothes – his other shirt had been ruined by the young blonde prostitute's cola "accident".

They had only planned on staying in Coyote's Rest for one night, but after the drunken horse race which had left the man named Emmett Pearce dead on the riverbank of Rambling Gulch, Quentin had decided that they would stay in town until Friday. He wanted to ensure that the next leader of the cowboys would confirm their acceptance of the bounty offer to eliminate the Rauders, the senior officer even going so far as to volunteer to foot the bill at Lorelei's Saloon, so that the grieving men could drink, fuck and gamble away their sorrows.

Quentin had handed the barkeeper one case of golden bucks, minus the cost of the three additional women who he had hired for his nightly romps. In a matter of hours, word of the open bar tab had swept across the small frontier re-enactment town, and the saloon was soon overflowing with drunken bacchanalia, with revellers passing out on the street and waking up in pools of their own vomit, only to stagger back inside for more.

The single solitary soul who hadn't partaken in the festivities was Liam, choosing instead to pay for his own overpriced meals at The Grand Chandelier Hotel down the road, coldly eyeing the free-for-all fuckfest as the bingers forgot all about their fallen friend.

Of course, as generous as Quentin's gesture had appeared, he intended to simply subtract the bill from the total bounty that was on offer. But, by and large, the gambit had paid off; Emmett's successor, a cowboy by the name of Harlan Reid, had accepted the proposition, turning his group of men into a bunch of hired killers.

After hours of silently watching the rolling fields of the farm belt rise and fall, Liam finally caught sight of the trading town of Rubicross, where diesel, cattle and produce flowed into Brimvale and the other settlements around South Tekota with a modest mark-up.

Despite having travelled east since dawn, the Shield Mountains had almost seemed to be a stain on the horizon that was somehow shrinking in the distance, yet now when Liam looked at the mountain range, he could make out the faint outlines of the trees which blanketed the range's south-facing side. The trees on the north face were markedly scarcer, courtesy of the windborne residual radiation from North Tekota's blast zone in years gone by.

Cruising in and out of the bustling streets of Rubicross, they stopped at the boom gate on the far side of Axemark Ravine's north bridge, where a pair of sentries emerged from the tinted-windowed checkpoint. One haughty guard swept a convex inspection mirror underneath the vehicle and peered inside each window while the other, a busty brunette, checked Quentin's identification.

He flashed his senior clearance badge from the Mayor's Office, along with a rare smile as a light rap resounded from the rear of the vehicle.

"Is he always this thorough?" Quentin asked the woman as he popped the trunk.

"There's not much else to do to pass the time here," she replied, returning his badge. "So whenever people cross into Brimvale, we make sure to give them the *full* treatment."

She simpered at him before following her colleague back to the security checkpoint while Quentin stared after her with his cold blue eyes, conducting an inspection of his own. The boom gate lifted, and they drove through, Quentin hungrily glancing up at the rearview mirror before gunning the engine into Brimvale.

Liam was glad to be back on the smooth asphalt once again as they sped down the highway that sliced through the suburbs. After having hit almost every pothole that the farm belt's dirt road had to offer, he felt like he had ridden a horse bareback all the way from Coyote's Rest, despite sitting in the leather seat that had served as his bed for the past week.

One noticeable benefit of the apocalypse was the light traffic. At first, the main arteries had been clogged bumper-to-bumper as people from the cities fled to the country, and people from the country fled to the cities, but as time passed and the abandoned vehicles were cleared, every lane had become an express lane, and the only times people actually slowed down was when they approached intersections. Thanks to their array of solar panels and their large reserves of diesel from Cloakwater, Brimvale's electrical grid was still functioning, but the few people who still drove a vehicle seldom paid any attention to the traffic lights anymore, so nobody ever knew what could come flying around the corner.

They breezed past Ferguson's Supermarket, whose doors now stood forever shut, although vendor stalls had been set up in the parking lot's concrete expanse to sell the meat and produce from Rubicross; the Pump and Go gas station, which rarely served customers outside the defence and public transport services; and a string of boarded-up bars, cafes and boutique fashion stores lining the street leading towards the town square.

Liam reached for his backpack on the floor as Quentin parked their vehicle behind the small column of other black SUVs. When Liam had first started working in the Mayor's Office two years ago, he hadn't been surprised to learn that, despite Brimvale's push to stockpile commodities and reduce their collective resource consumption, the senior officials were not catching a bus to work – despite expecting everyone else to – or even at the very least, carpooling.

"We've been staying at the hotel," Quentin began in a stern tone, breaking his silence as he lifted the handbrake and rolled up the windows. Liam glanced sidelong at him, unsure of who he was trying to convince, but the man was staring straight back with his cold blue gaze, "The entire time. We don't need to discuss what happens if you say 'no', do we?"

Liam withdrew his hand from the door. The chance to finally stretch his legs and to be back on home soil would have to wait for a few moments longer. *The nerve of this guy*, he thought to himself, eyeing Quentin's wedding ring.

"*Of course* we've been staying at the hotel," Liam supported the lie like the senior officer expected him to. "Where else would we have slept?" *Oh, I remember, in the fucking car*, he wanted to add.

Quentin gave a small nod of approval that was more towards himself than Liam as he took the keys out of the ignition, pausing to check his reflection in the rearview mirror.

Liam pinched the bridge of his nose, taking a deep breath as he stared out the window at the front steps of the town hall. He could have left the conversation at that. It would have been all too easy for him to just climb out of the vehicle, sling his backpack over his shoulders, and pretend that his extended stay in Coyote's Rest was just a humdrum, run-of-the-mill routine that he would simply have to get used to. But after being forced to sleep in the car for a week, he found that this job and his new responsibilities were things that he no longer cared for, and as such, he had far less to lose than Quentin.

"On one condition," Liam continued as Quentin reached for the door handle, seeing the adulterous man's pupils dilate in his otherwise dead gaze. "Next time, and I know there's gonna be a next time, I'm staying in the nicest accommodation money can buy, with three meals a day, all at your expense. Outside of that, you can do whatever the fuck you want." Liam smiled as he climbed out of the car. He looked back to see Quentin seething at him, raging in silence, before adding one more remark. "We don't need to discuss what happens if you say 'no', do we?"

He slammed the door, slung his backpack over his shoulders, and crossed the plaza, practically floating up the town hall's steps to the Mayor's Office.

Quentin the Unsmiling was *his* bitch now, not the other way around. Liam would never let himself be a pushover for anyone again, not since The Long Summer Night, no matter who the other person was. Archie Callahan had raised him better. Admittedly, he had learned more from the old war veteran that lived with him and Camryn Dawson than from his own parents, may they rest in peace.

He walked through the town hall's echoing marble foyer and pulled open the frosted glass door into the office, uttering a contented sigh at the first breath of cool air-conditioning. Dwight Jaskolski, a tall yet hunched downy-bearded blonde, turned away from his computer screen, wheeling his chair out from their shared workstation at the front of the room.

For the past two years, Liam and Dwight had been in charge of dispatching all of the mail and parcels sent around Brimvale and the various settlements of South Tekota, managing the bus routes which carried the deliveries, along with the driver rosters and vehicle maintenance schedules. He felt a pang of nostalgia, already yearning for the familiarity of his old administrative duties, but somebody had to fill the role that Lora Purcell had left behind.

"Liam!" Lora called, looking up from the desk of her new private office. The big-boned brunette ambled out of her open doorway and bounced past Dwight to greet him with an unreciprocated hug, wrinkling her nose slightly at his onion-like body odour. "I've missed you sooo much while you was away!" she exclaimed, although he could hear the forced affection in her voice. "You must feel *sooo* honoured with your new promotion! I used to *looove* travelling outside Brimvale. Meeting new people, sitting in on all of the important conversations with our trading partners… but Teddie needs me here now, and whatever he says, I follow."

Liam had always found it odd that Lora would address the Mayor so informally. He could understand it if she had been a senior officer, or if they had grown up together, but Mayor Ted Paxton was easily twice her age. Perhaps it was her way of subtly hinting that she was senior-level material. Now that she was the Mayor's personal aide, perhaps her subliminal messages had paid off.

"Yeah, it sure was something," he shrugged, looking past her towards Dwight, who sat patiently waiting for them to finish.

Underwhelmed by his answer, Lora caught his gaze and stepped to the side, letting the two friends shake hands.

"I thought you'd be back on Tuesday," said Dwight, cocking his head to the side, "What happened over there?"

"Same here," Liam raised his eyebrows, dropping his backpack by his desk and plopping down on his office chair as he explained the delay with the cowboy deal.

"Well, it's a good thing I was here to watch your back," Lora huffed dramatically as she leaned over a filing cabinet, apparently not done with him yet. "The boys decided it would be funny to play a prank on your desk while you was away, but I cleaned it up for you on Wednesday. I know how shitty it is to come back from a long trip, only to find everything turned upside down." She stared pointedly at the pair of them, knowing full well that they both had a hand in pranking her desk in the past.

"It was pretty funny," Dwight chuckled, averting his gaze from her glare. "We swapped all of the inks in your pens to red, hooked up elastic bands between your drawers and the desk frame, and then we put all of your pens in the drawers. So while you'd be looking for a normal pen, the drawers would keep slamming shut."

"Such a waste of time, and office supplies," Lora shook her head as Liam laughed.

"Speaking of which, where are the other guys?" asked Liam, looking around.

"I saw them in the break room a few minutes ago," Dwight waved his hand casually before glancing back at his computer screen.

"Are they *still* on lunch!?" Lora exclaimed, her cheeks reddening.

Just as she was about to march towards the break room, the office's front door swung open again, and Quentin strode in with a pair of new faces behind him.

"Good afternoon," he said mechanically, looking at Lora more than anyone else. "Is Ted around?"

"I'll get him," Dwight volunteered, not even receiving an appreciative nod from the senior officer as he disappeared around the corner.

Liam stifled a smirk, imagining that Quentin the Unsmiling had probably sat in the car fuming from their conversation until he spotted the two newcomers approaching the town hall, being forced to put on his friendliest face while fighting to keep his rage contained.

"Heyyy Quentin," Lora greeted him sweetly, her flushed cheeks fading. Her brown eyes conveyed false warmth as she turned to the two out-of-towners. "You must be the new recruits! I've heard sooo much about you!"

Naturally, Lora had made it her business to learn as much as she could about the pair of newcomers before they started, and, unable to keep it to herself, she had passed on their backgrounds to anyone who she could manage to corner into listening.

Shelton Turner, dark and stocky, hailed from The Gutter, as part of the Mayor's plan to reopen diplomatic relations with the garbage of Bushrock Flats, or at least with the organised groups who claimed to have had nothing to do with The Long Summer Night. Liam had already seen Shelton's test results for the internship program. He had scored well above his fellow Gutter Rats, and seeing the guy in person, he seemed both responsible and capable, just born on the wrong side of Burnshaw Forest.

Liam's heart heaved with a heavy sense of finality, knowing that he had no choice but to hand over his previous duties to Shelton. While he had sat contemplating in Quentin's car each night for the past week, Liam began to realise that he had just been fired from his old job. While Lora had been ecstatic about her new role, his promotion had felt like it was an unwarranted punishment, since he actually enjoyed his administrative tasks and the people he worked with, especially in comparison to riding along for diplomacy missions with Quentin the Unsmiling. He had thought of stepping down and reverting back to his previous job as soon as they were back in the office. The intern from The Gutter could have learned Lora's old role instead, but with the three-day delay directly prior to the meet-and-greet with the new staff, there was simply not enough time to back out now.

Bristol Hudson, on the other hand, was not part of the Mayor's internship program. The mousy blonde had been sent over from Sunken City, on Brimvale's east coast, in a bid to bolster the bond between the two settlements. She also happened to be Quentin's niece.

The people of Sunken City were mostly self-sufficient, although recent pirate raids from the escaped prisoners of Attiker Island on merchant vessels had begun to disrupt trade and threaten their territory. They were an important conduit for large fish caught by the inert Sovereign Rapture cruise ship anchored in Bellevue Bay, while also serving as a valuable trading port for the coffee merchants approaching from Guadasula. At any rate, they were far more viable as a coastal ally in comparison to Flintscray Port in The Gutter.

Interestingly, but not surprisingly, Lora had painted the pair of new-comers as a thug and a prude during her incessant speculative gossiping over the past few weeks, but they both seemed to be the same age as Liam, Lora, Dwight, and the other junior staff members in the office. And they seemed about as normal as anyone else would have been in a new working environment: nervously shifting their weight from one foot to the other, waiting to be introduced.

"Quentin, Liam, welcome back!" the stout and bushy-bearded Mayor Paxton called as he shuffled around the corner with Dwight. "And Bristol, Shelton, welcome to you!" he clasped each of their hands in turn before making the redundant introductions, at least from Liam's perspective.

Mayor Ted Paxton had once been a newcomer to Brimvale himself. When the missile hit North Tekota, the Sovereign Rapture cruise ship – or more commonly referred to as "The Rapture" – had been sailing off the coast. He had been one of the passengers on board, and one of the first to abandon ship after they anchored in Bellevue Bay. Upon seeing the Army Reserves' tyrannical chokehold on the food supplies, he had rallied every able-bodied citizen of Brimvale to rise up and remove them from power. Shortly thereafter, he had alleviated the food shortages with the cruise ship's catches of fish sustainably sourced from the deeper waters of Bellevue Bay. Lacking leadership in the Army Reserves' absence, it was only natural for everyone to elect him as the new Mayor, but he had become an entirely different man since then.

Reluctantly, Liam shook Shelton's hand, yet even as they muttered pleasantries, he could feel his apprehension of having a Gutter Rat in the office ebbing away. After all, Shelton's test scores had been phenomenal, and such a level of intelligence categorically could not have been capable of participating in The Long Summer Night. Still though, it wouldn't change how Liam felt about the rest of the people in The Gutter. One good egg could never hope to redeem a bad batch.

"Finally," Lora breathed as she greeted Bristol, "A girl my age! You have no idea how long I've been waiting for Teddie to hire someone who I can actually *talk* to. And your hair! It looks sooo good!"

"Thank you," Bristol managed to murmur, fidgeting with her wavy blonde hair as if it was a security blanket.

"Well," Mayor Paxton clapped his hands together, smiling a toothy grin through his bushy beard, "Shall we move this into the boardroom?"

"Actually, Ted," Quentin interjected, "I have to go. I didn't want to miss this, but I've got an urgent public relations opportunity with the guards stationed at The Ravine."

"Oh, absolutely," the Mayor nodded before adjusting his glasses, "Well, these two will still be here for you next week, but jump onto that opportunity while it's there!"

"Should I come with you?" Liam asked, suspecting that the senior officer's true intention was to meet with the busty brunette that he had been ogling at the checkpoint. *Jump on that opportunity indeed.*

Quentin clenched his jaw slightly.

"No, that won't be necessary," he replied in an uncharacteristically pleasant voice. "You've had a long week for your first day. Besides, I think you should take the time to get to know your new teammates first." With that, he offered his apologies to Bristol and Shelton before pushing the frosted glass door open and striding out into the hall.

Ollie, Bronson and Pedro rounded the corner just in time to see the door swing shut.

"Hello, you three," Lora said in a measured tone, "How was your lunch?"

"Good," answered Ollie Geary, a stocky green-eyed youth with parted brown hair, "How about yours?"

"Great," smiled Bronson Hopper, broad-shouldered with a light brown comb-over, "How about yours?"

"Fantastic," mimicked Pedro Pinto, hunched and lanky with glasses and an intentionally poorly-shaped bowl-cut, "How about yours?"

"Ugh," Lora uttered as everyone chuckled. She turned to Bristol, "See what I mean? I'm sooo glad you're here, these guys would've been the *death* of me."

"Hey, new people!" Ollie stepped forward to shake Shelton's hand, "I'm the CEO, welcome."

"Welcome to the party, he means," Bronson added with a well-practised straight face. "It's my birthday today. Hope you brought gifts."

"Hello," Pedro offered his hand to Bristol, solemnly bowing his head. "I live in the basement. I would like to request that you keep it down up here during the birthday party."

"Okay, you guys win," Lora groaned with a smile, giving into their antics. "But you three need to keep your hands off Bristol. She's mine. We're going to keep each other sane."

"If it was up to anyone else," Mayor Paxton chuckled aloud, "You three would've been gone a long time ago."

"Like that," Lora snapped her fingers with a grin that didn't entirely suggest that she was kidding.

The Mayor introduced the three as office assistants to the newcomers, but in reality, they were more like glorified handymen, wheeling bundles of mail and piles of parcels on and off the buses, performing routine engine checkups, in addition to any general maintenance and janitorial work. Chiefly though, they breathed life into the office, and so Mayor Paxton was always happy to look the other way whenever they bent the rules.

"Teddie," Lora began in her repulsively sweet voice. "It's Friday afternoon, and we have sooo many things to celebrate! Promotions, new people –"

"My birthday," Bronson added earnestly.

"It is *not* your birthday," Lora huffed, narrowing her eyes at him before turning back to the Mayor. "But, can we leave early? We'll go to Woozy's for a few drinks and get to know each other."

"I think that's a great idea!" Mayor Paxton exclaimed. "Normally, I'd invite myself and the rest of the seniors, but we old people need to be in bed by seven." He laughed at his own joke, the others joining in politely. "Well, I don't think it'd be fair on Quentin if the rest of us went without him, so we'll save the next round of introductions for Monday. You guys go and have a good time."

"Thank youuu," Lora's fake smile faded as she turned to Liam, "Are you gonna drink with us?"

Liam burned his gaze into her.

"No, I think I'll head home," he answered abruptly, picking up his backpack.

"But whyyy?" she asked, despite already knowing the answer. "You have your own promotion to celebrate!"

Part of Liam knew that she enjoyed watching him squirm for a decent excuse. The Woozy Rooftop Bar & Grill would be packed with drunks on Friday. She knew that he didn't drink, and couldn't stand being around those who did. Dwight and the other guys understood, having lost people during The Long Summer Night themselves, and they glanced at each other uncertainly, but Lora had just put the spotlight on him for Shelton, Bristol, and the Mayor.

"I mean, it's cool if you don't want to," Shelton shrugged, his gaze downcast.

"Yeah, there's always next week," Bristol agreed, her eyebrows furrowed slightly.

"But Quentin *did* say that you should get to know your new teammates," Mayor Paxton reminded him, taking Lora's side.

Liam looked at each of them in turn as they waited for his answer, four of them sympathetic, and the other four trying not to look offended. He forced a smile as his eyes came to rest on the Mayor.

"Quentin also said that I've had a long week for my first day," he replied, slinging his backpack over his shoulders. "I'm just looking forward to having a shower and going to bed."

"Careful," the Mayor held up a cautionary finger. "Because that's how you start getting old! No problem, Liam, thanks for putting in the extra hours. Have a good weekend. You earned it."

Liam nodded and left the office. Hayley, the blonde barista who worked across the street on the other side of the plaza, was busily stacking up chairs outside The Artisan's Roast Cafe. He veered to the left, taking a different road home so that he wouldn't have to talk to her. Usually, he would have enjoyed her company, since she treated customers like they were human beings, rather than hollow vessels bearing transactions. But not only was he in dire need of a shower, he knew that she would be eager to discuss the first week of his new job, and he simply would not be able to match her enthusiasm. He could feel her staring after him as he rounded the corner.

What brief elation he had enjoyed on his return to Brimvale had already been sucked out of him. It was so typical of Lora to embarrass him in front of new people. At least now that she was in her freshly refurbished private office, and he was out on the road, he would happily see a lot less of her. He had just been made the asshole of the office now though. The other guys knew better, but it seemed that she had already hoodwinked the new recruits along with the Mayor.

Scraps of metal from the Burnshaw Barricade glinted in the fading afternoon light as Liam walked home. In the aftermath of The Long Summer Night, workers from Stillborough had been contracted to build the makeshift palisade wall, which skirted the north end of Burnshaw Forest from Brimvale's east to west, in order to stave off any future assaults from The Gutter.

Nowadays, the guards only patrolled along the eastern and western sections of the wall. With the merchants in Rubicross offering higher salaries and better accommodation, Brimvale's guard personnel had become too thinly stretched to patrol the wall's midsection, although no one believed that anybody would dare venture through The Burning Forest to attack Brimvale now anyway, not since the women of the forest had moved in.

Passing by houses with overgrown lawns and untended gardens, Liam remembered when he had volunteered for guard duty years ago, even though all he could do was yell at the first sign of trouble, since he'd had no weapons training. He had to do something to get himself out of the house though.

One cloudy night, only a few weeks after the construction of the Burnshaw Barricade had begun, he and the other guards had heard motorbikes rumbling in the distance, and soon, a swarm of headlights cut through the towering grey trees. As quickly as they came though, the headlights disappeared, and there were men shouting over gunfire, followed by a deafening explosion. Then, there was silence. By the time all of the guardsmen had lowered their guns and resumed their patrols, a spine-chilling scream filled the night air as a huge bonfire erupted in the heart of the forest. It was a man's scream. They couldn't tell whether it was the same man screaming, but it had lasted until dawn. Liam would never forget the sound of the women laughing maniacally as their long shadows etched in flame flitted between the trees. From that day onwards, the woods became known as The Burning Forest, and the builders from Stillborough worked around the clock to finish the wall.

A shaggy stray cat growled at him as he turned the corner onto Roseview Court, the stray shooting off into the cover of an untended bush. Archie's bus was parked in the cul-de-sac at the end of the street. It was common practice for the drivers to bring the buses home after their shifts, saving them the hassle of having to walk to and from the town hall each day. As long as they kept the tanks full and the seats clean, nobody really seemed to mind.

Most of the houses in the court were abandoned, but it was the same story in every street, in every suburb. Most people had moved to Stillborough and Rubicross and other smaller settlements around South Tekota, starting new lives in the new world. The ones who stayed behind had decided to combine their households, not just because they were afraid of being alone, but also because some people couldn't bear the thought of setting foot in their own homes again. The haunting images of their lost loved ones strewn across the living room carpet, on the kitchen floor clutching a knife, or laying brutalised in their own bedrooms, would last longer than any bloodstain.

For Liam though, every time he walked through the front door was a reminder of what The Gutter had done to his parents. His anger had allowed him to be the brave one for his former neighbours. Archie Callahan, a fifty-something-year-old career sergeant, had taken Liam's parents' bedroom, waiting until the Burnshaw Barricade had been built before leaving to work on the railroad and sending food supplies back to the cul-de-sac; while Camryn Dawson, a fellow orphan of The Long Summer Night, had slept on his porch for weeks until she had finally agreed to take the guest room.

Liam's footsteps echoed on the wooden veranda of his brick veneer family home. He unlocked the front door and stepped over the threshold, forcing himself to look at the bullet holes that riddled the staircase. Archie had offered to patch them up, but only once.

"Liam?" Archie's drawl called from the kitchen, "That you?"

"Yeah," he replied, shrugging off his backpack by the stairs and following the steady *thock-thock-thock* to the kitchen.

"I heard what happened," the old war dog said as he chopped bell peppers, occasionally checking the deep-frying chunks of battered chicken on the stove. "How many drinks did Emmett have?"

"Emmett?" Liam echoed, wondering how the news of the cowboy leader's death could have reached him so fast, before realising that the veteran met a lot of different people on the bus each day. "I saw him with a beer."

"Just the one?" Archie stopped chopping for a moment, looking up to see Liam nod solemnly. He stroked the bristles of his rusty red and grey speckled beard, murmuring something indecipherable before focusing on the bell peppers again. "Tell me, why'd Ted send you over to Coyote's Rest, exactly?"

Liam recounted how Quentin Davis had delivered the Mayor's proposition, offering the cowboys a bounty of golden bucks in exchange for dealing with the Rauders.

"I'm surprised to hear he's doing something about the raids this time," Archie's lips curled disdainfully as he rotated a new batch of battered chicken into the frying pan, the oil hissing back. "But I'm not surprised to hear the pussy couldn't ask the cowboys for himself."

Liam knew that he still held the Mayor indirectly responsible for The Long Summer Night. While Archie had hated the Army Reserves' commanders of Fort Mason for starving the people of Brimvale during the months following the apocalypse, it was Ted Paxton who had organised the protests that had pulled the Army Reserves' patrols away from the suburbs. Archie's mother, and countless others, would still be alive today, if it hadn't been for the falsely acclaimed insurrectionist.

Archie wiped his hands on a dishcloth and stared out the kitchen window into the gathering darkness, momentarily forgetting the frothing frying pan.

"Ten full cases of golden bucks…" he said finally, turning to face Liam. "Why the fuck would *anyone* pay that much to get rid of somebody else's problem?"

CHAPTER 8 – DAMIAN

"Hey, Pops! Need a blue pill?" some punk Latino kid with neck tattoos called out mockingly from across the urban street, watching as Damian Bishop made his way over to the Red Light District in the early hours of the evening.

"Every fucking week…" Damian muttered under his breath. He was in his thirties, so he was certainly old enough to be the kid's father, but none of the broads he had bent over in his long list of sexual conquests would have ever been capable of spawning such a runt.

"Hey, I'm talking to you, Pops!" the kid shouted with a punch-worthy sneer plastered across his face.

"Fuck it," Damian decided, squaring his jaw. He stopped, his ice blue eyes glinting in the fading daylight as he stowed his dark shades into his black leather bomber jacket, looking up and down the sidewalk before pointing at himself and feigning incredulity, "Who, me?"

"What, you need your eyes checked?" the kid replied haughtily. "It's just you and me here, old timer."

It was one of Arturo Espinoza's boys, a petty hustler from Stepton Heights who was still caught in the limbo of knowing how to use a blade and not knowing when to use it; and right now was definitely not one of those times.

"How's business?" Damian asked, his leather jacket covering up his beefy physique as he crossed the street.

The kid started to quake, as expected, reaching for his back pocket.

"Doing good? Doing bad?" Damian shot a smug grin at the skinny runt when he saw the flash of steel as the switchblade flicked open, but it didn't slow him down. If anything, it made his dick hard. "Doing fuck yourself?"

The kid held the knife up, only for Damian to lazily swat it out of his hand like he was waving off a corpse fly. The cocksucker backed away, dumbstruck, looking down at his fallen blade like his little pin-dick had just been chopped off.

"Whatever, Pops, don't lose your teeth in the dairy section!" he yelled over his shoulder as he ran off like a bitch.

Damian watched the kid disappear around the corner with mild amusement. Five years ago, the Latinos wouldn't have even *dreamt* of setting foot in this part of town, unless they were paying customers, let alone try to set up their own mobile pharmacies. How the times had changed.

This used to be a nice neighbourhood, he remembered fondly as he resumed walking towards the convoy of whores parked only a few streets away.

He decided to take the long route; the route he always took whenever he had business to take care of. He hadn't been in business for the longest time, but the thrill of having a knife pulled on him had certainly set him in a nostalgic mood.

He passed by a vandalised convenience store on the corner, the laneway behind it looking like a mere extension of the store, with its festering garbage giving off a reek powerful enough to snuff out a stray cat. It was in that same laneway that Fabrizio Pasquale had given him his first handgun, back when Fabrizio was still only a made man.

Damian looked through the broken window of a beauty salon, with its slashed and gutted leather seats lying among the fragments of shattered mirrors and weathered magazines strewn across the floor. He remembered the women who would walk out with their perfectly permed and perfumed hair as he sat in the barbershop next door, not that he was ever interested in their hair, of course, but the effort was nice. Now, he found himself missing the perfume – far better than the rat piss that The Gutter's prostitutes smudged themselves with in between turning tricks.

The people of Little Italy were one thing, but he realised that it was the smells of the old neighbourhood that he missed the most. Turning onto the main avenue, the fruity aromas of creamy gelato from the ice cream parlour would have been the first scent to hit him, followed by the artisan bakery's freshly-made cakes and pastries, and the deli with its cured cuts of meat, cheese wheels and hanging sausages dangling over the counter.

Then there was the cafe where Fabrizio had sat ritualistically with his caffè macchiato every morning, watching the street's vendors setting up for the day, right up until the Ukrainians pulled up on smoking rubber and gave him some buckshot biscotti to go with his morning coffee.

Around this time in the early hours of the evening, one could smell the pasta sauce and garlic bread wafting from the kitchens of Giovanni's Bistro across the street. Damian could still picture the green, red and white-striped awnings hanging over the restaurant's windows, and the ashtrays on the red and white chequered tablecloths underneath the canopies lining the street. Both majestic and enticing, it had been the Mafia's centre for business and pleasure.

He remembered the night that Giovanni Vincenzo had sent his son, Luigi, to invite Damian up to the bistro's private rooftop bar. Top shelf liquor, top shelf women, he was a guest of honour. He had worked for the Vincenzo Family since he was a teenager, and they had finally deemed him worthy of a promotion.

No more hired muscle gigs. Cement shoes, shallow graves and acid baths were a thing of the past. They had forcibly vacated a logistics position at Flintscray Port, and they had squeezed their connections to ensure that he would be put forth as the perfect candidate with all of the necessary qualifications to fill the vacancy.

His job had been simple; let the family know when valuable shipments were coming in, and allow for a few items to be "misplaced". If anyone started breathing down his neck, they'd promptly be reminded of how lucky they were to be breathing at all.

Damian missed the organisation back then. Business was booming, and everyone paid their taxes. Gambling, prostitution, protection racketeering;

it was the golden era. They even had the law on their payroll. The local bacon patrol had some greedy motherfuckers, but they were just as keen to take their slice of the pie.

After Giovanni got sick though, the family fell apart, and everyone fought with each other like hyenas snapping at vultures over a dying corpse, each crew trying to take everything for themselves.

Now, the bistro was nothing more than a burnt-out husk of an old building, like the corpse of some failed business that had filed for fire insurance right before a freak accident, making it a piss and shit magnet for the Gutter Rats. The entire street had been defiled, with graffiti on walls and filth on floors. Beady bloodshot eyes stared out at him from the smashed windows of run-down shopfronts, junkies and tweakers ready to scuttle out and embrace the approaching night like cockroaches, on a single-minded search for their next fix.

Damian quickened his pace, not out of fear of the Gutter Rats; it was just a shame to see the old neighbourhood looking like a prolapsed asshole. The Red Light District up ahead had stayed the same though, abounding in sleazy bars and sweaty strip clubs and cheap whorehouses, the sidewalks crawling with hooker hawkers and prowling perverts, their leering faces obscured by the backdrop of flashing neon signs.

Instead of turning left at the intersection and heading into Bouncer territory, as he did most weeks, he turned right, towards a street-level parking lot surrounded by a chain-linked fence. A group of camper vans and RVs and gutted school buses had been arranged in a square along the inside of the fence, with four pickup trucks in the centre, parked back-to-back in an X formation. Sentries either stood in the truck trays or patrolled the perimeter, armed with assault rifles and shotguns hanging from shoulder straps.

Along this street, there were less hawkers and more gawkers, those who preferred to slink in the shadowy crevices in the surrounding buildings, cashless creeps hoping to catch a glimpse of the action.

Behind the four pickup trucks, a score of women and a handful of young men sat in a row of camping chairs in various stages of exposure, while slavering customers skulked this way and that, observing the supple meat on display like a pack of predators surveying its prey, as if any of them would be dissatisfied with their prize had they not been given a choice.

Zatar, the meat-hole mongering midget manager of the Velvet Convoy, despite his low stature, had high standards for those he brought along with him on tour. The broad-nosed little man would travel to every big city and small town across South Tekota, taking the most popular prostitutes and wayward women that each settlement had to offer, bringing them all on a sex tour around each depraved community. After sucking the local tricks dry of their pent-up sexual frustrations, along with their money, or whatever else they had to pay with, he would trade out the low-earning whores for newer, better quality investments, and move on to the next destination.

"Look at all these fresh new faces," one grimy-faced customer marvelled in a thick Ukrainian accent, shooting a grubby hand down a young redhead's frilly pink bra to grab a handful of her perky tits. She winced in pain as he squeezed roughly.

"There's a new batch of eighteen-year-olds every year, my friend," Zatar grinned, his grey-speckled beard parting. And, if the rumours could be believed, for the right price, one wouldn't even need to wait that long, either.

"No touching until after payment!" one of the guards yelled from the back of a pickup truck.

"*Relax*," Zatar waved up at the sentry as he approached the greasy-haired patron, who still had his hand beneath the woman's lingerie, enjoying the free sample while it lasted. "You like Cherry, huh? She came straight from Rookson City, a virgin to the industry." Zatar loved telling his whores' life stories; he found that it helped with the sale. He continued as the man squeezed harder, the redhead whimpering meekly. "Her father needs medicine, and we all know medicine doesn't come cheap these days. Her family thinks that she's going to join the miners at Cloakwater Cliffs, but she came here instead, to be your obedient servant, to hungrily satisfy your every desire… all for the low price of two hundred golden bucks."

Even as he examined the other women, the Ukrainian fished around in his pocket with his free hand, pulling out a wad of old currency.

"Here's two thousand," he said, thrusting the handful of crumpled bills at the pussy peddler. "Bring it to the Bankers in Gainstowe Park. You'll get your two hundred."

"I know this, and my many thanks," said Zatar, raising his thick eyebrows as he counted the money twice. He signalled to the timekeeper sitting nearby, who checked his watch before scribbling something into a book. "She's yours for the next hour. Enjoy yourself, my friend."

Wasting no time, the grimy-faced customer hauled the woman out of her chair and practically dragged her across the parking lot towards a free camper van, slamming the door shut behind him.

All around the parking lot, motorhomes and minivans rocked from side to side, suspension systems squeaking as clients got their money's worth. Slaps and screams – of both pleasure and pain – filled the night air.

Damian stood in front of the row of whores with his head cocked to one side, sizing up each of them as they sat stroking their smooth yielding thighs with lascivious and lustful gazes. Some of them uttered gasps and mewls as they groped their voluptuous breasts for him. He knew that it was all for show, but he didn't give a fuck whether they made noises or not, he was just there to get his dick sucked.

"Hey, Zatar," he called the meat-hole mongering midget over, "Which one of these new girls can rub her nose in my man-stache without messing up my jeans?"

"I have just the one for you, my friend," the hairy little man pointed out a black beauty in her late forties. She flashed a smile at Damian, sliding a finger in her mouth as Zatar sold her story. "We found Vivica in Rubicross. The man who owned her contract was willing to break it prematurely. He said that she was getting too old to work in their establishment… But with age, comes experience. Each one of her orifices has already been broken in; she has no internal walls left. She was built for rough sex. Only two hundred golden bucks, and if you manage to find a gag reflex, I'll give you a full refund."

Vivica rose to her feet as Damian pulled two gilded plastic chips from his pocket, paying the depraved dwarf. Her silky white lingerie was a stark contrast to her rich dark body, and her enormous tits overshadowed her slim waist as she led him to a nearby motorhome. Damian's cock was threatening to spear through his zipper by the time they climbed inside, and he found himself thinking that he might not be satisfied with just a blowjob from the ebony cougar.

He sat down on a grey suede sofa as she unhooked her bulging bra, her breasts spilling out like a pair of watermelons. She sank to her knees between his legs and undid his belt and fly using only her teeth. His rigid cock smacked her in the forehead the moment it was unleashed. Unfazed, she descended on his shaft without hesitation, her throat expanding to accommodate his girth, and soon her lips were brushing his ball sack, slurping back any excess saliva so that he was practically swimming in her mouth.

Damian leaned back, letting his mind wander as she sucked the shit out of him.

Two hundred golden bucks for an hour, he thought to himself, shaking his head.

Five years ago, he had women literally lining up to suck him off for free. The Mafia's territory was still in the process of being divided between the other gangs by the time the missile dropped in North Tekota and the world went to shit, but he still had enough cash set aside to start up his own brothel in Brimvale, and every decent whore in town was auditioning for a job. They all wanted to get out of Bushrock before negotiations turned violent, and he was their golden ticket.

Word must have gotten out about how he intended on bribing his way through the Burnshaw Barricade's checkpoint, because while he was out picking up the last of his chosen women, his house had been raided, all of his prostitutes had been shot – such a fucking waste – and his stash of cash was gone. One whore had managed to stay alive long enough to tell him that it was the Blacks from Gainstowe Park who had forced their way in.

Knowing that he would be shot dead at Brimvale's border if he turned up empty-handed, Damian had called on a couple of the guys he used to work with back in his hired muscle days. Manu "The Painter" rode shotgun while Winston sat in the backseat. With all of their artillery and ammunition, there was no room for anyone else.

Among the shattered remnants of the family, Winston was known as "The Street Sweeper", infamous for doing drive-bys with a minigun that had somehow "gotten lost" on its way over to Fort Mason. Six rotating barrels, each spitting eight rounds per second, were enough to saw a man in half.

Between the three men, sorely in need of some catharsis after the family had fallen apart, they had turned Gainstowe Park's neighbourhood into a warzone. Bodies in the street, cars riddled with bullet holes, and houses on fire. Although the massacre had been devastating enough to spark the Turf Wars across the rest of Bushrock, Damian had never quite managed to get his money back.

He stood up. *At least I can get my two hundred back,* he thought to himself. He grabbed the back of Vivica's head as she throated his cock diligently. Her fingers clutched his thighs, and he gave her a moment to prepare to have her face fucked. The veteran chocolate vixen looked up at him, nodding with her mouth full as her dark brown eyes glassed over.

Damian spread his feet apart and started thrusting savagely, determined to hit her gag reflex with his battering ram. Involuntary guttural croaks erupted from the woman as she took him balls deep to the chin, spit stringing from her mouth and latching onto her gigantic swinging tits. Her eyeshadow began to smear, but her fingers were still spread on his thighs, calm, even as he destroyed her esophagus.

He paused at the bottom of her throat, pulling her closer until she was nuzzling his man-stache. Challenging his endurance, her tongue snaked out underneath his cock to lick his balls, before trying to engulf his entire sack in her greedy mouth. It was too much for the ebony cougar. Her throat muscles tightened around his cock, and she began to sputter and choke. He withdrew his hands, and she pulled away instantly, dry heaving on the floor.

"That's the… first time… I've gagged in years," she wheezed in a husky voice before looking up at him with a grateful smile.

She rose up on her knees again, ready to throat him some more, when they heard a commotion coming from outside. Damian leaned over and stuck his fingers in between the window blinds, peering out to see someone banging on a caravan door nearby. Vivica resumed sucking as he watched.

He knew the guy. It was Claude, a Bouncer creep from the Red Light District. Damian opened the blinds wider to see his two fuck-buddies, Kelvin and Sonny, watching his back. The three were well-known for following women home after their shifts, but Claude was deluded enough to think that the whores who spurned him were just playing hard to get.

"You get your ass out here, Krystal!" Claude yelled, banging on the door again.

The sentries in the parking lot had their guns trained and ready on the trio, but none of them would dare pull the trigger without permission. After all, the Velvet Convoy were only guests in Bushrock, and the Bouncer gang as a whole had more firepower; in fact, they were the only gang in The Gutter that still had a steady supply of ammunition. There would be heavy losses on both sides.

Zatar, as was his custom, had already paid the Bouncers a rental fee to set up shop in the area, as a gesture of goodwill to make up for the lost business, but sometimes the Bouncers would get too attached to the regular girls who wanted to go on tour.

"Krystal, you fucking bitch!!" Claude pounded the caravan's window with his palm.

The door swung open, and a slim blonde emerged, hugging a green cargo jacket around herself, but without anything to cover her long pale legs.

"You stay the fuck away from –"

Claude cut her off, pulling her out from the caravan's doorway by her hair and dragging her down to the asphalt. Damian's cock went limp in Vivica's throat, and he pushed her away.

"What's happening out there?" she asked, wiping her mouth as he zipped up his jeans.

Damian kicked the motorhome's door open, tightening up his belt and descending the stairs as Claude backhanded Krystal across the cheek.

"Not the face, you idiot!" Zatar yelled, although he quickly raised his hands in smiling apology when Kelvin pulled a pistol from his waist, daring the hairy little man to say another word.

Sonny the short and stocky skinhead had his gun up too, standing ass-to-ass with Kelvin the lanky bug-eyed fuck-stain. The two Bouncers looked like they had just jumped on the Jet, a volatile cocktail of meth and ketamine with unpredictable destinations; either that or they had just missed the last boarding call and were in desperate need of a new ticket.

Several of the guards were already arguing back and forth, with some itching for an all-out gunfight with the entire Bouncer gang, while others called for removing Bushrock from their future tours altogether.

"FUCK THE GUTTER!!" a man aboard one of the pickup trucks shouted.

"FUCK THE GUTTER!!" another guard echoed.

The timekeeper quickly ushered the rest of the skittish whores still on display over to a school bus on the other side of the parking lot as more of the Velvet Convoy's sentries took up the cheer.

Damian's shadow fell across Krystal's swollen cheek as she knelt on the ground, tears welling in her eyes at Claude's feet.

"What the fuck do you want?" asked Claude, turning his head with his hand raised and ready to deliver another strike, his eyes raging like a short-fused serial killer.

"Nothing from you," Damian replied coolly, stifling a snort at the smell of cheap hairspray coming from Claude's parted brown hair. "I just thought it would be fun to take turns smacking her around. I paid to have a good time."

The slender Bouncer sized him up before lowering his hand with a sinister smile.

"Okay," Claude agreed, stepping back giddily, "Let's see what you got."

"How about you stand up for me?" Damian offered Krystal a hand as she broke out into a fresh sob. "And take off that jacket, let me see what you're hiding under there."

The chanting from the Velvet Convoy's guards had stopped, and now they were all pointing their guns at Damian instead. He wasn't a Bouncer. He was just a regular customer. They wouldn't need permission to shoot.

Reluctantly, Krystal stood, opening her jacket to reveal her pale naked body. She dropped the jacket to the asphalt along with the tears streaming from her cheeks. Damian spun her around so that she could face Vivica, who was watching with silent dread from the door of the motorhome.

"You've been a bad girl, haven't you?" Damian murmured into her ear, his hand on her slim hip, "Running away from your boyfriend like this."

More tears fell as she silently nodded.

"She *has* been a bad girl," Claude seethed behind them. "She's been a fucking bitch!"

"Keep running," Damian urged, spanking her bare ass with a meaty smack.

She staggered forward with the impact, looking back at him with confusion before hurtling towards the motorhome. Vivica caught her and pulled her inside, slamming the door shut.

Claude's fist smashed into the side of Damian's skull, just above his ear.

"Was that meant to be a punch?" Damian asked, turning around with an amused grin.

The Bouncer's jaw dropped in disbelief, and he fumbled for his gun. He would never have reached it in time though. Damian had been in enough street brawls to perceive his opponent's next move in slow motion, and deliver a lightning speed reaction. The only question was: what would be his counter-move?

A throat strike would leave Claude drowning in his own blood, while a punch to the chest could fracture his sternum, probably giving the guy a heart attack. But Damian only wanted to fuck up the guy's night, not everyone else's. He kicked Claude in the nuts so hard that the freshly-tuned choirboy got a good two seconds of air-time, sending his Adam's apple up into his mouth while he shrieked like the little bitch that he was.

Before either of the other two Bouncers could swing their handguns at Damian, one of the sentries leapt out of a pickup truck and pressed the barrel of a twelve-gauge shotgun into Kelvin's ear canal, forcing him down on one knee, while Sonny discovered that his shirt had suddenly sprouted an array of angry red dots. Whatever remaining Jet-fuelled bravado they had walked in with vanished at the sound of their cockless comrade crying on the ground as he rolled from side to side, holding his crotch. Jittering, they tossed aside their pistols and surrendered.

"I hope they do refunds here," Damian told the whimpering ex-man as he reached down, ripping the holstered handgun from Claude's waist. "Because the next time you pull your dick out, it'll be to piss blood at the urinal."

He tossed the gun over to the guards standing in the pickup trucks, hitting one of the men in the shoulder before it fell to rattle upon the tray. Good thing it was on safety.

"My friend!" Zatar called from across the parking lot, crossing the distance, "You want a job?"

"I want my two hundred back," Damian replied over the pitiful sounds of Claude wailing on the ground, the other two Bouncers on their knees, awaiting judgement.

"Of course!" Zatar handed his chips back with a smile. "What do you say? The pay is average, but it comes with *great* benefits."

"I'll think about it," Damian shrugged, pocketing the pair of golden bucks.

He knew that anyone else would have jumped at the opportunity to join the Velvet Convoy, especially with the consequences that would be waiting for him at Flintscray Port once they heard the news of his attack on the Bouncers.

"While you think," Zatar began as he nodded towards the window of the motorhome, where Vivica had pulled the blinds up to gaze back at Damian lustfully while she and Krystal fondled each other, "Consider allowing the girls to show their appreciation. Spend the night here, if you like."

The two women had unlatched the door and left it ajar. An open invitation. He was about to have a busy evening. One that would be filled with moans of pleasure as he pounded their dripping wet meat-holes into gaping craters while his mind worked to formulate a plan.

Finally, he was back in business.

CHAPTER 9 – ODESSA

Dess Sheridan, Garrett Ridley, and their armed escort of half a dozen Royce guards crested a rise in the farm belt's dirt road, their horses lazily treading through puddles and potholes as the vividly imagined re-enactment frontier town of Coyote's Rest came into view, crouching among fields of yellow prairie grass in the distance.

She squinted at the simple settlement basking in the morning sun. The Old West town was smaller than what she remembered, and without the charm that it once held. The rustic beauty of early settlers banding together to erect simple houses and places of business purely off the back of elbow grease and a dream of a better future, now just seemed like a pathetic cluster of poorly-built hovels. Or, perhaps the idyllic town she remembered had died along with Emmett Pearce.

The dirt road they had been travelling along was riddled with potholes after years of neglect, although Dess suspected that this might have been the case even before the world had ended. The potholes were full of mud, and great pools of water rippled in the slight breeze skating across the prairies, which would soon recede into the dry earth as the sun climbed higher into the sky.

They had spent the past few days alternating between cantering, trotting and walking their horses across the rolling fields of the farm belt, roughing it out at night in the prairies. They had seen heavy rain last night, but Dess was glad that they'd had the good sense to bring Nathan Royce's tents, despite Garrett's objections.

She had been surprised to see that even after the two years she had spent in Stillborough, there hadn't been any sizeable settlements established in between Rubicross and Coyote's Rest for them to stop in and stay for the night, other than a few lonely farmsteads standing sentinel over hectares of crops.

Dess had found herself grateful for the company of the armed escort, as the trip that she had originally planned with just herself and Garrett would have been markedly more isolated and vulnerable to an attack. She couldn't imagine how the farmers felt on a daily basis, yet despite the rumoured reappearance of the Rauders, they had only seen traders, farmers, and other travellers along the road. There was no sign of any raiders, although she assumed that the Rauders would not be brazen enough to be seen on the road between the two largest towns in the prairies so soon after their return.

"Damn," muttered Lloyd Price, one of the guards. He was wearing a black bowler hat with a comically narrow brim that did nothing to keep the sun off his face. It was the closest thing that he could find resembling a cowboy hat though, having wanted to fit in with the locals at Coyote's Rest. "If I'd have known we were this close, I would've rode on ahead before we made camp. My back's sore as shit from sleepin' on the ground."

"Sure you could find your way in the dark?" asked Blair Frost, a smile playing at the braided blonde's lips.

"Sure as shit found my way inside o' you," Price replied, hawking spit into the wind and wiping away the string of saliva that landed on his sleeve.

"And what kind of guard would you be," Kirk Boaz began, the bald black guard wearing homemade body armour trotting alongside Frost and smirking at Price, "If you left the people you was s'posed to protect?"

"One without a sore back, that's for damn sure!" Price scowled sullenly, eyeing the others before staring back at the town.

"Might have to give your back a break for a few days then," Merrick Werner, an unshaven curly-haired guard wearing a weather-worn flannel coat swayed in his saddle on Price's other side, winking at Boaz and Frost behind his back.

Dess had learned early on that the other guards loved to rile him up. Price was easily ruffled. But he had indeed slept with Frost. That much was true. As had Boaz and Werner. The three men would take turns keeping watch, sleeping, and burying themselves into the promiscuous blonde each night. Alix Carter and Nael Fletcher also shared a tent, although they mostly kept to themselves.

Dess glanced sidelong at Garrett and they kicked their horses into gear towards Coyote's Rest, with the six guards bringing up the rear, churning up clods of mud and sodden earth in their wake.

Garrett Ridley was one of the few railroad workers who had been smart enough to leave after they had rode down Wallace Pelletier, receiving his portion of the former foreman's stolen golden bucks and finding a safe and stable place to stay while they figured out what to do with their share of the money. He was younger than the others, now in his early twenties, but he had grown up quick, as had everyone else in the aftermath of the apocalypse.

Dess and Garrett had chosen to work as guards for Nathan Royce after he had pledged to finish the railroad with his remaining funds. For some of the workers, the construction project was merely a paycheck, but she and Garrett had known the importance of restoring the flow of diesel from Cloakwater Cliffs before Fort Mason's stockpiled supplies ran dry. Without fuel, every remaining civilised settlement would have eventually descended into darkness. Even Brimvale's solar array wouldn't be able to keep the spotlights on at night, and that would have spelt trouble for the sentries posted along the Burnshaw Barricade.

After the railroad was finished, and the raids from the Rauders had ceased, Dess left Rubicross for Stillborough, while Garrett stayed on with the Royce garrison. He had reasoned that he enjoyed the warmer weather of the prairies, but Dess suspected that he secretly harboured a penchant for danger. In a sense, she was grateful that he had chosen to remain behind, as he, of all people, would know whether the guards who were accompanying them would be trustworthy enough to sleep alongside when they stopped to set up camp each night.

They splashed through puddles of water on the main street into Coyote's Rest with barely a stir from the inhabitants. If they were raiders, the entire town would have been caught unaware.

Olaf Kaufmann, the general store trader, unlocked his door for business, placing his hands on his hips and eyeing them off speculatively. Washerwomen carried baskets of laundry behind Madame's Buxom Boarding House, while a scantily-clad prostitute did the walk of shame, crossing the street from Lorelei's Saloon.

Dess recognised the young woman. Lacey was one of the high school graduates who had given up working as an unskilled labourer on the railroad early on, opting for a life of making money on her back rather than breaking her back for money. From the look of her flabby arms and dry pale skin, it seemed that it was the only trade that Lacey had ever bothered to learn, but the few years of experience in her chosen profession had certainly taken their toll on her.

Bleary-eyed in the morning light, she shielded her blotchy face against their approach from the east, intimidated by the group of riders, yet intrigued at the prospect of new business.

"Dess? Garrett!?" Lacey exclaimed as she recognised them, bouncing with excitement as if her long-dead inner child had been brought back to life. "What brings you… oh, Emmett."

"Where can we find Harlan Reid?" asked Dess, not wanting to associate herself with the girl any longer than she had to.

"Harlan," Lacey smiled wistfully, the telltale gaze of a woman whose desires had been satisfied by his recent company. "You'll find him at Lorelei's. He practically lives there, now, along with all of the other guys, ever since…" she trailed off, suddenly aware of her present company again.

Dess climbed off her horse, leading it to the hitching post outside the saloon with the others following suit behind her.

"Will you be staying long?" Lacey asked, lingering after having served her purpose. Dess wondered if that made the girl a better prostitute, or a worse one.

"As long as I need to," she answered brusquely, knotting her horse's lead rope. She unshouldered her duffel bag, tossing it over to Carter and nodding towards The Grand Chandelier Hotel. "Check us in, could you?"

Carter, Fletcher and Frost carried the party's packs up the street, while Boaz, Price and Werner followed Dess and Garrett through the swinging batwing doors into Lorelei's Saloon.

Dustmotes danced in lazy spirals on the few beams of light streaming in through the grimy windows as their eyes adjusted to the relative darkness inside the bar. Lyle Beckett, the bespectacled barkeeper, was busily polishing glasses while his curvy daughter, Brandi, wiped down the tables, gingerly stepping from one to the next. Dark masses on the floor soon materialised into a group of bodies, many of the cowboys and cowgirls having drunk themselves to sleep, snoring up a storm.

Most of them were easily recognisable; Big-Stack Billy, Dante, Elwood. Others had changed drastically over the past two years, with Flem Wakefield having turned almost skeletal, his gaunt and emaciated frame bulging beneath his sallow skin.

"Hell of a welcoming party," Werner chuckled as they threaded their way through the mass of snoring bodies.

"Yeah," Boaz agreed, his boot narrowly avoiding a half-finished glass being cradled by one of the sleeping cowgirls, "Looks like we missed it though."

"We should've been here last night," Price shook his head, sorely disappointed that he had missed out on all the fun. He rubbed his lower back with a cheated scowl.

"The fuck are y'all doin' here?" a contemptuous voice came from one of the bodies on the floor.

"Jack," Garrett refused to lend a hand as the scruffy-bearded blonde struggled to sit upright. "Figured you'd wanna get back here soon as y'could."

"I'm here to mourn Emmett," Cactus Jack replied, grabbing hold of a chair and pulling himself to his feet. He glanced sidelong at the three guards standing behind Dess and Garrett, eyeing them off warily. "Y'all came a long way for nothin' if you think you're gonna drag me back to Rubicross."

"This the guy who started the fight with the Royce boys?" Boaz asked aloud, sizing up the slender green-eyed man.

"Ran his mouth to the wrong girl and got the shit kicked outta him," Werner confirmed with an amused grin, "I'm surprised him and his buddies could still ride a horse after what happened at The Oxhouse."

A few of the other cowboys groaned on the dusty floorboards, the sound of voices in the saloon shaking them from their sloshed slumber.

"Well, look who's outnumbered now," Cactus Jack gloated, although the handful of men and women waking up around them seemed as though they weren't even fit enough to fight their own hangovers.

"We ain't here for you," Garrett said out of the side of his mouth as he scanned the room. "But don't pretend you're here for Emmett. You came here to lay low for a while 'cause you got yourself in trouble."

"Don't pretend like y'all ever cared about Emmett, neither," Cactus Jack replied, his green eyes flicking between Dess and Garrett. "Runnin' away together like that..."

"Is that the story you heard?" Dess fired back, one hand on her hip. She could see why his mouth had gotten the shit kicked out of him. "Or just some bullshit you made up?"

Price, Boaz and Werner formed a tight semicircle around Cactus Jack before he could muster up a reply. He looked around at his friends on the floor, before deciding that riding his high horse wasn't worth what would happen next. Grumbling to himself, he headed outside with a pronounced limp.

Garrett pointed out Harlan, sprawled across a table in the back corner with half a glass of whiskey still in his hand. He and Dess were carefully making their way across the minefield of bodies when Father Norman fell off his chair with a loud thump, rousing himself and the rest of the cowboys from their sleep as the three Royce guards cracked up laughing.

Dess spread her hands wide across Harlan's table, leaning down and staring into his red-rimmed eyes as he stirred. He reared back at the sight of her, blinking himself awake. His hair was a mess, and he looked like he hadn't shaven or showered in days. He certainly smelled like it.

"Should I ask Lyle to fetch a bucket of water for you?" she asked, half serious.

"Prefer the taste of whiskey," he croaked, raising his glass and knocking it back in one grimacing gulp. Lyle set a glass on the counter, silently pouring another. Harlan wiped his mouth with the back of his sleeve as he stared up at her. "You came early. Have a drink with us."

Before she could answer, he pounded the table and called for another round.

"Let's go again, boys!" Big-Stack cheered, the boisterous red-headed brute clambering to his feet.

Slowly, the saloon came back to life, with Flem keeling over and vomiting on the floor. It was hard to believe that the bony man actually had anything inside him to regurgitate. Brandi narrowly avoided the splatter from the pool of bile, and with a disgusted sigh, she handed Harlan his drink and went searching for a mop while the hungover men and women began to call for breakfast.

"I'm not here to drink," Dess stood upright again. "Not until I see Emmett's body. At least save that one for when we come back," she nodded at his new glass.

Harlan swirled the liquor, eyeing it thoughtfully before pulling his hands away with a conscious effort, as if he was somehow magnetised to the whiskey. He reached for his umber brown cowboy hat hanging on the chair beside him, but paused as he noticed Garrett for the first time.

"Tell me that's not who I think it is," Harlan grinned, lifting himself onto unsteady feet.

"Good to see you, brother," Garrett returned the smile, extending an arm.

Harlan clasped his hand and pulled him into a hug. They had both attended the same high school back in Stillborough prior to the apocalypse, but being a few years apart, they hadn't actually interacted with each other until they had each begun to run out of food. While most people had struggled to survive during the food shortages, they had thrived, hunting game together in Stillborough Pines. Garrett was the tracker, and Harlan was the shooter. After they had cleared out the forest and it became apparent that the prairies had already been picked clean, they had decided to join the railroad's construction crew together in order to keep their bellies full.

Garrett looked back over his shoulder at Boaz, Price and Werner, guards who he still worked with in Rubicross, checking to make sure that they hadn't seen the two men hug. They were preoccupied though, eagerly helping a perky prostitute who claimed to have lost her bra.

"You boys take a break," Dess said to the three Royce guards, "Unpack and relax."

"You got it, boss," Price replied, his eyes still fixed on the prostitute. "You just let us know if you need us… for… anythin'," he added, before frowning at the floor, wondering if there was a better choice of words he could have used.

Werner slapped him over the head.

Harlan staggered to the front of the saloon, one arm around Garrett's shoulders, the other clutching his cowboy hat. In their absence, Flem crawled away from his mess on the floor, greedily sucking down the unattended whiskey like a man dying of thirst.

Harlan held up his hat to shield his eyes from the sun's blaze as they stumbled outside.

"I'll take that bucket of water now," he rasped, cranking the squeaky hand-pump on the rusty faucet above the horses' water trough and splashing himself with it, washing away the sweat and grime and alcohol emanating from his pores. He drank and cranked and heaved and drank some more. "I haven't left this place in days," he confessed, wiping his mouth with the back of his sleeve and staring up at the saloon before squinting up and down the street as if he was seeing it for the first time. "I was hoping you'd turn up soon."

"I started packing the day I got your letter," Dess replied, patiently waiting for him to sober up.

She knew how close he had been with Emmett. They had all been close, but after their circle parted ways following the manhunt for Wallace Pelletier, Harlan had chosen to stay with Emmett until the bitter end.

If it wasn't for her desire to investigate the curious circumstances of

Emmett's death, Dess knew that she would have been just as intent on destroying her liver as every other man and woman in Coyote's Rest while reminiscing about the good times they had shared with their fallen friend.

"You are planning on staying long?" asked Ingrid Kaufmann, a sunflower-blonde woman who had never managed to lose her European accent. She tilted her straw hat back, leaning on the railing of the saloon's veranda. "I take care of the horses, if you want."

Ingrid, Olaf's niece, owned the livery stable in town. The pair had been working in Coyote's Rest since before the world had ended, back when they predominantly served tourists who wanted a taste of the Old West.

Dess smiled, remembering that Emmett had once joked that Ingrid must have had an alarm bell that sounded off each time someone tied a horse to the saloon's hitching post.

"Much obliged," Garrett pressed a few golden bucks into her hand. "I don't know how long we're staying, but you come get me if we go over our tab."

She smiled and nodded before calling for her stablehand to help her with the eight horses.

Harlan shook the water from his hair before putting his cowboy hat on. Scraping himself back together, he led Dess and Garrett down the waterlogged street and around the corner towards Verne's Funeral Parlour.

The self-styled undertaker was a doddering old man in his seventies, perpetually dressed in a black suit with his white hair combed back, as if he had prepared himself for his own burial, refusing to retire until he joined his ever-growing list of clients in the afterlife. He stood motionless at the window of his front office, surveying the street like a forlorn shade, waiting for some external stimulus to lure him back into the land of the living.

"Ah, Harlan," Verne greeted them with his hands folded behind his back as they walked into the room's stale atmosphere. "I had been meaning to visit you today. There have been some slight additions to the overall cost. The burial suit you provided had to be tapered in…"

Dess tuned out of Verne's price-hiking prattle as she stared around his office. Antique furniture rested on low spider-thin legs, tarnished silverware adorned the coffee table, and faded floral-print curtains covered in mothballs flanked the windows. She would have mused that it all lent to the quaint character of the room, although the thick layer of dust blanketing the wall mirror, the picture frames, and even the floor, made it appear as though the office had been abandoned for years, and that Verne had some profound ability to float around the room to avoid leaving any footprints.

"We came to see Emmett's body," Dess cut across the spiel of vague hidden fees.

"Of course," Verne smiled at the interruption, gesturing towards an arched doorway.

He led them down a hall lined with rich display caskets made of mahogany, walnut and maple. The air grew colder as they continued, the familiar warmth of the prairies being replaced by clammy dread with each step in the echoing passage. Dess could feel gooseflesh forming on her arms. She knew that when she would see Emmett's body with her own eyes, there could be no doubt that he was dead.

Even now, the little girl inside her clung to a thin hope that this was all part of an elaborate scheme concocted by Emmett and Harlan to bring her back to Coyote's Rest. The stubborn man would extract an apology from her, the same one that they had both been waiting for two years to hear, *I was wrong and you were right*, and they would be together again.

But the woman that she had become knew the fool's fantasy for what it was. Taking a measured breath and flexing the slender muscles in her jaw, she summoned her resolve and marched into the preparation room.

Garrett stood on one side of the casket, bowing his head respectfully as Verne continued his hushed conversation with Harlan by the door.

"You want an extra two thousand!?" Harlan exclaimed, craning his head forward with his hands on his hips. "You're fucking kidding me, old man. You haven't even put him in the casket we agreed on. I grew up in Stillborough. I know fucking pinewood when I see it."

"Please," Verne cooed, smiling even as he stared into the storm, "With respect, I would ask you to keep your voice down in the company of the departed. Perhaps we can pursue further discussion back in my office."

Dess approached the casket as Harlan's outrage faded out of earshot.

Despite her determination to hold herself together, her lower lip began to tremble at the sight of Emmett's body, a sad and forlorn expression in her eyes, but with tenderness, too. *Handsome as ever*, she thought to herself, admiring the broad cheekbones and defined jaw line that she had fallen for all those years ago.

She fussed over his burial suit, although the undertaker had done a tremendous job already. Her hand reached down to hold his one more time, but she flinched at its cold touch. She pulled away, sinking down upon a swivelling surgical stool, wondering what she was even doing there.

Garrett sniffed, glancing at the open door before focusing on the task at hand. Moving to the head of the casket, he felt around Emmett's skull. A peculiar expression crossed his face as his fingers found something. He peered closely, parting the hair.

"Sorry, Emmett," he murmured under his breath.

Taking hold of the corpse's armpits, Garrett heaved its stiff upper back out from the casket. Dess gasped as Emmett's eyes and mouth popped open. The stench that spilled forth from his gaping lips was horrible. As much as she wished that she could turn away before the sight etched itself into her memory forever, she forced herself to keep watching.

"Head's been smashed in three places," said Garrett, his mouth set grimly. He pointed out one thick indent above Emmett's ear before combing his hair forward to reveal another just behind his widow's peak, with the biggest one on the back of his skull. "Unless he fell off his horse three times, that ain't how he died."

CHAPTER 10 – HARLAN

"That's the last cost you're gonna add," Harlan Reid grilled Verne as they stood in the ancient front office of the funeral parlour, the old man smiling back after hustling him over more minor details for Emmett's service. "And if you try to hit me with some other bullshit fee, we're gonna be hard-pressed to teach somebody else how to do your job for you."

"Of course," Verne replied in an infuriatingly soothing voice, his hands folded behind his back. "However, if you find that my work does not meet your high expectations, I have already documented all of the necessary instructions for my inevitable successor to prepare the departed for the journey beyond." He gestured towards his dusty desk drawer.

Harlan shook his head, exhaling in frustration. The old man was either calling his bluff with a bluff of his own, or he was ready to die. Everybody else in Coyote's Rest had regarded the funeral director as a kindly grandfather figure, despite his peculiarities. But he was a cunning bastard, humbly hiding his penchant for price gouging beneath his age.

"And another thing," Harlan began to bluster again as Verne raised his wispy white eyebrows with mild amusement, "That casket better be made of mahogany. I don't care if you have to use the case you got on display back there. I didn't pay good money for Emmett to be laid to rest in fucking pinewood!"

"Oh, Harlan," the old man scoffed softly. "Do you really believe that I would be so uncouth as to house our dearly departed friend in a cheap wooden box? The pinewood you saw is merely for temporary storage while I prepare him for his grand adventure. Emmett shall ride through the pearly gates in the most luxurious of limousines. My suppliers in Rookson City are handcrafting the freshly hewn mahogany as we speak, and they have assured me that the tailor-made order shall arrive within the month."

"The month!?" Harlan's cheeks reddened as he craned his head forward. "The funeral is next fucking week! If you –"

Harlan stopped, frowning. He sniffed at the stale air as a wafting stench of sun-dried bile and rotten eggs filled the room. Verne had his eyes closed, as if he was savouring the smell of a freshly-baked pumpkin pie, before he realised where the odour was coming from.

The underhanded undertaker hastily crossed the room to the hallway with uneven strides, doddering past the display coffins and stopping at the preparation room's doorway, his eyes widening in dismay.

Harlan loped after Verne, looking over the old man's shoulder.

Emmett, stiff with rigor mortis, was sitting upright and staring with his mouth open at the ceiling, as if he was in shock that he had just woken up to find himself laying in a casket. At the sight of the ghastly reanimation, Harlan instinctively ripped his umber brown cowboy hat from his head, momentarily fearing that his old friend might rebuke him for wearing it inside.

"Heathens!" Verne hissed, tottering into the room and glaring at Dess and Garrett incredulously as they huddled over the corpse, "Let the man *rest in peace!"*

"Sorry," Garrett mumbled, helping him reposition Emmett's body back inside the casket.

"Oh, what have they done to you?" Verne fretted beneath his breath as he fussed over the burial suit. "Your stitches have come undone, your hair is a mess…" he turned sharply to face Harlan by the door, hotly scolding him, "This is PRECISELY why I'm forced to charge you extra. More work, more costs. You can expect another bill on the morrow. And don't you *dare* threaten me again!"

"Go," Garrett said out of the side of his mouth, "I'll give him a hand."

Harlan rubbed his temples as they were shooed out of the funeral parlour.

"You wanna tell me why I'm forking out extra to this coffin-crook?" he rasped to Dess, fixing his hat back on his head as they re-emerged into the homely warmth of the prairies.

"We needed to have a closer look," she replied, not meeting his gaze, still visibly disturbed.

"I hope we get to see him one more time before he gets laid to rest," Harlan screwed his eyes shut and shook his head as if the macabre image might magically disappear. "Because that is *not* how I wanna remember Emmett."

Garrett caught up to them as they silently made their way back to the main street, which was now buzzing with life as the townsfolk went about their business, the morning sun beaming down in its full radiance.

Gloria Clementine flipped the hanging sign behind her feed store's shop door to "Open". Father Norman groggily staggered down the road to The Pilgrim's Respite Church to deliver yet another hungover sermon, for anyone who cared to hear it. Gemma Wagner brought a steaming mug of coffee to her husband, Shane, as he carried handmade display chairs outside his carpentry workshop.

Harlan snorted cynically at the only married couple in a town full of widowers and whores. As if on cue, the morning shift of prostitutes emerged from Madame's Buxom Boarding House and made their way over to Lorelei's Saloon.

Deputy Monroe sat outside the Sheriff's Office, the dour dark blonde woman with smiles rarer than a raw steak icily watching Lorelei's from across the street as the cowboys stretched and retched on the saloon's veranda, impatiently waiting for their breakfasts to be cooked and served before they would start their mourning's morning binge.

Harlan was about to make his way back to his glass of whiskey when Dess stopped in the middle of the street, a few buildings away from the crowd. She asked him to recount the events leading up to Emmett's death. Despite having been on a week-long drunken bender since the night that they had found his body, Harlan retold the story as best as he could remember; Big-Stack's cocky bet, Emmett agreeing to swap horses for the race… Everything right up until Billy rode back into town.

"You didn't ride out to watch the race yourself?" asked Garrett, squinting against the sunlight.

"No one did," Harlan answered before glancing uncertainly at the men and women milling about the entrance to Lorelei's Saloon. He shrugged, "It was raining. Most of us just watched from the veranda."

"Did you see anyone leave?" asked Dess, catching his moment of doubt.

"Yeah, anyone who had a date for the night," he snorted, shaking his head. "Look, everybody thought Emmett was gonna win anyway, no point waiting around just to watch the rain. When Big-Stack showed up first, we all thought maybe Emmett was only good at riding because of his horse. I don't know how long it took before we started worrying, but when Billy's horse came back without Emmett, that's when we got to looking. Found him… we found him face-down in the mud at Rambling Gulch." He took a shallow breath before wiping his mouth. "Fuck. I should've been there. Don't know why I wasn't. Maybe I could've done something."

Garrett clapped a hand on Harlan's shoulder, squeezing in sympathy.

"How could he be laying face-down?" asked Dess, her eyes flitting between the two of them. "He took the heaviest hit to the back of his head. That's gotta be the one that killed him."

"Well, it was wet out," Harlan shrugged Garrett's hand off, nodding his thanks. "Wouldn't be a stretch to say he was riding pretty hard and the horse slipped. He must've fallen off, hit his head on a rock and then rolled into place."

"I need to see where you found him," Garrett sniffed, getting back to business.

"Sure thing," Harlan obliged, knowing how good his ex-hunting partner was at reading the land. *Whatever brings them closure*, he thought. His whiskey would just have to wait.

"Should we bring the escort?" Garrett asked Dess as they passed by the crowded saloon, walking towards Ingrid's Livery Stable.

"No need," Dess shook her head, "Let them rest. They earned it."

"Royce sent some guards with you?" Harlan asked as Garrett picked up his pace heading into the stables. There was no hiding the sarcasm in his voice, "Big man, keeping you safe from the scaries in the prairies. Did you stay for dinner with him, too?"

"No, I didn't," Dess crossed her arms as she stared into the stables. She nodded towards Garrett as he spoke to Ingrid inside. "I needed him, and I needed some horses."

Harlan knew that he should have been happier to see the both of them, but he wasn't going to pretend. He would never forget how a piece of Emmett had seemed to have broken off after Dess left Coyote's Rest. He didn't smile as often. For a while, Emmett would buy two pints of beer and pause on his way back from the bar, before sliding the other glass across to Harlan, even if he already had a drink in his hand. Some nights, when Emmett was in a lighter mood, he would turn to an empty chair with a joke that would always die on his lips. For the past two years, Harlan had watched the man withdraw into himself, but he had stuck by Emmett all the same.

A few weeks after Dess and Garrett had left, some of the boys mentioned that they had seen them working for Royce, despite having plenty of money from the Wallace payday. It never made any sense to him why the pair hadn't just gone straight back to Stillborough.

"Well, you're safe here," Harlan turned away from her. "Don't need any guards to protect you from a bunch of boys who can just *buy* whatever they want."

Dess didn't bother to give him a reply, and they stood in stubborn silence until Garrett, Ingrid, and her stablehand, Flip, led their horses out.

"Everybody still use the same track at Rambling Gulch?" Garrett asked as they climbed onto their mounts.

"As far as I know," said Harlan, settling into the sweet spot on his saddle, his red stallion hoofing at the dirt impatiently. He hadn't been out for a ride since the night Emmett died. "With the amount of money they had riding on that race, I doubt they would've wanted to change the course."

The three of them tapped spurs into their horses, taking off at a canter as Ingrid ushered Flip back inside the stables with an unending list of chores that needed doing.

Harlan glanced sidelong at Garrett riding on his brown mustang. He was one of the many high schoolers who had come out of Stillborough and Brimvale, along with the skilled labourers who had a few years of trade experience underneath their belts, all of them looking for steady work on the railroad. Garrett Ridley had always been a bit of a loner, so Harlan doubted that the rest of the cowboys would acknowledge his return, but there was no denying that he was good at what he did.

They had hunted game together back in Stillborough Pines, and sometimes along the edges of Burnshaw Forest. Garrett was a natural at tracking down prey. They had teamed up plenty of times during the food shortages, first as part of a small group organised as a social exercise by Mr Cooper, one of their former high school coordinators, but after joining a few hunts with the other students – a bunch of loud and clumsy trigger-happy dopes – Harlan and Garrett had decided that they were better off branching out on their own. And they were. They brought a catch home every time they had ventured out into the forest.

They graduated from hunting game after Wallace Pelletier had stolen the golden bucks that had been set aside to pay the railroad workers, tracking the fat man across the prairies until the former foreman's heart gave out. Part of Garrett had died that night too though, seeing his hunting prowess being put to use on another human being, as despicable as that human being had been. Harlan tried to convince him that he had done a good thing, but the damage had already been done.

Garrett had aged considerably since then, despite being a few years younger than Harlan. His shoulder-length hair did him no favours, nor did his grizzled beard. But they would never have been able to find Wallace had it not been for Garrett's assistance.

Harlan had awoken the next morning after the manhunt to find that Garrett and Dess had split, along with Archie Callahan and several others. The most common reason in the handwritten notes that the more considerate retirees had thought to leave behind was that since the work on the railroad was over, there was no point in them sticking around. Nobody but he and Emmett really bothered to care about the people who had left. Everyone who had decided to stay behind was too preoccupied with their sudden fortunes and lavish self-indulgences to pay any attention to much of anything outside of their own hedonistic existences. Admittedly, Harlan had all too easily become one of them.

Garrett held up a hand just as they approached Legsnap Ridge, a sharp turn along a steep point in the track that was notoriously well-known for races ending prematurely and horses being put down. Harlan and Dess slowed their mounts to a trot, but Garrett stopped altogether, peering at something over the edge of the path.

Unnoticeable at first, they saw that a sizeable portion of the downward slope next to the track was a few shades darker than the rest of the surrounding rocks and gravel. Garrett jumped down, crouching on the ground, scrutinising the angle of the slope and glancing back at his own horse.

"We found Emmett up ahead," Harlan offered, but his words fell on deaf ears.

Garrett took a wide berth around the slope's dark patch to pick up a stick, the only sound in the gulch being the narrow stream burbling below, slightly swollen after last night's rains. He dropped the stick into an unremarkable hole in the earth that was no wider than a chair leg, and then withdrew it, measuring from his thumb to the end of the stick and glancing up at his horse again. He headed to the bottom of the small rockslide and surveyed the area like he was studying a painting before tossing the stick into the stream.

"Someone's horse slipped along here," he called up to the pair watching him work. "Whoever was riding the horse recovered without going down, and then they rode diagonally back up to the track."

"So he didn't fall off his horse here?" asked Dess, holding the reins of his mustang.

"No footprints," Garrett answered as he climbed back into the saddle.

"You sure the rain couldn't have washed them out?" asked Harlan, his stallion turning, ready to run again. "Been getting a lot the last few nights."

"I'm sure," Garrett replied as Dess tossed him the reins. "Whatever happened to him ain't happen here."

Garrett and Dess followed Harlan as he trotted farther up the path to where they had found Emmett's body, a relatively flat area by the stream. They dismounted, tying off their horses to a half-dead tree that occupied a niche in the wall of rock lining the other side of the track.

"If you fell off your horse," Dess mused to nobody in particular as they tied their knots, "You get yourself out of your stirrups and then tuck and roll, right? It doesn't mean you'll walk away without a scratch, but at least you're protecting yourself from any major damage. Sure, one knock to the head would've been plain bad luck. Two hits, yeah, he could've bounced into something else if he was riding hard, but three? Luck's got nothing to do with three."

"So what exactly are you saying?" asked Harlan, his head craned forward. "That he didn't just fall off his horse? How else do you explain why he's in a casket right now?"

"That's what we're here to find out," Dess answered, nodding at Garrett.

"Stay on the track," Garrett called over his shoulder, picking his steps carefully as he painted a mental picture. "Don't need any more footprints."

The pair watched from the path again as the tracker picked up loose stones and tested large rocks with his boot, pushing them with ease in the loose earth.

"Judging from the impacts," he indicated a series of indents along the riverbank, "Emmett fell right here. He tucked and rolled a few times, like any good rider would."

"We found him over there though," said Harlan, pointing half a dozen yards away.

His arm faltered as he shivered, an unbidden image of his closest friend laying face down in the mud flying into his mind's eye, blood mixing in with the rain in ruby red rivulets. For the past few days, Harlan had managed to numb himself from thinking about the whole ordeal, keeping himself busy by organising the funeral in between bottomless binges at the saloon. It was only as he stood there that he realised: Emmett had died alone. He turned away, blinking back tears.

"Looks like he dragged himself there," Garrett replied, crouching next to a pair of shallow narrow trenches. "Fall didn't kill him."

"Here's what I'm thinking," Dess peered up and down the track as Harlan discreetly wiped his eyes, "If he could stay on his horse during that slide back there, *if* that was him, but he fell off on a flat, then there must've been something else that knocked him down."

They looked around for any low branches, but the only tree nearby was the half-dead one hidden in between the rock face on the other side of the track where they had tied their horses, but none of its branches hung over the path.

"When you found him," Garrett began, his eyes focused on the ground as he left the riverbank and crossed over the path towards the rock shelf, "Where'd you hitch your horses?"

"It was raining," Harlan repeated with a hollow breath. "We were more worried about rushing him back into town than anything else."

Garrett tugged the slipknots that held the horses, passing the lead ropes over to Dess and Harlan before stooping beside the half-dead tree next to some dried horseshit.

"Well, *somebody* parked their horse here," Garrett concluded, looking up at the both of them. "And if you're tying up your horse in the rain, you're either waiting for somebody to come along, or you're sticking around to clean up a mess."

The trio shared a thought that didn't need to be said; regardless of how Emmett had fallen from his horse, someone had been there to finish the job.

CHAPTER 11 – BRISTOL

Dwight Jaskolski held the door open for her with his brown leather shoe as they exited The Artisan's Roast Cafe, coffee cups in hand. When Bristol Hudson had moved from her high-rise apartment in Sunken City back to Brimvale, her set of coffee mugs was among one of the first things that she had thought to pack. Throwaway cups were no longer being manufactured, along with almost every other previously mass-produced item, so if anyone wanted a barista-made coffee, they would have to bring their own cup.

Ever since halfway through her teenage years, coffee had played a major role throughout her life. Apart from being a breakfast staple, she had spent many late nights procrastinating on her studies with a steaming mug by her side. At home, she would hold a book in one hand and the other would be wrapped around her velvet red stainless steel thermos. When she had taken a gap year from college to accept an internship in the formerly-named Swanson City, the interview with her prospective employers had been over coffee.

Coffee had been the third wheel in just about any day-time social interaction, so it hit her especially hard when Brimvale had run out of the magic beans. At the time, she knew that she should have been more concerned about maintaining her food and water supplies rather than coffee, but it had been such an integral part of her life for so long, she had built up a dependency.

And so when she couldn't find any more, she crashed.

For weeks on end following the missile blast in North Tekota, she could barely get out of bed. The headaches were near unbearable, and the limited supplies of a nutrient-rich diet in the post-apocalyptic world did nothing to help correct her natural energy levels. She had known that the coffee shortage didn't mean that the world was coming to another tragic end, but it certainly felt like it had been; at least, it did for her.

Somehow though, she had made it through her caffeine withdrawals, even managing to hold herself together better than many of the other women who she had once worked with, especially the older and mature ladies who she had once respected as her seniors. Although, being an intern on a gap year from college, almost all of them had been her seniors. After living half their lives in the daily office grind, the slightest change to the middle-aged ladies' daily routines had thrown them all into complete disarray, and their workplace inhibitions had all but vanished, without any need for an apology email or a catch-up with the human resources department on Monday morning.

The inhabitants of the office towers and the high-rise apartments of Swanson City had a perfect unhindered view of the rogue missile strike, along with its ensuing mushroom cloud, and so anyone who usually made long commutes from the outer suburbs of North Tekota were able to watch as their family homes were obliterated in the blast. Many sought steamy comfort in the arms of a colleague, hoping to feel something again, while the once prudish middle-aged women of her company had jumped on every single opportunity with legs wide open and fallopian tubes tied shut.

Bristol had rejected the advances of all of the horny office guys who were desperate to find some relief from the sight of the chaos outside, even as the ensuing earthquake of the missile's impact shockwave had reached Brimvale and the piece of land that Swanson City rested upon had broken off and sank into the depths of Bellevue Bay. She knew that the men had already given up on the possibility of the world ever returning to some level of normality, so she doubted that any of them were ever planning on sticking around.

Luckily for some people, only a few of the city's older buildings had collapsed in the lurching plunge underwater. If it hadn't been for the ground being a gigantic slab of concrete, rebar and asphalt, the entire city would have crumbled. For others though, the fun times were short-lived, as they soon realised that the world wasn't going to end after all. Many of her former female colleagues around the same age as her were now raising children by themselves.

Bristol sipped from her mug in the morning sunlight as she and Dwight stepped out onto the sidewalk, grateful for the coffee merchants who had sailed from Guadasula to begin trading with them a few years after the apocalypse, and equally as grateful for her coffee addiction, since if it hadn't been for her caffeine deprivation which had led to her head-splitting migraines during those uncertain times, she might have also joined the ranks of single mothers aboard the loveless fling bandwagon.

"Good, right?" Dwight asked as he sipped from his own cup, standing kerbside and looking both ways before crossing.

It was an ingrained force of habit, she knew. There was no need for caution along the wide empty street. Nor was there any need for formal attire, yet they had both dressed the part for Monday morning.

Dwight, blue-eyed, in his early twenties with well-groomed sandy blonde hair, was garbed in a royal blue blazer and beige slacks, tailored to fit his tall and broad-shouldered frame, while Bristol had chosen to wear a loose-fitting grey pinstripe suit with a sky blue button-down shirt underneath. In passing, one might have assumed that they were brother and sister, with her wavy golden blonde hair and ocean blue eyes, had it not been for the height difference. She was borderline petite, while he stood a full head above her.

"Magical," she sighed heartily, crossing the street as the dopamine receptors in her brain threw a welcome back party. "It's hard to find a decent coffee nowadays. All of my favourite places are underwater now."

"Yeah, these guys definitely have a monopoly on the market," Dwight smiled, taking another sip.

The municipal square was well-kept, with neatly-trimmed low hedges bordering the manicured lawns on either side of the whitewashed concrete plaza. There was no doubt that a full-time caretaker was employed to ensure that the grounds around the town hall looked nothing like the suburbs of Brimvale, where the houses that had been abandoned for years were easily identifiable. Bristol had made short work of clearing old cobwebs and hosing the dust off her front porch when she had moved back to Brimvale, but the jungle of overgrown grass and garden beds were a different matter entirely; she estimated that it would take her at least a week to hack through it all by herself.

They passed underneath the long shadow cast by the town hall in the rising sun when a pale waiflike figure's hand shot out at them from behind one of the low hedges. Bristol stopped suddenly, almost spilling her coffee as she sidestepped to avoid the gnarled grasping fingers, backing into Dwight, who wasn't so lucky with his own mug.

The figure rose to its feet. Dark circles drooped from red-rimmed eyes set within the sharp angles of bony cheeks. The waif's hair was short, frizzy and greying, like the dusty tangle of cobwebs Bristol had cleared from her porch. A sleeveless dress that might have once been white some time before the world had ended hung from its skinny shoulders.

"Do you feel it, my child?" a wavering voice croaked from its cracked lips, waggling a crooked finger at Bristol. "It's coming for you. It's coming for all of us. We cannot hide."

"Fuck off, Priscilla," Dwight breathed exasperatedly, checking that his coffee hadn't splattered his clothes. He clucked his tongue at the sight of a brown stain on his beige pants.

"What's coming?" asked Bristol, furrowing her eyebrows.

Priscilla smiled at the question, her cracked lips peeling back from blackened teeth.

"Salvation, child!" her bleating voice broke as she spun in a circle in celebration. "Salvation is coming!"

"Get lost, before I call the guards," Dwight warned, stooping to dab at the coffee stain with a handkerchief.

"Who was that?" Bristol asked as she watched Priscilla dance away across the empty street, disappearing behind a row of boarded-up shopfronts.

"Just some crazy woman," Dwight answered, giving his slacks a final unsatisfied wipe of resignation before resuming their walk to the town hall's front steps. "We only tolerate her because she lost her husband and all seven of her kids during The Long Summer Night."

"That's horrible!" Bristol gasped, glancing back at the row of neglected shopfronts, *that poor woman.*

"Yeah," Dwight agreed reluctantly, sipping what was left of his spilled coffee. "We've all lost people though. To be honest, I preferred the guy who used to stand outside just staring at us for days at a time. At least he didn't talk shit to us."

"Does she have any other family?" asked Bristol, brushing loose strands of hair over her ear. "Where does she stay?"

"Who knows?" Dwight shrugged as they climbed the stairs. "Sometimes she's here, sometimes she's not. Every now and then, she vanishes for a few weeks, and *just* when we start to think we've seen the last of her, she comes back and eats some more children."

Bristol stumbled in shock as they passed through the town hall's echoing marble foyer, staring sidelong at Dwight.

"Got you," he laughed, turning the door handle on the frosted glass entrance to the Mayor's Office.

He held the door open for her as she stepped onto the grey carpet. The office was livelier than when they had left it, with Shelton Turner and Liam Caldwell now sitting among the desks and filing cabinets on the right. On the left was the entrance to the stationery room along with the water cooler and a leafy fake plant. Farther along the wall and around the corner were the senior officers' private offices, meeting rooms and the corridor that led to the break room. Dwight had given her a tour earlier, since they had been the only two in the office.

Bristol couldn't help but notice that Liam seemed uncomfortable sitting beside Shelton, the intern from Gainstowe Park and Liam's supposed replacement, since he was transitioning to Lora Purcell's previous role. Bristol wondered if Liam had social anxiety when it came to meeting new people, since he had declined the invitation to join them for drinks at The

Woozy Rooftop Bar & Grill last Friday.

Lora, wearing a pink and black business shirt, looked up from behind her desk, catching sight of Bristol and Dwight. She bounced out of her corner office with a wide smile, holding her arms out for a hug. Bristol hesitated for a moment before setting her coffee mug down on a nearby filing cabinet, sheepishly accepting the embrace.

"Good morning, you two," Lora chirped before shooting a pout at Dwight. "You went on a coffee run *without me?*"

"Don't you normally drink the office coffee though?" he asked, confused.

"How *are* you, lovelyyy?" Lora ignored Dwight's rebuttal, turning back to Bristol. Without waiting for an answer, she added, "Oh my gosh, I think I'm still hungover from Friday. I had *such* a great night!"

Bristol smiled and chatted politely, although she doubted that Lora could have been hungover at all, since she had spent the majority of the night nursing one drink while spilling her entire life story. She didn't mind Lora's overzealous friendship though. It was nice to have someone welcome her so enthusiastically in a new working environment.

Feeling excluded from the conversation between the two girls, Dwight quietly excused himself and joined Shelton and Liam in the shared workstation, breaking the streak of prolonged bouts of silence between the pair of newly-acquainted colleagues, to Liam's visible relief.

Like the rest of the junior officers who had joined them for drinks, Lora was in her early twenties, with shoulder-length brown hair and matching brown eyes. She was the same height as Bristol, although Lora might have been a few pounds curvier.

Lora had predominantly been raised by her mother as stepfathers walked in and out of her life, so she had instantly clung to the first stable fatherly figure that she could find in Mayor Paxton; or Teddie, as she preferred to call him. Despite the poor example set by her mother, rather than falling to the same cycle of burnt relationships and alcoholism, which had only been exacerbated during Brimvale's food shortages, Lora had instead dedicated herself to fighting for Teddie's cause, helping him rally disgruntled citizens throughout the suburbs of Brimvale and Stillborough until the previous regime of the Army Reserves were overthrown.

During the attack of The Long Summer Night, her mother had been seen fleeing towards The Burning Forest, but she had never returned, although Lora felt like she had lost her mother a long time before then. The absence of any family remaining after the end of the world only drove Lora to redouble her commitment to her new role in the Mayor's Office, while constantly looking towards Teddie to offer her guidance and support, both inside and outside the workplace.

Bristol was sipping her coffee to the tune of Lora's weekend when the frosted glass door swung open, with Ollie Geary, Bronson Hopper and Pedro Pinto swaggering into the office.

"Glad you could join us today," Lora criticised their late arrival, pointedly checking an imaginary watch on her wrist.

"We're not late if everyone else is," Bronson rolled his eyes.

"We were here an hour ago, we just went for a team breakfast," Ollie grinned as he dropped his bag by his desk.

"Why were you late for breakfast?" Pedro giggled, following the other two to their shared workstation.

Bristol wanted to laugh, but she thought against it at the sight of Lora's flushed cheeks. She didn't want Lora to feel as though she was being unappreciative of her friendship, and so she took another sip of coffee, hiding her smile.

The three boys were practically triplets, but in behaviour rather than in appearance; Ollie was staunch and stocky, green-eyed with parted brown hair; Bronson was broad-shouldered, handsome and hazel-eyed with a light brown comb-over; while Pedro, a few years younger than the other two, was a tall yet hunched and lanky teen, brown-eyed with glasses and a poorly-shaped black bowl-cut.

Together, they had been the life of the party on their night out at Woozy's, building on each other's jokes as if there was some competition between just the three of them. They had even poked fun at Harriet and Wilson, two of the Mayor's guards, who had just finished their shifts and had decided to have a drink with the junior officers, feeding Wilson an endless supply of shots while they presented Harriet with hypothetical sexual scenarios that were increasingly explicit, just to see where she would draw the line. Harriet returned raunchy responses, giving them just as good as she got, but Wilson soon had to excuse himself.

A bow-legged man was the next person to walk through the entrance. Bristol guessed that he was one of the Mayor's senior officers, Abhilash Shandar, judging from Lora's description of all of their co-workers. It seemed as though Lora had almost painted him into existence, her depiction matching him word-for-word. He sported a messy shrub of wavy black hair over a receding hairline, an eight-hour early five o'clock shadow of stubble, along with an excessive amount of golden bangles and rings adorning his hairy wrists and fingers. Lora had even predicted that he would be wearing a plain black shirt in an effort to hide his pot-belly.

"Heyyy Abhi!" Lora greeted him happily.

"Good morning," Bristol smiled, unwrapping one hand from her coffee mug just in case he wanted to offer her a handshake. It was their first time meeting, after all.

"Morning, morning," Abhilash replied as he passed by, his gaze lingering upon Bristol beyond an appropriate length of time.

"I should probably sit down somewhere," Bristol decided, clutching her elbow with her free hand as she took another sip of coffee. She shot a sideways glance at Abhilash, whose attention jerked back to refilling his bottle from the water cooler before tottering off towards his office. "I feel like I'm in the way here."

"Relax, just take it as a compliment" Lora comforted her in a hushed tone, also having caught the stare. Leaning closer, she added, "It doesn't hurt to butter everyone up. You never know when you might need someone's help." She winked, and her voice returned back to normal as she asked, "So, are you staying with your boyfriend?"

"I certainly hope not." Bristol recognised her Uncle Quentin's voice, and she turned to see him smiling warmly as the frosted glass door swung shut behind him.

She had turned down her Aunt Helen's offer to stay with them, choosing instead to live in her ex-boyfriend's long-abandoned house. She had lived with him there for a few months during her gap year from college, but after they had broken up and she moved to Swanson City, she wasn't ready to give up her independence, especially not after having lived on her own in her high-rise apartment for the past five years.

She wasn't sure why she had chosen her ex-boyfriend's house, out of all of the other abandoned houses that were available to her, but perhaps it was just her need for a familiar environment after being thrust into her new liaison officer role.

Perry Wisniewski, the ex-CEO of the company where she had spent her internship, had assumed the responsibility of Sunken City's lingering community. He had sent Bristol to Brimvale in order to strengthen diplomatic relations between the two settlements, in the hopes that Sunken City would receive support against the recent pirate incursions issuing forth from the escaped prisoners of Attiker Island, which have been threatening their security and impacting trade.

Despite the plethora of other people available for the job, each with more tact and experience in negotiating with business partners, Bristol had been selected for the role of liaison officer, since she was one of the few who had managed to keep her head straight and her emotions in check throughout the early stages of the apocalypse. Little had they known however, was that her comparative lack of poor decisions among those of her ex-colleagues had been due to the onset of her migraines stemming from her caffeine deprivation, which had prevented her from doing anything other than moping alone in her bed.

"Good morning, everyone!" Mayor Paxton poked his head in through the entrance as Harriet, one of his bodyguards, held the door open for him solemnly, almost as if she had been transformed into a different person while she was on duty. The stout Mayor's cheerfully chubby facial features were all but hidden behind a ball of hair, with black-rimmed glasses perched upon his nose and a mop of dark brown hair too thick to run a comb through falling across his forehead.

"Good morning," the staff echoed in a dissonant chorus.

"Back for more, eh?" the Mayor's bushy grey-streaked beard parted with a toothy grin at the sight of Bristol and Shelton acclimatising to the office. "I was worried the others might have scared you off!"

"Lora is *very* scary," Bronson called out from the corner of the room.

"We live in constant fear," Ollie confirmed gravely.

"I fear for my life whenever I see her!" Pedro added, struggling to keep a straight face.

"And so you should," Lora snapped, narrowing her eyes at the three troublemakers before reassuming her sweet tone. "Teddie, Rhonda and Abhi are already here, if you wanted to continue the introductions?"

"Right!" he clapped his fleshy hands together, rubbing them eagerly. "Let's get straight into the thick of things. We'll take this to the boardroom."

"Did you want me in there?" Shelton asked, moving to get out of his office chair.

"That won't be necessary," said Uncle Quentin, rather dismissively as Bristol and Lora followed him around the corner.

"Yeah," Teddie agreed, hanging back, "I think we're just gonna talk shop with Bristol for a little while. We'll call on you after we're done."

"Sure, no problem," Shelton replied, resuming his training alongside Dwight and Liam.

The boardroom was naturally lit with partially-transparent roller blinds drawn over the windows, offering a faint view of the plaza outside. A whiteboard occupied the left wall by the entrance, while a rectangular black table dominated the centre of the room, surrounded by a dozen faux-leather conference chairs.

Bristol followed her uncle around to the far corner of the room, taking a pair of chairs that faced away from the windows, realising as soon as she sat down that she wouldn't be able to enjoy the veiled view of the plaza, which Lora now revelled in. Teddie and the other senior officers filed in shortly afterwards, with the Mayor taking the head of the table, Abhilash sidling up next to Lora, and the third settling in beside Bristol.

"Welcome to *the inner circle*," Teddie's beard smiled as his fingers animated air quotes. "So, I try to run this as a democracy. We bring up any issues affecting Brimvale and hash it out until we can score a win. Have you already met Rhonda and Abhi?"

"Rhonda Moore," the senior officer swivelled in her chair, shaking Bristol's hand with a firm grip. She was in her forties, dark-skinned, toned muscles, with her thick black hair cut into a high fade. "Look forward to working with you."

"Vwe did meet earlier," Abhilash leaned back in his chair with his hands clasped behind his head, stretching his legs out not even one minute into the meeting.

"Alright!" Teddie tapped a quick drum roll on the table. "Lora, did you wanna bring Bristol up to speed for us?"

Lora nodded obligingly, opening her notebook and flipping through pages, landing on a neatly-written set of dot points. She started with the prairies, where there had been rumours of hooded figures descending upon the outlying towns, kidnapping settlers without a trace. Believing that the Rauders had been responsible for the abductions, Teddie had dispatched Uncle Quentin to hire mercenaries from Coyote's Rest to eliminate the threat.

Abhilash clucked his tongue.

"I am still suspicious of the mutants from Vwoodrow College," he ventured, puffing his cheeks with his eyebrows raised, still peeved by the result of some previous meeting.

"That's your opinion," Rhonda replied, leaning forward in her chair with one elbow on the table. "We all agreed that without a clear motive or a history of violence, the inhabitants of Woodrow College couldn't be held to blame."

"Vwell," Abhilash continued as Rhonda drew a patient breath, "They vwere unable to complete their education, and vwe all know it's very easy for any uneducated persons to fall into criminal activity. The numbers don't lie. I vwould not be surprised if the attacks continued even after these Rauders vwere dealt vwit."

Uncle Quentin frowned at the table as Lora nodded in feigned grave agreement.

Bristol couldn't help but wonder if the rest of them knew that she hadn't completed her own education, since she had taken a gap year from her studies to pursue an internship. But, if she had been given the same choice, she would have made the exact same decision; otherwise she would have been stuck at Woodrow College when the missile dropped in North Tekota, eventually turning into a mutant herself.

"In any case," Teddie shrugged, happy to repeat his reasoning behind Brimvale's intervention in the prairies, "It sends a clear message to *anyone* responsible for the raids that their actions will have consequences. It also gives some reassurance to the settlers out there that they're safe and we're looking after them. We wanna avoid any disruptions of food supplies from the farm belt, or diesel from Cloakwater. Besides, the Rauders are far from innocent, so if it turns out that they weren't actually behind the attacks, I won't be losing any sleep over it."

Abhilash bobbled his head from side to side and gestured for Lora to continue with a wave of his golden bangles.

"We're building a diplomatic relationship with The Gutt–" Lora caught herself, making a conscious effort to shake a bad habit, "Bushrock Flats. If our internship program is successful, we might be able to open up new avenues for trade and hire more skilled workers."

"And this is the reason why Shelton isn't in this meeting," Teddie explained, his bushy beard dancing with every syllable. "If the people of Bushrock Flats believe that there are opportunities available for them here in Brimvale, they might be more inclined to behave accordingly. We haven't had anything major from them ever since The Long Summer Night. Granted, those wounds are gonna take a long time for everybody to heal from, but now that we have a passable peace treaty in place under an agreement I've negotiated for, I think it'll be easier for us all to remember that we're all in this together."

Uncle Quentin cleared his throat at the mention of the agreement with Bushrock Flats. Rhonda shifted in her seat, expecting to hear more, but with an expression which showed that she knew better than to expect as much by now. Teddie smiled at Lora with a small nod for her to continue.

"On to Rubicross then," she started reading the next dot point, "There's been a report–"

"Just before we leave Brimvale," Bristol interjected, studying Teddie's eyes behind his glasses, "Are there any plans to address the recent aggression from Attiker Island? Sunken City's concern is that they'll ward off our trading partners and threaten our security along the coast, and in turn, our ability to serve as a trading port and a defensive buffer for Brimvale."

"I think at this stage," Teddie began before brushing his bushy beard for time to choose his next words, "The protection from our roaming patrols should be sufficient for now. I don't believe there's any real cause for alarm, especially since there haven't been any direct attacks on Sunken City or Brimvale."

That makes my job a whole lot harder, Bristol thought to herself.

"We won't ignore it though," said Uncle Quentin, although it sounded like more of a question than an affirmation.

"Oh no, of course not," Teddie agreed, looking back at Bristol. "At the moment, we're just concentrating our efforts on dealing with the trouble in the prairies, so we're having to shift some of our already-stretched guard personnel over to Axemark Ravine as a precaution to deal with any possible retaliation. This is only a temporary measure until the Rauders have been dealt with though, and then we can start looking at lending some assistance over your way to help out with the pirates.

"I'm sure we'd love to help out sooner," Teddie continued, glancing at Uncle Quentin. "But we're a bit short-staffed on the amount of guards that we can move around. I mean, we're running into difficulty retaining the guards that we have now, since Rubicross pays much better for more comfortable conditions. Not only that, but Rubicross are also paying higher prices for supplies of ammunition from Rookson City than what we're able to offer."

Bristol wrapped her hands around her empty coffee mug, which had long since turned cold. She didn't want to step on anyone's toes on her first day, but she knew that she would be betraying her duty as a liaison officer if she didn't try to resolve an issue that was preventing Brimvale from assisting Sunken City.

"Okay, so just a thought," she ran a thumb over her mug's handle as she framed her contemplation. "If you can to afford to pay mercenaries to deal with the Rauders, how come you're not able to match the wages on offer for guards in Rubicross? I'm still new here, so I might not have all the answers, but wouldn't it be better to designate a task force and deal with any threats as an inside job, rather than paying a premium to rely on outsiders?"

Uncle Quentin gave her an approving nod as Teddie combed his beard, clearly stumped. Lora glanced at Teddie and glanced away again, searching the room for an answer of her own before she began flipping through her notes, as if she had forgotten where she had already written the answer down.

"I had also been vwondering the same ting," Abhilash smiled across the table with his hands still clasped behind his head. "I'm glad Bristol has brought this up."

"I think she deserves a straight answer for that," Rhonda cut across Teddie's fumbling silence, swivelling in her chair to face Bristol. "Captain Karl Thornton took most of our supplies of ammunition from Fort Mason when he and his remaining soldiers were hired by the Royce Family. Whatever bullets were left has dwindled over the years of defending The Ravine and the Burnshaw Barricade. Now, we're faced with an ammo shortage, *on top* of a guard shortage. I'm sure that we could spare some guards to help you watch the shore, but they wouldn't do you any good since most of their guns are empty."

For a while, Teddie kept his eyes on the table. Admitting weakness was no easy thing. But Rhonda held her gaze on Bristol, keen to hear her thoughts. It took Bristol a moment to realise that she was now the object of everyone's attention. She reminded herself that the sooner she could solve Brimvale's problems, the sooner Sunken City would receive help.

"Well, it sounds like…" she trailed off, pausing to phrase her proposal carefully. "It sounds like Rubicross is your biggest issue. And I know we all rely on them for food from the farm belt and diesel from Cloakwater, but it's the truth. If you can't outbid them for Rookson City's supplies of ammunition, and if buying from Rubicross's reserves isn't an option…

Then maybe you should send someone to Rookson City to talk in person about purchasing their ammunition with some other means of trading; something that Rubicross can't offer."

Uncle Quentin exchanged a glance with Teddie.

CHAPTER 12 – EVELYN

"I'm leaving," Nathan decided, her broad-shouldered husband's unshaven face lined with determination as he threw his suitcase on the bed in the afternoon light.

"Don't you think you're overreacting?" Evelyn asked from their ensuite's doorway, smoothing out the folds on her low-cut navy blue shirt as she placed her hands on her slender hips, watching him unzip the battered brown leather suitcase. "Why can't you send someone else?"

"That's not how Rodney works," Nathan replied out of the side of his mouth, packing an armful of dark cardigans along with his brown leather bomber jacket, which blended seamlessly into the bottom of the travel-worn suitcase. "It has to be me."

She soured even further at his outdated sense of fashion as he piled bundles of vintage clothes into his luggage. Despite his youthful energy and appearance, he always insisted upon dressing like an old man. Some days, it seemed like she was married to a thirty-year-old trapped in a mid-forty-year-old's body, wrapped up in an eighty-year-old's clothes.

"You sent seven guards with Dess Sheridan," Evelyn reminded him, her shoulders stiffening as he continued stuffing his suitcase, "A woman who's more than capable of taking care of herself. You sent a dozen guards with Millie Quiggens. How is *this* any different?"

"Because," he began, pausing his packing and crossing the bedroom to take her gently by the shoulders, assuming his ever-composed tone, "They asked us for our help. Rodney never asks."

She sighed exasperatedly, feeling her rigid frame soften unwillingly in his firm hands. Her infuriatingly over-generous husband would be the ruin of them all. Always a sympathetic sucker for sob stories, he had sent a squad of men and women along with Millie Quiggens at her mournful request, if only to keep the distraught woman from crying aloud at Jeremy's birthday. During the lavish dinner, she had practically begged Evelyn for a garrison of guards to protect her ranch from the rumoured return of the Rauder raids, but when Evelyn had simply suggested that she move all of her cattle and ranch hands to Rubicross, where they would be much safer, Millie had turned to Nathan instead. She only had to ask him once, and he hadn't even thought to ask her for anything in return.

When Evelyn had asked her husband why he had been so quick to get rid of good soldiers, he joked that if Evelyn had her way, she would hoard every last resource in Rubicross, including the guards. After enjoying a cheap laugh at her sullen expense, he had reasoned that since Rubicross was the last place that the Rauders would think of raiding, he would rather send those same good soldiers to a place where they would actually be needed, because if Quiggens' Ranch were to indeed fall to an attack, then Rubicross, and all of their trading partners, would lose a significant portion of their supply of fresh horses and cattle meat. She didn't like it, but she supposed that there was some method in his madness, as maddeningly obscure as his method might have been.

Nathan turned back to packing his clothes, and Evelyn moved towards the second-storey window, sitting in her plush green armchair, tying her light brown hair into a loose ponytail as she watched the scattered clouds wandering through the pale blue sky.

Another shipment of diesel hadn't arrived on schedule. In fact, it hadn't arrived at all. For the past two years, the shipments of diesel from Cloakwater had arrived by rail each and every week; same day, same time, same amount. Like clockwork.

Until now.

Last night, a guard from Linchpin Station had barged into the dining room, interrupting their family dinner, and without even pausing to draw a single breath, he had shared his dreaded report of the second missing delivery, as if their lives depended on an immediate update.

Drunk, as always, her brother-in-law Jeremy had parted his lips from his glass long enough to absentmindedly suggest that perhaps they should stop selling their stockpile of diesel until the shipments recommenced.

"Finally, something we can agree on," Evelyn had replied. It had only taken five years.

Of course, it would mean blowback from their own customers, but it was far better to keep their fuel reserves stashed away for themselves, rather than sell their limited supplies to everyone else. Her mind flew back to the memories of taking Jeremy and Jordan into their home following the missile blast in North Tekota, only to watch her entire family starve and eat and starve and eat during the Army Reserves' period of rationed food supplies. Such was the price of sharing.

The rest of Rubicross had already heard about the rumours of the fuel shortage. The spread of gossip couldn't be helped. Their guards simply talked too much while drinking with the other guards at The Oxhouse. There was no sign of panic among the local population, since many of the other traders in town were well-stocked, and could afford to ride out a temporary diesel deficit; but it would be the other settlements around South Tekota which depended upon the constant flow of fuel that would be at their gates soon. Those in the farm belt, Brimvale, Stillborough, Sunken City and Rookson would all be hounding after them.

Eerily, it reminded her of the grocers and their families who had occupied and boarded up Ferguson's Supermarket in the early days of the apocalypse, unwilling to share their bounty of supplies with the outside world. Evelyn supposed that one key factor which would make all the difference was that what remained of the Army Reserves was now on their side of the walls.

"What if they've run out of diesel?" she asked suddenly, fearing the worst as she continued to stare out the window. Blackspout Trawl's oil fields had already been tapped into long before the world had ended. What if the wells had simply dried up?

Nathan scratched his cheek, his free hand holding the beginnings of a tightly-rolled business shirt. He thought for a moment before shaking his head.

"Rodney's been working on his oil tanker for the past two years," he reasoned, letting the shirt unfurl, shaking it out with a snap and then laying it back on the bed to start again. "I doubt he would have commissioned the work if he knew he would run dry of diesel before he finished."

"Then what if he's stockpiling it all for the oil tanker?" asked Evelyn. After all, it's what she would have done.

"No, that can't be it," Nathan shook his head again as he packed the rolled shirt into the suitcase and started on the next one. "He was generous enough to share his bunker's food supplies with us before the farm belt even had stakes in the ground. He wouldn't have cut us off without a good reason."

"Well, if he didn't cut us off, then it must have been the Rauders," she supposed. Millie Quiggens had said that the entire population of Torzal Arroyo had gone missing overnight. Granted, some of the outlying towns in the prairies had a grand total population of one, but perhaps Millie was right to be afraid, and Evelyn had been underreacting this whole time. Her eyes went wide as she looked back at her husband. "Please, don't go. Send someone else."

"I can't, and you know it," Nathan studied the contents of his suitcase, mentally checking items off his list. "We're business partners. We take the same risks, or there is no partnership."

She knew what he was going to say next, and he knew that he didn't need to say it.

After Wallace Pelletier had abandoned the railroad before it was finished, stealing Rodney Hamilton's golden bucks that had been set aside to finance the project, Nathan had taken the construction's completion upon himself. With no official request, and no promise of a reward, her husband had decided to finance Rodney's railroad, spending everything they had left on paying the remaining workers to finish the job that they had started.

With a substantial amount of Rodney's supply of golden bucks stolen by one of the few men he once trusted, and Nathan's family back to square one in the fledgling border town of Rubicross, Rodney Hamilton had decided to enter into an exclusive business partnership with the Royce Family.

Everyone was always eager to go into business whenever there were profits to be made, but once risks were involved, seldom few were willing to follow through on their end of the deal. Accepting that this was something that Nathan had to do for himself, if only to reaffirm his pledge to the partnership, Evelyn simply nodded her understanding, and Nathan smiled warmly as he sank his hands into the suitcase to create some more space.

"I'll pack the train full of guards," he reassured her, returning to the wardrobe for another armful of clothes. "I'm not sure how long we'll be gone though, so I'll be putting Jeremy in charge while I'm away."

"That *drunk*!?" she gripped her chair's armrests tightly, her fluster flaring up again, not even a moment after it had subsided. "Surely you can't expect that he'll be able to handle the responsibility of running the residence. He can't even handle the responsibility of being a father to his own son!"

Her husband, who always had a cheerful answer for everything, didn't turn around.

"Honestly, neither could I, if I'd have gone through what he did," Nathan muttered quietly, one hand leaning on the wardrobe's shelves as he stared at the floor.

Evelyn's lips tightened. She knew that she had just crossed a line. Rising from her armchair and moving silently towards her husband, she placed a gentle hand on his arm. Nathan took a deep breath and turned around. It broke her heart to see his handsome face crestfallen. It was a rare sight, but whenever he was sad, his crinkled laugh lines seemed to sag, and she would see the grey strands combed into his light brown hair, his youthful bubble bursting before her. He pulled her close and planted an understanding kiss of forgiveness upon her head, rocking her slowly from side to side.

"I'm sorry," she whispered into his chest. "I shouldn't have mentioned Jordan. But look." She turned her head to the side, staring pointedly at Jeremy's bachelor pad, the tiny two-room bungalow squatting next to the outer wall like some homeless person waiting for a handout. The curtains were drawn over her brother-in-law's windows, as ever at this time in the afternoon. "The party finished last week, but he's carrying on binge-drinking as if it's still going. At this rate, he'll be celebrating his birthday until it comes around again."

Nathan's hand dropped to her waist as he smiled fondly at the window, his cheeks filling out again. Perhaps he knew that partying non-stop for another year was exactly what his younger brother intended on doing.

"With all the success we've had," he began, speaking softly into her hair as she laid her head on his shoulder, "How could we deny our family from enjoying it? We invite complete strangers to eat and drink with us almost every week. Those same people wouldn't have even returned a smile in the streets if they thought they'd have nothing to gain from it."

"*You're* the one who keeps inviting those strangers!" Evelyn exclaimed, looking up at him incredulously. She didn't pull away from his side though. She was done arguing. It was just bewildering that he would use *that* as a reason to let his brother drink himself half to death each night.

"Look," Nathan smiled wearily at her, "Jeremy's been with us from the very start, before we had all this; before we even had the electronics store back in Brimvale. Sure, he might not be the same brother that I remember, but he's still my brother. I'm not saying that I approve of how he's been coping through it all, but at least it's better than seeing him moping around the estate all day, wondering what to do with himself without his wife and the daughter they would have had."

Evelyn was about to bring up Jordan again, but she thought better of it this time around. Nathan caught her hitching breath of apprehension though.

"The boy understands," he surmised, confident in his guess. "Everyone else in the family – even some of the staff – they're all happy that Jeremy can enjoy at least some level of comfort. Can't we just leave him be?"

And by "we", he means me, she knew.

Evelyn sighed, this time pulling away from his side, but only to stoop by the dresser to grab a few handfuls of black business socks. She packed them into the suitcase and compressed the rest of his clothes before straightening up again.

"I can put up with Jeremy's behaviour," she admitted reluctantly, looking out the window at his bachelor pad again. "But I still think that if you're going to put him in charge of running things while you're away, then his behaviour is going to have to change."

"That's exactly what I'm hoping for," Nathan replied, packing a stack of trunks next to his socks. "A bit of responsibility might be all he needs to make him ease up for a little while. Besides, he'll have you here to help him out, and I might only be gone for just a few days anyway, so it's not like it's the end of the world."

"No, we've already lived through that," she swept a strand of hair over her ear as she looked back at him. "So you know as well as I do, a lot can change in just a few days."

* * *

Evelyn's hand whispered down the staircase's railing towards the glossy white tiles on the ground floor, hearing the distinct *clack* of an opening shot breaking the pool table's rack in the games room.

She descended the last step and turned to the arched entrance on her right, seeing Ryan and Jordan on opposite ends of the pool table. Ryan's girlfriend, Zita Ortega, watched them play from a stool beside the fully-stocked bar, while Shirley Beaumont squeezed fresh oranges into a jug behind the counter, separating the pulp with a sieve.

One of the kitchenhands sat on a bar stool in the far corner, his white hat set down on the counter, revealing a thick head of wavy brown hair framing his pasty-white face, perhaps intended to be an afro, but it wasn't curly enough, and so his hair took on the appearance of an old bicycle bucket helmet instead. He was pretending to be engrossed in the game while occasionally sneaking furtive glances at Shirley and Zita. He was the first to notice Evelyn, shooting her a lopsided smile from across the room.

"Looks like you're stripes and I'm solids," Jordan announced with his cue stick in hand, peering down into the pockets of the pool table. He glanced up, looking past Ryan, and stood upright as he saw Evelyn standing by the arched entrance. "Hi, Mum!"

"Hi, Mum," Ryan echoed, turning around with his father's smile before concentrating on lining up his next shot.

"Hey, Mrs Royce," Zita smiled as she reached for her glass of orange juice.

"Evelyn," Shirley tossed an orange from one hand to the other behind the bar, "Want me to wrangle you up a drink?"

"Sure," she replied, moving towards Zita as Ryan drew back his cue stick, "That would be lovely."

No sooner had Evelyn placed her hand on the bar's counter than a loud voice erupted from behind her, causing her to spin around as Ryan hit the cue ball over the side of the table.

"Cody! Where the hell have you been!?" Mabel Brown, the sassy caramel-skinned sous chef stood by the room's entrance, brandishing a large wooden spoon. She had a thick build, but she wore her curves well, garbed in the standard chef's uniform of a diagonally-buttoned white jacket and chequered pants. "I don't remember saying you could go on break."

"Sorry!" the lanky kitchenhand slunk out of his bar stool, giving everyone another lopsided grin before pausing halfway across the room. Doubling back, he grabbed his hat off the counter and shamelessly ogled at Shirley's breasts in her black shirt one last time as she poured another glass of orange juice.

"Get your goofy ass back in the kitchen," Mabel punctuated her words with a smart smack of the ladle on his rump as he marched past. She shook her head with a hand on her hip, watching him pass by the staircase and disappear around the corner. "Boy breaks off faster than burnt crumbs on a puff pastry."

"My youngest is the same," Evelyn smiled, taking a satisfying sip of orange juice.

"Well, if I ever find a couple collars with a bell, I'll let you know," Mabel replied with a homely grin. She held the wooden spoon at a distance as she headed off after Cody. "Now I gotta disinfect this shit…"

"Zita," Evelyn turned to the olive-skinned girl sitting by the bar as Jordan sank a ball, "Would you mind taking a walk with me to the gardens? We can finish these outside."

"Sure!" Zita replied, grabbing her glass. "The weather's perfect."

She was a petite Latina girl, athletic, with natural caramel brown hair and dark brown eyes, only a few years younger than Ryan, but a few years older in maturity, as was always the case. They had met back when they were both teens, and she had just started working part-time in Nathan's electronics store after school. They still kept in touch with each other after the apocalypse rendered the necessity for the latest flat-screen televisions redundant, and their romance began to blossom. After the Royces had moved out west, Ryan and Zita often travelled between Rubicross and Brimvale just to see each other, since she still wanted to live at home with her parents.

"Everything okay?" Ryan asked as Jordan lined up another shot.

"Yeah, we're just gonna have some girl talk," Evelyn replied, suppressing a smile at her son's suspicion.

"Enjoy!" Shirley called from behind the bar, rinsing out the sieve as they left the room.

The weather was indeed perfect; not too hot, not too cold, with only a few clouds scudding across the pale blue sky. The guards watched from the walls as the two women strolled towards the gardens.

"I was wondering if you might be interested in a trip to Cloakwater?" asked Evelyn, cutting through the small talk.

"Isn't it dangerous to travel right now though?" Zita's dark brown eyes dilated, having heard the stories of the Rauders.

"It is," Evelyn agreed as they passed between the languishing purple coneflowers and dainty pink evening primroses, "But Nathan's planning on bringing Ryan along with him, and I was hoping that you might accompany them. Maybe you can keep those two out of trouble," she shared a smirk with Zita, both of them knowing how difficult the task would be. "You'll have plenty of guards travelling with you, so you'll be safe. I wouldn't let my husband and son go if I thought otherwise."

Admittedly, Evelyn was still apprehensive about Nathan's idea to bring Ryan, since she had grounded the two boys after their bar fight with a group of cowboys at The Oxhouse not long ago. Ryan needed some more time to mature, Jordan too, although Nathan argued what better way for Ryan to mature than to pull him out of his comfort zone and observe good business etiquette away from home.

"I'll have to ask my parents," Zita said solemnly after a contemplative sip of her orange juice.

"Of course," Evelyn replied. The Ortega Family had invited them over for dinner once, willing to share even in the midst of the food shortages. A mental image flashed in her mind, and she remembered how skinny her family had been back then, and the humiliation she had felt showing up at their door for a free meal. Not passing judgement, the Ortegas had insisted that they eat their fill, and ever since then, Evelyn had made sure that they were well taken care of. She put the memory out of her mind. "How are your parents?"

"They're fine, still living in Brimvale," Zita answered, before turning to Evelyn again. "When's Mr Royce planning to leave?"

"The day after tomorrow," Evelyn sighed as she glanced up at their bedroom window. She had managed to convince him to stay for one night longer than he had hoped, giving more time for him to tie up his affairs and for her to ensure that the staff were prepared.

"Okay," Zita replied as they rounded a corner, strolling through the colourful collection of columbines and bluebonnets. "I'll leave my overnight bag here and catch the late bus back to Brimvale. I'll be back tomorrow, I'll just tell Ryan first."

Evelyn tightened her lips.

"You might want to pack for longer," she advised, only just now realising it herself. *Just a few days*, she shook her head at her husband's comforting words. "I watched Nathan stuff his suitcase full. And don't worry about catching the bus back to Brimvale. Stay with us for dinner. Marv can drive you home afterwards."

"Thank you!" Zita smiled, finishing her juice and carrying the empty glass, bouncing with excitement at the thought of travelling outside of Brimvale and Rubicross for the first time since she could remember.

Evelyn let Zita head back inside the residence as she sat down on a garden bench, still nursing her own glass in the afternoon sun. The girl's heart was in the right place, and she was a good influence on her son, Evelyn knew. She just hoped that Ryan knew it too.

She stifled a smile as she heard Terry Delaney, one of the gardeners, grumbling to himself as he pushed his reel mower across the grounds. He was still miffed that he had been instructed to conserve diesel only this morning, just before he'd had the chance to cut the grass. Now, his diesel ride-on mower was collecting dust in the gardening shed while he was walking his manual cutter back and forth, having to stoop to empty the catcher every time he successfully made it from one side of the lawn to the other.

Evelyn realised that the staff would soon become her responsibility, since Jeremy was sure to screw up on his first day. She would have to ask Michelle Tan to take stock of their fuel supplies and possibly set a rationing plan for the coming days and weeks ahead, as there was no telling how long it would take for her husband to return and for the diesel deliveries to resume.

More pressing than that, Enrique Garrido, the event coordinator, would need to plan a small last-minute farewell dinner for tomorrow. She would have to invite the Ortegas, and perhaps Drew and Colin, along with the Mallory Family if they weren't busy.

"Mrs Royce?" a chirpy voice called out, interrupting her thoughts. She turned to see Bianca Beaumont, Shirley's fifteen-year-old daughter and Aimee's partner-in-crime. "Dinner's almost ready."

"I'll be there soon," she answered, examining the dregs of her orange juice as if it were an hourglass measuring her time in the gardens.

Evelyn finished the glass, resolving to make the very best of today and tomorrow, when she was suddenly overwhelmed with dread as she realised that after tomorrow night, she would have no idea when the next time her family would all have dinner together again.

CHAPTER 13 – JEREMY

Jeremy Royce coughed himself awake in the gloom of his dark bedroom. He pried an arm free of the women in his bed, massaging his hoarse throat, before reaching across another prone figure on his left for the glass of water that he had set aside for himself on his nightstand. It was empty, thanks to one of the women, so he reached for a half-empty bottle of vodka instead.

He took a healthy pull of Haydar's latest batch, suppressed a gag, and took another. It was a terrible substitute for water, but at least it was a fun substitute.

Haydar had given him a crate of vodka for his birthday, as he did every year. The queer little man living in the farm belt was practically swimming in the amount of vodka that he produced, and from the liquor's foul taste, it wouldn't have surprised Jeremy to discover if that was indeed part of the fermentation process.

Conjuring up the mental image of Haydar's fat hairy ass skinny-dipping in a vat full of vodka like some sweaty sasquatch sitting in a sauna, Jeremy failed to stifle his next gag, and he lurched over the naked blonde on his left to lean over the side of his bed, retching into a well-placed bucket.

The sweat-stained yellow bed sheets fell away as he sat up, revealing his gangly arms and a sparse brown tuft of ungroomed chest hair. Letting the dizzy spell wash over him, Jeremy poured another shot into the bottle's lid and downed it to wash out the taste of well-earned regrets.

Such was his morning ritual, although his mornings usually began in the late afternoon.

He hadn't always been a debauched, binging wreck of a man. In a past life, he'd had a stable job, working in Sunken City, back when it was known as Swanson City, and the streets were flooded with people and traffic rather than actually being flooded. After years of mind-numbing, soul-crushing service, he had been promoted from a glorified button-pusher to a supervisory role, and thus becoming the supreme overlord of his fellow glorified button-pushers.

They had even given his desk an ergonomic makeover, a status symbol to make him the envy of his underlings, although he suspected that it was only so graciously granted to ensure that he could no longer use his bogus backaches as an excuse to call in "sick" anymore.

The salary increase had been nice though. It wasn't enough to afford a brand new home for his pregnant wife and son, but it had been enough to convince the bank to increase the amount that they were willing to loan.

His plan had been to knock down their pest-infested weatherboard home in Brimvale, complete with its cracked paint, leaking roof, and the constant stream of tradesmen who kept the house from collapsing. He would then build a pair of brick veneer units in its place, sell one and live in the other, with a significantly-reduced mortgage. Sure, it meant that there would have been less space for his growing family, but with that would also come less maintenance bills, and mowing the lawn would no longer have seemed such a daunting task.

Jeremy and his family had arranged to live with his parents in North Tekota over the summer while the demolition and subsequent construction would take place. Jordan had been in his last week of school before the summer break though, so Nathan and Evelyn had agreed to take him on to manage the school runs. Jeremy had the old house to himself for the week, with every creaking floorboard bringing a wicked smile to his face, knowing that its time would soon be at an end.

Then, just as he was loading up the last of his furniture into the back of his station wagon, the rogue missile had dropped in North Tekota, and his plans for the future had disintegrated, along with everything else that had been caught in the blast radius, including his parents, his wife, and their unborn child.

He had driven to his brother's house to check in on Jordan, having resolved to make the trip to North Tekota straight afterwards, as his wife would still be expecting him. Nathan had tackled Jeremy to the ground before he could get back into the car, convincing him over his anguished sobs that if he went, the lingering radiation would render his son an orphan.

Jeremy had practically become a vegetable throughout Brimvale's food shortages, sleeping on an old couch in Nathan's garage for days at a time, lying motionless with his eyes closed, even while he had been awake. It had been his futile attempt to shut out the world, or at least, what was left of it.

But no matter how desperately he wanted to just sink into the upholstery of that old couch, forgotten and discarded, like every other dusty moth-balled inanimate object, the world had decided that it wasn't done with him yet.

So, when his brother had finally rolled up the garage door, letting the sunlight flood in and the gnats fly out, Jeremy submitted himself to whatever grand scheme the universe had in store for him. Nathan sprayed him with a garden hose until his stench became semi-bearable, before hauling him out of the imprint that he had left on the couch. Glancing back at the sweat-stained couch-angel in his wake, Jeremy realised that he had indeed been sinking into the upholstery, and his brother had pulled him out just in time, before he could be swallowed whole.

Nathan's voice had sounded like a foreign language trying to break through Jeremy's emotional barriers as they drove towards a destination that he neither knew nor cared about. Thankfully, Evelyn and the kids had already taken the trip, so it was just him and his brother in the car. Eventually, Nathan had reached into the glove box with a resigned sigh, pressing an old bottle of wine into Jeremy's hands. Seeing it as a way to numb the pain of his existential crisis, Jeremy unscrewed the cap and drank wholeheartedly, savouring the daze as the alcohol flooded his senses.

And just like that, whether Nathan had known it or not, he had given Jeremy a reason to live again.

Constantly fuelled by the thirst for his next buzz, Jeremy had slowly come back to life in Rubicross. Eating solid food and drinking water on a semi-regular basis, showering without the need for a garden hose, and waking up of his own volition, was just the beginning. Not pissing and shitting himself anymore was also a big win, for everyone. Next to return was his speech, as crude and insensitive as his jokes were at the dining table, followed by some personal hygiene, although that still needed work, and then, finally, his desire for the warmth of a woman.

His progression had plateaued there though. Months came and went with rarely a shift in his routine. Wake up, drink, pass out, with greasy food and greasier women in between.

Half-empty bottles of alcohol stood sentinel in the dim afternoon light filtering through the mothballed curtains of his tiny two-room bachelor pad. Half-eaten burgers and fries lay on the dresser, the latest addition to the all-you-can-eat cockroach buffet, while a shifting column of ants trekked their way across the mouldy carpet to gather around yet another unidentified stain.

Jeremy would have to call the estate's housemaids in again soon, but there was no need to rush. He knew that as soon as they finished the job, they would run off to Evelyn, who would be all too eager to learn of his latest depravities. It was almost a morbid fascination for her; she was obsessed with finding new reasons to admonish him for his black hole of self-pity.

He took another grimacing yet grateful swig of the vodka bottle. Whatever people thought of him now would not make a difference. His wife and unborn daughter would still be dead. He may as well enjoy the end of the world.

The woman on his left stirred. She was a brittle-haired blonde who might have been pretty once, but not for a long time. The same could have been said for the other two still dozing in each other's thin waiflike arms. Their dry papery skin, frazzled features and the distinct sweet and sour stench spoke of career prostitutes. They were off the clock though. There was no way he would have paid them. Whenever he spent money, he made sure that it was always put towards something that he would actually enjoy.

The blonde sat up with a dead gaze in her eyes, letting the sweat-dampened bed sheets pool in her lap, revealing her flat pale chest. Wordlessly, she reached for the bottle of vodka. The women were there for the free alcohol, nothing else. He knew it, they knew it, but it was a win-win scenario. He was not nearly tipsy enough to take them up on their end of the deal this early in the day though.

There was no way to know how long he had been celebrating his birthday, since all the nights seemed to blur together into one long party ever since that old bottle of wine, but he hadn't seen the decorations outside for a while. He figured that if he just kept drinking the nights away, eventually there would be another occasion to celebrate, and he would fit right in with all of the other guests again.

His head jerked at the sound of a knock on the bungalow's front door, and he threw aside the bed sheets. The blonde made no move to conceal herself, mechanically taking another pull from the bottle.

Bleary-eyed and staggering, Jeremy pulled his jeans on, ducked underneath a black shirt and shut the bedroom door behind him. He seldom had any visitors, so he knew that it would be important.

Half-focused, his red-rimmed eyes scanned over the living room and kitchen.

"Just a second," he croaked, stooping to gather empty bottles of Stillborough beer from the coffee table and piling them beside the overflowing trash can.

He stacked plates with spaghetti leftovers from an unknown number of nights ago into the sink, gave the laminate countertop a quick wipe with a crusty sponge that simply smeared a rainbow of mould into the bench, and gargled a glass of water before drinking its foreign purity. He almost threw up again.

Guess this'll have to do, Jeremy thought to himself as he flattened his unkempt brown hair and tested his vodka-and-vomit breath. He stalked over to the door and opened it up to see his brother patiently standing outside.

"Can I come in?" Nathan looked him over and offered him a smile.

"Of course," Jeremy stood aside, letting his brother through, who surveyed the front room with mild interest, his green eyes settling on a skimpy neon-orange dress strewn over the couch.

"Let's get some light in here," Nathan suggested, not commenting on the dress.

Jeremy tugged on the curtain's cord obligingly, squinting and shielding his face from the afternoon sun as it burst through the dusty blinds and into the room. After his eyes had adjusted, he quickly snatched the dress off the couch.

"Sorry," Jeremy mumbled, pondering what to do with the dress. "If I knew you were coming, I would've…" he trailed off, swallowing dryly.

"No need to apologise," Nathan replied, waving him off with a grin. "I'm just glad you're having a good time."

He settled onto a kitchen stool and gestured for Jeremy to join him. Jeremy wondered whether his lifestyle of debauchery had finally caught up to him. Perhaps Evelyn would get her own way after all. Ever since he had moved into Nathan's garage back in Brimvale, Jeremy had been a burden on the family, and he wasn't exactly setting a shining example for the kids.

"I wanted to ask you for a favour," Nathan scratched his bristly cheek before clasping his hands and turning to face him.

"Anything," Jeremy replied, eager to make a payment towards his mountainous debt.

"I'm taking the train over to Cloakwater Cliffs the day after tomorrow," Nathan began, gauging his brother's expression before continuing. "And I've decided I'd like for you to keep things running here while I'm gone."

"*Me?*" Jeremy asked in disbelief. "Why would you want…? Does your wife know?"

"She knows," Nathan answered with a chuckle. "She wants to kill me, but she knows."

"Welcome to the club," Jeremy replied, his gaze dropping to the floor with a half-smile.

The two brothers laughed aloud, echoing around the small bachelor pad and rousing the women in the bedroom as they continued to take turns with the vodka.

"How long will you be gone?" asked Jeremy, hoping to hear a clear end date before he would reluctantly take on the responsibility.

"Couple days," Nathan shrugged before shaking his head, "A week, maybe. I don't know what's been happening over there or what we'll be riding into."

"But you'll be bringing your guards, right?" asked Jeremy, his knee beginning to bounce of its own accord.

"There's no way Evelyn would let me go without them," Nathan's laugh lines deepened as he snorted. "I'll probably be safer than you."

Jeremy glanced out the window at the two-storey residence, and even then, he could feel Evelyn's eyes upon the bungalow, seething in silence from her bedroom window.

"Definitely safer than me," Jeremy gave his brother a wry grin. He thought to himself for a moment, and he figured that it couldn't hurt to make a request of his own. "When you go, would you mind taking Jordan along with you?"

"Jordan? Yeah, no problem," Nathan replied without hesitation. "I was going to bring Ryan with me anyway. Those two are inseparable, so that's an easy decision."

"Like we were, at their age," Jeremy remembered, although he felt like his mind was reaching back into someone else's memory.

"*Were?*" Nathan raised a playful eyebrow. "We still are. I couldn't get rid of y–"

A metallic clang resounded from inside the bedroom, and a disgusted squeal pierced through the door.

One of the girls must have kicked the bucket of vomit over, Jeremy assumed, glancing over Nathan's shoulder. *Hopefully it was the same girl who drank my water last night.*

"I'll let you get back in there," Nathan stood with a wink, walking back towards the front door and noticing the three pairs of women's shoes beside the crate of Haydar's hooch. He looked back at his brother with his hand on the doorknob. "Oh, just one other thing before I go. Would you mind slowing it down a bit while I'm away?"

Jeremy's dopamine receptors wanted to shriek in protest at Nathan for even making the suggestion, but he managed to keep his mouth shut, offering a simple nod. The gesture was easy enough, but whether he could actually follow through on his promise was another matter entirely.

He shut the door behind Nathan and considered Haydar's birthday gift. Pulling out a fresh bottle of the clear spirit, he held it aloft in the afternoon sun's rays streaming in through the window as he listened to the women complaining that they had run out of vodka in the bedroom.

Jeremy swallowed dryly as his mind proposed one last hurrah.

CHAPTER 14 – ODESSA

Just like every other building in Coyote's Rest, the Sheriff's Office had been conceived and constructed in vivid detail. Every facet of how a typical frontier town's law enforcement station would have appeared had been devised and designed meticulously. A cast-iron furnace squatted opposite the slightly lopsided entrance, faded and yellowed "Wanted" posters lined the wooden walls, and dusty old cowboy repeaters hung on a gun rack above the Sheriff's desk.

Based on appearance alone, the room's furnishings would have been enough to impress any average metropolitan tourist who had come to visit for a weekend getaway of historical rediscovery, but the building's true character lived invisibly. It was in the groaning floorboards, it was in the ill-fitted window frame that whistled every time the wind blew, and it was in the creaking wooden chair that had survived years of leaning back on its hind legs as an amateur thespian Sheriff had kicked his boots up on the desk.

It was also in the pair of rusty-hinged holding cells that lined one side of the room. Both ruddy iron cages were complete with a stained pisspot, a lumpy thin mattress raised barely a foot above the hardwood floor, and a barred window set in the mismatching brick wall, just large enough to let the fading sunlight in, affording a grand view of the gallows outside.

One of the cells was complete with its own forlorn prisoner, idly rattling his cage with a tin cup, hoping that the constant clattering would summon someone who would actually believe his unconvincing version of events. This was no low-paid failed actor however, or a guest who had been stowed away for being drunk and disorderly at Lorelei's Saloon.

This prisoner had been locked up for murder.

The front door swung open, scraping the floorboards, and Dess stepped into the room. Sheriff Byron Ashby, a pudgy blonde man with pig-like blue eyes who had been irked at the idea of having to keep watch over the prisoner, uttered a sigh of relief.

"Thank God you're here," he said, leaning back in his chair with a wooden creak. "I was about to shoot that tin can outta his hand, and at this point, I wouldn't've cared if I missed."

Big-Stack Billy stopped rattling the iron bars of his holding cell, staring at Dess with stony contempt. Only last night, he had been drinking and gambling in the saloon, as ever, when Dess, Garrett and Harlan had confronted him. He had laughed at their accusation in that boisterous way of his, although he had been the only one laughing. No one believed that he would have been able to win the horse race against Emmett Pearce without cheating in some way, but killing him and making it look like an accident was far beyond cheating.

Those who were loyal to Big-Stack, regardless of whether they believed the accusation to be true, had placed their hands on their holstered pistols, ready to defend a friend, while Lyle Beckett reached for a shotgun behind the bar and Toby the piano player had signed off mid-tune with a fleeting downward key slide, grabbing Brandi and ducking out of sight.

The armed escort of Royce guards however, already had their weapons drawn and ready for action before the drunken Big-Stack and his boys could even unbutton their gun-belts' straps. *They had actually been useful for something other than drinking jugs of beer every night like they were on a holiday*, Dess remembered thinking to herself.

The saloon had been in an uproar as Billy was dragged across the main street to the Sheriff's Office, but Harlan had served to calm the crowd down somewhat, explaining the horseshit that they had found at the scene of Emmett's death. The other cowboys' threats had soon descended into disgruntled dissent, murmuring theories of who the real killer – if there had been one – could have been, while others had agreed that it would not have been beneath Big-Stack to have murdered Emmett, having been in races against Billy themselves, where he had kicked their horses off-course, breaking shins at Legsnap Ridge, or simply whooping and hollering madly as he chased them around Rambling Gulch's horse track with a lasso.

Big-Stack stood and spat at the creaking floorboards as Dess approached his holding cell, ignoring Byron's indignant yell. She observed the towering burly redheaded brute through the bars with indifference before dragging a pair of wooden chairs across the floor, one at a time, setting each chair up to face one another, purposely taking far longer than necessary.

It served to vex the murderer, as was her intent, since he had probably realised by now that his time was limited, having watched the shadow of the gallows platform stretch across the ground outside all afternoon, drawing closer to the two cell windows of the Sheriff's Office with each passing hour.

Dess sat down, putting her boots up on the other chair, reclining wistfully and staring out the front window as if he wasn't even there. Big-Stack Billy cleared his throat impatiently, and she glanced at him, studying the restless hothead again, before turning her attention back towards the main street and eyeing the saloon.

Billy had been one of the skilled workers who had signed up for the railroad's construction project, along with herself, Emmett Pearce, Harlan Reid, Garrett Ridley, Archie Callahan, and countless others. She and Emmett had known him prior to the railroad though. They had worked together in the old sawmill at Cape Huxley before the missile dropped in North Tekota.

They had stayed away from him back then, keeping their distance even when he had followed them to the railroad. He was a bully when he was sober, and even worse when he was drunk, with the muscle to back him up in a fair fight. Usually though, the fights weren't fair, and he often played the victim whenever an anonymous complaint was submitted. Little had changed over the years.

"Listen, lady," Big-Stack began, gripping the bars and gritting his teeth, "I don't care what you *think* happened. I didn't kill your boyfriend."

Same old Billy, Dess thought to herself, *pleading his innocence after being caught out*. She admired the cage that he was trapped in; it was almost as if his hand was caught in a cookie jar that had pulled him all the way inside.

"You never liked Emmett, did you?" she asked, breaking her silence.

"Nobody did," Billy replied, clenching his jaw. "Stubborn son of a bitch was too quiet for his own good, always wantin' to keep to himself, but never passin' up on the chance to put one of us down."

"Were you mad at Emmett because he didn't wanna be your friend?" Dess asked, stirring him up. Like most brutes, she knew that he would be quick to anger, and quick to make a mistake.

Big-Stack scoffed at the idea.

"Who would wanna be friends with that quiet little runt?" he asked, averting his gaze. She could tell that his ego was hurt.

"I'd gladly count myself as one of Emmett's friends," Sheriff Ashby chimed in from behind his desk on the other side of the room.

"No surprise," Billy replied derisively.

Nobody took the Sheriff seriously in Coyote's Rest. It was no secret that Byron Ashby had been one of Brimvale's few police officers who had managed to survive the brutalities of The Long Summer Night, but only because he never even showed up to the protests. He had claimed that he was too busy defending the suburbs from the depraved and deranged drug addicts from The Gutter, but not surprisingly, no one had come forward to applaud and affirm his apparent heroic efforts afterwards.

What had been surprising however, was when he had made the decision to move out of the relative safety of Brimvale, coming to Coyote's Rest of all places, where he would need to deal with any threats arising in and out of town. Soon after he had taken up the mantle of Sheriff though, it became clear that he had merely come for the prostitutes, who had followed the money when the railroad was under construction.

Deputy Monroe however, was the real authority figure in town. The dour dark blonde woman sat ritualistically outside the Sheriff's Office every day from morning until evening, cradling her rifle, watching and waiting for the chance to use it.

Dess gave Byron a reproachful glare for his interruption, and he quickly resumed his poorly-disguised act of pretending not to eavesdrop.

"So, there was no love lost when you killed him, then?" Dess prompted, looking back at Billy with mild interest.

"I DIDN'T FUCKIN' KILL HIM!!" Big-Stack shouted, slamming the bars with his callused hands before pacing around the small cell angrily. "I won that race fair and fuckin' square. Ain't my fault he fell off his horse and died."

"How much did you bet you were going to win?" Dess asked, unfazed by his outburst as she resumed her line of questioning.

Billy stopped pacing and turned back, his fierce blue eyes narrowing at her.

"A lot," he glared, working his jaw slowly. "But I never had the chance to collect, since he fuckin' died on me."

"Maybe you made a side bet to win with someone else?" Dess suggested.

"Why the hell would I make a side bet?" Big-Stack fumed. "I was gonna get paid when I won. And if I lost the race, I'd have to pay up double." Then, with his internal wheels slowly turning, he added, "If I *did* make a side bet, it would've been against myself. And if I wanted to lose, why the fuck would I have killed Emmett?"

Dess glanced outside again as a cowboy stumbled out of Lorelei's to retch over the veranda's railing into the horses' trough before heading back inside the saloon for more. She agreed that a side bet would have been a stupid idea, although knowing Billy, she wouldn't have been surprised.

"After I won that damn race," Big-Stack muttered under his breath, "Seems like everyone *but* me's gettin' paid."

"What was that?" asked Dess, turning her attention back to the prisoner.

"Oh, Harlan didn't tell you?" Billy asked contemptuously. "Word around town was the kid was about to go bust that same night. Everybody's been runnin' dry on chips, but he was about to get himself kicked outta Darlene's boardin' house for not payin' rent. Mornin' after the race, Emmett's room's been raided, his stack of chips is gone, and Harlan's got enough money to pay Darlene in full."

Dess rubbed her chin, frowning as Billy stalked over to his cell's pisspot and unzipped his jeans. She knew that Emmett's funeral service had been costing Harlan an arm and a leg, but she had never thought to ask him where all the money had come from.

She remembered her conversation with Nathan Royce back in Rubicross, who had said that Emmett had been wanting to go into business together with him for the longest time. She knew how Emmett was with money, always thinking ahead and planning for the future, so it was safe to assume that he would have been saving his golden bucks in preparation for any capital outlays.

"Couple days later," Big-Stack said out of the side of his mouth as he sprang a leak, "Harlan makes a deal with some uptight shit-stain from Brimvale. Apparently we're s'posed to be a bunch of hired killers now. Everybody's gettin' their share of blood money, and *I'm* the motherfucker who gets thrown in jail."

That was news to her. Harlan had never mentioned anything about a deal with Brimvale, much less becoming a group of mercenaries for hire.

"Who raided Emmett's room?" she asked, bringing Billy back on topic.

"Fuck knows," Big-Stack shrugged, shaking his cock and turning back to face her, taking his time to stow it away and zip up. Byron clucked his tongue and folded his arms, but he held his silence. Dess raised her eyebrows at Billy, unimpressed, waiting for him to continue. "Someone who knew about Emmett's death before I did. Every man, woman, horse and dog went through his room. Anyone who says they didn't is a fuckin' liar."

"Speaking of liars," she began, playing her last card, "I think you lied about winning the race fair and square. We saw track marks evidencing a slide down Legsnap Ridge, a few hundred yards from where Emmett's body was found."

"It was rainin'," Big-Stack swallowed. She knew why he had to cheat at playing cards; he never had a strong poker face. "Fine," he admitted hotly.

"I kicked his horse. But it was my fuckin' horse anyway. And he didn't die at Legsnap Ridge, did he?"

Dess pulled her feet from the second chair and faced him front on, considering his story as the setting sun shone through the barred window behind him, the sudden glare causing her to avert her gaze.

"The only thing you got on me is I kicked my fuckin' horse," Billy continued, taking advantage of her uncertain pause. "And if you're gonna string me up for that, you'd best leave town before you get *yourself* put on trial for murder."

Byron knocked his chair over as he clambered to his feet.

"How dare you threaten a lady!?" he asked menacingly, or as menacing as the impotent Sheriff could be.

"Save the act of chivalry, Byron," Big-Stack said scornfully. "We've all heard the stories of how you need to whip whores in the bedroom just so you can get it up."

Sheriff Ashby reddened, but before he could form a response, Dess stood abruptly.

"We're done here," she decided, placing the two chairs back in front of Byron's desk.

"Good," Billy grunted. "You gonna let me go, now?"

The Sheriff turned to Dess with the same question on his mind.

"I'm gonna see if his story checks out," she told Byron. "It wouldn't hurt to keep him locked up in here for a few more days though."

"A few more days!?" Big-Stack hollered as they heard the tell-tale sound of a heavy vehicle's engine brakes outside, "The fuckin' funer–"

Dess scraped the front door open to drown out Billy's indignation. A bus from Brimvale kicked up a cloud of dust on its way into town, cruising down the main street and parking in front of Ingrid's Livery Stable, opposite The Grand Chandelier Hotel, causing the horses to neigh and whinny in their stalls. She only knew one driver who would be mad enough to navigate the potholes from Rubicross to Coyote's Rest, but she was glad to see Archie Callahan behind the wheel again all the same.

Old faces stepped off the bus, laden with suitcases, rucksacks and duffel bags, shuffling towards the hotel. Some she knew from the sawmill at Cape Huxley, others she recognised from the railroad, along with a few that she couldn't quite put her finger on. Like her, after the work had dried up, they had all opted for a more peaceful life away from the prairies; but now they were back, here to mourn Emmett's passing.

Edwin Yun Park alighted among all of the other people who had come to pay their respects. The slender middle-aged Korean man was a neighbourly ex-doctor who now made simple home remedies for minor ailments, and in his spare time, he was one half of the two community leaders who made the important decisions on behalf of Stillborough. Dess assumed that Taryn Remington must have remained behind to run things while he was away, but then again, Taryn was never much of a people-person.

Shane Wagner, the carpenter, and his wife, Gemma, moved to embrace Edwin, both of them overjoyed to see him after having been away for so long. Dess couldn't believe that it had already been a year since the young couple had married and moved to Coyote's Rest from Stillborough. She remembered that Edwin had been especially supportive of their decision to make a life for themselves out in the prairies, even giving them a few golden bucks to help them set up shop.

She had heard that Shane had built and painted custom signs for every building that ran a business in Coyote's Rest, for free, as a demonstration of his handiwork upon their arrival. Although the entire town already knew what each building had to offer by that point, the gesture must have paid off, as Shane and Gemma seemed to be doing quite well for themselves.

Dess wanted to greet the new arrivals, to thank them for coming, and to say that it meant a lot to her that they had, but who was she kidding? She wasn't Emmett's wife. She couldn't even call herself his girlfriend anymore. It wasn't her place to thank them for their support, despite the romance that they had once shared, and the last thing that she wanted to seem was pretentious.

Reagan Dempsey, the owner of The Grand Chandelier Hotel, sporting a receding hairline and a pencil-neck set in between his wide shoulders which gave him the appearance of a turtle peering out of his shell, stooped and rubbed his hands eagerly at the sight of all the newcomers who would be staying at his hotel.

Dess's stomach turned at the thought of all the people who would profit from Emmett's death; Reagan, Verne, Father Norman, and even Flem, the town's alcoholic gravedigger. They were all scavengers clawing for carrion as far as she was concerned, but she was sure that they were not the predator who had made the kill.

She took a deep breath, her gaze hardening as she refocused her thoughts on finding Emmett's murderer.

Archie stepped down from the bus, stretching his back after the long drive and readjusting his khaki-coloured trucker cap before making eye contact with Dess. As the old war dog smiled and began to approach, she nodded at him, before briskly making her way towards the saloon. Archie faltered, choosing instead to stay back and monitor the luggage being unloaded from the bus's storage compartments, shooting her a curious sidelong glance.

Dess squeezed her way through the crowd that was now forming outside Lorelei's, tipsy onlookers emerging from the saloon with their drinks in hand to survey the new arrivals. Perhaps this had been a frequent tradition for anyone who had worked in Coyote's Rest prior to the missile dropping in North Tekota; a bunch of tourists jumping off a bus to check in at the hotel while the slack-jawed locals eyed them off from the veranda's railing, wondering who among them would make an easy target for a price hike.

Dess walked into the saloon, the batwing doors squeaking shut, open, and shut behind her. The room was near empty with most of the patrons gathered outside. Lyle and Brandi took advantage of the brief respite, clearing away as many empty jugs and glasses as they could, pushing in chairs and wiping down tables, hoping to make sure that the saloon was in a semi-decent state before the wave of new customers arrived.

She spied Garrett in one of the booths, sitting opposite Flem Wakefield, with their half-dozen of armed escorts keeping watch from another booth nearby, or as watchful as they could be after the few empty jugs of beer that Lyle was now gathering from their table.

Dess moved to sit beside Garrett, who gestured for Flem to excuse himself to the bathroom and come straight back. They watched with pity as the gaunt emaciated man shambled out of his seat and tottered towards the corridor in the back corner of the room, placing a hand on the wall to steady himself.

She remembered when Flem and his family had first shown up to work on the railroad. He was a lively ex-soldier whose food rations had dried up the moment he had decided to leave the Army Reserves, which was sometime in between the missile levelling North Tekota and the events of The Long Summer Night. His beautiful wife and two daughters had formed part of the mobile construction camp's cooking and cleaning crew, while he and his teenage son toiled on the tracks. Flem and Archie had served in the military together for years, so he and his family often joined them for dinner each night.

Normally, the travelling construction camp was never far away from the rest of the labour force, unless they were working nearby a town or a settlement, and all the rustic amenities that it had to offer. Flem and his son had decided to take a rest day soon after they had reached Quiggens' Ranch. Given that Millie Quiggens and her brother, Ernie, were scrimping on security, it was common for the workers to stay behind and volunteer to keep watch on their days off.

It was a sad day for all of the labourers when the Rauders raided the ranch, killing the men and taking the women. Flem had only survived because he had hidden his son in an empty stall in the stables, but it had been at the expense of his wife and daughters, who he was unable to reach in time. Emmett had beaten Ernie Quiggens half to death for his failure to protect the people, but the damage had already been done. As satisfying as it had been to see him suffer, killing Ernie would not bring their people back.

There wasn't much left of Flem once the railroad had reached Coyote's Rest. The man had turned to drink instead of revenge, lazily drifting through life until his next buzz, finding solace at the bottom of a bottle, however many bottles it took. Dess never imagined that he would have let himself shrink into such a scrawny ruin, yet here he was.

"Want a drink?" Garrett offered over the sound of Lyle washing glasses behind the bar.

The prematurely-aged tracker must have known by now that she would decline, but it had become a habit. Dess refused to take another handout from Garrett. He had given her his share of golden bucks from the Wallace payday shortly after they had reached Rubicross. He had reasoned that he didn't deserve the money after his tracking skills had led to another human being's death, and so he decided that she should have it. He was glad to know that she had put the money to good use, setting up her firewood business in Stillborough, even though she really only needed a hatchet to get started. His money was still waiting for him though; whenever and if ever he chose to forgive himself.

"I'll buy us a round," she replied, calling for three glasses of bourbon before relaying her conversation with Big-Stack.

"Story lines up," said Garrett, sniffing. "Billy couldn't've won without cheating, but there wouldn't've been any point in him hanging around to kill Emmett if he was already in front."

"Maybe he was scared of being disqualified?" Dess suggested as Brandi brought their drinks. It hadn't taken Lyle long to pour, but that was the advantage of being some of the only customers in the room.

"Rules've changed since we been here," Garrett exhaled, relishing the bourbon's burn. "Ain't a crime to be kicking a horse during a race from what I heard. Whoever makes it back to the saloon first is the winner, ain't matter how they win. Emmett would've had to honour the bet."

"So if anything," Dess ventured, letting her drink breathe for a while, "Billy would've wanted to keep Emmett alive, or at the very least, until he got paid."

"There had to've been a third rider," Garrett stroked his scruffy beard. "Already talked to Ingrid. Her stablehand, Flip, tends to fall asleep when he's meant to be watching the horses at night. Someone could've taken a horse out and put it back without him waking up."

"So if it wasn't Billy, then who?" asked Dess, the ice cracking in her glass.

"Ain't ruling him out just yet," Garrett replied before taking another sip, "But we should start thinking about some other suspects. Like who stood the most to gain from Emmett's death, because when he died, Big-Stack stood the most to lose."

"Nathan said he was planning on going into business with Emmett," Dess remembered their conversation in the garden at Royce Estate. "You think Bruce Mallory had something to do with it? Remove the competition?"

Lyle's ears pricked up behind the bar at the mention of Mallory, the bespectacled man shutting off the sink's tap and listening in, despite his sore need for fresh glasses and jugs.

"Ain't ruling him out neither," Garrett's keen eyes stared at the ice melting in their drinks.

"And you mentioned Cactus Jack was in Rubicross recently," she frowned sidelong at Garrett as he nodded slowly. "What are the chances he met up with Mallory while he was in town?"

"You think Bruce paid to have Emmett killed?" Lyle interrupted, drying wet glasses with a hand towel.

"Would you put it past him?" Dess replied with a question of her own as Garrett weighed up the possibility.

"Brandi, honey, could you take over for a minute?" Lyle directed his daughter to the sink before sidling out from behind the bar and approaching their booth. The lanky man looked over his shoulder before bending down with his hands on his knees and lowering his voice. "They still talk about killing Bruce, you know; Big-Stack, Cactus Jack, Dante, Elwood, Gabe, and all the rest. They call him *the one that got away*. As far as they're concerned, Bruce helped Wallace Pelletier steal the money, and that he might've pocketed some of it himself."

"So you think Mallory's innocent?" Dess raised an unconvinced eyebrow.

"I think," Lyle began, pushing his glasses up the bridge of his nose as he studied the pair of them, "If any of these men and women could get within firing distance of Bruce, they'd shoot him. And that's before he could ask them to kill a man they all looked up to."

"Money changes things," Garrett replied before taking another sip of his bourbon.

"Who do I have to fuck to get another beer!?" Blair Frost yelled from a nearby booth, the rest of the Royce guards laughing as Merrick Werner waved an empty jug overhead.

"Money *does* change things," Dess agreed, turning to face Garrett again as Lyle collected the empty jug and headed back to the bar. "It changes people, too."

They looked up as Flem emerged from the bathroom, stumbling back to the table.

"You said you were outside the whole time during the race?" Garrett pushed the third bourbon towards him, the ice already melted.

"Like I told ye," Flem replied, wrapping both of his hands around the glass and slurping greedily before deciding to knock it back in one breath.

"Do you remember who was watching with you?" asked Dess, pulling her own drink out of his reach.

Flem's silver-grey eyes stared up at the roof thoughtfully, licking his lips before shrugging his bony thin shoulders. Dess took a mouthful of bourbon. She didn't want to ask the next question, so Garrett did.

"Was Harlan with you?" he asked, dreading the answer.

Flem started to nod, then frowned and shook his head.

"He was out on the veranda for a little while…" Flem answered before shaking his empty glass, eyeing them off speculatively. "I'm real thirsty, can I get another drink?"

"Answer the damn question," Dess said hotly, but even as her fist clenched on the table, Garrett slid his own glass towards him.

"Harlan 'n' most others left sometime afore Big-Stack came back," Flem recalled as soon as he had the drink in his hands, taking a throaty gulp of Garrett's bourbon. "He must'a gone out in the rain though, 'cause when I seen him back inside, his clothes were all wet 'n' his boots were muddy."

Dess and Garrett exchanged a glance. Neither of them wanted to continue. Dess knew the question she wanted to ask, but she didn't want to hear the answer. She took another drink before flexing the slender muscles in her jaw, levelling her gaze at Flem.

"How long was Harlan with you?" she asked finally.

"Couldn't'a been more'n a minute," he answered.

CHAPTER 15 – HARLAN

At the rear of The Pilgrim's Respite Church, a modest shell of rugged timber, the reimagined frontier town's burial ground was packed shoulder to shoulder. Prior to the recolonisation of the prairies, Culmination Graveyard had been purely ornamental, artificially adding to the quaint theme of Coyote's Rest, filled with the headstones of imaginary cowboys and folklore legends, but without any actual occupants inside.

However, during the many raids upon the outlying towns that had sprung up along the railroad, the residents had begun using the grave markers as templates to indicate where to dig burial plots, scratching out the original tombstones' inscriptions and carving in new epitaphs for the deceased. They worked by row and added a unique symbol on each of the headstones to differentiate the real resting places from the fake, but only after Flem Wakefield had too much to drink one day and dug up the same grave twice.

As little as Emmett Pearce had wanted to do with the vast majority of them, all of the inhabitants of Coyote's Rest had come to pay their respects, although there wasn't any other place to be, since all of the business owners in town had agreed to close up shop for the morning. After the blessed two years of peace from the Rauders' attacks, funerals were no longer a common occurrence, but they still observed the same traditions.

Harlan spotted Shane Wagner, the diligent carpenter, standing in the gang of gathered grievers with one lean arm wrapped around his frigid wife, Gemma, alongside Connie Coleman, the friendly hotel clerk, and Connie's perverse pencil-necked boss, Reagan Dempsey. There were washerwomen from the boarding house; prostitutes, also from the boarding house; visitors who had once worked along the railroad, now employed as guards posted in Rubicross or along The Ravine; men and women from the various settlements spread throughout the farm belt; ex-mill workers from Cape Huxley who had moved to Brimvale and Stillborough; even some from as far out as Rookson City were in attendance.

Most of them were dressed in black suits and mourning gowns, but for Harlan, Dante, Elwood, Gabe, and many of the other cowboys and cowgirls from Coyote's Rest, black dress shirts and dark leather chaps or denim jeans – faded and rubbed raw from years in the saddle under the hot sun – were the best clothes that they could conjure up.

Emmett's casket was resting on timbers over the open grave. Harlan had soured at the sight of the simple wooden box that the funeral director had given him. For a man who worked so closely with the dead, Verne certainly had no trouble flirting with the idea of joining them. At the last moment, the underhanded undertaker had swapped his promised case of finely-carved mahogany for a hastily-stained heap of cheap pinewood from Shane's workshop, the crafty old codger claiming that his suppliers in Rookson City had experienced a delay in sending the custom-made casket, and that the display case had been damaged beyond practical pallbearing integrity when they had tried to use it instead.

Of course, a refund was out of the question, because Verne had supposedly paid his suppliers – if they even existed – in full in advance, which Harlan had also been regretfully foolish of doing.

The frugal display of orange and purple flowers arrayed around the grave did nothing to hide the pinewood, although knowing the yellowed grasslands of the prairies; they had probably collected more flowers than what was growing in the entire surrounding area of Coyote's Rest. All told, a piss-poor effort from everyone, but at least they were here.

A raven cawed plaintively from the roof of the church, attracted to the scent of death upon the air, scrutinising the proceedings with a haughty stare. Brandi Beckett bowed her head beneath a veil between her father,

Lyle, and Toby, the piano player, who pulled out a handkerchief for her at an opportune moment during the priest's burial rites.

Father Norman had settled into a monotonous droning while leading the mourning mass, robotically reading soothing words from a sheet of paper, an excerpt from the book that he no longer believed in. The wind riffling the weather-worn page had more resonance than his recitation. With the present company however, nobody really seemed to care.

Most of the believers had abandoned their religions when the world had ended, and their lives, or the lives of their families, had been destroyed. And who could blame them? Some had stayed true though – the masochists – thinking that it was all part of some divine test. The trials of the supposed Judgement Day had lingered long after the end of the apocalypse, but surely anybody who still clutched onto the fanciful idea must have realised by now that the day of reckoning was well and truly over.

Anyone who still flaunted their beliefs nowadays was only doing so for appearance's sake, simply using their position as a guiding hand to coax what they wanted out of people who were still desperate enough to believe in something. Although, after having spent years alongside people who relied on primal pleasures just to get themselves through the night, Harlan of all people knew better than to question anyone's coping mechanisms.

Elsewhere in the crowd, he spotted Gloria Clementine, the silver-haired feed store owner who had happily given away the town's blacksmith equipment to a pair of shit-pushers from Rubicross years ago, standing alongside Darlene, the boarding house matron.

Darlene Sobol, a thickset blonde woman in her fifties who had grown thicker and richer with each and every one of her premeditated divorces, had been a whore back in Brimvale throughout the food shortages. After acquiring a taste for speedy settlements in return for her sexual favours, she had moved to Coyote's Rest during the railroad's construction, in the hopes of earning extra cash without much competition.

As more whores moved out to the prairies however, she had put herself in charge of the old Madame's Buxom Boarding House instead, insisting that everyone call her "Madame" and charging the other whores for conducting their business in a place where they could work from home.

Then there was Reagan Dempsey, the owner of The Grand Chandelier Hotel, who had been overjoyed at the sight of all the mourners coming into town. Although he had the most expensive real estate in Coyote's Rest, he still relied heavily upon tourists travelling through the prairies in order to meet his overheads.

Harlan narrowed his eyes at the skinny balding middle-aged man, wondering if he might have had something to do with the murder, knowing that Emmett had plenty of friends from out of town. Then, as they came to mourn his death, Reagan would profit by offering the only decent accommodation – by an outsider's standards, at least – in Coyote's Rest. Harlan soon disregarded the thought though, knowing that Reagan wasn't smart enough to figure out how to save his failing business by himself.

He remembered back when Reagan had been charging the whores of the town half-price for lodging, on the condition that they only carried out business in their own rooms and not in those of the guests; it was less work for the housemaids. The arrangement had kept his head above water for a while, until he had thrown it all away.

Too proud to pay the prostitutes, Reagan had instead tried multiple times to offer free lodging to the whores who would fulfil his fantasies. Some of the women were willing, but his fetishes had proven to be so perverse that every prostitute in town soon chose to stay at the boarding house instead, which costed the same amount of money and allowed them to conduct their business wherever they liked.

Just about the only person who wasn't present at the funeral was Big-Stack, who still remained a key suspect in the ongoing investigation. Dess had posted two of her Royce guards to watch the prisoner so that Sheriff Ashby and Deputy Monroe could attend the funeral, believing that the mere sight of Billy at the service would incite a lynch mob.

Garrett was on the other side of the casket holding Ingrid Kaufmann as she wept into his shoulder, with Olaf and Flip nearby.

That's my boy, Harlan thought to himself.

Archie, Dess and a few of her friends from Stillborough stood alongside

Garrett. Harlan knew that they had made some progress into investigating the cause of Emmett's death, but he didn't want to ask them about it just yet. For the first time since arriving in Coyote's Rest, they had finally seemed to be loosening up, at least, with others. Harlan had thought that their old friends who had arrived yesterday on the bus would have helped to break the ice somewhat, but Dess, Garrett, and even Archie, had been giving him the cold shoulder ever since the new arrivals came off the bus yesterday.

Harlan hadn't thought too much of it at the time, but last night in the saloon, before he had even sat down with his first glass of whiskey, Dess had confronted him about the extra golden bucks that he had come across after he had been claimed by many to be almost broke. He thought that he had kept his financial situation under wraps, so he was taken aback by her blunt question.

"I'll admit it," he shrugged, holding his drink loosely in his hand, "After we found Emmett's body, the first thing I did after getting him back into town was breaking into his room to take his money."

"Wow," Dess replied, one hand on her hip, "I see you've got your priorities in order."

"Don't – you fucking…" he had to take a breath to recompose himself. "If I hadn't done it, some other fucker would've. And I needed those chips to pay for his funeral, especially with Verne's bullshit." He took a sip of his whiskey before adding, "Besides, it's not like Emmett needs the money anymore, anyway."

Dess frowned at him with an unyielding stare, choosing her words carefully, better than he had chosen his.

"It was nice of you to pay for the funeral," she said in a measured tone, ice in her voice, "But the rest of those golden bucks don't belong to you."

"Who should the money belong to, then?" Harlan asked, recalling the argument he had overheard between Emmett and Dess the night that they had ridden down Wallace Pelletier and distributed the stolen golden bucks fairly among the rest of the railroad workers. When Dess had argued that they weren't entitled to *everything* Wallace had taken, Emmett had asked her the exact same question.

Dess hadn't answered Harlan, and she seemed to linger, glaring as she waited for him to either apologise for evoking a repressed memory, or to admit to something that he wasn't aware of.

She hadn't spoken a word to him since then, but he assumed that they had been too busy catching up with the others in the saloon, reminiscing about old stories and fond memories that they had shared with Emmett. Today, he simply thought that they must have been nursing some well-earned hangovers, and none of them were in the mood to talk. But still, he couldn't ignore the feeling of a rift, growing like some invisible chasm that was keeping them apart, and the distance between them in the crowd at the funeral being bridged only by Emmett's casket spoke volumes in itself.

Eventually, Harlan realised that Father Norman's monotonous droning had died, as if the ambient rumble of a diesel generator had suddenly coughed and spluttered its last fumes before the lights went out, realising its absence more than its presence. Everyone looked towards Dess, expecting her to make a speech, but she simply shifted her weight with her eyes downcast.

After a few minutes of silence, with some of the mourners scanning the crowd to see if anyone else would say something for Emmett, Harlan stooped in between Dante and Elwood as they each picked up one of the long straps trailing out from underneath the casket. Dess, Garrett and Archie snatched up the straps on the other side, pulling tight as the timbers suspending Emmett's box over the open grave were removed.

Harlan locked eyes with Dess, offering a nod towards her, yet receiving nothing in return. She must have been holding a grudge against him for having reminded her of the argument that she'd had with Emmett over two years ago, the night before she had left town; the same night that marked the last time either of them would ever see each other alive and well.

Slowly, the six volunteers unravelled the straps, lowering the casket into the ground.

"Go easy, Emmett," Harlan whispered as he sprinkled dirt into the grave.

As much as Harlan hated Verne, he was grateful that the old man had invited them all into the viewing room of his funeral parlour, where they could see Emmett one last time before his casket was closed. Although Emmett's face seemed to have shrunken and his hair had grown longer, it was a far better sight to remember him by than the state he had been in after Dess and Garrett had pulled his carcass upright in the casket, with his eyes staring and mouth wide open.

He had overheard some of the cowboys debating the body's warped appearance in a hushed conversation, a few of them believing that fingernails and hair simply continued to grow long after someone's death, although Verne had explained – with a morbid fascination – that the skin of the deceased tightened due to dehydration, retracting from the hair and nails, which then seemed longer in comparison.

Harlan found himself beginning to wonder why he had accepted Quentin Davis's bounty offer to hunt down and kill the Rauders, given that the cowboys knew so little about death. They all talked a big game, but he questioned whether any of them would be man enough to pull the trigger on someone else.

* * *

He lingered long after the other funeral attendants had left, watching the steady shower of earth as Flem kicked his shovel into the nearby mound of dirt while drinking from his hip flask. Scoop, toss, swig, repeat. It was mid-afternoon by the time Harlan realised that even Flem had left the graveyard. He started heading back towards the boarding house, the sun's rays shimmering over the dirt road of the main street, when he spotted Dess and Garrett heading into Ingrid's Livery Stable.

Harlan paused just outside the entrance before passing under the cool shade of the barn. That first whiff of fresh horseshit in an enclosed space would never get old.

"… I don't wanna believe it either," he overheard Dess saying. "I don't even wanna ask the question. But we do this, and we'll know whether it's worth asking."

Garrett cleared his throat and tipped the brim of his black hat at Harlan

172

as he stepped inside the stable. Dess looked around at Harlan, flexing the slender muscles in her jaw as she wondered how much he had heard.

Their pair of horses whinnied as Flip, the stablehand, testily tried to coax them into biting their bridles' bits.

"You're not gonna say goodbye, first?" Harlan asked. The Royce guards weren't with them, and neither was their luggage, but he had always fantasised about what he would have said if he had caught them in the act of leaving town unannounced.

"Ain't like that, brother," Garrett answered, averting his gaze, "Just heading out to Rambling Gulch again."

"Flip, come help tack mine up next," said Harlan, grabbing a saddle and an old blanket as he marched over to his red stallion's stall where it hoofed idly at the sandy floor.

The teenage boy with the mullet sighed as he reluctantly crossed the stable, being lumped with yet another task to add to his list of chores which he still hadn't had a chance to work on yet.

"Company couldn't hurt," Garrett shrugged. Then, glancing at Dess, he asked, "Should we bring the escort?"

Dess iced Harlan over with her brown eyes, still refusing to speak a word to him directly, although she was staring straight at him when she made her reply.

"Absolutely," she crossed her arms as Flip brushed the red stallion's back roughly.

Garrett sniffed, nodded, and loped over to Lorelei's to find the Royce guards, hoping that they hadn't already sunken too many jugs of beer between themselves, although it was a thin hope, since the day was now well past noon.

"Still mad about last night?" Harlan asked into the void of silence as he padded and saddled his horse. No answer from Dess as she began preparing other horses for the escort. "Guess that's a *yes*, then," he winked at Flip as the boy passed the saddle's girth beneath the stallion's belly for Harlan to buckle and tighten the strap on the other side.

He checked that the stirrups were hanging low and let Flip fiddle with the reins and bridle before leaning against the wall of the stall, staring at the day outside. He supposed that he could have helped Dess prepare the extra half dozen horses, but only if she were to ask him nicely.

The other funeral attendants – who had already changed out of their graveside outfits and were now lounging and drinking along the railing of the saloon's veranda – watched as the six Royce guards headed into the stable. Taking their lead, a few of the onlookers began to wander into the barn, asking if Flip could prepare a few more horses for them as well.

"Fucking hell," the stablehand muttered under his breath before running to fetch Ingrid.

"Y'all ridin' 'round the track?" asked Cactus Jack, grabbing a blanket and saddle and throwing both over the nearest horse.

"You bet," said Harlan, mounting up on his red stallion before anyone else could claim it.

Excitement rippled through the crowd gathering in the stable as Ingrid emerged from her office, happily accepting payments from anyone who wanted to celebrate Emmett's life by riding past the scene of his death.

A few of the cowboys volunteered to help the overworked stablehand, grooming and tacking the horses, while others leapt onto their saddles and pulled up any woman who was willing to ride tandem. Archie smiled from the saloon's railing, raising a bottle in salute, along with the other spectators who were still marginally sober enough to know better.

Harlan's red stallion trotted out alongside Garrett's brown mustang, following Dess's lead, with the half dozen Royce guards trailing behind. The crowd parted to let them pass, some having to wait until the first batch of riders would come back before they would get their turn. Elwood, having drunken too much too quickly, climbed up onto his saddle only to fall off on the other side, letting someone else take his place with a woozy wave, insisting that he would join the next batch of riders before he began snoring beneath his hat.

They rode past the buildings at a steady pace towards the start of the racetrack, Dante giving a few of the first-time riders tips on the fly before Dess held up her hand, halting the rest of the horses behind her as she clutched the reins and checked the small golden watch on her wrist.

"Fuck, fuck, fuck," breathed Lloyd Price, one of the Royce guards, as he snuck past Harlan and Garrett, his horse slowly driving forward with its own course in mind.

Cactus Jack already had his tongue in his passenger's mouth when Dess took off at a gallop, Harlan and Garrett kicking their spurs into their mounts and trailing after her.

"Eat shit, Price!" Kirk Boaz laughed as the rest of the guards left him in the dust.

Apparently Price's horse had decided that it was time for an afternoon snack, grazing off to the side of the track as he flailed his stirrups and tugged at the reins impotently.

"Least you made it farther than Elwood!" Lacey called from Gabe's saddle as they rounded the first corner.

"Whose idea was this?" Harlan yelled into the rushing wind with a grin as he rode side by side with Garrett.

"That'd be Dess's," Garrett replied, his shoulder-length hair whipping wildly beneath his wide-brimmed hat.

"Well, it was a good one," Harlan admitted, only just now realising that he was still in his attire from the funeral. "Any reason why she's –" *being a bitch*, he wanted to say as they ducked under a tree branch, "Not talking to me?"

"I ain't getting involved," Garrett answered, keeping his eyes on the path. "That's one for you two to work out."

"Slow up!!" Harlan shouted ahead as Dess neared the sharp turn on Legsnap Ridge. She pulled back on the reins at the last possible moment, her horse skidding on all fours, before rocking to the side and galloping off again. He glanced sidelong at Garrett, "She's riding like she put a stack of chips down. What the hell's she thinking?"

Harlan slowed his stallion to a trot, easing into the turn with Garrett on the inside edge. When they picked up the pace on the other side, Harlan held his horse to a canter, with Garrett keeping stride behind him. Heavy footfalls thundered the track as the other horses caught up and passed by, kicking up clods of earth, the riders whooping and hollering.

There were more cowboys and cowgirls than there were guards. Dante was casually riding side-saddle while flirting with one of the out-of-towners; Lacey cheered as she held Gabe's hat high in the air, catching the wind; and Cactus Jack was thrusting one hand up his passenger's blouse as she squealed and laughed in delight.

Dess had already disappeared into the distance by the time they all began slowing down, approaching the scene of Emmett's death, the path broadening and flattening next to the riverbank as the narrow stream gurgled by. Bowing their heads in silent respect, those who were wearing a hat held it to their chest, while others upended the contents of their hip flasks onto the ground.

Harlan looked up at the cloudless sky, willing the image of how they had found Emmett's body out of his mind. He wanted to remember his old friend how he had been in life, not how they had seen him in death.

He smiled as the memories came back to him, recalling that whenever Emmett would get up to buy another round at Lorelei's, he had a habit of elbowing Harlan as he sat back down, holding Harlan's beer aloft with a sly grin to see if he would push back and spill his own drink. Whenever Emmett was feeling down about Dess and it was Harlan's turn to buy, he would get them a pair of triple whiskeys. A couple rounds later and they would be roaring with laughter as they staggered back to the boarding house, trying their best to sneak past Madame Darlene's room before she tried to lure some young cock into her bed.

"Go easy, Emmett," Harlan echoed, following the Royce guards as they pushed their horses through to the other side of the crowd.

A shadow had fallen across Dess's face by the time they had reached her at the main street's intersection. She was staring past the gallows towards the Sheriff's Office. Harlan figured that it was time he offered her an apology for bringing up a bad memory, so that maybe she, too, could focus on the good ones she had shared with Emmett.

"How long?" Garrett asked as they pulled up next to her, cutting off Harlan before he could even start to make amends.

"Seven minutes, fifty-three seconds," she replied, refusing to break her stare. It was almost as if she was speaking to the row of ornamental nooses dangling from the gallows.

"Hey!" Harlan exclaimed cheerfully, "You almost broke the record! Imagine if you took the run without one of them Royce horses."

Garrett shifted in his saddle uncomfortably as Dess flexed the slender muscles in her jaw.

"What's the big deal?" asked Harlan, the smile fading from his face. "You wanna set a new record? I'll let you try with mine, if you want. He's warmed up. Just don't take that corner too hard with him. He's a heavy son of a bitch. He'll go over."

No response. He turned to Garrett for answers.

"Talked to Flem," said Garrett, sniffing. "Time's too close to what Big-Stack's was."

"So what?" asked Harlan, searching his face for a better explanation.

"So," Garrett looked at Dess. "Big-Stack wouldn't've been able to attack Emmett, park his horse, finish the job and get back to the saloon on time."

Still puzzled, Harlan turned to Dess, who had finally decided that it was time to break the silent treatment.

"Big-Stack's innocent," she concluded, staring back at him.

CHAPTER 16 – DAMIAN

Damian Bishop leaned into the corner as the armoured truck swung left, the cargo tinkling as its contents shifted inside the pair of green plastic canisters on the metal floor. He felt like a kid again, running errands for the higher-ups; pick-up, drop-off, keep your head down and tell me if anyone fucks with you. The only difference was: if anyone fucked with him now, he wouldn't need to tell anyone.

He grinned to himself, remembering the Bouncer who had squirmed on the asphalt, holding his crushed nut sack in the parking lot for the whole Velvet Convoy to see. Sure, it was one less potential customer for Zatar, but nobody was going to pay for a banged-up broad. Being in the same line of work, Claude the choirboy should have known better than most; cash comes first, product comes second, and the customer comes last, if at all.

Barry Sutton, the chunky uptight boss of the docks at Flintscray Port, had been a little less understanding when he heard the news. His face had been purple with rage in his third-storey dockmaster's office as he bellowed at Damian for assaulting one of the Bouncers' representatives, their only trading partners; the one group of people who were keeping the Flints fed with real food, rather than having to resort to begging for scraps from the Ukrainians like every other poor son of a bitch in The Gutter.

The fringe of Barry's skid-mark brown comb-over had flapped around like a furry butt plug in a strip club as he yelled, blaming Damian for the entire altercation, including the Velvet Convoy's subsequent confiscation of the three Bouncers' weapons.

Damian couldn't help but chuckle, even while he was getting chewed out. The running joke around the docks was that Barry's ass was tight enough to burst a cluster of hemorrhoids, like a set of overgrown pimples in a vice. The tighter he clenched, the angrier he got, and the angrier he got, the tighter he clenched. Seeing Barry wriggle around in his office chair uncomfortably while spewing garbled profanities made Damian imagine his crusty ring of squashed grapes as some all-powerful volcano of wrath.

The chuckle had escalated into laughter, and soon, Damian was roaring loud enough for the rest of the boys working down in the yard below to hear. He had never respected Barry as a boss, mainly because he had never needed to. Damian was there as the Mafia's liaison, Barry was beneath him. Although, since the Mafia was no longer around to enforce his position, both of them had quickly realised who was really in charge. By the time Damian's laughs had died down, Barry's purple face had reverted back to its natural puffy red.

Barry had reminded Damian that his Mafia buddies wouldn't be able to help him out of the mess he had gotten himself into, and if he ran into any trouble, there was only one crew in his corner now; the Flints, the same people who had given him food and shelter since the apocalypse began, even after they no longer had a need for him, or more accurately, after they no longer had an obligation to suffer his presence.

Barry had offered him a simple choice; he could stay with the Flints, make up for his mistakes and continue to enjoy their protection, or he could leave Flintscray Port and deal with the Bouncers on his own.

It was an easy decision for Damian, and Barry had all too happily busted him back down to hired muscle. Then, like a bad joke, Barry had decided to send Damian along on the next delivery run to the Bouncers. *Some protection*, Damian grinned smugly.

The armoured truck took another turn, and the cargo tinkled again. They were transporting a batch of ammunition. Every gang in The Gutter had run dry of bullets in less than a year during the Turf Wars, and there was no chance that the people of Brimvale would ever consider a trade deal to rearm them, so the only supplies of fresh ammunition had to be shipped in from the coast.

The ex-convicts from Attiker Island had ties to the Bouncers, so the pirates topped them up regularly to ensure that their business interests in the Red Light District were taken care of. The Flints were the conduit, or in other words, the scapegoat if things went wrong. If any of the cargo was reported missing, the Flints would be held directly responsible. They were paid handsomely for facilitating the logistics though, not receiving any bullets of their own, but a steady stream of real food and golden bucks kept everyone happy.

The pair of canisters slid across the metal floor as the driver brought the truck to a stop. Damian glimpsed one of the Bouncers' sentries posted on a rooftop through the narrow back window. He wasn't looking forward to meeting whoever was accepting the delivery, but he had made a conscious effort to appear as placid as possible.

Dressed in dark jeans, a black leather bomber jacket, matching black sunglasses and holding a thermos full of shitty coffee, he was just another grunt going about his day.

The driver's overburdened boots squealed in wheezing agony as they crunched across the asphalt outside, Donnie pounding three times on the rear hatch. Damian unbolted the doors and threw them out wide to see the curly-haired Donnie huffing and puffing after the brief waddle from the driver's cabin.

Damian was grateful for having chosen to wear sunglasses; they hid the disgust in his eyes as they traced over the sweat stains pooling out from the big butterball's underarms on the moderately cool day. The man had a constant look of apology about him, as if there was nothing he could do about the reeking stench of body odour mixed in with candy constantly chasing him like a shadow, wherever his hoard of sugar might be.

Damian knew Donnie Lombardo from the years they had both spent working in Little Italy. Donnie used to be the driver for the local ice cream parlour, delivering creamy gelato and frozen treats all over Bushrock, although none of the merchandise ever reached the customers, mostly because Donnie had trouble with leaning out of the window. Despite his complete lack of sales, his boss never complained about the amount of money he was bringing in, because Donnie was using the truck to run deliveries on the side for Fabrizio Pasquale, and a sweaty sasquatch driving an ice cream truck made for the perfect cover. Today was just another regular day for Donnie.

"You're late," an accusing tone came from the sidewalk, just beyond Damian's field of vision in the back of the truck.

"I'm sthorry, I'm sthorry," Donnie apologised profusely with one meaty hand in the air, waving his thick sausage fingers, "Had sthome troubles with the engine."

Damian knew the real reason for their late arrival though. It wasn't the engine or Donnie's fault at all; it was Damian's. As he had sat in his throne room earlier that day, Damian had decided that he would rather let the Bouncers stand on the kerb and wait for a while, like a bunch of ugly-ass street hookers desperate for a John, instead of rushing through his morning dump just to suit their schedule.

"Yeah, I'll bet," the accusing voice carried on. "Any truck would run into engine troubles hauling your lard ass."

A couple of other voices sniggered from the sidewalk.

Donnie mopped his forehead with a handkerchief as he mumbled a reply.

"What'd you say to me, you fat fuck?" the Bouncer asked, taking on a menacing tone.

Damian had planned on staying in the back with the cargo, but now he was curious. He stepped down from the truck and turned to see the speaker, whose scornful demeanour quickly changed. It was Claude, backed up by his two fuck-buddies, Kelvin and Sonny, the same three guys from the Velvet Convoy's parking lot.

"Hey, it's the eunuch!" Damian greeted them cheerfully. "No hard feelings about the other night, right fellas? Certainly not from you, I wouldn't think," he grinned at Claude, painfully reminding the short-fused Bouncer just how superbly his crotch had levitated off Damian's boot.

"You got a lotta balls coming over here after what you did," said Kelvin, the lanky bug-eyed fuck.

"You're damn right I do," Damian replied, grabbing his nut sack through his jeans, "And a delivery. Now, do we wanna do business, or were you waiting all morning just to talk with my good friend here?" He gestured towards Donnie, who was flustered, but relieved that someone else was doing the talking for him.

Claude the choirboy ground his teeth, but snapped his fingers for one of his lame-brained lackeys to check the delivery. Taking a few long moments to recognise his cue, Sonny the short and stocky skinhead perked up and came forward to place a weight scale on the truck's lip, meticulously checking that the dial was set to zero. Damian pushed one of the green plastic canisters towards him and stepped back, letting the dopey dunce crack the lid open and pour the bullets into the scale's container.

Damian put one hand in his pocket, sipping from his coffee thermos with the other, grimacing at its coppery taste while taking in the surroundings. Without the neon lights buzzing overhead, the Red Light District was just another empty street in the day time. Red carpets, velvet ropes and burly security guards adorning the entrances of the popular clubs were nowhere to be seen.

The only signs of life came from a brothel across the street that needed no security; the 24/7 Cum & Go. It was the one whorehouse in town that never closed, offering discounted prices for anyone desperate enough to make it past the foyer. They had an extended happy hour for chubby-chasers that would run all morning, but what you saved on price, you lost on dignity.

The women there had lost all hope of a better life, along with the reasons that they had clung on to like a mantra to get themselves through the first few months of their hole-for-hire careers. They were now women who had already given away anything special they might have once had to offer; giving up on their dreams and settling to be mere plugs for the depraved bums who wanted to give their carpal tunnel-riddled hands a break but couldn't afford any better.

This is where whores go to die, Damian grinned to himself.

A fat cow wandered out of the barn and onto the concrete paddock of the sidewalk, dressed in a furry pink scarf and a leopard-print bodysuit that was stretched to the absolute limits around curves that it hadn't been designed to flaunt. She noticed the men standing around the rear of the truck and shot a lascivious wink in their general direction as she lit up a homemade cigarette, hoping to catch at least one potential client.

Damian noisily suppressed a gag and turned away.

"What happened?" Kelvin asked in a derisive tone, his eyes big enough to be mistaken for a pair of cue balls, "You lost your nerve?"

"Could say that again," Damian jerked his head towards the other side of the street. "That your wife over there?"

Donnie erupted in an involuntary titter, his titties trembling, but he stopped himself short when he saw that nobody else was laughing. He feigned looking up and down the street instead, having to swing half his upper body in the effort, only to glance back at the bovine creature. Twice.

"That can't be right," Sonny muttered to himself, checking a scribble on a note against the figure on the weight scale. "The numbers are off," he called over his shoulder, picking up the canister again and shaking empty air.

The trio of Bouncers reached for the pistols that they had tucked in their waistbands, despite having had their old guns confiscated by the Velvet Convoy the other night. Damian wondered how many weapons the Bouncers had at their disposal. He supposed that it wasn't the amount of guns they had that would make a difference though, it was the amount of bullets.

"You stupid cunt," Claude sneered, his voice dripping with scorn. "You've been talking shit this whole fucking time and you wanna come up short?"

The eunuch raised his pistol at Damian's forehead, resting the end of the barrel just above his sunglasses. Donnie started backing away, until Kelvin switched his sights to the butterball instead. The leopard-print cow across the street let out a high-pitched moo and lumbered back into the barn.

"Come on guys," Donnie pleaded, the armoured truck bouncing slightly as he fell to all fours on the asphalt. "There's gotta be sthome kind of misthtake."

"Give me a fucking break," Damian sighed as he casually slurped from his coffee thermos. "Would it kill you guys to do a bit of math? Try checking the other canister before you start waving your little pin-dicks around."

"It doesn't work like that," Sonny replied, although even as he spoke, his dopey blue eyes strayed back towards the weight scale, as if there was a setting or dial that he had never noticed before.

"So make it fucking work before we have a problem," Damian shrugged, still smiling at gunpoint. "You got a pencil? Write down the number, weigh the other canister, add the two together. Think you can handle that?"

The other two Bouncers looked to Claude for guidance, who reluctantly nodded his head. Sonny took out his pencil and jotted down the number on the weight scale before pouring the bullets back into the empty canister and turning to measure the other container.

With Claude's gun still trained on him, Damian moved closer to the weight scale to read the dial. Sonny wrote down the second number and scratched his bald head, struggling with the sum. At a glance, Damian could see that the number still wouldn't add up to the total that they had been expecting. The Flints had under-delivered, and now he and Donnie would be held responsible.

"It's short, fuckhead," Damian groaned with impatience, Sonny still tapping his pencil on the truck's lip. "Stop, before you give yourself a migraine."

"You're in a hurry to die," Claude the choirboy snarled, his head cocked and frowning at the numbers while struggling to do the math himself. In the end, he gave up and refocused his attention back on Damian, happy to accept that the delivery was off.

"We all gotta go someday," Damian replied as he set his coffee thermos down on the truck's lip. "Least I still got my balls."

"Oh please," Donnie begged, still on his knees. "Oh please oh please oh please oh please oh please."

Damian put both his hands up, withdrawing the other from his pocket and pulling out a grenade with the safety pin dangling from the ring around his thumb.

"SHIT!!" the other two Bouncers yelled in unison, eyes wide and bodies frozen like a pair of college kids caught fucking in a bathroom stall.

Claude's gun rattled in his shaky hand.

"I could just throw it," Damian said in a measured tone, his fingers holding the safety lever at bay. He shrugged at the eunuch, "Or, I could let you shoot me, knowing that as soon as my corpse drops the ball, you die straight after. He probably lives though."

Damian nodded towards Donnie, who was still kneeling the farthest away from the grenade's expected blast radius, sweat streaming from his forehead down his pudgy cheeks and dripping onto his titties.

"Or, probably not," Damian continued, now holding the grenade over the weight scale, which was still brimming with bullets. "Shit, this would be like watching a firework factory explode. Would be a great light show for anyone standing a block away behind a brick wall... Yeah, on second thought, you definitely wouldn't live," he grinned at Donnie.

"What the fuck do you want, man?" asked Kelvin, not sure whether to lower his gun and try to run, or stay, shoot, and die. His voice broke as he pleaded, "Just let us go."

"What *do* I want?" Damian mused, taking pleasure in pondering the question while the other four men hung on every word, doing their utmost not to piss him off. "A plate of lasagne and some garlic bread to go with it would be nice. An old-fashioned that doesn't taste like cat's piss, served by a topless nineteen-year-old with titties too big for one hand. And some decent head to top it all off."

"You want us to suck your dick?" asked Sonny, a little too eager.

"Fuck no," Damian frowned at the window licker. "Who knows where your mouth's been. What I want is to find out who stiffed us on the shipment." He looked at the grenade, admiring it in his hand. "If I let this go, and the five of us give this street a meat shower, then they get away with stealing your cargo. Next delivery day, our boys are staring down the barrel again, and whatever mooks they hire to replace you three are short of more ammo. Nobody wins."

"Do you really think we're just gonna let you go?" asked Claude, his voice shakier than the grip on his pistol.

Damian smirked, his free hand shooting out to grab the choirboy by his hair, the gun falling out of his hand as Damian pulled Claude's wide-eyed face next to the grenade hovering above the weight scale full of bullets.

"My coffee's losing steam," he looked at his thermos disapprovingly, "So I'm gonna make this real fucking simple for you simpleminded fucks. If I have to drink that shit cold, I may as well drop the ball and die right now. I'm gonna give you until the count of four. What's it gonna be?" he asked, silently counting with his fingers lifting off the grenade's safety lever.

"Okay!" the eunuch screamed above the pair of Bouncers yelling behind them. Damian had barely lifted his second finger. "Just give us the bullets, we'll say the count's right, you do whatever the fuck you need to do."

"Oh, you can bet on that," Damian grinned, letting go of Claude's hair and shoving him away from the truck. "You can keep whatever's in the weight scale, but this other canister's mine now. Call it a gesture of goodwill for having to deal with your bullshit."

The eunuch opened his mouth to say something else, but after Damian lifted his ring finger off the safety lever in warning, he thought better of it.

"You girls ever played fifty-two pick up?" Damian asked with his back turned to them. Without waiting for an answer, he held the grenade over the half-empty canister and tossed the weight scale out of the truck with a crash on the asphalt behind him, the bullets tinkling as they rolled in every direction. He cocked his head around the side of the truck. "Time for lunch, Donnie, let's get the fuck outta here."

"Give me a sthecond," Donnie panted, rocking back on his haunches to stare up at the clouds and gasp in gratitude before clambering to his feet, hoisting himself up with one hand on the rear wheel. "I sthwear, I'm about to have a fuckin' heart attack…"

"Oh, and one more thing," Damian said over his shoulder to the three Bouncers as he picked up his coffee thermos and climbed back into the rear of the truck, kicking the empty canister off the truck's lip to join the spreading mass of ammunition, "Don't you ever threaten to suck my dick again."

Still gripping the grenade between his thumb and little finger, he waved a cheery goodbye to the dumbstruck trio as Donnie hurriedly closed the rear hatch and waddled back to the driver's cabin. Damian set his thermos down on the seat, bolted the doors, and re-engaged the safety pin on the grenade.

Standing by the narrow back window, he picked up his coffee again as the truck rumbled to life, raising the thermos in a victory toast. The diesel engine's exhaust enshrouded the Bouncers in smoke, and soon, they receded into the distance as they began picking up the bullets, confused as to what the fuck had just happened.

Sitting back down, Damian screwed the lid back onto his thermos, giving the slugs inside a dense watery rattle as he pondered what to do with the rest of the bullets in the canister.

CHAPTER 17 – ADRIAN

He shaded his dark brown eyes from the blinding blaze of the merciless midday sun, its brilliant beams bouncing off every surface it could reach, reflecting its radiance at him as if the great celestial body itself had been employed by Captain Thornton to assist in administering Adrian's punishment.

Seldom few guards enjoyed walking the walls while the sun was at its peak. The ultraviolet rays above were one thing to contend with, but more irritating were the harsh glares from the metal rooftops shining up from below, making it difficult to keep a watchful eye on their surroundings.

For leaving his post during Jeremy Royce's birthday celebrations, Adrian Wakefield had been assigned to midday patrol along the top of the estate's walls, a job that was usually reserved for someone who was licensed to carry a firearm, or at the very least, a crossbow. Armed with only a baton and a pair of binoculars, Adrian had effectively become a glorified meerkat, unable to do anything but duck and scream at the first sign of trouble.

He was glad that he'd had the good sense to bring his old sun-bleached blue and red baseball cap with him when he had abandoned his self-piteous father back in Coyote's Rest, but his hat did nothing to protect the back of his neck from the savage sunrays.

His constant shade of sunburn must have been bad enough to draw attention, because it wasn't long before Sadie, Nathan Royce's eldest daughter, had broken her customary silence around him. The first time that she had ever spoken to him on a personal level was on the night of Jeremy Royce's birthday party, and that was only because he'd had that unfortunate run-in with Anton Snyder.

As drunk as she had been on that night, Sadie knew – or more likely, heard from someone else – that she had been the reason for Adrian's reassignment to midday patrol, and while she couldn't convince Captain Thornton to lighten up on him, she had offered him a pair of shades, a wide-brimmed hat and a jar of aloe vera gel. Some of the well-intentioned gifts came with a catch though. The sunglasses were floral-framed, and the hat was striped pink and white, made for strolling in a garden rather than patrolling as a guardsman.

Adrian had happily taken her up on the offer of aloe vera gel though, but only on one condition: she would have to rub it on for him. He had only been half-serious, but to his surprise, she had agreed, and so each night, he would practically run back to the barracks, shower off the sweat and grime from his sweltering shift, change into some loose casual clothes, and wait for her to meet him at the end of the alley between the garden shed and the generator's access panel behind the warehouse.

It was perhaps the only place in the entire estate that was mutually accessible for both of them without attracting any attention from others, while also being secluded enough for them to enjoy some measure of privacy, although she still insisted on making their clandestine encounters quick every time they met.

Adrian was more than happy to agree to any condition she set. He couldn't imagine what would happen to him if word had somehow managed to get back to Captain Thornton that he was flirting with the boss's daughter, especially since he was already high up on the captain's shit list. He could tell that Sadie, too, was both nervous and excited at the risk of being caught.

Every time they met behind the warehouse, she would shoot him a guilty smile, hurriedly exchanging whispered greetings before cracking open the jar of gel and rubbing the aloe vera into her hands. Apparently that wasn't the only thing that seemed to excite Sadie. He had once caught a glimpse of her biting her lip as he removed his shirt to reveal his lean build, but she had flitted behind him before he could look twice.

The first kiss of the soothing gel had been heavenly upon the back of his neck, even as her trembling hands involuntarily swatted at his sunburn. He often found himself wondering whether she had ever been with a guy, although he doubted that she would ever have had the opportunity, given how overprotective her family was of her.

He supposed that it was both good and bad. On the one hand, she would not so easily grow bored of their all too brief encounters, but on the other hand, he suspected that it would never amount to anything beyond that. Sometimes, he felt like he was a mere peasant boy trying to court a princess. Still, he didn't mind working the midday patrol if it meant that he could spend a few minutes alone with her at the end of each shift.

His shift was far from over though.

From where he stood above the wooden gates set within the east wall, he could see the faint outline of the north bridge spanning the width of Axemark Ravine, along with its security checkpoint on the other side, which guarded one of the few entrances into Brimvale. He often wondered whether there was some other lowly-paid guard staring back at him, counting down the seconds until the end of the day.

He didn't bother to lift his pair of binoculars up to his eyes. There was no need to check. He knew that on such a cloudless day like this, the sentries would all be inside the guard post, leaning back in their chairs and watching the bridge from the air-conditioned side of tinted windows, rather than risk getting sunburnt outside.

Adrian waved off a particularly persistent blowfly before wandering over to the southeast corner of the ramparts, listening to the sounds of drunken laughter coming from The Oxhouse on the other side of the street, a bar where most of the guards in town would ritualistically spend the majority of their spare time and money.

Farther down was a row of commercial storefronts, whose internal shop walls had been knocked down to house Drew and Colin's Metalware, so that their furnace, living area, supply of raw materials and finished products were all housed underneath the one roof. They had picked the perfect location for their business too, since anyone travelling to and from Brimvale via public transport would need to board and alight at Rubicross's only designated bus stop, which happened to be right outside their store.

To the south of Royce Manor, across a usually-empty dirt lot and over the street, were the school grounds of Rubicross Elementary, where the Snyder Family had set up shop, having repurposed the school's gym into a giant strip club, and the old classrooms into the private suites of a brothel.

Laszlo Snyder had named his nude gallery The Mezzanine, and branded his brothel as Backstage. They were appealing monikers to his clients, giving everyone the innocent impression that they were simply visiting the local theatre for a live performance, with an opportunity for VIP guests to meet some of their favourite cast members behind the curtains. And for the price of three hundred golden bucks, anyone could become a VIP guest, even if it was just for an hour at a time.

The naming convention must have been popular with the women working there too, because the venue boasted a full roster of entertainers every night. Adrian supposed that they must have felt better about themselves being referred to as performers who were paid to put on a good show for their audience, rather than being called a bunch of strippers and whores.

Though admittedly, a visit to The Mezzanine seemed less smutty than a visit to a strip club, Adrian had never been there himself, nor did he intend on visiting. He couldn't see the appeal of being intimate with the same women who put their bodies on display and made love to every other man in town.

Worse than that, he didn't want Laszlo's son, Anton, reporting his visit to Sadie. Adrian didn't get the feeling that the two were particularly close, but Anton Snyder seemed like he was the saboteur-type, who would actively work to push others away from Sadie in order to ensure that he was closer than anyone else.

Adrian's friends had been there though. Reece Jensen and Simon Yu had been sensible, hanging out by the main stage to watch the free shows, having smuggled in a hip flask of bourbon to mix their own drinks in the bathroom rather than splashing chips for the overpriced watered-down beverages at the bar. Stacey Sherman, on the other hand, had spent a month's worth of his cadet wage on lines of shots, along with cocktails for the ladies, extended lap dances and a VIP pass to Backstage. He ended up paying for a second hour too, which proved just as fruitless as the first, as he sat on the bed the entire time trying to rouse his whiskey dick. While it wasn't a story most people would have openly bragged about, Stacey was definitely not most people, and he couldn't resist giving every detail about his first time with a naked woman.

After laughing his ass off at the story, Adrian supposed that being a proficient pervert wasn't a prerequisite to having a good time beyond the gates of the repurposed Rubicross Elementary, but as slim as his chances were with the boss's daughter, he still didn't want to risk his connection with Sadie over a visit to the venue.

Farther to the south and west was an array of single-storey houses and clusters of commercial properties that had been taken over by groups and families of less significant merchants. The rest of the trading town of Rubicross was otherwise largely-abandoned, as most of its previous inhabitants had preferred the relative safety of Brimvale, Stillborough and Rookson City.

Adrian looked back at the dirt lot next door with idle curiosity.

Everyone had scrambled to get into defensive positions when they heard the crash late last night, only to discover that Haydar, the perpetually-drunken potato farmer from the prairies, had managed to drive his faded blue pickup truck all the way from the farm belt into Rubicross, with his rusty white caravan in tow. He had either misjudged the distance on his approach or he was proudly announcing his arrival when he rammed the front end of his old blue bucket into the concrete wall of the estate.

The comically short round man was eventually able to conquer the inflated airbag, hauling himself out of the crumpled wreck and bellowing into the night, as loud, hairy and unintelligible as an escaped circus bear. Everyone had thought that he was yelling garbled and pained profanities, but when they peered over the parapet, he simply appeared to be singing in his native tongue, swaying to some imaginary music with one hand in the air and the other around a bottle of his own special batch of vodka.

Every so often, he would take a stumbling swig and slur his demands for diesel at the crowd of guards lined up along the wall who simply watched him with amusement. Adrian had overheard Terry Delaney, one of the estate's gardeners who always seemed to shadow the guards, laughing with Javier Cortez and Wade Griffin, joking that this was the closest thing to an attack that they had seen ever since the Rauders' raids years ago.

While the engine in Haydar's pickup truck had been spewing smoke a short distance away, his tall and brawny bodyguard, Omar, had parked a red semitrailer nearby, pitching an awning from the roof of the rusty freight container to a set of large poles that he had embedded into the ground.

Now as Adrian watched, the bald brown bodyguard with a black goatee was frying up some sweetly-spiced meat and scalloped potatoes in the shade of the canvas. There was no sign of the infamous Haydar around, but it was safe to assume that the pudgy little man was sleeping off a hangover inside his motorhome. With the front end of his pickup truck still squashed against the wall, it seemed as though they were planning on staying for a while.

"That smells incredible," Devon sighed as she sidled up next to Adrian, lured by the sizzling meat wafting on the breeze, "You think they're trying to smoke us out?" she asked with a wry grin.

Devon Bailey was in her mid-twenties, former Army Reserves, like many of the other guards in Rubicross. She was over a half-decade older than Adrian and his friends, but she preferred the company of the cadets over the guards her own age, who only seemed to be interested in one thing, even though they had long since given up on the idea of getting into her pants, preferring to satisfy their primal pleasures through payment in place of patience.

She was also one of the few guards who preferred to walk the walls during the midday patrol. It allowed her to enjoy the sun, while avoiding some of the men in the garrison whom she had a distaste for; although being ex-military, she was dressed far more appropriately for the part, with an

M4 assault rifle slung across her vest while wearing a tactical scarf and a pair of mirrored sunglasses beneath a desert camouflage cap, her glossy black ponytail flowing out from the back.

"If that's their plan," Adrian salivated as he caught another seductive smell of the savoury-seasoned scalloped potatoes and the sweetly-spiced strips and slabs of succulent meat. He swallowed his spit and licked his lips to keep himself from drooling. "It's working. I'm tempted to head out there for dinner instead of going back to the barracks."

"You sure you don't have somewhere else to be after your shift?" she smiled coyly.

Adrian glanced around nervously, making sure that no other guards were within earshot. Devon had caught him one night. Suspicious of his behaviour after their shifts, she had watched him disappear behind the warehouse, where Sadie had coincidentally wandered shortly after. Devon had promised not to tell anyone else, but she would smirk at him every night when he came back to the barracks with the telltale scent of aloe vera after his "evening stroll".

"Security detail, move out!" Captain Thornton's commanding voice boomed from the middle of the estate's grounds.

Adrian had been so busy focusing on the perimeter that he hadn't noticed the guards assembling into a boxed formation in the courtyard below. The sharp-eyed captain marched at the centre of the group, alongside Mr Royce and his family. Also among the detachment was the easy-going Lieutenant Dina Grady, or more commonly known as the human resources department of the barracks whenever Captain Thornton was being particularly harsh on one of the guards. There must have been half the garrison with them, although it made sense, since the sole purpose of their employment was to ensure the safety of the Royce Family.

Adrian and Devon watched from the southeast corner of the ramparts as the procession approached the gates. Sadie's light brown hair caught the sun as she peered around at all of the guards posted along the walls, until her hazel eyes found Adrian's. He gave her a small nod, so as not to draw suspicion, and she returned a timid smile before averting her gaze.

Following her eldest daughter's focus, Mrs Royce studied the pair of guards curiously before the procession passed through the gates.

"You might not want to hear this," Devon said softly in his ear, "But I'll tell you anyway, because I don't want you getting your hopes up... She knows she can't be with you."

Adrian swallowed, and nodded. He had already suspected that it might have been the case. But to hear somebody else saying it out loud and confirming it, the thought didn't hurt any less.

"But hey, enjoy it while it lasts!" she added, clapping him on the shoulder, making him wince as his shirt tugged on his sunburn. "Not everyone gets to know the boss's daughter on a personal level."

Devon lingered for a moment, waiting for him to say something in response. He simply nodded again with a smile, which faded the moment she squeezed his shoulder and resumed her patrol.

Adrian leaned on the parapet as he watched the detachment of guards leaving the estate, marching north towards Linchpin Station. He had never learnt how many other guards were employed by the Royce Family, but he figured that with half the garrison accompanying Mr Royce to visit his business partner in Cloakwater, along with the team who had been assigned to protect Quiggens' Ranch and the armed escort dispatched to Coyote's Rest, there would certainly be some double shifts to be spread across the remaining guards.

It was a necessary evil though, as they would eventually run dry of diesel to power the generators if the deliveries didn't resume soon. They had a sizeable surplus of fuel in the warehouse, since fortunately, Mrs Royce was extremely insistent on stockpiling resources, which would at least guarantee them electricity for a few months longer than anyone else in Rubicross, and the rest of South Tekota, for that matter.

But it was those same fuel reserves that painted a target on the estate. Adrian knew that more and more angry customers, like Haydar, would eventually run out of diesel and come knocking.

If the rest of the settlers and labourers living in the farm belt suddenly stopped working to protest in Rubicross, then diesel wouldn't be the only shortage that they would be facing. They, along with everyone else in South Tekota, would soon be running low on food supplies as well. Fuel was one thing, but food was another. Other people who depended upon the constant supply from the farm belt may not have had the foresight to plan ahead, having learned nothing from the apocalypse.

If and when that day would come, everyone caught outside the walls would be desperate to get inside, and with a half-staffed barracks, Adrian would want more than just a baton in his belt whenever he was out on patrol.

CHAPTER 18 – NATHAN

Their footsteps crunched along the gravel road in the open air, the serene blue sky stretching across the picturesque landscape like a great cerulean canvas. There wasn't much to see in terms of buildings on the north side of Rubicross. Away on the left was the pothole-plagued dirt road that traced a lazy meandering trail through the farm belt towards the prairies and Coyote's Rest, while on the right were the Shield Mountains in the far distance overlooking the settlements of Stillborough and Brimvale. Vast and vacant fields of swaying yellow grass covered everything in between.

They could have easily taken a truck and saved themselves the trouble of sweating in the sun while swatting at the occasional irritating insect, but Nathan preferred to walk. Linchpin Station wasn't all that far away, given that the Royce Family's estate had once served as the nerve centre for storing and distributing building materials along the northern edge of the prairies during the railroad's construction.

Besides, it allowed him to spend a few more minutes surrounded by his family in the sun, something that, despite their abundance of success and leisure time, they rarely engaged in together nowadays. He supposed that with the kids growing up and beginning their own lives, along with the ever-growing barrier that Evelyn had placed between herself and his brother, their family outings would soon join the other treasured memories of the past.

It was a beautiful day for a walk though. A mild breeze rippled through the surrounding swathes of grass, which were abounding with the remaining wildlife that had managed to outlive the apocalypse. Birds of prey soared high above, wheeling and calling, waiting for the procession to pass so that they could swoop down on the unsuspecting rabbits, snakes and lizards in the fields below.

His youngest daughter, Aimee, intermittently sung to herself with a spring in her step, unaware that everyone – including the guards – were listening to her as they marched, keeping them all in high spirits. Nathan didn't recognise the song, but she was always making up new music, refusing to allow her melodious voice and rhythmic talent go to waste on echoing someone else's lyrics.

Ryan, his broad-shouldered son, had insisted on carrying both of the suitcases, while his olive-skinned girlfriend, Zita Ortega, trailed along behind him chatting with Sadie. Jeremy had also decided to join them for the walk, looking pale and scruffy in the midday sun. It was a rarity for him to be awake this early in the day, but it was uplifting to see him spending some father-son time with Jordan before their departure. Evelyn walked by Nathan's side, clutching his hand tightly, still grappling with the idea of letting him go.

In Nathan's opinion, he had been delaying the inevitable trip to the west for far too long, but Evelyn had been successful in imploring him to stay for just one more night, giving her enough time to organise a small farewell dinner. While he would have settled for a quiet meal with just the family, he knew that part of the reason for the extra night was because she was still holding on to the thin hope that Rodney Hamilton's operations in Cloakwater Cliffs had simply experienced a hiccup, and that he would soon send word of when the diesel shipments would resume.

Nathan had argued that Rodney, despite all his eccentricities, was a prudent man, and that he would have sent someone the first time that they had missed their scheduled delivery. It was what he himself would have done if he had been in the same position. But, all the same, he had delayed his departure, if only to make his wife happy.

He had attempted to alleviate Evelyn's apprehension though, bringing fifty guards with them to pack the train, enough to make any roving band of Rauders prowling the prairies think twice before approaching them. Evelyn, despite being a renowned hoarder, had been all too glad to part with nearly half the garrison, and had insisted that he bring more, just in case. Nathan had smiled to himself as he replied that if they brought any more passengers, he would have to catch the next train.

In the months leading up to the railroad's completion after Nathan had taken over the project, one of the workers had coined the name for Linchpin Station due to it being the cornerstone of the planned diesel distribution network, although on a darker undertone, the name had been intended to pay homage to the lynch mob of men and women who had tracked Wallace Pelletier across the prairies.

The thief's grave marked the exact spot where the railroad workers had hauled his dead body out of his would-be getaway car. With neither the strength nor motivation to move him anywhere else, they had unceremoniously dumped him on the ground for the vultures to pick through. After work had resumed on the railroad, the sight of Wallace's headstone growing in the distance as the tracks moved inexorably closer to the site of his death brought the workers a level of satisfaction that could only have been achieved through vigilante justice.

After the railroad was finished, the concrete wall surrounding the station had been built with the intention of ensuring that Wallace's grave would stand sentinel outside the entrance, as a grim reminder of greed's reward. It was only fitting that Wallace kept vigil over the very literal end of the project that he had attempted to abandon.

Nestled against the foot of a sheer sun-bathed cliff wall, Linchpin Station was little more than a brick storeroom attached to a wooden guard tower. Idling in the train yard was one of the two trains that ran along the railroad. Nathan imagined that the other train was sitting stagnant and sidelined on the other end of the tracks in Cloakwater.

Over the course of an average week, empty barrels from various settlements around South Tekota would be sent back to Rubicross and loaded up onto the stationary train while waiting for the next delivery to arrive, so that once Rodney's train crew pulled into the station, they could jump straight onto the next train back to Cloakwater without any unnecessary delays. The arrangement had run like clockwork over the past two years, which was the reason why they had been so concerned when the past two deliveries hadn't been received.

As instructed, the station's attendants had loaded up the last fortnight's collection of empty barrels onto the open-air cargo carriage, as whatever the situation was in Cloakwater, they didn't want to arrive empty-handed.

The sentries in the lookout tower above the station lazily waved down at the approaching procession, but straightened up as soon as they spotted Captain Karl Thornton among the crowd. Their hands whipped up to their foreheads in salute at breakneck speed, almost as if they were trying to give themselves a concussion to demonstrate their dedication to the guard captain.

Having enjoyed the interruption in freight and the subsequent light duties over the past few weeks, the station's attendants on the ground level broke out broomsticks and began brushing the dust off the platform, a task that had conveniently been left until an authority figure could bear witness to all of their hard work and diligence despite the downturn.

Barbed wire fences with spiked barricades stood on either side of the railroad's tracks, extending into the western horizon to ward off any Rauders who would be brazen enough to attempt to sabotage the rails, but still, ever-thorough, Karl barked orders for six members of the detachment to sweep the train and the surrounding area before giving the all-clear for the Royce Family to approach.

Ryan stopped in the shadow of the guard tower, turning with the pair of suitcases and almost taking Sadie out at the knees.

"Bye girls," he said brusquely to his two sisters, to which Aimee stopped singing.

"Is that all you're gonna say?" she glared with one hand on her hip.

Ryan glanced sidelong at Zita, and then at the fifty guards surrounding them, his cheeks beginning to blush. He shrugged.

"Bye Uncle Jeremy," he grinned sheepishly, "Bye Mum."

"Don't think you're getting away without a kiss," Evelyn replied in an accusing tone, her hand slipping out of Nathan's and catching their son mid-turn.

Ryan's red cheeks intensified and his smile widened guiltily, bowing to kiss his mother's cheek, before dropping a suitcase on the ground to shake his uncle's hand and give his sisters a half-hug.

"That's a little better," Aimee brushed her dark blonde hair back over her ear, "I might actually miss you now."

"You're not getting soft on me, are you?" he teased, before turning to Sadie. "See you when we get back."

"See you. Be safe," she replied in a small voice, her shoulders slumped. She gave him a fleeting smile which disappeared the moment he looked back at the idling train.

"Bye Mum," Jordan planted a kiss on Evelyn's cheek before hugging Jeremy, whose eyes kindled as he beamed back at the fine young man his son had grown into.

Decidedly done with any further farewells in the company of the guards, Ryan picked up the other suitcase and boarded the train. Jordan hugged Sadie and Aimee before thumbing the straps on his backpack and following after his cousin.

"You keep those boys out of trouble, okay?" Evelyn told Zita, who smiled and nodded diligently, glad to have been invited along for the journey.

Nathan suspected that it had been his wife's idea for Ryan to have brought his girlfriend. Evelyn wasn't about to let her husband and two boys leave town for a few days without someone that she could trust to keep tabs on them. He wondered how many other people she would have sent if he had chosen to bring Jeremy along as well.

Nathan's head jerked when he realised everyone had turned towards him, all of them watching and waiting expectantly.

"You guys go on ahead," he addressed the guards first, waving them off, "I'll hang back for a while." Apprehensive at the thought of leaving the people whom they had shown up in force to protect, the guards filed towards the train platform, watching from a short distance instead. Nathan turned to

Aimee with a warm smile. "You keep practising that song until I get back. I'd like to hear it when it's finished."

"Who says it isn't ready now?" she gave him a coy grin. He returned her smirk, cradling her in his arms.

"And you take care of your mother, okay?" he asked Sadie, who nodded obediently. She had always been the shyest of their three children, but also the one who seemed to take after him the most. "I'm very proud of you," he added warmly, the same words that would always coax a smile out of him back when he was her age.

It did the trick; he caught a glimpse of her pearly whites as he pulled her into an embrace.

His brother stood awkwardly off to the side, in the shadow of the wooden lookout tower, not wanting to impose. His forehead was slick with sweat.

"You need a drink, you look terrible," Nathan chuckled, his crow's feet crinkling.

Jeremy burst in a fit of nervous laughter before his gaze turned downcast.

"I've cut myself off," he replied, almost apologetically.

"I didn't mean stop altogether," Nathan suddenly felt a pang of sorrow for his brother. At his request to slow down on the drinks, Jeremy had completely cut out one of the few things that still kept him going. "I just meant for you to pace yourself, that's all."

"It's only until you get back," Jeremy swallowed dryly, taking his eyes off the platform and looking back up with brave resolve, "I can manage."

"Well, I appreciate the commitment," Nathan replied, and he was about to leave it at that, but seeing the determination in his brother's eyes reminded him of someone else. "I almost forgot to mention!" he exclaimed, "If Dess Sheridan gets back from Coyote's Rest before I come back from Cloakwater, make sure she stays in town for a while. I've got business with her, and I really don't feel like going on a day trip to Stillborough straight after this."

"I'll take care of it," Jeremy nodded, wiping the sheen of sweat off his forehead with the back of a clammy hand. "And I promise I'll – I'm going to try my best to make sure that when you get back, the place will be exactly as you left it."

"Don't try too hard," Nathan winked at him, "Business is boring without a bit of change."

He shook his brother's sweaty hand and clasped his arm before turning to his wife, who had been waiting patiently. Her shoulders stiff and rigid, Evelyn looked as equally nervous as Jeremy. Even now, she was reliving the nightmare of the last time that Nathan had left "for just a few days". Her eyes were welling with tears as he drew near, but he knew that she wouldn't cry in front of the girls.

"Everything's going to be alright," he reassured her, holding her close enough to feel her shuddered breathing, speaking softly into her hair as she wiped her eyes on his shirt. "There's nothing to be scared of. We've come a long way from our all-or-nothing days. I'm going to meet Rodney, ask him what the hold-up is, and then we'll come home with a train full of diesel. Failing that, we'll come home with Plan B."

She pulled away from him, her cheeks wet as she stared up into his cheerful green eyes.

"You never have a Plan B," she sniffed, fussing over the creases in his shirt. "Just make sure you come home."

"I promise," he replied, before leaning in to plant a kiss on her lips long enough to make Aimee mock a dry-heave.

They parted, his wife's brown eyes crinkling as they laughed together. Nathan savoured the sight of her smile before turning to approach the crowd of guards on the platform.

The train's engine hissed and clanked as it rumbled to life, and a pair of engineers exited the driver's carriage to conduct their final checks. It was typically a day-and-a-half's journey to Cloakwater Cliffs via train, so the two drivers would need to work in shifts. Neither of them had ever driven along the railroad before. They had received the same training as the crew from Cloakwater, but they were only ever intended to be the back-up drivers in case something ever went wrong, and although the current situation certainly called for an emergency, they took their time looking over the checklist on their clipboard just to be sure.

Karl waited by the entrance of the passenger carriage with Lieutenant

Dina Grady, a curvy yet toned dark woman, a former officer of the Army Reserves and his most trusted subordinate to lead the guard detachment in his absence. Evelyn had asked that Karl go with them instead, but Nathan had been inflexible when he insisted that the guard captain should stay behind to watch over his family.

"I want you all to remember that you are not going on a vacation," Karl called out to the assembled guards, his commanding voice echoing as it collided against the cliff wall. "Until you get back to base, there is no downtime, for anyone. You will remain vigilant at all times, even while you sleep. You will not dream unless ordered to do so by the lieutenant. Clear?"

"Sir, yes, sir!"

"Clear?"

"Sir, yes, sir!"

The pair of engineers exchanged a concerned expression, wondering if the captain's speech also applied to them.

"Over to you," Karl nodded at Lieutenant Grady. "Good luck, soldier."

Dina saluted Karl, before turning to Nathan.

"After you, sir," she gestured towards the train's doors.

For a moment, Nathan was dumbfounded by the formal ceremony of the occasion, feeling half a soldier himself over a simple train ride, until he realised that fifty people were waiting for him to board the carriage.

He grinned sheepishly and stepped inside. The air was relatively cool compared to the warm breeze of the prairies. The doors into the passenger cabin were already open. With two seats on either side of the aisle and shelves for hand luggage above, this section of the train had been designed to cater for an emergency evacuation, if something ever were to happen to the settlements on either side of the railroad.

Nathan had always thought of the inclusion as more of a benefit for Cloakwater, since the inhabitants of Rubicross would just make a beeline for Brimvale if they couldn't hold the town against an attack, but Rodney's engineers had been in charge of building the trains while the railroad was under construction. Perhaps Rodney's true intention was to add the option of being able to call on Rubicross for a garrison of guards if evacuating

Cloakwater wouldn't have been possible.

Nathan smiled to himself at yet another reminder of just how crafty the old codger was.

Lieutenant Grady stepped in behind him, and Nathan strode the length of the passenger cabin, towards the second pair of open doors at the other end of the carriage, leading to the private compartments.

"I want eyes looking out of every window," the lieutenant railed off orders to the guards as they shuffled onto the train, "Even if that means you're staring at the cliff wall all the way to Cloakwater. If *anything* looks suspicious, I wanna know about it."

Naturally, there was a mad rush for the seats that offered a view of something other than the cliff wall.

There were two VIP compartments on either side of the corridor which led towards the dining carriage. Granted, the best cabins weren't necessarily located in the best position, since the guards would be marching back and forth through the corridor as they went to and from the dining carriage during each meal service, but it sure beat being stuck next to the train's engine.

Nathan passed by the first set of VIP cabins, hearing Ryan and Zita talking on the left, and Jordan unzipping his backpack on the right. He found his battle-scarred brown leather suitcase waiting for him inside the second compartment on the left, lying flat on top of a wooden bench.

He stooped to catch hold of a pair of salvaged car seatbelts dangling from either side of the bench. Strapping his suitcase in securely, he sat down on the cracked leather chair screwed into the wall next to the window, opposite a neatly-made small bed. Almost like a cheap motel on wheels, it wasn't the most luxurious of accommodations, but on this side of the apocalypse, it was the best way to travel.

Nathan looked out the window at his family gathered on the train platform. Evelyn stood between their two daughters, clutching Sadie's arm. Aimee, who had kept everyone's spirits uplifted with her meandering melodies during the march, was now crestfallen. For a moment, he didn't want to leave. He wanted to take his suitcase and walk back to Rubicross with his family. They could wait for Dina to come back with a report. But it was too late, the brakes had already been released, the engine was whirring, and the train was moving.

The rails groaned under the tonnes of weight shifting over them, plumes of black smoke shot up into the air as they left the station, and the wheels' steady clacking over the tracks were slowly building a rhythm. Jeremy was the first to wave, still in the shadow of the guard tower. Nathan held his hand up to the glass, watching his three girls shrink in the distance, the view of the platform soon replaced by the swaying yellow grass of the prairies.

A light rap came from behind, and he turned around, realising that he had left his door open.

"Sir," Dina stood at the entrance with the ingrained posture of someone who had served at least a decade in the military, "I'll be in the opposite compartment if you need me."

"Thank you, Dina," Nathan stood up to slide the door shut as she about-faced and strode into her room.

He looked around at his plain compartment, although there was nothing of interest. *Should have packed a book*, he chided himself in hindsight. He knew that he had forgotten something. Touch-screen entertainment during an extended travel was certainly a thing of the past. He would have to borrow a novel from Rodney on their way back.

Sighing as he scratched the bristles on his cheek, Nathan considered sitting in the leather chair to gaze out the window again, but he knew that watching the world fly backwards would soon make him feel queasy. He kicked off his shoes and lay back on the bed instead.

Closing his eyes, he wondered what troubles awaited them at Cloakwater Cliffs. He ran through hypothetical scenarios in his mind. Considering the rumours of the Rauders' return, and Millie Quiggens's claim of the entire population of Torzal Arroyo going missing overnight, he couldn't rule out the possibility of Cloakwater being under siege.

Rodney's people might not have had enough time to reach the train station, especially if the Rauders had attacked from the north, so their best chance of survival would have been to shelter inside Hamilton's Lair,

Rodney's underground bunker, and simply ride out the storm. If the people of Cloakwater were being held captive in their own town, a strike force of fifty armed guards would certainly make a difference.

Another possibility was Evelyn's idea that Rodney had decided to stockpile his diesel production, choosing to build up his own reserves in preparation for his oil tanker's completion. The vessel had been Rodney's pipe dream, which would enable him to scour the coast for other survivors and settlements, and perhaps even some semblance of a government while he was at it.

Nathan had never seen the work in progress, but during Rodney's last visit to Rubicross, the old industry warhorse had assured him that it was under way.

"I've got the eggheads doing the legwork," referring to Rodney's crew of engineers, the same engineers who had pieced together his trains from a combination of abandoned vehicles and freshly-smelted ore from the Tuskiron Mountains.

If it was true that Rodney was stockpiling his diesel, the halt of supply would only be temporary, as no matter how big the oil tanker was, it could only hold so much. Nathan still doubted that this could have been the reason for the disruption though. Any business partner worthy of a business partnership wouldn't just cut operations after two years without some form of prior notification. Granted, Rodney was a strange old man, but he still knew how to run his business.

Who knows? Nathan thought to himself. *Maybe the train in Cloakwater just ran into some engine troubles, and they've been waiting for us to come this whole time.*

Just as he was settling down comfortably at the idea, the most dreaded possibility flew unbidden into his mind. *What if Rodney's found another buyer?* Diesel was liquid gold prior to the apocalypse, and now, even more so. Nathan would need to be prepared to negotiate. There was no telling what prices people would be willing to pay, if indeed Rodney had found some other settlements to trade with.

Even in Rubicross, after the Royces had chosen to stockpile their own supply, some of the other well-stocked merchants in town – like Laszlo Snyder – were quick to fill the initial unmet demand for diesel, selling a portion of their own reserves at grossly-inflated prices. They had claimed that it was only to curb any chances of civil unrest, but Nathan knew that they were just jumping on the opportunity to price gouge the vulnerable communities who had been left without juice for their generators to light up the darkness.

Even Bruce Mallory hadn't hesitated to climb aboard the bandwagon, turning a nice profit on his family's stockpile of fuel. Nathan had expected better of the Mallory Family, but Bruce had always been quick to take advantage of any opportunity, regardless of its morality. Although, had he been in Bruce's position, Nathan didn't doubt that he would have done exactly the same thing.

Despite the other merchants' best efforts to undermine the Royce Family's control over the supply of diesel, the civil unrest had still come knocking. Admittedly, it was only Haydar crashing his pickup truck into the concrete wall of the estate, but his drunken tirade had been fuelled by his desire for diesel.

Nathan silently hoped that Haydar would be the only instance of angry customers that they would encounter. Jeremy was more than capable of handling a single drunken man, especially if – and he supposed that it wouldn't be a bad thing in this case – they drank enough together to slur the same language. Perhaps dealing with Haydar first would be a great stepping stone for Jeremy to transition into taking charge while Nathan was away.

* * *

With all of the thoughts running through his mind, Nathan felt as though he had only settled down to rest for no longer than a few minutes, but when he opened his eyes again, darkness had already fallen outside.

He stood and stretched, setting off a chain reaction of crackles and pops from his stiff joints. The black night sky was studded with stars steadily making their way across the window, shedding light on the dark contours of the land. He strained his eyes, searching the rushing terrain outside for a landmark or a settlement to indicate how far they had travelled, but the silhouettes of the few isolated structures that he laid eyes upon were unlit, by torchlight or candlelight.

His first assumption was that they were the abandoned hovels that came and went as the railroad's construction crew had passed through, although with the diesel shortage, the inhabitants may have simply just run out of fuel to burn at night.

Nathan slid his door open and lumbered out into the corridor, hearing the clink of silverware in the dining carriage as he lurched against the train's speed. Through the pair of doors to his left, he could see Ryan and Jordan leaning on the bar, sizing up a bottle of bourbon as Zita watched the pair of boys with pursed lips from a table at the front end of the carriage. A dozen guards sat in booths, shovelling food into their mouths as they stared out into the night.

Dina's door slid open on the other side of the corridor, and the lieutenant stepped out into the passage. Nathan felt as though she had been waiting for him to wake up, or more likely, she had heard his joints popping from her compartment.

"Sir, fancy a late night snack?" she asked him, her brown eyes determined not to stray towards the food on offer as a chef checked the buffet's bain-maries.

"Please, call me Nathan," he smiled, still unsure of how long he had slept. "Care to join me?"

She returned his smile and politely gestured for him to lead the way. He opened the doors to the dining carriage, his hunger hitting him the moment the first whiff of fried fish, sautéed vegetables, roasted pork and stewed minced beef wafted towards them.

He had barely taken one step into the carriage when static crackled from the speaker system overhead, punctuated by heavy breathing.

"BRACE FOR IMPACT!!"

CHAPTER 19 – BRISTOL

Bristol Hudson's white and pink sneakers squeaked across the marble floor as she walked through the echoing foyer of the town hall, carrying her empty coffee mug in one hand and hugging a stack of notes with the other. While her footwear didn't exactly match the formality of her grey pinstripe slacks and white three-quarter-sleeve blouse, her morning meeting had required a pair of shoes with reliable grip.

Just as she was sizing up the office's frosted glass entrance, a silhouette appeared behind it, turning the handle. Saved from the trouble of juggling her bundle, her sigh of relief soon became a frightened gasp as the door flew open, arcing in a swift semicircle to crash into the adjacent wall, spraying shards and bouncing the metal door frame back into the jamb's latch.

Her notes dropped from the crook of her elbow as her hand shot up to shield her face from the explosion of glass. Peeking through her fingers, she watched as Bronson Hopper stepped through what remained of the door where the opaque glass panel had once been, his shoes crunching over the frosted crystals scattered across the marble floor.

"Whole place is falling apart," Bronson laughed aloud, his handsome face twisted with callous contempt.

Pedro Pinto hunched through the door's metal frame behind him, the lanky late teen giggling, although his eyes widened when he saw Bristol frozen in the lobby. His smile waned as he stooped to help gather up her notes. She accepted the stack of pages with a trembling hand.

"Bye Bristol," Pedro muttered, almost apologetically. He lingered a moment, wanting to say more, but he thought against it, starting after Bronson towards the exit instead.

Ollie Geary appeared at the shattered entrance next, opening the door slowly and sweeping the glass shards aside with the bottom of the metal frame. He kicked the remaining fragments down the hall.

"Hate to leave you here with that psycho," he jerked his head back at the office, the fringe of his parted brown hair swishing sideways across his forehead. "But we're outta here. Maybe see you around."

"I don't understand," Bristol replied, finally breathing air back into her lungs, "What happened?"

"Probably she'll tell you whatever she wants you to hear," Ollie shrugged, holding the door open for Bristol.

She stepped through the doorway onto the grey carpet uncertainly, seeing Lora Purcell pacing behind her corner office's glass walls, her newly-dyed blonde hair contrasted against her flustered red cheeks. Bristol turned back to Ollie, hoping for an explanation, but he was already halfway down the hall, the broken door slowly swinging shut between them.

Bristol cautiously advanced through the workplace, passing by Shelton and Liam, neither of whom would offer her an explanation either. Shelton Turner was working away behind his computer with his headphones on, nodding his head to music that he had downloaded well before the internet had shut down. Liam Caldwell, on the other hand, was swivelled around in his chair with his arms folded, watching indifferently as Lora hyperventilated, fanning her face with her hands and looking as though she was on the brink of a breakdown.

Bristol set down her notes and empty mug on a filing cabinet nearby, her eyes on Lora as she reached for the private office's door handle, but instead, her fingertips brushed against twisted metal, the broken handle discarded on the floor a few feet away.

She knocked softly on the glass, snapping Lora out of her agitated state. Lora looked up from her pacing and heaved a deep breath to recompose herself. She opened the door without a greeting and trudged back behind her desk, slumping in her chair.

"Hey, you okay?" asked Bristol, bracing herself for a flare-up.

Lora looked up at her with a resigned expression, but before she could reply, something behind Bristol caught her attention.

"Where the fuck does he think *he's* going!?" Lora squealed, staring daggers through the open blinds of her office's internal window. "We was *supposed* to be leaving for Rookson City this afternoon, and he's just gonna abandon us too?"

Bristol turned back to see Liam leaving the office, with Shelton sliding his headphones off one ear and looking around at all of the empty desks, equally bemused and just as new as Bristol was to the workplace. She closed the door swiftly yet softly, recognising the need for privacy from the rest of the staff. Thankfully, it was lunch hour, so only a few of their colleagues remained as she scanned each of them through the internal office's windows, trying to piece together what had happened.

Abhilash Shandar sipped water behind his desk in his own office, slouching bow-legged in his chair with an entertained expression, as if he was watching a live soap opera unfold. He noticed her gaze and spilled his water down his black shirt, mustering up an awkward wave of his excessive golden rings and pausing to consider whether he should clean himself up in the bathroom. He chose to stay at his desk and dab at the stain with a handkerchief instead, not wanting to miss the show.

Dwight Jaskolski emerged from the break room corridor, the tall blonde passing by Lora's corner office without so much as a glance. He sat down at his desk and resumed working like nothing had ever happened. Shelton soon followed Dwight's lead, simply shrugging at the whole ordeal and slipping his headphones back on.

Bristol sat down opposite Lora, whose face was now buried in her hands. She had dyed her hair blonde last week – "for a change", she had claimed – although Bristol couldn't help but notice how similar the colour was to her own. She had thought to ask Lora where she had managed to find hair dye after the apocalypse, but she had been afraid that her question might cause offence.

"Maybe he's just going out for lunch," Bristol said gently, trying to sound reassuring.

Lora exhaled heavily, staring down at her desk as she massaged her temples with her thumbs.

"He wants to be part of the *boys' club* and quit with the other three?" Lora asked before snorting scornfully at her own question. "Let him. It doesn't matter anyway. It's not like we *actually* needed him to come with us to Rookson. He was just meant to tag along so that he could learn how to do my previous role. It would've been nice if he said something *before* he decided to abandon us though… Two years of working together and he doesn't even have the *decency* to say goodbye. I seriously feel sooo betrayed right now!"

Bristol sat listening, thinking of how best to ask what had happened, but she decided to hold her silence instead. She hadn't known Lora for very long, but it had been long enough to know that she would vent about it in her own time.

"Ughhhh… I feel like I'm gonna have a migraine," Lora complained, her face emerging from behind her hands, gazing at Bristol before getting to her feet and opening the door. "Can you come with me? I haven't had lunch yet."

The question was more of a demand than an invitation, but Bristol followed her lead all the same. She, herself, hadn't eaten her lunch today either. In fact, she hadn't eaten anything at all, unless a cup of coffee counted as breakfast.

Lora turned and reached for the handle to shut the door behind them, only for her fingers to scrabble at the twisted metal instead.

"MOTHERFUCKER!!" she screamed, seething at the broken door handle on the carpet.

Dwight straightened up in his chair at the outburst, although with practised restraint, his eyes didn't leave his screen. Shelton stopped typing at his keyboard, his furtive glance over his shoulder suggesting that his music hadn't been loud enough. Abhilash shifted his attention back to the pair of young women, greedily sipping his water, ready for Act Two of the live soap opera.

"Come on, let's go," Bristol urged, quickly ushering Lora out of the office before she could damage her workplace reputation any further.

Fresh air seemed to do Lora some good, her bright red cheeks fading as they walked between the manicured gardens that bordered the whitewashed concrete plaza.

"I can't believe they would just vandalise government property like that," Lora said aloud, "I bet they only done it because they know we're short on guards at the moment. Everyone else is too busy doing their jobs and watching the walls to worry about what's *actually* happening inside Brimvale. I can't wait to tell Teddie later though, they're not gonna get away with it." She gasped excitedly, turning to Bristol. "Oh my gosh, how funny would it be if they got arrested?"

Bristol chose not to comment, but she had found a way to prompt her indirectly.

"Why were they breaking the doors?" she asked unobtrusively. "I don't understand."

"Honestly… neither do I," Lora replied, narrowing her eyes and shaking her head. "The three of them have been so fucking petty ever since I got my promotion, but Bronson has been the absolute worst. Like, yesterday, I don't think you was there, but I asked him to do the *tiniest* thing for me, and he started complaining. And it wasn't even that hard, like, I would've done it myself, but I've just been so *busy* lately."

"What was it?" Bristol asked, still treading lightly.

"Ugh, it doesn't matter," Lora breathed exasperatedly. "The point is, when your senior asks you to do something, you do it, yeah? And there he was just bitching and moaning that it wasn't his responsibility. Like, hello? This is why you're employed? To do the tasks that get delegated to you. I don't think any of them ever really seemed to understand that. Like, actually doing the job that they was hired to do was beyond their comprehension. Come to think about it, I'm actually *glad* they're gone. Now everyone will be able to get some work done without them interrupting all the time."

"So, what happened yesterday, that's why they left today?" Bristol asked, trying to coax some more information out of her.

Lora glanced at her bewilderedly as if Bristol had just asked her to repeat herself.

"Nooo, today was something *else*," she huffed, as if there was an ongoing list that she had been keeping. "Today, Bronson admitted to defacing government property, and when I asked him to clean up his mess, that's when he threw his little temper tantrum. The other two left because they're like, best friends or whatever. The three of them joined together, and now they can be unemployed together. I really hope they get arrested for their outright vandalism, because then they can share a jail cell together for all I care," she laughed maliciously as they crossed the wide empty street to The Artisan's Roast Cafe.

Bristol's stomach turned. For the brief time that she had worked in the Mayor's Office, it seemed to her that Lora was much closer to the three boys who had just left, engaging with them far more often throughout each day than what she did with Dwight, Shelton and Liam. The idea of her taking pleasure at the thought of misfortunes that might await her former colleagues made Bristol regret accepting the lunch invitation, even with as little choice as she had been given in the matter.

They entered the style-conflicted cafe, which sported a homely library theme on the left, with community-sourced books packing the shelves lining the walls. They had a "leave one, take one" policy on novels with each order, but it wasn't difficult to imagine an avid reader settling into one of the form-hugging beanbags or a deeply-cushioned chair, ordering a new hot beverage to accompany every new chapter on a continuous loop, until they had travelled the world of an entire story from cover to cover.

The other side of The Artisan's Roast was furnished with trendy black business sofas arranged in private meeting areas, along with evenly spaced wood-grain tables and chairs. The cafe clearly catered towards two crowds of customers; an ordered section for those busy people to whom time was always short, juxtaposed against a laid-back refuge for those who knew that life was too short to be busy.

As the soothing aroma of roasted Guadasula beans filled her nostrils,

Bristol instantly realised that she had left her coffee mug back in the office, remembering that the era of throwaway cups was long gone.

She began to feel out of place. In a conversation, she could delay an answer by taking a sip. She could hide behind her cup if she felt that her facial expressions might betray her true feelings. And, if nothing else, she could wrap her hands around the mug and draw serenity from its warmth. In a way, her coffee mug was her security blanket, and now she was caught in an uncomfortable situation without it.

Hayley, the barista, greeted them pleasantly, and by name; the staff of the Mayor's Office made up the majority of the cafe's customers, and so it was management's policy to ensure that they were well looked after. Although, since the coffee shop was one of the few in South Tekota that still remained open for business, they would have no trouble keeping customers, but the extra mile towards client satisfaction was always a welcome experience.

Lora ordered a creamy tuna melt sandwich from the display case and searched among the black business sofas, pondering which one would offer the best vantage point of the town hall. Hayley laid a hand on the back of the display case, smiling patiently as Bristol made up her mind.

"I might just grab a quick bite to eat," Bristol swallowed, her mind racing for an excuse to leave as she pointed out a ham and cheese sandwich, "I umm – oh, toasted please – I dropped my notes in the hall earlier, and I want to make sure they're all in order before this afternoon's meeting."

"Oooh, good thinking!" Lora exclaimed from the window before addressing Hayley, "Can I get mine to-go as well?" She smirked as she turned back to Bristol, "I wanna see Teddie's reaction when he gets off lunch and sees what the boys done to the office. I can't *wait* to hear what the other seniors say when they find out four staff members quit on the same day!"

Bristol furrowed her eyebrows slightly. Something wasn't adding up. She hadn't picked Liam for the social type, especially not to the extent that he would quit in solidarity just to follow a trend.

"Was Liam close to the other three boys?" she asked, watching Hayley fumble as she loaded the ham and cheese sandwich into the toaster. "I mean,

I wasn't there for the whole thing, but it seemed to me that he must have hesitated before he left the office, otherwise he would have left at the same time, right?"

"Who knows what he was thinking?" Lora shrugged, her satisfied smirk vanishing. "He's too quiet. Him *and* Dwight. If either of them two was ever that close to the other three, they sure didn't act like it whenever I was around. But if he really decided to quit, which I'm sure he did, I guess we can't blame him if he doesn't know what's best for his own good. I'm just angry at myself that I recommended him to take my old position in the first place. And I only done that because I felt *sorry* for him. I thought it would bring him out of his shell, but clearly it didn't, and clearly he isn't very grateful for everything I done for him."

Hayley shot Lora a reproachful glance as she served up their takeaway lunches on scraps of brown paper towel, which thankfully hadn't yet become a thing of the past. Plastic and polystyrene containers though, were remnants of the single-use civilisation, which ironically would live on long after the survivors of the apocalypse met their inevitable ends.

"Thank youuu," Lora smiled sweetly as she handed over enough golden bucks to cover both meals.

"Oh, you don't have to," Bristol blushed, pulling out her own gilded plastic chips.

"It's fiiine, hun, seriously, don't worry about it," Lora replied, pushing her stack of golden bucks towards Hayley insistently. "First round's on you when I get back from Rookson City though!"

Bristol smiled in polite agreement, stowing her money away before realising that she was now obligated to spend even more time with Lora outside of work. Hoping to avoid any further conversation on the topic of their ex-colleagues, she was grateful that Lora had decided to hurry back to the office in eager anticipation of the senior officers' reactions when they would return from their lunch break.

They entered the marble foyer to find one of the guards, Wilson, standing in as a janitor as he methodically swept the frosted glass fragments into a dustpan under Rhonda Moore's watchful eye, who stood with both hands on her hips, scanning the floor for any stray shards. She turned at the sound of their approaching footsteps.

"Young ladies," she began in a stern tone, "Would you mind explaining why security was not sent for immediately after this occurred?"

"It was Bronson," Lora replied quickly, as the office's air conditioning breathed through the gaping hole in the door, "But he was leaving the building, so I thought..." her voice trailed off under Rhonda's raised eyebrow.

"You thought...?" Rhonda prompted, waiting for Lora to finish her sentence. After a few long moments of silence, the senior officer completed it for her, "You *thought* that the threat was gone, so you *thought* that there was no need for security?" she surmised. Lora nodded apprehensively. "And if he had come back with a weapon, what would you have *thought* then?"

Lora seemed to shrink under her glare.

"I'm sorry," flecks of tuna melt sandwich flew from Lora's mouth, which Wilson quickly swept up into his dustpan. "I didn't know what to do. That's the first time I've ever seen something like this happen."

"That's precisely why we have standard operating procedures," Rhonda replied, relentless, "So that you know how to respond to any situation, regardless of whether it's your first time or your hundredth time. If you want to earn your place among the other senior officers, I would suggest that you familiarise yourself with them."

"Abhilash was here as well," Bristol blurted out. Lora shifted uneasily, but with a sigh of relief as Rhonda turned her fierce gaze. Feeling as though she had been caught in the harsh glare of twin spotlights, Bristol immediately regretted having said anything, although there was no other choice now but to continue. "He would have known the standard operating procedures, right?"

"Never rely on others to do your job for you," Rhonda frowned before addressing them both. "If you can't handle the responsibilities of the position that has been given to you, then you don't belong in your position. I expect you both have some work to do."

Rhonda turned to resume supervising Wilson's efforts, kicking a glass crystal in the direction of the dustpan as it caught the light. Bristol and Lora exchanged a sheepish glance. They turned to head back inside the office when Teddie and Uncle Quentin bustled up the steps outside. Teddie was flushed – or at least the small portion of his face that was visible – and breathing heavily from his brisk pace. Lora seethed at the sight of Liam flanked by the Mayor's guards, Harriet and Butch, as they followed the pair of officials into the foyer.

"Head on in, girls," Teddie wheezed, bending forward slightly with one hand tenderly massaging a stitch in his stout side, his bushy beard bristling as he breathed air back into his lungs. "Thanks, Rhonda," he added, straightening up as Bristol pulled the shattered door frame open. "Lora, I'd like a private chat with you in my office. Bring your lunch with you."

"Of course! What's this about?" she asked, shooting a backwards glare over her shoulder at Liam as he lingered in the hall with the pair of senior officers and the three guards, wondering how much he had told them.

Bristol silently went back to the filing cabinet where she had left her stack of notes and coffee mug, pretending to rifle through the papers as she chewed her sandwich. Abhilash was leaning over the water cooler, but he stood up as Teddie and Lora passed by. Bristol furrowed her eyebrows with distaste as he stared after them, probably hoping to catch some snippet of conversation to add to his day-time drama.

Then, unexpectedly, he spoke up.

"Teddie," Abhilash called before they could round the corner, "If you're planning to ask Lora about those three bedfellows who all left today, I vwas here for the whole ting." Teddie stopped and turned to listen, with Lora sneaking another bite of her tuna melt as Abhilash continued, "Bronson vwas surely out of line. He had made graffiti in Lora's office, and refused to clean it, even vwhen Lora vwas vwilling to accept his apology. The other two chose to quit along vwit him." He grinned, soaking up the attention and glancing back at Bristol, making sure that she was a witness to his glory. "But, I had alvways tought they needed to be fired anyvway; they vwere notting but a nuisance for everyone here. If you need some reliable replacements, I know of a few suitable candidates in the market who all vwould be ready and vwilling to join us."

Teddie looked to Lora, who confirmed Abhilash's testimony with a solemn nod. The Mayor heaved an audible sigh of relief, having been spared the trouble of grilling her in his office. He brushed his bushy beard and turned back to Abhilash.

"Okay," Teddie clapped his hands together, "Let's reach out to those people and arrange a few interviews. In the meantime, let's have the drivers load up their own mail and parcels to be dropped off along their bus routes."

With a jingle of his golden jewellery, Abhilash bobbled his head from side to side and tottered back to his own office in triumph, probably fancying himself a hero who had saved the day. Bristol took another bite of her lunch, looking back at her stack of papers. As she chewed, she pondered what kind of graffiti Bronson could have left in Lora's office, as she couldn't recall seeing anything that might have been out of place.

Her musings were short-lived though, as a pair of sneakers appeared on the carpet next to her own by the filing cabinet. She looked up to see Teddie smiling at her through his grey-streaked beard. She would have returned the smile if her mouth hadn't been full of bread, ham and cheese.

"Welcome back, I hope your morning meeting went well!" he said cheerily. "I see we've got a lot of ground to cover," he gestured towards her notes.

"Yes," Bristol nodded, covering her mouth and gulping her food down so that she could reply. "They had a number of things they wanted to bring to your attention. I'll just cover the important points today, and we'll work through the rest during the week."

"Sounds like a plan! How much time do you need?" he asked, glancing at her sandwich. "Quentin and the others should probably be getting on the road soon."

She considered her half-eaten lunch. She had already skipped her breakfast in order to catch the bus on time for her morning meeting in Sunken City.

"I'm ready now," she lied, resolving to wrap up what was left of the sandwich in the brown paper towel, her stomach rumbling in protest as she dusted crumbs from her fingers. She didn't want to hold up the rest of the team; her meeting would be far less pivotal than theirs in Rookson City.

Teddie nodded his understanding, looking at her with a mixture of appreciation and sympathy behind his black-rimmed glasses, before calling the other seniors over to the boardroom. Lora, Rhonda, Abhilash and Uncle Quentin filed in after them.

Bristol quickly scanned through her handwritten pages as the others picked out their preferred conference chairs around the big rectangular table. She had already highlighted the key items for discussion, so contrary to what she had told Lora, the order of her notes had no actual bearing on the briefing.

"Thank you all for your time today," she began, looking around the room. It wasn't her first time presenting to a group in a formal setting, but the butterflies fluttered around in her empty stomach all the same. She was speaking on behalf of her entire community now. She drew confidence from her uncle's patient gaze, and took a deep breath. "Perry Wisniewski from Sunken City wanted me to pass along his gratitude to the good Mayor for giving them a voice in shaping the future of Brimvale. He looks forward to working together closely for our mutual benefit."

Teddie nodded his approval, the faint glint of a warm smile shining through his beard.

"Well," he said, charmed by the praise, but remaining modest, "We give our thanks to Perry too, for his cooperation, and to you especially, for agreeing to be the liaison between our two communities."

"There will be a common theme to all of the items on today's agenda," Bristol continued, pushing past any further formalities, conscious of the time. "Their most immediate concerns are based largely around the recent diesel shortage from Rubicross."

She made a point of referring to the concerns as "their" concerns, as her uncle had advised her not to think of Sunken City as the sole place that she was representing now, but rather, she was representing Brimvale while she was in Brimvale, and Sunken City while she was in Sunken City. His reason had been that it made people care more when she collectively included those who she was presenting to, rather than letting her language convey which side she was taking.

"Yes, yes," Abhilash waved his golden bangles dismissively. "Everyone is feeling the effects of the diesel shortage. They are not the only ones who all are dealing vwit this problem."

Uncle Quentin glared at him across the table for speaking out of turn.

"It's true," Bristol agreed, tactfully stroking his ego, "Many communities are struggling for diesel. But much of Sunken City's economy relies on having fuel to offer their trading partners. Without it, we're going to experience more shortages than just diesel."

"What if we gave them a loan of golden bucks?" asked Lora. She savoured the spotlight as everyone turned to listen to her proposal. Straightening up in her chair, she continued, "They could use the golden bucks to continue buying whatever they're buying from their trading partners, and when the diesel starts flowing again, we recover the debt *and* collect interest on top."

"That might work," Rhonda replied in an unmoved tone, "If the Sovereign Rapture's fisher folk and the merchant boats from Guadasula could use golden bucks to run their engines."

"What are the main commodities Sunken City imports again?" asked Teddie, scratching his beard.

"Mainly large fish and coffee beans," Bristol answered, hoping that at least one of them shared her enthusiasm for good coffee. "Sunken City has their own fishing traps, but it's only enough to sustain their community. The catchment areas were never designed to generate an excess supply for the rest of Brimvale, out of fear of overtaxing the natural ecosystem."

"We'll survive without fish and coffee," said Uncle Quentin, to her disguised dismay. "Plenty of food in the farm belt. Sunken City can provide for themselves," he shrugged at the others before turning to Bristol. "The diesel shortage is only a problem for The Rapture and Guadasula, not for us. If either of them were smart, they would have stockpiled their fuel, like everyone else. It's up to them whether they want to accept another form of payment. They can always take the golden bucks for now and use it to buy diesel when it's available again."

Bristol swallowed at the thought of struggling through another coffee shortage.

"I agree, to an extent," she replied. Her uncle raised an eyebrow, and she had to look away as she explained, "Most of us won't feel the effect of a decline in fish and coffee. These are luxuries that we don't necessarily *need* to survive. But Perry isn't as concerned about the impact on commodities as he is about the impact on communities. Having dealt with the inhabitants of the Sovereign Rapture for the past few years, I *know* they'll be too stubborn to accept anything other than fuel. Perry stated that they might turn to trading with the pirates if they have no other choice."

"I know Murray Rankin's stubborn," Teddie combed his fingers through his beard, remembering his time aboard the cruise ship anchored in Bellevue Bay. "But he wouldn't be *that* desperate, would he?"

"I say, let them," said Abhilash, leaning back with his hands clasped behind his head. "Vwhat's the vworst that vwould happen? The pirates get some fish?"

"The pirates don't need to trade for anything," Rhonda replied realistically, leaning forward with one elbow on the table. "If they want something, they'll take it by force. If the people aboard The Rapture are foolish enough to believe that a bunch of escaped prisoners would supply them with fuel just so that they can continue to live freely on their floating paradise, they're in for a rude awakening. Anyone who could afford to be on a luxury cruise ship prior to the apocalypse would have *something* valuable hidden away. The pirates would know that, or they would be quick to believe it, and The Rapture would be allowing those criminals to sail in on a Trojan seahorse."

There was an audible silence in the room. Lora seemed as though she had a question forming on her lips, but she would not dare to risk being rebuffed a second time.

Rhonda completed the thought for them all.

"It's not just about trading fish for fuel," she explained, turning to Abhilash. "The Rapture is the high ground in Bellevue Bay. The strategic position that it offers would leave Sunken City vulnerable to long-range assaults. And if Sunken City falls, there's nothing to stop the pirates from moving inland."

Each of them stared around the room, knowing that it was true. Axemark Ravine and the Shield Mountains served as natural defences to raids from the west and the north, while guards patrolled the Burnshaw Barricade which separated Brimvale from Bushrock Flats to the south. The coast however, was wide open, with only the people of Sunken City standing sentinel against the sea.

Bristol's shoulders relaxed in light of Rhonda's insight. Only now, did any of them realise just how vital a part the coastal community played in maintaining Brimvale's security.

"While we're on the subject of an attack," Bristol broke through the silence, seeing her chance to capitalise on their newfound concern, "Without diesel to power their generators, Sunken City's sentries won't be able to spot anything at night."

"It would be an open invitation to a raid," Rhonda nodded.

"What if we gave them a supply of diesel?" asked Lora, chancing another proposal. Teddie and Uncle Quentin exchanged a glance. "Not much," she added quickly, "But just enough for them to run their generators."

"Not an option," Uncle Quentin said bluntly, Lora's eyes turning downcast. He almost didn't elaborate, but remembering that his niece was in the same room, he explained, "If we say that we want them to use the fuel to watch the coast for us, they could extort us in exchange for the protection they're providing. If we don't specify what they should use the fuel for, they'll use it to trade. If we give them enough to do both, we won't have enough reserves left to keep our own lights on at night, mobilise our troops if an attack does come, *and* still have enough barrels left over to buy ammo from Rookson."

Teddie sighed in reluctant agreement. They had no choice but to stay the course with trading a portion of their diesel reserves for Rookson City's ammunition. With reports of Rubicross beginning to run dry of their own stockpiled supplies, other settlements in and around Brimvale would soon panic and protest over the lack of diesel.

They only had a handful of ammunition spread across their defence force to deal with any civil unrest; but they also had the advantage in the bid for bullets now, being able to offer Rookson City something that Rubicross no longer could.

With the rest of the fuel reserves, they would be able to stretch their stockpiles out for a few more months before the protests would begin to break out in Brimvale, but a supply of ammunition would be a sure deterrent.

In the meantime, Sunken City would simply have to persevere.

CHAPTER 20 – LIAM

They were driving northbound along the wide empty highway towards Griften Pass, the road that cut a path through the Shield Mountains. Liam sat in the back of Quentin Davis's black SUV, idly staring out the window as they passed by boarded-up furniture warehouses, vandalised luxury car dealerships, and the occasional string of abandoned restaurants.

Columns of gleaming metal – Brimvale's solar farm – glinted in the distance away on the right as the panels caught the early afternoon sun. The collection of energy-converting components was comprised of residential and commercial rooftop solar systems. If there had been one thing that the Army Reserves had gotten right during their brief reign, it was the decision to assemble a labour crew of roofers, electricians, mechanics and welders to dismantle every solar array in Brimvale, aggregating them into one centralised location and plugging them all into the local substation, bringing the electrical grid back online.

If it hadn't been for the military's enforced food shortages and their subsequent endorsement of prostitution in exchange for extra rations, the project probably would have served to divide the common people; pitting those who had the foresight to install their own rooftop renewable energy generators against those who had always been dependent upon the convenience of public infrastructure, making them all much easier to intimidate into compliant servitude.

Instead, many of Brimvale's surviving citizens had chosen to unite against the act of procurement, citing the Army Reserves' initiative as outright theft and oppression of their rights to their own personal property. And so, when the food-motivated labour crew had come to collect from one of the suburbs, a rabble of peaceful protesters had formed a blockade at the entrance of their quiet middle-class neighbourhood.

Liam remembered learning that Dwight Jaskolski's asthmatic older brother had been among the crowd, demanding that the people of Brimvale be treated with respect, and given the choice of whether to donate their solar systems to the cause, rather than being viewed as holders of resources and assets that were to be stockpiled and exploited.

Acting upon orders from their commanding officers, the labour crew's escort of soldiers soon began firing rubber bullets into the crowd to disperse the protesters, one of which had struck Dwight's brother square in the chest and caused him to suffer a fatal asthma attack. The news of his death quickly spread across Brimvale, and a few weeks later, served as the basis of the markedly less-than-peaceful protests outside the town hall during The Long Summer Night. Archie Callahan later told Liam that the young man's death had also been the reason why many of the soldiers had refused to fire upon the crowd a second time, abandoning their positions in solidarity.

"I used to looove that seafood place," Lora Purcell pointed one of her freshly-painted pink nails out the front passenger seat's window.

Liam frowned at her manicure and newly-dyed blonde hair. *Only* she *would be that much of a narcissist to stockpile enough cosmetics to outlast the apocalypse.* He rolled his eyes and crossed his arms before looking back towards the solar farm, wondering what life in Brimvale would have been like if Dwight's brother hadn't died that day.

"Good oysters," Quentin agreed, glancing out the window. "Full of liquor, with big fat lemons on the side."

"Don't worry, Liam," Lora said condescendingly, turning around in her seat with a fake smile plastered across her chubby face. "He just means the brine inside the shell. There's no *actual* alcohol in oysters. Although I did have an oyster in a Bloody Mary shot glass once," she turned back to Quentin with an unnecessary flick of her new hair. "It was absolutely *magical*. I sooo wish I could have one again."

"Might have to ask Woozy's to add it to their menu," Quentin replied, before glancing up at the rearview mirror. "You're not a fan of alcohol, Liam?"

The senior officer smiled at him, or rather, he attempted to smile. His facial expression was less of an outright glower and more of a resting bitch face, although his cold blue eyes still demanded that Liam reciprocate the civil gesture.

Get fucked, Liam thought to himself as he stared back out the window. He knew that both of them were just putting on an act for one another, being overly nice to him for fear of what the other might think if they both treated him as per normal.

The vehicle's wheels rumbled as they crossed the bridge over Flagmire Creek, the near-stagnant man-made brook that flowed eastward at a snail's pace from the Fairstream Reservoir's spillways, eventually emptying out into Bellevue Bay.

Liam suspected that if he wasn't in the back of the car, then these two buddy-buddy brown-nosing bitches soon would be; Quentin eager to cheat on his other half and Lora eager to please the senior staff. Liam had spent the past few days dreading the thought of accompanying them both to Rookson City, but at least he could take some solace in the high probability that he would be cock-blocking the pretentious pair throughout their entire trip.

Normally, there wouldn't have been a need for Lora at all, as Liam was supposed to be taking over her role, but since this deal with the people of Rookson was so important, Mayor Paxton had declared that her presence was necessary, perhaps even essential to the negotiations. In light of the recent diesel shortage plaguing South Tekota, their plan was to offer a portion of Brimvale's fuel reserves to Rookson City in an attempt to outbid Rubicross for new supplies of ammunition.

As if it was her own story to tell, Lora happily explained the tragic backstory behind Liam's opted life of sobriety to Quentin. The senior officer pretended to care as he fiddled with the climate control, moaning with feigned empathy until the story was finished, like a low-key misogynist listening to the pain of menstrual cramps.

I never should have told her about my parents, Liam sighed through his nose, regretting ever having trusted her as someone that he could have confided in. He had realised far too late that Lora loved latching onto every opportunity to spread gossip to anyone who would listen. Only hours after sharing the details of his loss with her, he had left the office to order a coffee from The Artisan's Roast Cafe, only to be greeted by Hayley the barista expressing her condolences. He supposed that the violent nature of his parents' deaths couldn't be changed regardless of how many times Lora retold his story, but at least it had served to shed light on what type of person she really was.

The forested peaks of the Shield Mountains disappeared from view as they neared Griften Pass, a narrow two-lane chasm that had been blasted into the rock at the lowest point along the mountain range, which was still at least three storeys high. The engines of the black SUV and their trailing military escort were amplified as they entered the cleft, the sheer cliff faces on either side blocking out every other ambient noise.

Liam recalled that prior to the world ending, his father had been one of the construction workers who were contracted to excavate the Stillborough Tunnel, which would have eased the congestion along Griften Pass for any traffic travelling between Brimvale and Woodrow College, and North Tekota beyond, but the project had been scrapped due to frequent cave-ins. Luckily, his father had escaped many of the tunnel's collapses unscathed, although his luck unfortunately hadn't carried over into The Long Summer Night.

Rounding a slight bend in the road that obscured the chasm's exit from the entrance, Quentin slowed down a few car-lengths from the highway's T-intersection, pulling up to a security checkpoint's boom gate, where a pair of guards emerged from a concrete outpost nestled against the cliff wall. Quentin flashed his identification at one guard while the other inspected the vehicle. Satisfied, the sentries moved on to the armoured truck behind them.

"I still don't get why they have to check vehicles *leaving* Brimvale," Lora huffed as she watched the sentries shrinking in her side mirror.

"Keeps them awake, I suppose," Quentin replied, stowing away his senior officer badge.

The landscape north of the Shield Mountains was far less barren than Liam had anticipated. He had thought that the radioactive fallout borne on winds from North Tekota would have wiped out any traces of wildlife and vegetation, and while that was partially true towards the west, he could still see birds flying between thickets of trees beyond the highway, and farther towards the north and east were denser patches of overgrown forest. If anything, the flora and fauna had thrived in the relative absence of people travelling outside Brimvale.

As he surveyed their surroundings, a bus hurtled towards them from the west along the highway. It was one of theirs, which was strange, as Liam wasn't aware that a bus route existed between Brimvale and any settlements west of Griften Pass, even though he and Dwight had been tasked with managing the bus routes for the past two years.

As far as he knew, Woodrow College, the home of the mutants, was the only semi-civilised settlement out that way. If the bus had come from the prairies, the driver would have only been taking the long way around, since the bridges over Axemark Ravine would have saved hours of travelling time. He made a mental note to ask Dwight if there had been any new routes added to the public transport network.

The pair of guards signalled to the security checkpoint to lift the boom gate as they prepared to inspect the incoming bus.

"Finally," Lora breathed exasperatedly as they turned east along the highway, as if a few minutes of waiting for the security guards to do their job was the worst inconvenience she had encountered today.

Earlier, she had scolded Bronson Hopper in the middle of the workplace for playing a prank on her new private corner office. Most of the seniors had been on their lunch break – apart from Abhilash, the spineless frog-faced fool – so Lora had free reign to say and do as she pleased. Sensing a storm brewing, Dwight had left the room, knowing how her temper tantrum would play out. Shelton, too new to get involved, put his headphones on and turned back to his work, but Liam, Ollie and Pedro had watched everything happen from their desks, sitting in judgement.

Bronson had used a pencil to draw a big smiley face, along with "Cheer up, buttercup!" on the inner office blinds of Lora's internal office window, leaving the blinds open and waiting patiently for her to close them again. It was his way of telling her to stop taking her new job so seriously. Personally, Liam had found it funny, and long overdue. He agreed that she had to be taken down a peg before she became even more of a bitch than she already was, although she was probably too far gone.

Lately, she had been taking offence at even the slightest of provocations, constantly reminding everyone beneath her position the power and responsibilities of her newfound authority, and how they all should be following her orders without question.

Just yesterday, Lora had engaged Bronson in a particularly scathing argument, which would have set the precedent for his decision to walk off the job today. She had ordered Bronson to take inventory of all of the ammunition in Brimvale, by speaking with each individual guard and taking note.

When Bronson had asked why the commanding officer couldn't just request all of the guards to take stock of their own bullets and then send her a report, she had launched into a profanity-laced frenzy, calling him an ever-questioning subordinate who never wants to do any work.

Liam had volunteered himself to take on the task instead, since his new role was basically public relations anyway. Plus, it would have bought him a few weeks of blessed peace outside of the office, where he wouldn't have to put up with her shit. He soon realised that Lora was merely on a power trip when she denied his offer, placing him on a pedestal instead, and holding him up as a shining example of what the other juniors should strive to emulate.

"I honestly don't care what any of you think," Lora had told Bronson earlier while staring daggers at Ollie and Pedro, who laughed from their desks, only infuriating her more. "You really don't understand the responsibilities my new position carries. I am not your friend, I am your – *fucking hell* – you are reporting to me. And I shouldn't have to remind you of that. You need to either respect my authority or get out, because I don't have time for your fucking games anymore!" She poked her finger at Bronson, "And you know what the worst part is? I actually *wanted* to help you grow your career here. If you only waited for a few more months, I could've gotten you a way better position than fucking handyman, but I definitely won't be doing *that* anymore."

"Would it make you happy if I just quit instead?" Bronson had asked, unrepentant.

"HA!" she laughed derisively, "Please, spare me your idle threats. Now get in my office and clean up your fucking mess." Bronson shrugged, walking into her office as ordered, when she slammed the door behind him, trapping him in as she decided to launch into another tirade. "Furthermore…!"

The glass walls had done nothing to dampen her tea kettle screech. Bronson had simply sat on Lora's desk the entire time, listening patiently to her crazed rant, amused like a kid watching a clown at the circus getting ready to perform his next trick. When she was done, he walked out with a big grin and snapped the handle off her door on his way out, with Ollie and Pedro leaving along with him. Lora screamed in frustration and was hyperventilating by the time Bristol had walked into the office.

Liam found himself in the back seat of the SUV again as Quentin swerved to avoid a pack of feral dogs crouched around the carcass of a mauled deer, their bloodied muzzles snarling at the pair of passing vehicles.

The forest was thick on both sides of the highway, but Liam could still see smoke against the sky, high up on the right. *Probably a chimney from Ridgesaddle Inn*, he thought to himself. He hadn't been there personally, but Archie had told him that the tavern in between the last two peaks of the Shield Mountains was a safe haven for anyone caught outside a settlement after dark. Supposedly, it offered a spectacular view of Bellevue Bay, but it also served as a pit stop for some of Rookson's roving bands of mercenaries, who sometimes waylaid travellers while conveniently claiming no affiliation to the city; like anyone incapable of defending themselves in the wilderness would be able to file a complaint afterwards.

It was the reason why Bulldov, Butch and Wilson had been assigned to escort them in an armoured truck on the road to Rookson. They could be targeted and ambushed by the mercenaries or other groups of highwaymen just for the diesel in their engine, not to mention Rookson City itself. Who knew what type of people lived there?

Liam was happy to have them along for the ride though. At least he would have *someone* who he could bear to be around when they arrived. He had patrolled the Burnshaw Barricade alongside Bulldov back when the wall was first built.

The guard had only been eight years old back then, but his story was legendary among the survivors of The Long Summer Night. After witnessing the deaths of both of his parents, Bulldov had jumped his backyard's fence and broken into his neighbour's house, taking weapons from their gun collection. Without wasting any time, he jumped back over the fence, shot the intruders inside his home, and then worked his way down the street, saving several civilians from certain death.

When the story had reached the remnants of the Army Reserves in Fort Mason, former Sergeant Butch Gorman had left his commanding officer, who refused to train a child to become a soldier. Arguing that Bulldov had no one else who would steer him in the right direction, Butch took the boy under his wing instead, insisting that he be granted an honorary guard position along the Burnshaw Barricade, keeping him occupied before post traumatic stress disorder could kick in.

Bulldov was treated like a celebrity among the other sentries, who were more than happy to have him, and he and Butch had eventually worked their way into the ranks of the Mayor's personal security team.

Liam wondered why he couldn't have just ridden along with their escort instead. He would have enjoyed the company far better. Come to think about it, he was beginning to regret that he hadn't simply quit in solidarity alongside Bronson, Ollie and Pedro.

He had followed the three boys outside, ignoring Lora's outburst from her corner office as he stepped over the broken glass in the marble foyer, finding them celebrating their newfound freedom in the whitewashed concrete plaza. Pedro was pissing on the manicured lawn while Ollie and Bronson laughed at Priscilla, the pale shadow of a woman who sometimes lingered outside the town hall.

"Your day will come," she had warned in a wavering voice, waggling her crooked finger at them, "And you cannot hide from that which comes. *All of you will answer for your sins!*"

"I think my list of sins is too long for 'that which comes'," Ollie had scoffed, "Probably they will skip me."

"My list will break a record," Bronson boasted proudly, "They'll throw a party."

"And I'm still filling my list!" Pedro yelled with glee, dashing towards Priscilla, the waiflike figure breaking into a run. The lanky late teen giggled like a maniac as he gave chase, but he soon slowed to double over in laughter, letting her escape across the street and around the corner.

"Are you guys okay?" Liam asked as he approached Bronson and Ollie.

"More than okay," Ollie answered with a wide grin on his face, walking towards Pedro, "That place will be shit without us anyway."

"No regrets," Bronson smiled blissfully before chuckling, "Maybe just one regret. I should have written on the other side of her office's blinds: 'court in session'!"

"But where will you go now?" asked Liam, jerking a thumb back at the town hall. "You might not want to stick around after breaking that door."

"Probably we'll check out the protest in Rubicross," Ollie shrugged, picking Pedro up off the ground.

"I heard they're giving away free food and drinks," Bronson added, already convinced of the idea. "Maybe it'll be fun. You should come with us. Fuck this place."

Liam hadn't thought about quitting at the time, but he also hadn't been looking forward to accompanying Quentin and Lora to Rookson. He had savoured the thought of seeing the Mayor's Office struggle to replace four staff members simultaneously, but he knew that it only would have placed a heavy burden upon Dwight, having to train Shelton by himself, along with managing every other administrative task that he had been shouldered with.

Ultimately, Liam had rejected their offer, reasoning that he didn't want to be around any of the drunken protesters that were sure to be there, choosing instead to track down Mayor Paxton, fetching him and Quentin from The Woozy Rooftop Bar and Grill during their lunch break, and giving them his version of events. He already knew that Lora would get away with alienating three of the staff, but it was all worth it, if only to see the reaction on her face when they returned to the office with him in tow.

The forest opened up on the right as they approached Bellevue, the once-idyllic bayside town. Many successful businesspeople and retirees had chosen to live there prior to the apocalypse, taking a speedboat to work in one of the bigger cities on either side of the bay or simply spending the day by the beach. The white sands and the laid-back lifestyle of the locals had once attracted many passing cruise ships throughout each year.

Now, it was a ghost town. Without a wall to protect them from the scavengers who lived in the forest on the north side of the highway, all of the inhabitants had either abandoned their homes or died while trying to defend them. Liam imagined that it would have been like living under constant threat of The Long Summer Night, never knowing when the next strike could be.

Quentin hit the brakes as they came across a fallen tree on the highway. It was long enough to cover the entire road, including the shoulder on the far side. He clenched his jaw as he turned the steering wheel and reversed the car, drawing level with their escort. Butch wound down his window just enough to reveal his eyes beneath his old green army helmet.

"Feels like a trap," Quentin said in a hollow voice, speaking through Lora's window.

"Sure does," Butch agreed. "Safest bet is to turn around and head back to Brimvale."

"That's not an option," Lora replied, crossing her arms in her seat. "We need to get to Rookson. You have no idea how much is riding on this deal. Can't we just cut through this thing?"

"We *could*," Butch answered, his eyes narrowing as he stared across the road. "It would take some time though. At least two of us would have to put boots on the ground, and I don't like the look of that forest."

"Liam could go," Lora decided, turning in her seat. "Right, Liam?"

"It's *your* meeting," Liam replied, his voice dripping with resentment. "Volunteer yourself if it means that much to you."

Waves of shock, confusion, anger and betrayal contorted her features as she stared back at him, her cheeks flushing red.

"Any other options?" Quentin cut across Lora before she could open her mouth.

"Turn around and head back to Brimvale," Liam repeated the sergeant's suggestion, even as he knew that any proposal carrying a hint of logic would fall upon deaf ears.

"Cut through the town," Butch turned to check his mirrors. "Road's back there. We'd have more cover, so it's better than being caught out here, but not by much."

"You lead the way," said Quentin, winding up the passenger window. His jaw was still clenched as they cut across the median strip, heading back towards the entrance into Bellevue.

Unlike Brimvale and all of the other inhabited settlements in South Tekota, nobody had ever bothered to clear the abandoned vehicles from the roads of Bellevue. A luxury car riddled with bullet holes stood in the middle of the street, the driver's side door wide open, allowing families of raccoons and other wildlife to come and go as they pleased. On the same block, a sedan was crumpled against the side of a small cafe. Its airbags had most likely failed to deploy, since all four of the occupants were still inside the car.

Liam stared around as they slowly weaved through the wrecks. All of the roads were stiflingly narrow from overgrown bushes creeping out of front yards and nature strips; dull shards of broken glass adorning the weathered entrances of houses and businesses gave evidence that they had been raided a long time ago; and all of the speedboats docked along the jetties in the distance had either been sunken or stolen. Anything of value had already been scavenged, and nature had begun its slow reclamation of what was left.

They turned down a long residential road with double-storey houses sporting shattered windows on both sides. Finally, they had a clear run eastward. All they had to do was navigate through to the other side of town and get back onto the highway.

They began driving slowly until Quentin glanced up at the rearview mirror.

Jolting upright in his seat, he pounded the horn in both short and prolonged blasts, calling for Butch's attention. Liam turned around to see something that hadn't been there a moment ago. A rusty yellow school bus was blocking the intersection behind them.

A series of whooshes and crashes filled the air, like a gigantic whip was being cracked all around them, as towering wooden telephone poles fell from between the houses on either side of the road, blocking their way forward and back.

"Get us the fuck out of here!!" Lora screeched at Quentin.

He thrust the gear stick into reverse and slammed the accelerator, but the rear wheels spun impotently against one of the telephone poles that had rolled underneath the SUV. There was no space for them to build enough momentum to climb, and no room to move.

"Nothing we can do," said Quentin, gripping the steering wheel with white knuckles and keeping his eyes on the back of the armoured truck. "Get ready to run."

Liam looked for their assailants with shaky dread, but he didn't have to look for long. Guns were pointing at them from every house – rifles mostly, but pistols too – poking through the broken second-storey windows. Even the bus behind them now had a row of gunmen standing between the seats, aiming their weapons at the SUV like a mobile firing squad.

What now? Liam would have asked, if he thought that either of the two fuckwits in the front seats had a brain between them.

As if in answer to his unspoken question, a megaphone's speaker crackled in the distance:

"GET OUTTA THE VEHICLES WITH YOUR HANDS UP!!"

CHAPTER 21 – ODESSA

There was no "grand chandelier" in the hotel at Coyote's Rest. The oversized ornament had fallen from the lobby's ceiling during the ensuing earthquake of the North Tekota missile's impact shockwave, lying broken on the hardwood floor like some great glass octopus, and a replacement was out of the question, since chandelier makers weren't exactly easy to find in the post-apocalypse. Rather than changing the hotel's name though, Reagan Dempsey simply encouraged the guests to imagine the splendour whenever they walked through the double doors of the front entrance.

Dess sat alone by one of the lobby's front windows with a perspiring pint of heady brown lager from the hotel bar, looking out onto the main intersection that ran between Ingrid's Livery Stable, Lorelei's Saloon, and the gallows outside the Sheriff's Office. Despite the influx of hotel guests that Emmett Pearce's funeral had brought, the place was relatively empty, since everyone had soon realised that the hotel's drinks were watered down and overpriced.

Besides the hotel's clerk and bartender, her only company was Alix Carter, a slender brunette with shoulder-length hair, and Nael Fletcher, a rugged bald Englishman. They were the only two of the six Royce guards who hadn't been spending their entire days drinking at the saloon along with the rest of the cowboys and cowgirls in town, but only because Carter and Fletcher had been too busy with each other in their hotel suite.

Dess took another sip of the Stillborough lager, savouring its nutty bitterness. It was definitely one of Errol Chandler's, but she had forgotten the name her older neighbour had given the brew. She pondered it for a moment before becoming aware of herself drifting off again. Insignificant thoughts had somehow managed to occupy the forefront of her mind, continuously drawing her focus away from the task at hand. Despite her annoyance at her own inability to concentrate, she found that it was far easier to think about other things, but she knew that it was time to put her mind towards why she had come to Coyote's Rest in the first place, and why she still hadn't left yet.

She gathered her thoughts, compiling her evidence, and began examining all of the pieces of the puzzle, one by one.

The funeral invitation lay before her on the wooden table, crumpled and creased from her constant fidgeting. She considered unfolding it again, but she had read it over and over so many times, the words were already imprinted in her retina.

It is with my deepest regrets… Harlan's letter began to echo in her head. She always came back to a specific sentence though. *A stubborn man, through and through…* As headstrong as Emmett Pearce had been, it was an odd choice of words to include while paying tribute. Perhaps Harlan had written the invitations to the funeral with feelings of frustration still fresh on his mind.

In the saloon, Flem Wakefield had told Dess and Garrett that he had overheard a proposal from a representative of Brimvale to hire the cowboys as mercenaries, killing the Rauders in exchange for ten full cases of golden bucks. It was a lot of money, but Emmett had planned to turn down the offer. Dess would have been proud of him in that moment, but Harlan had been bitter about it. Apparently it hadn't been the first time that Harlan had entertained the idea of becoming killers for hire.

"I wouldn't say it was an argument," Flem had croaked as he recalled the first disagreement between the two men. "But for a few weeks afore Emmett died, they weren't exactly the best of friends as they were."

Dess then remembered her conversation with Big-Stack, who claimed that Harlan had accepted the proposition from Brimvale on behalf of the rest of the cowboys, refusing to honour Emmett's initial decision to decline.

A stubborn man, through and through… Granted, it had been two years since she had last seen her old flame, but Emmett was nothing if not inflexible, even for her. She hated him for it. She loved him for it. Once his mind was made up, there was no way to convince him otherwise. Harlan must have known it too.

Was that *your way of convincing him?* A tear tracked down her cheek as she pondered the thought, and she rubbed it away angrily, glaring across the intersection at Lorelei's Saloon in resentment. She didn't want to believe it, but she couldn't argue against it either.

Who stood the most to gain from Emmett's death? Garrett's statement from the other night posed the question in her mind.

It was Harlan who had assumed command of the cowboys; it was Harlan who had hired them out as mercenaries for Brimvale; and it was Harlan who had managed to solve his money problems by raiding Emmett's room and taking his stash of chips. For Harlan, it was all too convenient that Emmett hadn't lived through the night.

"Couldn't'a been more'n a minute," Flem's words echoed as he had recalled Harlan's presence on the saloon's veranda with the rest of the crowd, followed by the sight of his wet clothes and muddy boots shortly after the horse race had ended.

Only one question remained: what was Harlan doing in the rain?

She could picture him standing beside the half-dead tree at Rambling Gulch, raindrops coursing off the wide brim of his umber brown cowboy hat as he hid within the niche of the rock face that lined the side of the racing track, holding a thick fallen branch, patiently waiting for Emmett to ride past. The night was dark and wet, and Emmett would have been riding hard to catch up to Billy. He wouldn't have seen it coming until it was too late.

Dess took another swig of the heady brown lager, swallowing bitterly. Errol's nutty brew flooded her brain's synapses, beckoning to her, begging for her to try and remember its name and take her mind off all of this. She swept the plastic pint off the table, sending it to the floor with a clatter.

Carter and Fletcher were on their feet in an instant, hands on their pistols as they scanned the lobby and its windows for any signs of danger. The bartender simply grumbled behind the counter, huffily setting about to find a mop to clean up the mess on the floor.

"Let's go," Dess said as she checked the pistol holstered on her thigh, her expression resolute. She marched across the lobby, through the double doors and down the hotel's front steps onto the dirt road.

The pair of Royce guards only had a vague idea of where they were going, but they followed her all the same, unsure of what to expect, but certain that there was going to be trouble. They flanked Dess as she strode towards Lorelei's Saloon.

Horses whinnied in the depths of Ingrid's Livery Stable as diesel generators fired up one by one throughout the Old West re-enactment town, lights flickering on in each building to ward off the darkness of the approaching night. Dess squinted against a swirl of dust as it blew through the main street, her face steadfast and lined with determination.

"Hey, you fuckin' bitch!" Big-Stack bellowed from the small barred window of his brick-walled holding cell. "Let me the fuck outta here!!"

Deputy Monroe sat outside the Sheriff's Office with her rifle lying across her lap, her dour expression unchanging as she watched the trio make their way towards the saloon. Judging from their long strides full of purpose, she knew that it wasn't for a social visit. She nodded at Dess when they made eye contact, but Monroe made no move to prevent the impending clash. If anything, she was looking forward to dealing with whatever would come afterwards.

Two cowboys stood on the veranda on either side of the saloon's entrance, holding the batwing doors open for a prostitute that they intended on sharing for the next few hours. The pair of men let the doors swing shut, shouldering past Dess and the two guards in their haste as the pistol-packing trio entered the drunken atmosphere of raucous laughter and squeals of delight.

"I got a son your age, if'n you're interested," Flem's scratchy voice floated over the upbeat ragtime rhythms of Toby's piano chords in the front corner beside one of the grime-covered windows.

Brandi Beckett smiled politely, as she always did, eyeing Verne and Father Norman's glasses before Lyle called her over to serve another tray of drinks to the guests who Dess recognised from Stillborough. Reagan was happily entertaining the out-of-towners, having given up on trying to coax them into spending their booze money at his hotel's bar, with Edwin Yun Park, Shane Wagner and his wife, Gemma, among the people grinning and leaning in intently as he spun up another absurd story about one of the many eccentric guests that he had hosted over the years.

At another table, Garrett was whispering something into Ingrid Kaufmann's ear, making the blonde European woman blush and smile, while Archie Callahan and Gloria Clementine were trading tales of their youths over an early dinner.

In a booth, the other Royce guards – Boaz, Frost and Werner – were topping up Price's beer every time one of the passing prostitutes caught his attention, only for him to turn back and wonder why he was unable to keep up with the round.

Dante, Elwood and Gabe were at the dice tables, each with a woman in their lap and stacks of golden bucks arrayed across the green-felted tabletop. Cactus Jack had lost all interest in the game, his cup of dice unattended while he slurped body shots off a prostitute's slender stomach as she lay across the wooden bar counter.

None of them remember Emmett, Dess frowned in disgust. This was the town that she had abandoned two years ago. Seeing what had become of it, she was glad to have left. Her only regret was in not inviting Emmett to come away with her, no matter what compromise she would have had to make to convince him.

Harlan emerged from the bathroom corridor in the back corner of the saloon, slapping Lacey's rump as she fixed her skimpy black dress, letting her rejoin the crowd before he sauntered over to Lyle for another whiskey.

Dess flexed the slender muscles in her jaw, marching through the dice tables to join Harlan by the bar, the pair of Royce guards following in her wake.

"Take it outside," Fletcher shoved Cactus Jack a few steps towards the exit as Carter helped the body-shot woman down off the counter.

"Make that two doubles," Harlan told Lyle as he noticed Dess standing beside him. "I'm surprised to see you're still here. I thought you'd left town without saying goodbye again."

Despite her urge to grab the back of his head and slam his smiling face down on the bar, Dess held her anger at bay. She had one more question for Harlan. She would give him one final opportunity to prove his innocence before she concluded that he was guilty beyond reasonable doubt.

"The night Emmett died," she began, scrutinising every detail of his face, watching for a gesture or some involuntary tic that might betray his story. "Flem said he saw you disappear just after the race started, and later, your clothes were wet and your boots were muddy."

"What the fuck is this, Dess?" Harlan asked as Lyle handed him the pair of neat whiskeys. Reconsidering his offer to buy her a drink, he decided to knock one back and sip the other.

"Just answer the damn question," she shot back, one hand on her hip.

The chatter nearby died down as other people began to listen in. Cactus Jack was still seething off to the side, one arm draped around his woman as he watched the exchange. Garrett sniffed and turned away from Ingrid, his attention focusing on Dess and Harlan, with Archie soon following his gaze.

"I had to take a piss," Harlan shrugged before leaning back against the bar, his voice loud enough to satisfy their eavesdropping audience. "Bathroom was locked, so I had to head out into the rain to use one of the outhouses instead."

"Thank you," Lyle interjected as he wiped down the counter before pouring another serve of drinks, "For not pissing all over the wall outside."

"We asked you to tell us *exactly* what happened on our first day here," Dess reminded Harlan, ignoring Lyle's attempt to ease the tension. "Why did you leave that part out?"

"I didn't think my bladder was so damn important," Harlan replied with a confused grin, bringing on a low chuckle from some of the cowboys.

"But that wasn't the only part you left out, was it?" she stared at him relentlessly. At his silence, she shared the missing pieces of information that she'd had to find out for herself. His disagreement with Emmett over the bounty offer from Brimvale; his sudden fortune of golden bucks that had come from Emmett's room; and his acceptance of Brimvale's deal after Emmett could no longer oppose his views.

"Fine, fuck it," Harlan shrugged. The piano music had died some time ago. The whole saloon was listening in now. He set aside his drink and craned his head forward. "I didn't know what I was doing with my life. I was thinking about joining Emmett when he went into business doing whatever he was planning on doing, but I didn't have a clue what I was gonna do in the meantime. I was down to my last chips, and going for a walk in the rain seemed like a good idea."

"Can anyone vouch for that walk?" Garrett called out from across the room, clenching his jaw as he studied the crowd.

Harlan grimaced and shook his head, only just now realising how bad his alibi was.

"I just needed to be alone for a while," he answered in a dejected tone before grabbing his whiskey off the bar and taking another sip.

"You know how this looks, right?" Dess asked in a quiet voice, but the entire room still heard it. "Why didn't you just tell us all of this from the beginning?"

"I've been hitting it hard ever since he died," Harlan muttered, gesturing to Lyle for another as he downed the rest of his second whiskey. "I'll admit I forgot most of what happened until you brought it up."

"Hear, hear!" Flem raised his glass in agreement, but he was alone in his cheer.

Dess wasn't convinced either way. The motives were there, and his excuses were weak. She had come to Coyote's Rest to find out who killed Emmett, and she didn't like the answer. Despite having everything short of a confession, Harlan was either a very good liar, or she was simply being too naive. She might have left it at that. A dubious death that was better left unsolved, to prevent any further heartache among her old circle of friends.

She might have, if only he hadn't been irking her with his constant barbs ever since the day they rode into town.

"I know you had your heart set on killing for money," she narrowed her eyes, uncertain whether the money she was referring to meant Emmett's savings or Brimvale's bounty. Her words were dripping with venom all the same. "And I know he was a stubborn man, through and through… But you didn't have to *murder* him for it."

Something inside Harlan snapped.

His blue eyes raged with fire, and he raised his hand as if to strike her. He turned and slammed his fist down on the bar counter instead, cracking the wood. Garrett and Archie were on their feet in an instant, along with the rest of the Royce guards, but the cowboys and cowgirls outnumbered them easily, and they were all gearing up for a fight.

"You have no fucking idea," he growled menacingly. "You, you, and you," he stared daggers at Dess, Garrett and Archie each in turn, "You left us when Emmett and I needed you the most. It was just the two of us watching each others' backs out here. You think it was a fucking cakewalk trying to keep these motherfuckers in line after we all felt like we didn't have a purpose anymore?"

"Come on now, son," Archie's soothing drawl came as he tried to take control of the situation before it got out of hand. "We all got our own lives to lead. But we're all friends here, remember that."

"I was a better friend to Emmett than any of you fucking cocksuckers," Harlan raged on. He turned back to Dess, spit foaming at his mouth. "And you think I killed him!? I loved that man like a brother! Ask anyone here if they believe your bullshit story. They'll laugh you outta town. Now that I think about it, don't you three have somewhere else to be? How about y'all fuck off back to wherever the fuck you've been hiding for the past two years. Then you can quit acting like you actually gave a shit about Emmett."

Dess had heard enough. She stepped back, unbuttoned the strap on her holster and pulled out her pistol.

"Say that again," she dared him, setting her sights between his eyes.

Harlan stared down the gun's barrel as she thumbed the safety off. He lifted his chin, puffing his chest out, ready to take what was coming.

"The only reason I haven't pulled this trigger already," Dess began before he could open his mouth again and seal his fate, "Is because I haven't found more concrete evidence to back up what I know to be true. And you better hope that day never comes. Because if it does, you'll *wish* I ended you today."

"Never gonna happen," Harlan snarled back at her, "Because it never fucking happened."

"Enjoy spending all of his money," Dess replied, stowing her pistol away and turning her back on him as she shouldered her way through the stunned crowd towards the exit. "I hope it was worth murdering your own friend."

"You're the one waving the gun around," he spat, boring his gaze into the back of her head, *"Friend."*

* * *

"Just stay one more night," Archie pleaded in the stable as Fletcher peered out into the gathering darkness, warily watching the saloon from the big barn's entrance.

Dess had already sent Carter to fetch their things from the hotel. She had packed her duffel bag long before confronting Harlan, having had the foresight of knowing that she wouldn't want to spend another night in Coyote's Rest after she levelled her accusations against him.

"Come on now," Archie continued, readjusting his khaki-coloured trucker cap as he glanced around the stable for an angle that would convince her to stay, "The bus is right outside. You can sleep in there if you want, and I'll drive you back to Rubicross in the morning. Leave the horses here. Nathan won't notice if a few have gone missing. They'll probably be put to better use around here anyway. They're just getting fat in the Mallory stables."

Flip, the impudent stablehand, was groggily preparing their horses for the evening ride, having been roused from his sleep while he was supposed to have been keeping watch. He looked up hopefully, more than happy to stop working and get back to sleep.

"Thanks, Archie," Dess said out of the side of her mouth, snapping her fingers at Flip as she passed the saddle's girth underneath the horse that they were tacking up. "But I don't think I can spend one more night in this town. I've stayed long enough. I've gotta get outta here."

"Alright, if you insist," Archie replied, accepting defeat. "I'll see you on the road in the morning after I get all the passengers on the bus. You wave me down if you need a lift, y'hear? Actually, just wave me down, so I know you're okay."

"What makes you think you're gonna pass me?" Dess offered him a thin smile.

"Oi, company," Fletcher called from the door, drawing his sidearm at a pair of silhouettes approaching through the darkness.

"Put it away," Garrett's voice came as he and Ingrid materialised in the pool of light beneath the barn's entrance.

"I will wait you," Ingrid said softly, planting a kiss on Garrett's scruffy cheek before she disappeared through a side door.

Archie whistled when she was gone, shooting a wink at him.

"Think I'm gonna stick around for a while," Garrett stared around at the horses in their stalls, seeing them all with a new perspective. "Got a good thing here, ain't no sense in leaving."

"Don't worry, I get it," Dess replied, dusting off her hands and offering him a handshake. "I'll let Nathan know you're staying. Thanks for riding with me. This would've been a hell of a lot harder without your help. Write me if you hear anything else about –"

"Emmett," Garrett finished, his keen eyes studying her, "Will do."

"Yeah, Emmett," Dess echoed, although she had been meaning to say "Harlan". She looked over her shoulder as Carter entered the barn with their bags. "You be careful, Garrett."

"Likewise," he replied. "You best get moving now though."

CHAPTER 22 – HARLAN

"What the fuck are y'all staring at?" Harlan demanded, his voice piercing through the stunned silence lingering in the saloon in the wake of Dess's accusation.

She had already left the bar, along with Archie Callahan and the two Royce guards who she had walked in off the street with to spout her bullshit, but the other four guards lingered for a while, talking among themselves in one of the booths as they finished off their round of beer, probably watching and waiting to see if he would go after her.

"Don't tell me you believe this shit," Harlan rounded on Garrett and Ingrid as they moved towards the exit.

"Ain't matter what I believe," Garrett replied, clenching his unshaven jaw as he stopped to hold one of the batwing doors open for Ingrid. "Ain't gonna bring him back."

Garrett studied Harlan for a moment with his keen blue-grey eyes before his gaze dropped to the floor in a mournful mixture of doubt and disappointment. And then his ex-hunting partner was gone, loping off into the night, the two doors creaking in farewell as they swung shut, open and shut again.

At least they had the balls to say goodbye this time, Harlan swallowed, gut-punched.

Feeling the eyes of everyone in the room upon him, he turned back to Lyle Beckett, slowly running his hand across the surface of the bar counter and feeling the split where he had cracked the wood in his rage. Not surprisingly, Lyle made no move to pour him another drink.

"Self-service, huh?" Harlan muttered as he reached over the counter to snatch up a bottle of whiskey sitting on the bench top.

Lyle backed away with his hands up, letting him have the bottle while mentally deducting the cost from Quentin Davis's healthy bar tab.

Toby tried to break the uneasy silence by drumming out a lively tune on the piano. Harlan took a few strides towards the front corner of the room and kicked him off his stool, the chords ending in a swift crescendo as Toby careened to the side, dragging his fingers up the ivory keys. Taking a pull from the whiskey bottle, Harlan eyed all of the onlookers in the saloon.

"Anyone else think I killed Emmett?" he growled, wiping his mouth with the back of his shirt sleeve. Nobody dared to speak a word, quietly withdrawing into themselves as he began stalking through the crowd. "Don't be shy now. How long we all been friends? You think I'd kill any one of y'all?"

Apparently the shoddy wooden walls, floorboards and ceiling were far more interesting than him. Everyone preferred to admire the rustic craftsmanship of the shitty watering hole rather than meet his gaze. He shoved Cactus Jack backwards into one of the green felt-topped dice tables.

"You think I'd kill you?" Harlan demanded. He palmed Dante and Elwood in the shoulder as they sat in their seats before elbowing Gabe in the torso, making him drop his drink on the floor and stumble backwards into the bar counter, clutching his chest and wheezing air into his winded lungs. "You? You? You?"

Brandi Beckett ducked through the double doors into the kitchen while Lacey and the rest of the whores left their prospective clients, huddling together near the staircase in the back corner of the saloon in terror.

"You got nothing to fear from me, ladies," he reassured them unconvincingly before taking another menacing swig from the bottle. He wiped his mouth with his sleeve again. "Have I ever pulled a gun on *anyone* here?" He waited for someone to speak up before answering his own question. "No."

"Emmett wasn't shot," a lone quavering voice rose up from one of the tables.

Harlan rounded on Reagan Dempsey. The hotel owner with the receding hairline sat with his lanky hairy arms on either side of a lager that had been nursed for so long that it was already room temperature. The pervert's pencil-neck set in between his skinny stooped shoulders gave him the appearance of a turtle peering out of his small shell as he dared to speak out. Just as Shane and Gemma Wagner and all of the guests from out-of-town got up to leave, Harlan flipped the table, sending Reagan's beer flying, spraying the crowd as they shrank towards the batwing doors.

"You accusing me of killing my friend?" Harlan snarled, pulling his pistol from his holster.

"You needed money, and he had it," Reagan patronised from his seat, having the audacity to frown and smile while he said it, as if he was talking to a child.

"Let me ask you something," Harlan growled as he pointed his gun at Reagan's head. The son of a bitch sure wasn't smiling anymore.

The crowd's steady creeping towards the exits turned into a mad stampede as they screamed out of the saloon. Many of the whores holding their breath in the back of the room seized their chance to escape, rushing through the bathroom corridor and out the back door or up the staircase to lock themselves in the private rooms, although the majority of the inhabitants of Coyote's Rest elected to stay behind, either curious to see how all this would play out or hoping to see Reagan's brains splattered across the wall.

"Are we friends?" Harlan finally asked once the rumble of fleeing footsteps faded and the last of the doors slammed shut upstairs.

Reagan's wide eyes wildly searched the room before he shook his head, his chest deflating as he realised that nobody was coming to help him. He held his quivering hands up and turned his head to the side, as if his skull's temple could magically deflect a bullet at point-blank range.

"So if you think that I could kill Emmett," Harlan paused to take another pull of the whiskey bottle before pressing his pistol into Reagan's temple, his hot breath pervading the trembling hotel owner's senses. "A man who I loved like he was my own brother… What the fuck do you think I'd do to you?"

The colourless coward's crotch sprang a leak as Reagan began to piss himself, sobbing in his seat with his head sandwiched between the saloon's wooden wall and the gun's barrel. If he indeed had a turtle's shell to retreat into, now would have been the perfect time.

"ENOUGH!!" Archie thundered from the entrance, summoning his commanding tone from his former days as an Army Reserves sergeant as the batwing doors creaked back and forth in time with Reagan's jerky whimpering sigh of relief. Archie whipped out his own gun from the back of his belt, taking aim and staring down Harlan. "We might not have any evidence of Emmett's murder, but we'll damn sure have evidence of Reagan's!"

"Safety's still on," Harlan said out of the side of his mouth as he savoured the sight of Reagan looking down at the mess he had made of himself and hanging his head in shame. Satisfied, Harlan straightened up, pointed his pistol at the ceiling and pulled the stiff trigger impotently before holstering his sidearm.

"Much as I feel like killing anyone who accuses me of doing shit I didn't do," he continued, glancing down at the circular imprint of the gun's barrel on Reagan's receding hairline, "I'm not a killer. Not yet. That's about to change though." Harlan grabbed his umber brown cowboy hat off the back of a chair as he marched towards the exit, calling over his shoulder, "Gear up everybody, we're going hunting!" He looked back at Archie, challenging the ex-military man as he craned his head forward. "Move aside."

"You've never killed anyone before, but I have," Archie threw back, the old war veteran still holding his gun steady. "If you're planning on going after Dess, I swear, you won't even feel yourself hit the floor."

Harlan shook his head as he took a deep breath and donned his hat. His former friends were a constant stream of disappointment.

"I'm not going after her," he exhaled, before knocking Archie's wrist aside with the whiskey bottle and clocking him across the jaw with a fist.

Archie stumbled backwards and tripped over Cactus Jack's outstretched boot, the former sergeant landing on his elbows, his gun letting off a stray slug that crunched through both ends of a wooden barrel, embedding itself into the wall. Harlan stared down at the old man, his head lolling around in a daze as Toby crawled over to kneel by his side.

"How's that floor feel, asshole?" he asked, fixing his cowboy hat.

Without waiting for an answer, Harlan left the saloon, punching through the batwing doors and descending the veranda's steps two at a time into the night. He marched across the street, curious onlookers drawn by the gunshot's blast soon scurrying away again at the sight of him. With no sign of Deputy Monroe manning her post, he brazenly walked into the Sheriff's Office with his whiskey bottle in hand, catching Byron Ashby bent over his desk as he scrambled to load his rifle.

"Harlan!" Byron exclaimed, still fiddling with his repeater, as if he had any time left. "Don't you come any closer."

"About time one of you fuckers came to visit me!" Big-Stack yelled from his cell, the towering redhead brute gripping the ruddy iron bars like a gorilla poising to break out of its cage.

Harlan shoved Byron over the table, the rifle's rounds tinkling as they rolled off the desk and spilled across the floor.

"What do you think you're doing!?" Byron yelled, squirming on top of his desk with his fat ass in the air, staring back at Harlan like he was waiting for a spank. "Monroe! Monroe, get the fuck in here!!"

"Billy's innocent," Harlan answered, grabbing the set of keys from Sheriff Ashby's hip and tossing the shrapnel across to Big-Stack's holding cell.

"No fuckin' shit," Billy grunted under his breath as he reached around the bars, jamming each key into the cell door's lock.

"I ought to arrest you for assaulting a police officer!" Byron shouted indignantly as he turned around, finally accepting that he wasn't going to get the spanking that he so desperately craved.

"That's about the only thing anyone here's guilty of," Harlan snorted as Big-Stack jangled the right key into the lock. "And Billy's already done my time for me."

The rusty hinges screeched as the big cowboy kicked the cell door open, sauntering out and stretching his limbs, glad to be back in the free world again. Harlan grabbed the sheriff's old repeater and tossed it over to Big-Stack. Byron's pupils dilated in terror as Billy crossed the room in two strides, holding the butt of the rifle menacingly between the sheriff's pig-like eyes.

Harlan took another pull of the whiskey bottle before he stooped to pick up the scattered rounds from the floor, stuffing them back into the ammo box and pocketing it on their way out.

As expected, Byron didn't say shit. He was just glad that they were gone.

The rest of the cowboys and cowgirls were forming up outside Ingrid's Livery Stable, while Olaf Kaufmann stood out the front of his general store, happily declaring that he was having a flash sale on rechargeable LED lanterns, boasting thirty-hour life spans along with a generous two-hour warranty.

With Deputy Monroe still missing in action, Harlan and Big-Stack approached the hunting party, catching sight of the four remaining Royce guards who were busily tying their gear down on the backs of their horses.

"Thought we might join you," said Blair Frost, the slim blonde who was both easy and hard on the eyes, depending on who was looking, "If you don't mind us tagging along."

"Sure your boss won't fire you for not guarding Dess?" asked Harlan, suspicious of anyone who had thrown in with Royce, past or present.

"Maybe," Kirk Boaz shrugged, bald, black and bored with what the world had become. "No shortage of work for hired guns though."

"Company couldn't hurt," said Big-Stack, sizing up Frost as she swung one of her long legs over her saddle.

Harlan was about to ask another question when he caught sight of his own red stallion tacked up and ready to go, walking out of the stables alongside a brown mustang, with Garrett holding both horses' lead ropes.

"Thought you'd be long gone by now," Harlan remarked as his stallion snorted.

"No," Garrett shook his head, "Made that mistake once. Ain't making it again. I'm with you, brother."

"We're hunting *people* tonight," Harlan put a hand on Garrett's shoulder, his eyebrows raised beneath the shadow of his umber brown cowboy hat before hoisting himself up onto his saddle, "Rauders. You good with that?"

"They gotta die someday, right?" Garrett replied as he handed Harlan the reins and mounted up on his mustang. "Better sooner than later."

"I'm ridin' Emmett's horse," Big-Stack declared, not humbled by his brief incarceration in the slightest. "I won it, it's mine now."

Harlan exhaled before taking another pull of his whiskey.

"Go get the man his horse," he ordered Flip, spotting the impudent teen's mullet in the crowd. The boy ran back into the shadows of the stables, muttering curses beneath his breath.

"And I want my damn money, too," Big-Stack added, always pushing his luck. "Five thousand."

"It was three," Harlan reminded him coldly as he wiped his mouth with the back of his shirt sleeve, "And you can forget it. That money went towards paying for Emmett's funeral."

"Don't you cheat me outta my winnin's," Big-Stack menaced, "Ain't my fuckin' fault Emmett died."

"He'd still be alive if you hadn't insisted on racing," Harlan whirled his stallion around, spurring it forward to knock Billy off balance. "You want your money back? Go talk to Verne. That old fucker made twice as much." He pushed Big-Stack aside with his horse again at the sight of Flip emerging from the barn with Emmett's beautiful black fox trotter mare. "And one more thing; if I see one mark on Emmett's horse, you'll be walking back to Coyote's Rest. Understood?"

"Yes fuckin' sir…" Big-Stack grumbled as he snatched the reins off Flip.

"YEEHAW Y'ALL!!" Lloyd Price whooped as he whipped his mount into motion, almost falling back onto his ass as he took off. "Let's crack some fuckin' skulls!"

The rest of the cowboys and cowgirls cheered and hollered after him. Harlan and Garrett spurred their horses forward in unison, and the nostalgia settled in just as the whiskey began to kick up a buzz. While the manhunt for Wallace Pelletier had left Garrett prematurely aged; for

Harlan, chasing a person across the prairies was one of the greatest thrills he had ever experienced.

You wanted me to be a killer, Dess, Harlan reflected as he took another swig of his whiskey bottle. *Well here I am.*

CHAPTER 23 – JEREMY

For every fire that Jeremy Royce managed to extinguish, two more would blaze up from the ashes, as if he was battling some flaming hydra that had taken on the horrible form of a constant stream of meetings and impromptu requests coming at him from all angles, at all hours of the day. He had been plagued with the guards; the house staff; the chefs; the warehouse managers; even Enrique Garrido the event coordinator, whose only complaint had been that there were no upcoming events for him to coordinate. It seemed like every living soul in the estate had some vague need or urgent request, each one of their demands completely trivial and unrelated to one another, apart from them all requiring his immediate attention.

It was as if Evelyn had secretly called a staff meeting, encouraging them all to send their suggestions, problems and petty grievances in Jeremy's direction, plotting to overwhelm him with the workload in his first week of taking charge of the Royce Family's affairs. As much as he had been willing to take on the full responsibility of running the residence, he had soon been left with no other choice but to ask his haughty sister-in-law to help bear the burden.

Evelyn had sat back and smiled in scornful satisfaction the moment he had made his plea. She even ridiculed him openly in front of some of the house staff – who had awkwardly averted their gazes – for not being able to handle the task his brother had entrusted to him, before suggesting that she take over the role for him completely so that he could comfortably return to his lewd and lackadaisical lifestyle.

Jeremy was ashamed to admit that he had given her proposal some consideration. He would have been all too happy to withdraw back into his comfort zone again, where he was emperor over everything within the walls of his dusty moth-balled two-room bungalow, without having to worry about anything that occurred outside of his dingy domain. But as tempting as Evelyn's offer had been, he had declined, choosing instead to give her control over the decision-making regarding the rationing of supplies, which she was so well-known for anyway; along with money management; drafting new rules for the house staff during the protest; and any other important tasks that he didn't want to be held accountable for.

He couldn't decide whether he had chosen to keep at least some of the responsibility thrust upon him only because he wanted to spite Evelyn, as if his stubbornness to surrender completely would prove to her that he still had some redeeming qualities left within him, or if he just wanted to avoid disappointing his older brother any more than he already had.

Jeremy had always been content to live in Nathan's shadow, even before the world had ended. Nathan was a firm believer of giving back to the community after achieving his own success, whether his generous gestures were in the form of donating a portion of his old electronics store's profits to charities, or hiring unnecessary staff just to give them a helping hand. He had a knack for inspiring others to follow him, and possessed either great business acumen or an extremely persistent stroke of good fortune. Admittedly, it was sometimes vexing that both brothers had never been equally as blessed, but after all these years of living together, perhaps some of Nathan's luck or logic had finally rubbed off on him.

Jeremy was sitting on the grey couch of his bungalow's living room, his back to the horizontal strips of afternoon sunlight streaming in through the recently-dusted blinds, when a knock came from the front door.

On the first day of his new role, Jeremy had been handling the household's affairs in one of the small offices within the bowels of the grand double-storey residence, but whenever he would emerge to go to the bathroom or to simply stretch his legs, members of the house staff would see it as an opportunity to swarm him with a flood of new requests.

After a few short hours, he had given up on the idea of having an office, and he decided to make a few requests of his own. The housekeepers assigned to clean up the mess in his bachelor pad had the worst of it: removing the stacks of dirty dishes that had piled up over the past few weeks, exterminating the various colonies of pests that had thrived on his leftover meals, and attempting to scrub the mouldy unidentified stains out of his carpet until their arms were sore.

He had instructed one of the kitchenhands to cart what was left of Haydar's vodka crate into the warehouse, along with any other beer, wine and liquor they could find. By the time they had finished the job, it was almost as if his bungalow had been burgled by a bunch of clean-freaks, but he was also amazed to see the amount of extra space that had been hidden away beneath all the booze bottles and forgotten food scraps for so long.

"Come in!" he called, although at this time of the day, he knew what was coming. The knowledge still didn't stop him from bouncing one of his lanky knees and wiping the sweat of his clammy palms onto his moss green corduroy pants in anxious anticipation.

Cody Palmer, the pasty-white apprentice chef, juggled his load as he entered the bungalow with a lopsided smile, shutting the door with a bump of his bony backside. He set a tall glass of milk and a plate of freshly-baked honey-glazed buttermilk biscuits down on the coffee table.

It was strange, but the combination of milk and cookies had been helping to hold Jeremy's cravings for alcohol at bay. It did nothing to stop him from waking up queasy and shivering with cold sweats each morning, but at least the regular snacks managed to keep his unrelenting dopamine receptors at the back of the queue of never-ending naggers knocking on his door.

Cody lingered in the room, staring at Jeremy, who quickly snatched up one of the biscuits and took a bite.

"Delicious," he said around the crumbling mouthful as he chewed. The inside of the cookie was still warm and gooey from the oven. "You'll be a proper chef in no time!"

"I had a question about that," Cody replied, neither he nor his lopsided smile leaving.

"Sure, go ahead," Jeremy covered his mouth as he spoke, but it was more to stifle a yawn than to hide the morsels in his teeth. *Apparently I'm the one who's in charge of promoting people now.*

"When I'm a chef," Cody continued, leaning against the laminate kitchen counter and staring wistfully out the window at the residence, "Does that mean I'll be able to date some of the other staff?"

Jeremy reached for the glass of milk and took a quick swallow to keep from choking.

"I'm not sure what Evelyn's policies are on that," he offered his favourite line which seemed to solve the majority of his problems, even if it didn't solve the problem itself. "You'll have to take it up with her."

"Okay," Cody stared at Jeremy while scratching his nose, as if he was waiting for an alternative answer to satisfy himself with.

"I'll see you tomorrow, Cody," Jeremy broke the uncomfortable silence in the room as he set the glass back down.

Wiping his milk moustache, he was about to get up and open the front door to usher the boy out when the apprentice chef finally realised that their time was done, leaving of his own accord with a dreamy look in his eyes. Jeremy shook his head in bewilderment as he set the plate of cookies in his lap. He couldn't tell whether somebody else had put Cody up to the question or if it was a genuine request.

Nathan had never been this busy, at least as far as Jeremy could remember. Jeremy usually missed most mornings, and he would spend the majority of his waking hours binge-drinking behind closed curtains, so he didn't really have a benchmark to compare the busyness of his brother's business against.

They should have reached Cloakwater by now, he supposed as he washed down another gooey biscuit with the glass of milk. He wondered whether Jordan was making the most of his time with Nathan and Rodney Hamilton, his brother's business partner, listening and learning from their trade talks, as Jeremy had encouraged him to during their walk to Linchpin Station.

He dusted his fingers off and brought his dishes over to the sink, determined not to let his freshly-cleaned bachelor pad fall to nauseating neglect again, at least not while he was sober. *Whatever they're up to in Cloakwater, I'm sure they're having a better time than me.*

Glancing at the sun hanging low over the western wall across the courtyard, Jeremy decided that his day full of meetings and trivial requests was finally done. Leaving his dishes on the rack to dry and throwing a threadbare black coat around himself before locking up, he went for a walk in the late afternoon air. It was still warm outside, so there was no need for the coat, but Jeremy had found that it served to stave off the shakes somewhat.

Normally, he would have been enjoying a greasy lukewarm breakfast at this time of day, nursing a hangover until the next wave of alcohol kicked in. With the sounds of music and laughter coming from the protest over the wall however, he was certain that there were dozens of other people who had carried on his daily tradition. He smiled thinly at the irony of being asked to sober up while everyone else had a good time.

Having endured the week-long affair of drunken revelry sounding from the other side of the concrete walls, Jeremy finally decided that it was time to see what all the fuss was about.

He motioned to the guards stationed in the gatehouse to open up. It was odd to see the storey-high wooden doors closed, as Nathan often stated that everyone was welcome to visit and share the news of what was happening around South Tekota, or at the very least, share a meal. But when the first few protesters had arrived to join Haydar outside the walls, keeping the gates shut at all times was one of Captain Karl Thornton's first security mandates.

One of the gigantic double doors creaked open just wide enough for Jeremy to slip through the crack before it swung shut behind him with a deep wooden *clack*, its closure emphasised by the sounds of heavy iron bolts sliding into place.

Unlike the pre-apocalyptic world, there was no maniacal mob parroting a megaphone or mindlessly looting other places of business that had nothing to do with the diesel shortage. There were no picket signs or angry banners being paraded through the streets. There were no rocks or debris being hurled at the guards posted along the walls. This was a peaceful protest, for now at least.

The crowd in the dirt lot next door was growing, with tents pegged into the ground, awnings hanging over makeshift stalls and marquees shading barbecue grills and playing card tables. It was more of a festival than a protest, with circles of people sitting cross-legged on blankets, laughing and drinking as they listened to musicians playing acoustic guitars and tapping rhythms on bongo drums.

Haydar was selling his hooch from the back of a rusty red semitrailer. The perpetually drunken potato farmer was making money hand over fist from all of the young men and women lining up, happily giving discounts to anyone who stooped to give him a kiss. Most of them opted to plant a quick peck on his balding forehead, but some were drunk enough to give the queer little man a cheeky tongue wrestle before laughing as they staggered back to their friends. His face was flushed, either from all the smooches or all the alcohol, but he was grinning and proudly yelling something merrily unintelligible all the same.

Jeremy swallowed dryly as he watched bottles of booze pass from one person to the next, their sighs of satisfaction as they slaked their thirst like an open invitation for him to set aside his newfound inhibitions for one night and join in on the fun. He spied an open spot in one of the circles and began to walk towards it when a small boy in an oversized black college hoodie darted in front of him, looking up at Jeremy with beady black eyes before snatching a sizzling sausage from one of the barbecue grills and disappearing into the crowd.

Faltering for a moment, Jeremy took the strange boy as a sign to turn around and head back to the estate, willing himself to put one foot in front of the other, remembering his promise to Nathan. Just as he was about to reach the corner of the concrete walls, the party fading from his peripherals, a familiar voice floated above the revelry.

He stopped and stared past the tents and pickup trucks and people leaning against the wall to see a flash of dark blonde hair. Frowning slightly, he kept his eyes on the prize as he moved through the crowd towards the makeshift stage, which was a piece of string tied to four wooden stakes in the ground beside the wall.

As he approached, the singer's voice soon became clear and her face materialised. It was his brazen teenage niece, Aimee, along with her bandmates, Bianca Beaumont and the Mallory kid, playing proudly outside the walls of Royce Manor for all of the people gathered.

Aimee was surprised to see her uncle among the crowd, but she kept on singing without missing a lyric, gripping her microphone with a glad smile. Finishing the song, she motioned for her bandmates to continue playing before thumbing off her microphone and moving towards the edge of the stage to talk with her uncle.

"I thought it was you," Jeremy said hollowly before glancing over his stooped shoulder and lowering his voice. "What would happen if your mother found out you were outside the walls? How did you even get past the guards?"

"Are you kidding?" she asked, brushing her hair back over her ear. "It's so much fun out here! Meeting new people, eating and drinking the night away… Now I can see why you always stay out late every night!"

"I'm different," he replied, rather unconvincingly. "Besides, you're too young to be drinking. You should probably take it easy before you get into trouble."

"You never do," Aimee shrugged, smirking as she awaited his reaction.

She had the makings of Evelyn's quick barbs, which were easily disarming when coupled with Nathan's easygoing smile. He knew that he couldn't discipline her without looking like a complete hypocrite and losing any respect she might have held for him.

"Fine," Jeremy conceded, swallowing dryly as he looked around at the crowd, "But I never saw you. And send the Mallory kid over here for a second."

"It's Jake," she smiled victoriously before beckoning the drummer over as she seamlessly slid into Bianca's verse.

Jake Mallory was a slender teenage kid with mane-like windswept hair.

Cool, calm and quick to flash his boyish smile, it was easy to see why he got on so well with the two girls. Jeremy was about to burst his bubble though.

"If anything bad happens to either of those girls," he summoned the most menacing tone he could muster as he towered over Jake at the edge of the makeshift stage, "I'll take you all the way up to North Tekota and make sure the same thing happens to you."

Having said his piece, he spun on his heel and moved back through the crowd while the Mallory kid tried not to shit his shorts. Jeremy wiped the sweat of his clammy palms onto his corduroy pants. He wasn't accustomed to threatening teenagers, let alone even confronting somebody else. Knowing that the kid's fear wouldn't last forever though, he made a mental note to assign some guards to watch over Aimee from the wall whenever she was seen out in the crowd.

Passing by a large tent, Jeremy came across a long line of minivans, motorhomes and gutted school buses, all arranged in a wide arc that bordered the southern edge of the dirt lot, with some of the vehicles rocking back and forth as customers got their money's worth. Zatar's Velvet Convoy was working in full swing, with dozens of young women along with a few scantily-dressed men fondling themselves in a row of camping chairs, ready and willing to serve the drunker members of the crowd who were eagerly browsing their wares.

Zatar, the depraved dwarf, was constantly touring the countryside for business and pleasure, always looking for new talent to keep their old customers coming back for more. Jeremy knew from experience that his whores catered to every fantasy and desire, for the modest hourly price of two hundred golden bucks. While Rubicross was a regular destination on their tour, it seemed like they were digging their heels in for quite some time, happy to draw revenue from what looked to be the beginnings of a drawn-out protest while equally as affected – perhaps even more so – by the diesel shortage.

Just across the street was Laszlo Snyder's Mezzanine, which would certainly be missing out on a large chunk of all the profits to be made while the Velvet Convoy was in town. Even so, as much as Laszlo and all the other brothel owners around South Tekota hated whenever Zatar and his shagging wagons rolled in to set up shop, their businesses would have been crippled by now without his frequent deliveries.

Jeremy had heard that a scientist somewhere in Rookson City had discovered a way to replicate birth control pills – the lifeblood of the industry – using Zatar as a bulk-purchasing customer and distribution retailer to every settlement they served, and with the arsenal of artillery adorning each guard in the pickup trucks escorting the convoy, only a waylayer with a death wish would ever think to stop them.

He began to wonder whether Laszlo was offering a discount, as he usually did whenever Zatar and his fuck-trucks made an appearance. Even as he pondered the thought, Jeremy's feet were carrying him away from the crowd in the dirt lot and towards the gates of the old Rubicross Elementary.

I've earned this, his subconscious mind argued before he could even begin to reason with himself. He had spent all week listening to trivial complaints and resolving petty problems. *Why shouldn't I be allowed to relax for just one night?*

Not a single drop of alcohol had passed his lips since taking on his new responsibilities. That was reason enough to celebrate.

CHAPTER 24 – EVELYN

Somebody had to take charge of the Royce Family's affairs in Nathan's absence, but Jeremy was the worst possible candidate Evelyn could think of. Although he had lasted a little longer than she had originally anticipated, she knew that he would eventually crumble under pressure. The man was utterly incapable of handling any form of responsibility. For the past few days, the drunken fool had been making a mess of trivial tasks, delegating the more difficult decisions to her, and all the while ignoring the most important issues.

She had let out a prolonged sigh of relief when her useless brother-in-law finally begged her for help, although she hadn't felt a single ounce of pity for him as he stood dishevelled and distraught before her, overburdened by the weight of having to earn his keep – for once in his miserable life.

While he hadn't given over complete control of the residence's responsibilities, which by right should have been hers in the first place, he had at least seen the sense in letting her oversee the rationing of their stockpiled supplies, budgeting their finances during the halt of trading activities, and – with Karl Thornton's assistance – establishing a set of security protocols to ensure that the staff were kept safe from the dangers of the protesters lurking just beyond their walls.

Her plan to overwhelm him with the house staff's flood of petty complaints had worked, and now she could finally begin taking care of business, although if she was being honest, she had already begun long before Jeremy had even thought to approach her with his tail between his legs.

Evelyn sat alongside Michelle Tan in the spacious rosewood furnished and scarlet carpeted library on the ground floor, one of the few rarely-frequented rooms in the residence which offered ample and undisturbed desk space for them to pore over the plethora of warehouse inventory ledgers, stocktaking summaries and future food and diesel projections.

They had to tighten up their expenditure on new supplies in the absence of their usual income, while also balancing the needs of their essential employees, which was no easy task. Which workers were essential? To what degree would each of their needs vary? And exactly how long of a timeframe were they planning for?

At least Michelle was the right person for the job. Proactive, astute and highly organised, the Royce Family's former personal accountant turned inventory manager had previously worked in Sunken City in a role that largely consisted of planning, budgeting and forecasting. She was pretty, too, lithe and petite with high cheek bones, although she never mentioned her personal life, at least not to Evelyn, keeping every conversation strictly professional.

As instructed, Michelle had reviewed their historical figures of food and fuel supplies along with their current stockpiles in order to set a rationing plan for the estate.

"It's difficult to tell," Michelle began, turning in her chair as they sat in front of the neatly-stacked piles of handwritten receipts. "All of the dinner parties and events skew the numbers. Enrique was able to provide me with a calendar of celebrations and occasions, so I've excluded those dates from my calculations, but there are some weeks with significant turnovers like we see here," she leafed through one of the ledgers, indicating where supplies of salted fish and fresh produce plunged and rose again considerably. "This leads me to believe that there were some events that he hasn't recorded, and it also doesn't take into account any surprise guest visits or food wastage."

"I see," said Evelyn, her lips tightening as she racked her brain to remember if any of the outlying dates held any importance. "I suppose food spoilage and Nathan's donations don't help us out much either."

"That's where we're covered," Michelle replied, indicating another stack of ledgers. "I've made sure that the warehouse managers keep a record of anything that passes through the doors for whatever purpose. I just wish that the kitchen staff were equally as diligent about tracking how much food is thrown out each day."

"I could ask Mabel to nominate one of the kitchenhands for the job?" Evelyn suggested.

"I'd prefer to assign one of my warehouse managers," Michelle replied brusquely.

No nonsense, no explanation, just straight to the point. Evelyn liked that about her. Of course, the counterproposal didn't require an explanation. People were either capable of performing their duties, or they weren't. Just like in Jeremy's case. She nodded her approval.

"And how are we with the diesel?" Evelyn asked, scanning the piles of notes for a projection of their fuel levels.

"That's a lot easier to estimate," Michelle answered, plucking out a single piece of paper filled with her calculations. "We either sell it or burn it, and at our average burn rate, I'd say we'll have power for at least a few more months. At the moment, my main concern is the food. It'll take some time to track our current rate of consumption before I'll be able to provide an accurate forecast, but in the meantime, I'd appreciate it if someone could inform me whenever we have guests."

She folded her hands on the desk and turned back to Evelyn, a habitual gesture from her accounting days to indicate that their business had concluded.

"Great work, Michelle," Evelyn stood, taking care not to disturb any of the piles. "I don't think we'll be accepting any guests for some time with what's happening outside, but I'll be sure to keep you informed if we do."

"Thank you," she replied, straightening up her stacks on the desk, meticulously ensuring that they were all in perfect alignment to some invisible grid.

Evelyn left the scarlet red carpet of the library and stepped out onto the glossy white tiles leading to the entrance hall. A faint *clack* of pool balls resounded from the games room. She half-expected to see Ryan and Jordan playing a match before dinner as she rounded the corner of the arched entrance, yet the room was empty, and the rack was still in a perfect triangle.

Despite the amount of staff that they had working in the manor, every room felt empty in her family's absence. She missed Nathan's cheerfulness every time he irked her with some new act of completely unnecessary generosity. She missed the boys' voices, laughing and jeering as they competed against each other. She even missed Zita Ortega, Ryan's perceptive and tactful girlfriend, despite only talking with her on rare occasions.

Her own daughters had grown somewhat distant lately. Admittedly, Aimee had always been an independent child, but Sadie had started to disappear unannounced as well. At first, Evelyn had thought that she was just off searching for her younger sister, but she always returned alone, smiling to herself. Evelyn suspected that there must have been a boy involved, and her mind unwillingly conjured up an image of Anton Snyder when he had invited Sadie to accompany him for a drink on Jeremy's birthday.

Evelyn was sitting with her eyes closed on one of the bar stools beside the counter, concentrating on suppressing the vile thought when another ghostly *clack* struck sharply from behind. Her eyes snapped open as she jumped out of her seat, whirling around to face the pool table, only to see Marv grinning in one of his trademark Hawaiian shirts, holding a cue stick.

"Sorry, couldn't resist," he laughed, stroking the black bristles of his pencil moustache before lining up another shot. "You seem a little edgy, everything okay?"

Marvin Devereux was a slightly chubby black man, a former prize-fighter who had spent all of his winnings on living the good life, until he was eventually forced to live modestly again. He was in his sixties, but his decades of training had followed him into retirement. Evelyn had witnessed his dormant physical prowess first-hand during one of the more terrifying Rauder raids on Rubicross.

They had been attacked in the dead of night, back when the trading town was still a mere fledgling settlement in the post-apocalypse, long before they had their concrete walls to keep them safe. A savage gang of scavengers had forced their way inside, ransacking the residence from room to room, hacking and slashing at anything that moved and stuffing their packs with anything that didn't.

Marv had been leading Evelyn and her family through the kitchens towards one of the service doors when a machete-wielding madman emerged from the walk-in freezer, his blade dripping with blood. With lightning speed, Marv deftly dodged the swing of the machete, sidestepping around the Rauder and throwing a single neck-snapping punch, instantly killing their would-be attacker before his knees even had the chance to buckle.

"Everything's fine," she breathed, letting her shoulders relax as she sat back down on the bar stool. "You just caught me off-guard, that's all."

"My career was built on catching people off-guard," Marv chuckled coolly before sinking the eight ball into a side pocket and suddenly losing his interest in the game. "Say, you wouldn't happen to know why Jeremy headed outside the gates, would you?"

Evelyn frowned at him. Marv shrugged nonchalantly as he hung up his cue stick, and she sighed in exasperation. The staff had all been grumbling over being barred from venturing out into town until further notice, especially since the Velvet Convoy had arrived; and here was Jeremy, undermining their security protocols so that he could party with the protesters. She would be sure to tell Nathan how devoted his brother had been towards managing the crisis in his absence.

"I'll have a word with him," she replied, although she was tempted to instruct the guards to let Jeremy stay outside until Nathan came home.

"Dinner's ready," Shirley Beaumont called as she opened up the dining room's double doors on the other side of the hall. "Any chance either of you have seen Bianca around?"

"Same chance of me seeing Aimee," Evelyn smiled, her frustration with her useless brother-in-law fading.

The two women shook their heads at each other, sharing a knowing expression as they entered the dining room. All four of the mahogany tables inside were convertible, each seating twelve when fully extended for formal occasions, and comfortably seating eight when folded on a hinge into a square for casual meals. Enrique Garrido turned and happily raised his wineglass at them from his seat on the square table closest to the kitchen. Marv clapped the fusspot event coordinator on his fleshy shoulder and sat down beside him, reaching for the bottle of merlot and pouring glasses for Evelyn and himself before passing it across the table to Shirley and Michelle.

Evelyn had taken to dining with the senior members of the house staff following the first doleful dinner on the day that Nathan had left for Cloakwater. The silence had been suffocating between herself and Jeremy – the only other person to show up on time – while they waited for the girls to arrive.

As if on cue, one of the front doors creaked open and shut with a soft thud. Sadie peered into the dining room and glanced back at the staircase, biting her lip before bashfully joining the others around the table. She settled in beside Evelyn and wiped her hands on a table napkin before spreading it over her lap. There was a fragrance about her that reminded Evelyn of Ryan's aloe vera hair gel, although she dismissed the aroma as another faint *clack* of the pool balls.

"Just the six of us then?" asked Enrique, glancing at the three empty place settings that had been squashed together before holding his wineglass aloft as he turned to check whether anyone else had crept into the hall behind Sadie.

"Yes," Evelyn nodded at the waitress lingering by the service door, who promptly disappeared into the kitchens. "Jeremy won't be joining us, and the girls will eat whenever they decide that they're hungry."

"Like a pair of stray cats, those two," Shirley commented before taking a sip of wine.

"Three, if you count Jeremy," Marv sat with his arms folded as he lounged in his chair.

The service door opened again with Mabel Brown supervising a small crew of caterers as they emerged from the kitchens, bearing a pair of boiled blue crabs surrounded by sticks of butter along with tartare and aioli dipping sauces, plates of mashed potatoes garnished with parsley and chives, creamy scallop fettuccine dusted with parmesan cheese, and a roast chicken basted with lemon and garlic butter.

Michelle's concern over food wastage was a distant memory as she savoured the seductive smells of each dish. Marv sat up in his chair again, pulling one of the blue crab platters closer to him and Enrique. Shirley had her eyes set on the seafood fettuccine, but she allowed Evelyn the honour of breaking into the meal, masking her salivating lips with another sip of merlot as the creamy sauce oozed into the pasta's fresh crater.

Ignoring the food, Sadie turned aside to exchange whispers with Paige Spencer, a button-nosed kitchenhand with wavy strawberry blonde hair, the pair of girls giggling at some secret joke.

That's not like her, Evelyn noted as she handed the pasta tongs to Shirley.

"Hey, Mabel," Marv called the sassy sous chef over to his side, holding up his empty wineglass with a faint smile playing at his lips, "Can I get a refill?"

"You know damn well I'm not here to pour your drink, old man," she replied with a hand on her hip.

"So sexy, and yet so cruel," Marv chuckled as Enrique reached for the bottle and topped him up. "At least somebody around here loves me."

"You better shut your mouth before your dentures fall out, grandpa," she warned playfully as Marv held a hand to his chest, consoling his broken heart. Mabel shook her head with a smirk before turning her ire on Cody, the lanky pasty-white kitchenhand lingering by the door with a lopsided grin as he eyed Paige leaning down beside Sadie. "Cody, you goofy ass, stop staring with your damn mouth open and get back in the kitchen."

He nodded obediently, scratching his nose and staring for a few more moments before quietly slinking out of the room. The rest of the caterers soon followed in his wake, and Mabel raised her eyebrows at Paige. Noticing the sous chef's gaze, Sadie cut their whispered conversation short before Paige could get in trouble.

"Bon appétit!" Mabel smiled at them gracefully before glaring at Marv and mouthing "asshole" as she shut the service door.

It was impossible for Evelyn to hide her grin as she ate. The past few nights had been full of banter, and she found herself wondering why she hadn't dined with the senior members of the house staff more often. It was almost enough to take her mind off Nathan and the boys, but not completely.

She tuned back into the dinner conversation as it turned towards the protest outside, which had grown in numbers since Haydar's first appearance.

"… and now with the Velvet Convoy, there's even more reason to come," Enrique remarked before cracking a crab leg open and sucking out the meat.

"In more ways than one," Marv smirked, licking his fingers.

"They can camp outside all they like," Michelle said as she carved into a moist roast chicken breast, "But the diesel from Cloakwater won't flow any faster."

"And they certainly won't be getting any of our supplies," Evelyn added, popping a mollusc in her mouth.

"Do we have enough supplies though?" Sadie asked, unsure of who to turn to, so she looked to her mother.

"We're still working out the food," Michelle covered her mouth with a napkin before swallowing, "But we have *plenty* of fuel and golden bucks to buy more, if need be."

"I'm sure we can outlast them," Marv winked at Sadie as he washed down the crabmeat with a sip of wine. "They'll either run out of food before us, or they'll get bored and leave."

"I wouldn't bet on it," Shirley replied as she twirled fettuccine around her fork. "I've seen a few of the protesters coming straight from the farm belt, and it looks like some of them have brought everything they own."

"I'm just glad that at least for once," Evelyn began as she spooned a ladle of creamy mashed potato onto her plate, soaking up the remains of the seafood pasta sauce, "We aren't the ones footing the bill for the biggest event in Rubicross."

* * *

A light breeze whispered through the colourful array of columbines and bluebonnets as Evelyn sat on a garden bench, enjoying the subtle floral scents as she digested her meal in the warm evening air. The peace and tranquillity of the gardens were somewhat cheapened by the rabble's raucous ruckus rising over the walls, but over the past few days, Evelyn had managed to tune out the noise somewhat.

Imogen Hainsley was still hard at work, even at this hour, morosely pruning wilted flowers with a pair of secateurs. She had a matronly figure, with her blonde hair falling in curls over her wide-sleeved dress. The middle-aged woman had never married. She had been quite content to live out a quiet life with her elderly mother in the suburbs of Brimvale. For as long as Evelyn could remember, Imogen and her mother had endeavoured to keep their garden in pristine condition, even after the end of the world.

But when The Long Summer Night came, tweakers from The Gutter killed her mother and had their way with Imogen, leaving her broken and depressed, like a sunflower that stopped reaching for the sky, staring earthwards instead, searching for its roots in the dirt to bury its shrivelled golden crown beside them. She could have wandered off into The Burning Forest along with all of the other disenchanted women and victims of that dreadful night, and no one would have been surprised.

A creature of habit however, Imogen had been seen working in her front yard the very next day, battered and bruised, yet still pruning her rosebushes all the same, where they later learned had been the site where she had chosen to lay her elderly mother to rest.

After the Royce Family had moved to Rubicross, Nathan took a trip back to Brimvale to hire her as soon as they had a garden to tend. Evelyn was surprised when she heard that Imogen had accepted his offer, but she couldn't imagine the heartache of having to spend so much time around her mother's grave each and every day. Come to think about it, after everything that had occurred during The Long Summer Night, Evelyn couldn't imagine how *anyone* could still bear to live in Brimvale.

She felt a chill despite the warmth in the air, and she began to head back to the residence, when a guard's shout sounded from atop the front wall. Moments later, one of the storey-high wooden gates creaked open, and a pair of silhouettes slipped into the estate.

Did you think I wouldn't catch you and your whore, Jeremy? She marched across the grounds towards the two figures, who promptly stopped in their tracks at the sight of her. Evelyn's pace faltered as well. Either Jeremy's stooped posture had stripped him of a foot of height, or he was still somewhere beyond the walls. The silhouettes' hair swished in the night as they searched for a place to hide, and Evelyn's eyes widened in horror as their faces began to materialise.

"What were you two doing outside!?" her voice broke as she yelled. Aimee and Bianca shrank closer together. "Don't you know how *dangerous* it is out there?"

"It's not dangerous at all," Aimee was the first to speak, swelling her chest defiantly and stepping in front of Bianca, sparing her from Evelyn's wrath. "They're just normal people out there. You'd even recognise a few of them."

"They are *protesters*, Aimee," Evelyn breathed exasperatedly, "They want what we have in the warehouse, and it's only a matter of time before they get violent!"

"We know, and that's what we're trying to prevent," Aimee replied, brushing her curtain of hair back over her ear. "Violence is the last thing on anyone's mind when they're singing and dancing and having a good time, and that's exactly what we gave them!"

"And what if something happened to you?" Evelyn crossed her arms, her shoulders stiff as stone. "What if someone held you hostage and demanded that we hand over all of our supplies for your release? Or worse, what if they just *took* you and nobody said anything, because nobody knew where you were. *We never know where you are!*"

Another guard's shout sounded from above the gatehouse, and one of the big wooden doors creaked open again. Jeremy sauntered back into the estate with a glazed grin, which disappeared the moment he laid eyes upon Evelyn.

"Uncle Jeremy knew where we were," Aimee replied in a soft voice, glancing guiltily over her shoulder at her uncle.

"Get inside. Now," Evelyn menaced, her lips tightening as she stared daggers at her drunken brother-in-law, "I'll deal with you two later."

Aimee and Bianca promptly obliged, practically running back towards the residence. Jeremy opened his mouth to explain, but Evelyn held up her hands, not interested in hearing the half-cocked excuse he was sure to spew at her.

"Why am I not surprised?" she asked as the shabby wretch of a man staggered in place just to stand up straight. "Getting drunk with the very people who could attack us at any moment… And putting my daughter in danger!? Your brother would be so disappointed. He gives you chance after chance and you just let him down again and again."

"Listen," he began, his gangly frame swaying underneath him.

She folded her arms and raised her eyebrows, steeling herself to have the patience to hear him out before she would call for the guards to drag him back outside the gates. There was nothing he could say to change her mind.

"Well?" she asked, her face drawn with disdain.

"Just listen," he held a long finger in the air, showing a toothy smile as he looked up at the sky. But besides the noise from the riffraff outside the walls, there was nothing more to hear. He looked back at her before she could say anything further. "Listen to the people, their laughter, their singing. They're having fun out there. They're celebrating life without diesel. *This* was the response they needed. Not something born out of hate, or fear, but love."

Evelyn narrowed her eyes at him. He was speaking coherently for someone who could barely stand.

"They're our loyal customers," he continued, imploring her with his head tilted at an abnormal angle. He couldn't even see straight. "We need to show them that we still care about them when they aren't giving us money. Maybe we could even give them a gesture of goodwill, for everything they've given us over the years. Some food and drinks from our warehouse would keep them thinking that it's a party rather than a rally. And it's much better to have them chanting lyrics instead of chanting protests."

He was almost beginning to sound like Nathan. Give everything away and expect nothing in return. If it had been anyone other than Jeremy making the suggestion, perhaps she would have entertained the idea.

"No," Evelyn said flatly, unconvinced. "I'm not giving your friends any more free food and drinks. Tell them they'll have to feed themselves for a change. And the same goes for you."

Jeremy swallowed dryly, blinking and staggering, certain that he must have misheard her.

"Guards!!" she yelled.

CHAPTER 25 – LIAM

They had arrived in Rookson City a few days ago, which had been largely uneventful compared to the powder keg standoff at the surprise residential roadblock in the seemingly abandoned bayside town of Bellevue. One flash of Quentin Davis's senior officer badge was all it had taken for their ambushers to have a change of heart, at least according to Quentin. Of course, it had nothing to do with Sergeant Butch Gorman opening up the gunner's hatch on the roof of the armoured truck, swivelling the mounted turret in a slow circle and announcing on a bullhorn of his own that he was more than happy to saw them all in half.

The mobile firing squad in the rusty yellow school bus blocking them in from behind had quickly ducked out of sight, and the rifles and pistols pointing out of broken windows on either side of the suburban street began to waver as they awaited their leader's instructions, wherever the voice on the megaphone had come from.

Lora Purcell had curled up into a petrified ball in the front passenger seat of their black SUV, while Liam had lain down flat on the floor in the backseat, his only solace being that Quentin and Lora would most likely be the first to die in the shootout.

Emboldened by the presence of their military escort however, Quentin had decided to play the hero, holding his ID out the window, as if anyone in their right minds would have approached the pair of vehicles to take a closer look.

Then, a garage door's screech of metal had resounded from one of the double-storey houses, revealing a black-and-white SUV emblazoned with "state trooper" on the front quarter panels. Four former highway patrolmen emerged from the garage, dressed in weather-worn dark tan uniforms that were adorned with blue epaulettes and red shoulder patches.

Archie Callahan had warned Liam about the highwaymen. Officially, they had been hired as one of Rookson City's roving bands of mercenaries, assigned to guard the road between Brimvale and Rookson after their law enforcement unit no longer held the same authority or government salary in the lawless post-apocalypse. The reality was that they were just a bunch of brigands, accustomed to accosting anyone caught unarmed on the road, swiping their supplies, executing the survivors, and claiming that they had been the first on the scene in the wake of yet another horrible "random" attack.

Under the watchful gaze of Butch's mounted machine gun barrel, they had done their best to appear imposing, hooking thumbs into their belts and spreading their elbows wide as they approached. For Sergeant Gorman however, they were just giving him a bigger target. One of the former officers approached the SUV while the other three unsuccessfully searched for an opening in the gun turret's armour plating.

"Mr Quentin Davis," the chevron-moustached trooper with dark sunglasses read as he scanned the ID. "I'm gonna need you to step out of the vehicle."

"What for?" Lora asked, unfolding from her defensive ball in the passenger seat. "You was the ones pointing your fucking guns at us."

"That was for our protection," the officer replied matter-of-factly. "Now step out of the vehicle."

"Don't," Liam cautioned, reaching past Quentin's shoulder from behind and slamming the central door lock with his palm. As much as he would have loved to watch what he suspected was going to happen, it was against his own self-interest. "He knows you're in charge. He'll use you as a meat-shield until you order Butch to stand down."

"I'm just trying to do my job," the trooper reasoned, his eyes on Quentin.

"Sure you are," Quentin said as he withdrew his ID badge. "That is, if your job is to patrol the highway from the houses of Bellevue's backstreets."

"Not much of a choice nowadays," the officer replied, looking back at his three partners and glancing up at Butch again, wondering what was taking so long. "Can't afford to burn fuel on the road anymore ever since the diesel stopped coming from Rubicross, so we've been funnelling everyone through town inst–"

"That's not our problem," Liam interrupted from the backseat. They had to get moving soon. He could tell that the officer was just stalling for time. A well-placed bullet from one of the second-storey windows on either side of the street could take out Butch at any given moment, and then they would lose the slim amount of leverage that they had. "But if you let us go, we might be able to fix it."

The highwayman combed his moustache in consideration, his interest piqued.

"Exactly," Lora perked up, latching onto the idea as if it was her own, "If you want more diesel, we was just on our way to meet with Victor MacDougall to offer him some of Brimvale's fuel reserves. You don't want to be the ones who got in the way of that, do you?"

"We could turn around," Quentin shrugged, even though their vehicles had been blocked in from both sides. "We'll just have to tell Victor we missed our appointment because we couldn't get through the only blockade between Brimvale and Rookson."

"I'm sure you can appreciate the gravity of the situation," Lora added, rather unnecessarily. She was practically bouncing in her seat at the thought of being able to talk their way out of the mess.

The trooper swallowed, staring into the SUV and scanning their faces for a lie before returning to his three colleagues for a whispered conversation, each of them occasionally glancing back at the pair of vehicles. The chevron-moustached officer soon signalled to the house with the open garage, and a voice on the unseen megaphone instructed the rest of their people watching from the broken windows on either side of the suburban street to stand down and reset the trap on the road.

Of course, they never had an appointment with Victor MacDougall. That had been a bluff, along with the bullets in Butch's mounted machine gun.

The guards posted along the massive concrete walls of Rookson City had held them at gunpoint when they arrived, confiscating their weapons and vehicles upon entry through the gigantic rust-covered rolling gate. Shortly afterwards, a not-so-friendly welcoming party whisked Brimvale's diplomats away to a trio of suites in the hotel tower of the Golden Buck Casino, while strategically placing their three guards, Butch, Bulldov and Wilson, in different rooms on different floors, with unlimited access to round-the-clock room service.

Liam had a fair idea that there were cameras in each room, ensuring that they were all on their best behaviour, but at least the view was nice. He could see Brimvale beyond the office towers and apartment buildings of Sunken City on the far side of Bellevue Bay, along with The Rapture cruise ship in the bay itself, dead in the water as its ant-sized inhabitants idly lounged upon the sprawling pool deck.

Rookson City had once been a popular tourist destination, offering a pristine white sand beach with a backdrop of busking musicians, street entertainers and craft stalls along the wide esplanade; the Rookson Board-walk Mall was packed with high-end fashion stores, seaside restaurants and cafes, with plans to add an entertainment complex featuring a double-storey arcade centre, a virtual reality playground, and cinemas with the largest screens in South Tekota; and of course, the Golden Buck Casino, where the currency of the post-apocalypse had originated, with its golden stag emblazoned upon every entrance, signboard and casino chip, in case anyone ever forgot where they were sinking their life savings.

Now, the coast was abandoned, with a huge concrete wall sealing off the esplanade from the rest of Rookson. The wall surrounding the city had been completed with various building materials sourced from the construction site of the mall's planned extension, with enormous prefabricated panels and welded sheets of metal embedded into the ground, patched together and fortified by a thick layer of concrete and steel rebar.

Besides being prized for its vault of casino chips and defensive capabilities,

Rookson was also well-known for its ammunition factory. The roving bands of mercenaries in the city's employment would routinely scavenge the abandoned outlying towns farther to the east, bringing back scrap metal and fertiliser which would be melted down and purified, then recycled into bullets at Hardy Munitions and sold across South Tekota. The fortress-like city had prospered upon its formidable pillars of military, industrial and commercial might, but an unprecedented shortage of diesel was their Achilles' heel.

"What the fuck is taking them so long to see us?" Lora asked, her cheeks flushed red with impatience. She held up her thumb and forefinger, her eyes flicking between Liam and Quentin. "I am seriously *this close* to just grabbing our shit and leaving."

They were sitting in the lounge of Quentin's business suite during their daily midday meeting. The rooms that they had been given were most definitely reserved for the high rollers of the old world, affording spacious blue-grey suede couches, black marble tabletops, a fully-stocked minibar, and double-plated glass windows to ensure that each guest settled their debts before leaving the casino hotel.

Liam had sincerely hoped that Quentin the Unsmiling would be forced to foot the bill for all six rooms at the end of their stay, but to the man's marked relief, the bellhop had informed them that Victor MacDougall always offered complementary accommodation to all of his esteemed guests. All Quentin had to do was ensure that he was worthy of Victor's esteem.

"They're posturing," Quentin replied, sipping from a tall glass of soda water and savouring it as if he was sucking on a lemon. "Gives the impression their time's more important than ours. They also want to see how desperate we are."

"They can posture all they want," Liam sat with his arms crossed, waiting for the meeting to end. He wanted nothing more than to leave the reeking smell of prostitution that was permeating throughout Quentin's room. Even more frustrating was that they had been talking through the same conversation every day since the moment they had arrived. "Their supply of diesel is dwindling, and our supply of bullets is the same as it was last week. Their mercenaries are running on fumes, and our buses are still running as normal. Their generators are about to die, and our entire grid is powered by solar. They need this deal more than us."

Lora scowled at him. She was still bitter that he hadn't blindly followed her orders to volunteer himself to clear the fallen tree from the highway outside Bellevue, despite how vulnerable he would have been if he had left the vehicle. For the rest of the ride to Rookson, she had cited his blatant insubordination as the sole reason why they had been ambushed. Apparently the mercenaries were completely blameless in the matter since they had only been following orders, unlike Liam. Nevertheless, she knew that he was right about the Rookson Council. And he knew that she knew, because she kept her snarky mouth shut.

"Every day that goes by," Liam continued, hoping to hammer his point home today so that they wouldn't have to repeat the same mundane monotonous meeting again tomorrow, "Our position strengthens, and theirs weakens. In a couple of weeks, we could offer them one fifth of the fuel that we're willing to give them now, and they'd still take it."

"Maybe Lora's right," Quentin conceded, to her palpable pleasure. She could care less about what she had finally gotten right, as long as she was given the credit. "Maybe it's time to leave."

"I'll pack my things," Liam stood immediately and headed for the door.

He was halfway across the room when the suite's doorbell rang. Standing in the corridor was the bellhop, breathless, as if he had just run from another suite at the other end of the hall.

"The Council will see you now," he panted the moment Liam opened the door. "Follow me."

* * *

Liam followed at a distance, but he could almost feel the brooding intensity of Quentin's glowering frown as they were led through a series of passageways that grew narrower and less inviting with each turn, the circular patterns of the casino's warm red carpet giving way to a grey vinyl floor.

"Where the fuck are you taking us?" Lora breathed exasperatedly as they reached an intersection and turned down yet another service corridor.

"To see the Council," the bellhop replied, keeping his eyes fixed on the path ahead. "We're almost there now."

At long last, they reached a pair of plain grey double doors, one marked with "Stage Door". The bellhop turned the handle and gestured for them to enter. Liam glanced over his shoulder, looking back at the way they had come. He had remembered the first few turns since leaving the casino's carpet, but after that, the passageways became a labyrinth. Retracing his steps would be near-impossible, and it seemed that Quentin and Lora were weighing up the same dilemma.

"Let's get this over with," Liam decided, sighing through his nose as he quickly became aware that he was going to have to be the first to walk through the shadowy entrance, if only to deny Lora the satisfaction of giving him the order and watching as he followed through on what he would have done anyway.

He led the way into what appeared to be a gloomy warehouse, warily eyeing plywood frames, stacks of black crates, and columns of metal cables reaching up towards dull pulleys obscured by the dark ceiling. The stage door creaked as the bellhop swung it shut behind them, sealing their fate.

The sound of their footsteps was dampened by the soft wooden floorboards, as if the cavernous room wanted nothing more than to swallow them whole in the oppressive silence. And yet, the silence threatened to explode as one of the warehouse's walls materialised into a pair of gigantic curtains.

A buzzing drum sounded from somewhere behind the curtains, and twin circles of light traced symmetrical patterns across the heavy red velvet fabric before sweeping towards the centre to reveal a thin opening. Peering through the crack, Liam stared out at rows upon rows of dimly-lit plush red theatre seats. The vast majority of them were empty, but there were a few in the front row that were occupied.

"What is it?" Lora whispered as she crept forward, overcome by her own curiosity.

"Don't be shy," a whiskey-cured voice called out from the audience on the other side. "You are all welcome! Shall we begin?"

As Lora stared out through the drapes, Liam pulled back one side, presenting the members of the intimate crowd with an eyeful of the nosy bottle blonde gawking back at them. She shot Liam with an indignant glare as he gestured for her and Quentin to step out onto the stage.

Perking up and putting on her all too familiar fake smile, Lora willed herself forward, summoning an overly-friendly wave as Quentin the Unsmiling trailed in her wake, still wearing his perpetual frown of disapproval.

Liam dropped the curtain behind them, preferring the company of the inanimate props and set pieces wreathed in shadow compared to whoever had staged this unnecessarily elaborate meeting. He crept around the side, keeping to the darkness of the wings as Quentin and Lora made their introductions to the near-empty auditorium under the harsh glare of the spotlights, not even aware of his absence, not that they ever cared for his presence anyway.

"I hope you'll forgive our tardiness in receiving you," the whiskey-cured voice came again from a bald man in a black suit sitting in the front row, his handful of Rookson Council cohorts spanning out on either side. "We've been preoccupied with other pressing matters."

This must be Victor MacDougall, Liam concluded. Only the richest man in South Tekota would be arrogant enough to drag less than a dozen people into a theatre hall for a conference rather than a more appropriately-sized meeting room.

Victor began introducing his Council, but Liam didn't pay any attention. He doubted that he would be able to remember any of them, even if he had any interest in making the effort. They were all carbon copy corporate pigs, people who had never worked a day in their lives, whose fathers had all met each other at some exclusive golf course for the elite and planned out careers for their children so that they could carry on the family tradition of profiting off the backs of others who traded their lives for peanuts, knowing that they would never reach the top of the corporate pyramid, no matter how many asses they kissed or toes they stepped on.

"I see that Mayor Paxton isn't with you," Victor remarked, his face obscured in the dim lighting contrasted against the illumination of the stage. "Does this proposal mean so little to him that he doesn't feel the need to attend?"

"He's preoccupied with other pressing matters," Lora blurted out rather aggressively before quickly tightening her lips and deferring to Quentin.

"I'm sure he is," Victor replied with subtle sarcasm as one of the Council members murmured a sly joke to another. "To business, then! Our mercenaries have informed us that you'd like to make a gift of Brimvale's fuel reserves. How gracious of you."

"Not a gift," Quentin's stony face cracked into one of his rare smiles, "An exchange."

"An exchange?" Victor raised his eyebrows, wrinkling his bald head in feigned confusion. "And what exchange would that be? A cultural exchange? An exchange of information?"

"An exchange of commodities," Quentin answered, his smile plummeting back into the black pit he had pulled it from. Then, to ensure that he wasn't purposely misconstrued any further, he added, "Bullets."

"Ah, bullets!" Victor exclaimed, leaning back in his chair. "You see what happens when you use your words, Quentin? We actually get somewhere!"

Liam snorted as Quentin clenched his jaw. Perhaps Victor wasn't as completely full of himself as Liam had thought him to be. Or perhaps the man was just trying to bait Quentin into a pissing contest. Maybe that was the reason why none of the other Council members were talking; they had already been out-pissed.

"Is that how you plan to deal with the Rauders?" Victor mused, tapping his chin with his index finger. "I only ask because we've had troubles with the cannibals from Grismorne attacking our scavenging parties lately." He held up a hand when Quentin opened his mouth to speak. "Let Lora answer for a change. I'd like to hear more than five words at a time."

"We've hired mercenaries to deal with them," Lora replied, glancing sidelong at Quentin for some hint of approval. "Maybe you could do the same."

"Mercenaries are such lovely creatures, aren't they?" Victor smiled in the dim light. "There's not a problem in the world you can't fix with a person who kills for money! Provided you have the money, that is. Thank you for the advice, Lora. I need more people like you in my Council." Then with a serpentine smirk, he added, "I'd make you my queen if you decided to stay, even just for a while."

Liam rolled his eyes at the false flattery, having suffered the company of fake people for long enough to set off his bullshit radar at the slightest hint, and Victor was laying it on thick. Lora, on the other hand, was lapping up the praise and attention.

"I only wish there was seaborne mercenary crews for hire," Lora attempted to change the topic, even while she was still blushing at his proposal. "Then we could deal with the pirates that have been threatening our coast."

"Ah, so you need the bullets for the pirates," Victor crossed his legs in his seat, nodding at one of his colleagues as if they had placed a bet. "Well, if you like, I can negotiate for a ceasefire with the pirates so that they leave your coast alone. If you give some consideration to staying here in Rookson, that is."

"What's your connection to the pirates?" Quentin broke his silence.

"Six words!" Victor exclaimed, the other Council members sniggering. "Well done, Quentin. You'll return to Brimvale a changed man at this rate. To answer your question, there is no connection. But our sheer military strength would be enough to make the pirates think twice about attacking."

Tired of listening in from the shadows, Liam stepped out from the wings and onto the stage. Not into the spotlight though. He wanted to avoid staring into the glare. He sat down on the curtained apron instead, his feet dangling over the side.

"If you're strong enough to intimidate the pirates into a ceasefire," Liam began, eyeing the Council members dubiously, "Why are you having trouble with the attacks from Grismorne?"

"*There* you are!" Victor laughed, turning his bald head from side to side, studying his associates to see if they had suspected this plot twist in his private play of politics.

The man was completely hairless. Even his eyebrows were gone, his serpentine blue eyes set within the slightly sagging folds of his chubby pink-tinged face like a human-sized naked mole rat.

"I was wondering where the third member of your party had disappeared to," Victor continued, still wearing his smile of surprise. "I thought you might have gotten lost somewhere in the service corridors. The difference, my boy, is that the pirates are on the water, like ducks in a shooting gallery, whereas the cannibals strike from the trees. And besides, there's no reasoning with those savages from Grismorne."

Liam was still unconvinced, but the answer seemed to satisfy Lora, who glared at him for interrupting their diplomatic affairs, as if talking to other community leaders wasn't part of the role that she had supposedly given him. He followed Quentin's lead for a change, keeping his mouth shut, so that he wouldn't be held responsible for screwing up the ammunition deal.

"I expected at least a few more questions from you," Victor eyed Liam with disappointment before waving his hands. "Okay, I'm bored! Let's talk numbers."

"Twenty barrels of diesel, twenty canisters of bullets," Quentin answered, clenching his jaw as he prepared to be congratulated for adding two more words into his sentences.

"Do you know how much diesel it takes just to produce *one* batch of bullets?" Victor scoffed. "Twenty barrels gets you ten cans!"

"Twenty cans," Quentin repeated sternly, testing how desperate they were for fuel, "Fifteen barrels for getting greedy."

"Fine, fifteen!" Victor conceded, knowing when to cut his losses. Running his own casino and watching gamblers lose everything over the years afforded him that insight.

"Ten cans today," Quentin added, his cold blue eyes staring, "The other ten on delivery."

The other Council members glanced sidelong at Victor as he clambered to his feet, placing his hands wide on the stage's apron. Liam stopped swinging his shoes over the edge of the platform. They had already agreed on the numbers, but it didn't seem like they were about to shake hands.

"Done, but on one condition," a slow smile started spreading across Victor's pink face. "Lora accompanies the diesel delivery to Rookson. Where she will stay."

CHAPTER 26 – DAMIAN

Damian Bishop lounged on the charcoal grey sofa in his second-storey office turned bedroom with a self-satisfied grin across his square jaw as he considered his black leather bomber jacket hanging on the wall by the door. It was one of his favourite pastimes, back when the Mafia had him pretending to push pencils for the port; lazing by his office window and waiting for the black-and-white wall clock to hit half past four before he fucked off early.

Other than keeping an eye on the day's manifests for luxury cars, expensive suits and dresses, and any other big-ticket items that had a tendency to mysteriously vanish in transit, there was very little else that his old job had demanded of him, and so he would spend the majority of his "workdays" sleeping off hangovers, or slurping a coffee while he watched the ships dock and dump their loads like a flock of rusty cocks stopping by a brothel.

But now that the coffee was shit, the manifests were all the same, and he couldn't find a bartender who could mix a decent old-fashioned if his pipe depended on it, there wasn't a whole lot of things that he could do to pass the time other than sit in silent contemplation, but at least today's topic of contemplation gave him plenty of reasons to smile.

"I can't believe you fucked up the ONE thing I asked you to do!" Barry Sutton, the chunky red-cheeked boss of the docks had blustered in his office earlier, one of his piggy eyes twitching as another crusty cluster of hemorrhoids burst.

Word had somehow managed to get back to Flintscray Port that the latest delivery of ammunition to the Bouncers had been light, and Barry clearly wasn't taking it very well. Part of Damian had known that he wouldn't have been able to trust Claude and his two fuck-buddies from the Red Light District to report that the bullet count had been precise, but it was precisely what he had been counting on.

"You're off deliveries, you stupid son of a bitch!" Barry yelled, to Damian's pleasure. He had graduated from being a delivery boy decades ago. "I want you to find out who fucked up the shipment, otherwise it's your ass on the line!!"

"Not really," Damian yawned back.

"NOT REALLY!?" Barry swept his ornamental mug full of stationery off his desk in a fit of fury, the cheap cup exploding against the wall and sending pens flying in every direction.

"Not really," he repeated casually, chuckling as he imagined the bloody shit-stain around Barry's asshole when he would later have to bend down and clean up the mess, like a big red brown eye angrily glaring around the room. "Sure, I might've been sitting in the back of the truck, but who's running the show here? Not me."

"Are you fucking threateni–"

"You know it as well as I do," Damian interrupted coolly.

Barry swallowed his indignation, and his purple shade of anger had seemed to fade as the truth of it slowly dawned across his bloated face. Regardless of whoever had been responsible for the botched delivery, the pirates from Attiker Island would want to make an example out of the port's leader as a warning to the rest of the Flints that nobody was untouchable, while also serving as a reminder of who was really in charge.

"But I've got it all under control," Damian went on in the least-derisive tone he could muster. "So relax. If there's one thing I can guarantee, it's that I'll have things back to the way they used to be around here."

Of course, he hadn't just been talking about Flintscray Port. That was only part of it. He was referring to the rest of Bushrock. He still yearned for the good old days, back when the Mafia was in control, and after his brief bout of nostalgia walking through the streets of Little Italy on his way over to the Velvet Convoy the last time they were in town, he had cooked up a plan that was sure to cripple each one of the would-be gangs that had popped up to squabble over their own piece of the pie. And like any good pie, every piece was bound to crumble after Damian's cream filling.

"Yeah, well you fucking better," Barry had grumbled grouchily as he considered his shattered mug and the mess of pens spread across the floor, "And I want that thieving motherfucker's dick on my desk so I can shove it up his ass before we turn him over to the pirates. I want them to *know* who does the fucking around here!!"

"I'm sure they already know 'fucking around' is what you do best," Damian grinned as he had left Barry's office, leaving the door wide open to hear the barrage of garbled profanities following him down the metal staircase and all the way back to his quarters.

Agitating Barry was another one of his favourite pastimes, simply because of how easy it was to rile him up. Damian's parting barb had fallen just short of what he had been tempted to do though: flop his cock out, lay it on the desk with a big meaty smack and wait for Barry to realise who the thieving motherfucker was.

The groaning of the metal walkway as it strained under heavy footsteps announced Donnie Lombardo's arrival long before the butterball's meaty hand knocked on Damian's door. He sighed, folding his arms and glancing up at the clock on the wall. 4:19.

"Door's open," he said reluctantly. *Who the fuck walks into somebody's office right before knock-off time*, he wondered rhetorically as the door handle turned.

The former ice cream man huffed and puffed his way into the office, bringing his thick body odour's sugary stench along with him. Sweat glistened across his forehead and soaked his grey polo shirt, the cotton cloth clinging to him like a wet newspaper. Damian wondered how many pounds the man would have lost if his own sleeping quarters were up on the second storey too. But who was he kidding? The bolts holding up the walkway outside would have snapped off years ago.

"Where… can I… sthit down?" Donnie lisped between gasps of air, one fleshy hand on the wall and the other holding one of his thunder thighs.

Damian's eyes looked over his own office with a dubious expression. Neither of the chairs on either side of his desk would hold Donnie's weight, not even the desk itself, and he wasn't about to give up his spot on the sofa for the sweat-soaked sasquatch.

"I'm about to head out soon," he replied, still stretched out on the couch. "Catch your breath and make it quick."

"Randy's walkin' around the yard," Donnie panted, glancing out the window, "Asthkin' everybody about the other canisthter."

Barry must have called in his resident brown-noser, a shit-munching schmuck by the name of Randy Wratchet, to launch a second investigation into the missing shipment of ammunition. It was the same guy who never knew how to look the other way back when Damian had been tipping off the Mafia about luxury items whenever they came off the ships. The only difference now was that Randy had Barry's unhindered support.

"What fucking canister?" Damian cocked his head, feigning incredulity.

"The canisthter," Donnie repeated, straightening up and mopping his forehead with the back of his arm, "Those fuckin' Bouncer basthtards sthold usth out. They sthaid we took the half the bulletsth. You gotta hand it in before we get in trouble."

"I still don't know what you're talking about," Damian frowned quizzically, glancing at the clock on the wall again, wondering how long this was going to take. "What are the rest of the boys saying?"

"Nobody's stheen shit," Donnie shrugged his immense shoulders, his neck momentarily disappearing from existence. "Only that both the canisthters got loaded up into the truck like they do every other time. Everyone was off havin' lunch when we came back."

"And you haven't talked to Randy yet?" asked Damian, sitting up now.

Donnie's loose chins practically hit his ears as he shook his head from side to side.

"But I can't avoid him forever," said Donnie, reaching up and wiping the sweat off the back of his neck. "What should I do if he comes knockin' on my door?"

"So nobody else has seen shit," Damian replied in a measured tone as he rose to his feet, eyeing Donnie, and as gigantic as the man was, he seemed to shrink under the weight of Damian's gaze. "Why should your story be any different? I think those Bouncers might have gotten their facts wrong, because I haven't seen shit either."

Donnie's eyes widened as he met Damian's stare, finally nodding his comprehension.

"Now," Damian tested, squaring his jaw, "You were saying something about a canister?"

"What fuckin' canisthter?" Donnie replied, faking a flummoxed frown.

"What fucking canister," Damian echoed with a grin, turning the door handle and ushering the witless witness out. He left the door open for a while, in the thin hope that Donnie's reeking musk would follow him out.

Damian glanced up at the clock again. 4:23. *Fuck it, close enough.* He lifted his heavy leather jacket off the wall and zipped up, giving the room a quick once-over before closing the office blinds and heading out onto the metal walkway.

The dockyard below was a gigantic seaside concrete quadrangle, surrounded on three sides by walls of shipping containers that the port crane had stacked up like a bunch of building blocks, each rusty container serving as either retrofitted living quarters or as a barricade against the rest of the sorry bastards who were still living in Bushrock.

It was a simple but effective setup that had allowed the Flints to survive the Turf Wars, without having to plead for mercy while deep-throating a gun barrel. The only way in or out – besides the sea – was through the kill-box, a single bloodstained shipping container that had been dropped in sideways between the double-thick walls, open at both ends, where they could cut down a raiding party into bite-sized chunks of fish bait.

The rest of the boys were working down in the dockyard, dragging their feet like they were still getting paid by the hour, monotonously checking for leaks in the network of pipes that connected the rows of black-painted water tanks of their bootstrapped water desalination plant. At the height of the Turf Wars, some of the bootleggers from Chinatown had bargained their way inside the fortified port, talking about their little science project like it was a working visa, reasoning that Brimvale could cut the water to The Gutter at any moment, and all any of them would have left to drink would be shit and seawater.

After the water tanks had been set up, Barry had chosen to keep all of the dockhands employed long after the boats from the outside world stopped coming. They worked the same hours every day, even though apart from checking the pipes for leaks, their only task was to facilitate the occasional ammo shipment – whenever the fuck the pirates felt like making an occasional ammo shipment.

Despite the daily drudgery of fucking around all day, the men who had grown accustomed to clocking on and off for a living had figured that they may as well stick around, working to defend the one place that they all shared a mutual hate for, as long as they were still getting paid.

Rat-Shit Randy was questioning a couple of dockhands who were being less than helpful in his investigation, their blunt responses stopping a few words shy of outright telling him to fuck off. Thanking them for the riveting insight into the case of the missing bullets, Randy happened to catch sight of Damian heading out into town, and promptly rushed over to intercept.

The neatly-combed and clean-shaven crumb had always been out of place among the Flints. He was more like a passing salesman who had overstayed his welcome, hawking his wares – despite having nothing to offer – to anyone who was unfortunate enough to be in earshot. Wearing a striped tie over his carefully-ironed collared shirt, he was dressed like he was on his way to a job interview, or off to some cheap crab-hopping titty bar with a bouquet and a box of chocolates for his favourite stripper in the hopes of scoring a free lap dance.

"Damian Bishop!!" Randy called in a voice loud enough to make a deaf man cringe. His fugazi face was full of fake smiles as he speed-walked to the port's exit, racing Damian to the kill-box before he could make his escape. "Just the man I wanted to see! I have some questions for you."

"Better keep up then," Damian replied out of the side of his mouth as he pushed past Randy and entered the maw of the shipping container, his footsteps reverberating around the rusty blood-stained bottleneck.

"I wanted to ask you about the missing canister," Randy's voice echoed before they emerged into the commercial car park's concrete expanse on the other side.

Abandoned delivery vans and semi-trailers stood tall among the rusty pickups and paint-worn sedans in the staff parking lot. Gunless sentries stationed along the top of the shipping container wall kept watch over the chain-linked fence lining the perimeter, as if they would be able to drop down to ground level and chase off any vandals who felt like breaking a few windows just to let off some steam.

As proof of how useless the guards were, mounds of weather-worn glass crystals were strewn around almost every vehicle in the parking lot. This was how it had always looked though; a dumping ground full of stolen cars and cars that weren't worth stealing.

The armoured truck that they used for ammunition deliveries stood closest to the port's entrance. If Donnie had his way, he would have parked it right outside his living quarters to save himself the walk, but the truck wouldn't fit through the kill-box.

"What fucking canister?" Damian asked as he marched through the parking lot.

"There's no need for that language, Damian," Randy chided, shuffling as he struggled to keep pace while attempting to confront him from the side. "The Bouncers reported that they only received *one* canister, but the workers on the dock said that they loaded up *two*. Does that strike you as odd?"

"Nothing surprises me nowadays," Damian replied, skirting past the boom gate and heading east towards Chinatown without breaking stride.

"You were the only person in the back of the truck with those canisters," said Randy, alternating between walking along the asphalt and the kerb of the narrow footpath just to stay abreast. "Any chance one of them might have been misplaced?"

"We made the drop as planned," Damian answered as they cleared the corner of the parking lot, passing under the shadow of a building and out of sight of the sentries. "If you wanna find out what happened to those canisters, you're talking to the wrong guy."

"So tell me," said Randy, loosening his tie, "Who should I be asking?"

"The three mooks who took the delivery," Damian replied, focusing on the details in his peripherals with every piss-stained alley they passed by; each dark and uneven lane filled with the remnants of sawn-off fire escapes, overflowing garbage dumpsters, and walls that were covered with more graffiti than brick.

"Language, Damian," Randy reminded him as they crossed the street to the next empty block. "And if you're expecting me to ask the Bouncers to verify that their own report is correct, then I'm sorry to say that won't be happening. Now, I'm just trying to make sense of all this, but, you were the last person to see the two canisters together. So tell me, why did the Bouncers only receive one?"

Damian's boot heels scraped to a sudden stop outside the hollowed-out carcass of an auto repair shop that crouched between a bunch of abandoned warehouses and empty factories. He raised an eyebrow at Randy.

"Are you calling me a thief?" he asked, his jaw squaring up and his ice blue eyes frosting over at the insult, as true as the accusation might have been. "You probably could've picked a better spot for it."

Rat-Shit Randy's eyes went wide as he stared around at all the empty buildings standing in the shadows of the late afternoon. His head had been so far up his own ass that he hadn't been paying attention to their surroundings at all, much less had he predicted Damian to suddenly become so defensive. If he wasn't careful, his life could end right here in front of the derelict auto repair shop, his blood pooling across the oil stains on the concrete, with only the vehicle lifts and the overturned red tool chests inside the ransacked garage to stand as witnesses.

"N-no, that's n-not what I meant," Randy stuttered, putting on a brave face and resisting the urge to piss himself. He stared at Damian's black leather bomber jacket, searching for a way out as if the answer was written somewhere within its seams. "I think I'll let you get back to your afternoon stroll. We can continue this conversation later. How long will you be in town for?"

"What are you, my fucking mother?" asked Damian, taking a step forward.

"No, no. Just making friendly conversation," Randy took two steps back, almost tripping over the kerb. He desperately needed to retake control of the situation, as if he ever had it, but he wasn't about to bitch and moan about Damian's language a third time. Then his eye twinkled, and he took on a different tact. "Would you say, a couple hours, give or take?"

"If I come back tonight," Damian menaced, catching his drift, "And there's *one thing* outta place, I'll rearrange your fucking face. Got it?"

"So," Randy began with his eyebrows raised speculatively, "I have your permission to search your quarters, then?"

"Don't act like you had the balls to ask," Damian replied, his lips curling in disgust, as if the man had just shit himself. He wouldn't have been surprised if it was true.

"Very well, thanks for the chat," said Randy, retreating even farther into the street. "Enjoy your night out on the town."

"Felching motherfucker," Damian muttered under his breath, watching the worthless weasel looking back over his shoulders while he speed-walked home.

Chuckling as he turned in the other direction, he thought to himself that Rat-Shit Randy's idea of a "night out on the town" probably involved paying double price just to tongue-punch the fart boxes of the used-up whores at the 24/7 Cum & Go after the daily gangbang creampie happy hour. *He'd lick that shit up like a stray kitten laps milk.*

Damian wasn't on his way to the Red Light District tonight though. He was headed somewhere else, but he would have to cut through Chinatown first. There wasn't much left of the waterfront district after the Turf Wars. Most of the red-pillared and green-tiled arches lining the north side of the street were still standing, but they had been decorated with bullet holes. All of the street food vendors, bootleg stalls, laundromats, overpriced restaurants and karaoke bars either got shot to shit by the Blacks from

Gainstowe Park, or they went out of business in the mass exodus that followed.

Some of the refugees fled north, bribing their way past the Burnshaw Barricade into Brimvale, with the surviving members of the Wu Family opening up a rooftop bar somewhere in the commercial district. Most of them couldn't afford the cover charge though, and so they boarded one of the deep-sea fishing vessels docked at the wharf and either made port at Rookson City or sailed out to open water.

Damian had the same idea for a while, jumping on board a ship and seeing how far out he could get before he fucked up the engine, but not with the pirates from Attiker Island patrolling the gulf. The remnants of the Red Tigers had probably thought the same thing, with their members soon defecting to the other gangs around The Gutter, just as the Mafia had done.

The Red Tigers had been the real business owners of Chinatown, running protection rackets for anyone who posted a sign above their store. The big money came from their deep-sea fishing though. They would use the boats as a front for illegal immigrants coming up from Guadasula, sometimes coming back to port with more crew and less fish than they had left with.

They had a great alliance with the Latinos as a result, and an understanding with the Flints, since Damian was in charge of checking the manifests whenever they unloaded their haul. That "understanding" came in the form of Damian's all-access pass to the back-alley brothels, the rub-and-tug massage parlours, the gambling spots, and the warehouses stacked with fireworks and counterfeit merchandise.

He had been living the good life; right up until the Blacks began to suspect that the Red Tigers were responsible for the massacre in Gainstowe Park after they had tracked Damian's car back to one of the unmarked clubs. His three-man drive-by had sparked the Turf Wars that swept fire across Bushrock, raining bullets and death on anyone caught on the wrong side of a double-brick wall.

Gainstowe Park still had the worst of it though.

The retaliation from the Red Tigers was like an impotent cuck husband making sweet love to his wife after Damian's crew had run a train on it, but even then, their staggered hit-and-run fully-automatic lead sprays had been enough to drive the survivors of the ghetto raids into a single fortified warehouse lot.

As Damian walked past the charred remains of the used-car dealerships that marked the border between Chinatown and Gainstowe Park, he could plainly see that the neighbourhood still hadn't recovered even after all these years. It was a wonder how some of the rundown houses hadn't collapsed or been reduced to piles of ashes. One weatherboard home's front wall had more holes than a cheap whore's fishnet stockings, and another looked like the withered husk of a chain smoker's lung, although the crackheads and dope fiends that still lived inside probably never even noticed the difference.

Scorched earth, motherfuckers, he grinned to himself before whistling a tune. He wasn't sure if he had ever killed the group of home invaders who had stolen his cash and killed his whores, but he damn sure had gotten his money's worth.

He rounded a street corner and came across a scattered group of shambling corpses, all at different stages of decay. One bloodshot-eyed woman was limping down the road, running with the left half of her body and dragging her dead right half along the asphalt. A ginger-haired teen was alternating between scratching his scalp and anxiously checking his blood-encrusted fingernails for bugs. Another addict was lying with his spine contorted over an overturned washing machine, jerking his limp cock furiously at anyone who made eye contact. And underneath a burnt-out sedan riddled with bullet holes was one sorry son of a bitch stuck balls deep in a K-hole, his wide eyes wildly trying to signal for help, the rest of his body completely frozen.

"Hey, man!" one of the tweakers yelled as he caught sight of Damian and attempted to approach. The junkie was bent over backwards with his head craning up at the sky, as if he was about to be swept away by the tailwind of a low-flying airliner. "You got some Jet for me, man? I'll suck your dick, man!"

Jet was the nasty new mix of meth and ketamine that the Latinos from Stepton Heights were pumping into The Gutter, and Damian had just stumbled upon a friendly street full of their happy customers.

What is it with all these guys trying to suck my dick lately? Damian wondered, slightly amused. He poked the tweaker off balance on his way past, sending the fiend reeling into the asphalt.

"Just try it, man," the addict called after him, the weight of his entire upper body resting on his skull, watching upside-down as Damian walked away. "Close your eyes, man. It feels the same, man!"

One box-braided youth in his early twenties was bouncing a basketball across the end of the street when a junkie scuttled up behind him on all fours, sniffing at his heels like a dog searching for drugs. The young man jumped before turning around to slam the ball down on the tweaker hard enough to hear his front teeth snap off on the asphalt.

The basketball bounced away, rolling towards Damian, who stooped to pick it up as he considered the youth. He was lean and muscular, wearing a white singlet and black jeans. *He'll do.*

"Nice throw, kid," said Damian, tossing the ball up and catching it. "Got a name?"

"Markeith," the youth replied, holding his hand up for the ball.

"Seriously?" Damian frowned with a grin. "Did your mother have a lisp when she mumbled 'Marcus' to the nurse?"

"What?" Markeith's arm faltered in the air, and he stepped over the addict on the asphalt as he was gathering and swallowing his snapped teeth in a solemn effort to grow them back.

"I said," Damian tossed him the basketball, "Do you wanna make some money, Markeith?"

The kid's eyes went wide, and he almost missed the ball.

"Fuck yeah!" Markeith smiled, not even doubting the offer for a moment. He was the perfect candidate. "What do I have to do?"

"First, I need you to stash this," Damian winked as he unzipped his heavy leather jacket, reaching into his two well-stitched inner pockets and pulling out a pair of pillowcases bulging with the stolen bullets.

That felching motherfucker can turn my place over, Damian grinned as he handed over the ammunition. He never had any intention of saving the bullets for himself.

"Yeah, I can do that," Markeith hugged the basketball against his hip with his elbow as he held the pillowcases aloft, trying to peer through the cloth as if there were diamonds inside.

"You keep this to yourself. Got it?" asked Damian, although he already knew what he could expect of the kid as he motioned for Markeith to lower the bags. "You find some guns to fire these with, and I'll have some *real* work for you, where you can start making some *real* money. Maybe buy your girl something nice."

"I mean, I don't have a girl, but I'll take the money," Markeith answered, still dumbfounded by the sheer luck of the opportunity that had apparently fallen into his lap. "Hey, I didn't get your name?"

Damian had been waiting for him to ask. The answer he had prepared wasn't exactly crucial to the second phase of his grand plan. It was more like the garlic bread to a plate of lasagne; the orange peel to an old-fashioned; and the set of titties too big for one hand to a topless nineteen-year-old.

"Wratchet," he replied with a smug grin. "Randy Wratchet."

CHAPTER 27 – BRISTOL

Nobody had been expecting to see Bristol arrive back at the Mayor's Office until sometime after lunch, so when she rushed into the echoing foyer of the town hall and burst through the newly-installed hardwood door in the middle of the morning, the sleepy junior staff were jolted wide awake as they looked up from behind their computer screens.

"Running late or running early?" Dwight quipped with a smile, spinning around in his office chair and wheeling away from his desk.

"Yeah, aren't you meant to be over at Sunken City today?" Shelton asked beside Liam, both of them peering over the wall of their shared workstation.

"Is the Mayor here?" Bristol asked breathlessly as she paced towards the water cooler to fill up her empty coffee mug.

"As far as I know," Dwight shrugged, swivelling in his chair as she passed by. "Want me to get him?"

"Heyyy lovelyyy, good morning!" Lora called, happily bouncing out of her private office and holding her arms out for a hug. "I've missed you sooo much while we was in Rookson. Oh my gosh, I have sooo much to tell you!"

"Lora, hey, could you call a meeting?" Bristol replied, neglecting to return the embrace as she straightened up to take a drink of water.

"Sure, hun, what's up?" Lora asked, lowering her arms but still firmly rooted to the spot, wanting to hear the news before anyone else. "Maybe we can grab some coffee first. Orrr, have you already eaten your breakfast? I still haven't yet and I'm absolutely *famished*."

"No, not yet, but I really –" Bristol could barely get more than a few words out before Lora assumed her agreement and began walking towards the front door.

"Great! Let's go grab something to eat," she chirped over her shoulder. "Relax, nobody's gonna be looking for you until after lunch anyway, which should give us *just* enough time to catch up. I've been saving some extra juicy gossip for today and I wanted *you* to be the first person to know."

Bristol's heart was pounding and her hands were trembling, and the last thing she wanted to do was leave the office to get breakfast, coffee, or anything else for that matter. She was still standing beside the water cooler even as Lora reached the hardwood door.

"Lora, please," she began, hoping against hope that she wouldn't be offending her co-worker by spurning her overly-friendly advances. "This is an emergency. Whatever you have to say, it can wait."

Lora's cheeks flushed red as her hand slipped from the door handle. She tightened her lips and shot Bristol with a disgruntled glare. Dwight promptly swivelled back to his computer screen, but it was blatantly obvious that Shelton and Liam were attempting to subtly continue watching the exchange as Lora stalked back across the grey carpet towards Bristol.

"Fine, I'll call your meeting," Lora simmered with her arms folded across her chest. "I didn't realise my life was sooo unimportant to you, but whatever."

"Lora, I didn't mean –" Bristol's eyebrows furrowed in apology.

"It's fine," Lora curtly cut her off as she marched past towards Abhilash's office. "Just remember, it's your shout at lunch because I actually fucking paid for your shit last time." She took a moment to recompose herself, her bright red cheeks fading, before knocking on the open office door. "Heyyy Abhi!"

"What happened?" Liam asked from his desk. It was the first time he had spoken to Bristol since the day they had met.

She stared back at him, still dumbfounded in the wake of Lora's pendulum-like mood swing, and then a sudden flood of thoughts washed over her like a wave hitting the shore. Her stomach was rumbling quietly. Just as quiet as the shore had been. She had skipped breakfast in order to catch the bus on time for her morning meeting in Sunken City. But she had never even stepped off the bus. Maybe it was for the best that her turning stomach was empty, otherwise her breakfast would have been all over the grey carpet of the office floor by now.

"Bristol?" Liam was on his feet now. Dwight and Shelton turned their gazes back to her, their faces filled with concern.

Feeling the weight of their stares, she took a small sip of her coffee mug, hiding her ashen face behind the cup before gawking down at the strange taste and remembering that she was only drinking water.

"There's been an attack," she finally murmured, almost in disbelief as she said it, still struggling to process the image of the bullet-riddled bodies laid along the sidewalk of Broadbeach Road and bobbing up and down in the waters of Bellevue Bay.

"Where?" Dwight asked, both he and Shelton getting to their feet alongside Liam. "Sunken City?"

Bristol swallowed and nodded, just as she had when one of her former colleagues from the coastal community made his hasty report to her, standing on the sidewalk and shouting over the noise of the idling bus while her gaze was fixed upon the bloated corpses of fallen sentries being fished from the shallows.

"Are they part of the meeting?" she recognised her Uncle Quentin's voice through the noise of her memory as he and the other senior officers appeared from around the corner.

Bristol wanted nothing more than to hug her uncle in that moment. To be reassured that everything was going to be okay. But she knew that this was the workplace, and she had to remain professional at all times. Her uncle didn't even know what had happened yet, so how could he possibly reassure her of anything?

"Let's keep senior business among the seniors," Rhonda declared, both Dwight and Shelton wilting under her authoritative stare as they returned to their seats. "We can decide whether the juniors need to be briefed on whatever this is about."

"Agreed!" Mayor Paxton clapped his hands, rubbing them together and smiling beneath his bushy beard at Liam, who was still on his feet. "Liam, let's get you back to training up Shelton. You two don't usually get a lot of time in the office together, so let's use the time we have."

Sighing through his nose, Liam looked as though he was about to say something, when he shrugged and caught hold of the back of his office chair instead, sitting down with a dispassionate expression that clearly stated he didn't believe that his opinion would matter much to them anyway.

Abhilash was flicking switches on and off in the boardroom, seemingly stumped as he intermittently stared up at the dark ceiling lights and studied the four switches in the wall's electrical cover plate. Having failed to crack the correct combination, he clucked his tongue and tottered towards his preferred conference chair beside Lora, stretching his feet underneath the big rectangular table as the other senior staff members filed into the room.

Closing the door behind her, Rhonda flicked the four switches on with one deft sweep of her hand. Abhilash noisily cleared his throat as the ceiling's bulbs shone bright, supplementing the natural light coming from the overcast sky outside.

"You're back early!" Teddie kicked off the meeting as Bristol set her coffee mug down on the table between her Uncle Quentin and Rhonda. "I have to admit, I'm glad we're doing this before lunch. I'm super keen to hear the details about the ammunition deal with Rookson, but let's hear from our friends on the coast first!"

"Sunken City was attacked last night," Bristol said flatly, colour slowly returning to her face as she came to grips with reality.

What cheerful air Teddie had brought with him into the boardroom dissolved immediately, yet Lora still had her arms folded above her notebook, sullenly gazing at Bristol from across the black table.

"By who?" asked Rhonda, shifting in her seat.

"The pirates from Attiker Island," Bristol answered, fidgeting with her coffee mug as she recounted her former colleague's report. "The city ran out of diesel for their generators to power the spotlights on the rooftops a few days ago, but the sentries could still hear the boat engines approaching last night. They caught the pirates trying to steal some of the fishing traps and they opened fire… but it looks like we lost more than them."

"How many?" Teddie asked as he brushed his bushy beard, eyebrows frowning beneath his thick mop of hair.

"A dozen, maybe more," Bristol replied while staring at the table, fighting an internal battle to push away the scarring memory of watching the bodies being dragged out of the water and onto the shore. She hadn't dared to ask who they were. "They're practically defenceless at night now. They can't see anything. They've said that they either need *something* to help them hold the coast, or they'll abandon Sunken City completely, leaving the rest of Brimvale vulnerable to raids from the pirates."

"Wisniewski said that?" Uncle Quentin clenched his jaw beside her.

"Someone I used to work with," Bristol answered before taking a sip of water.

"I vwould prefer to hear Perry's official statement," Abhilash scoffed, his golden bangles rattling against each other as he leaned back in his chair with his hands clasped behind his head.

"Wisniewski doesn't watch the coast," Rhonda pointed out, her eyes scanning each person in the room. "His people do. If that's what they're saying, then that's what we're dealing with."

"Why do they even need diesel in the first place?" Lora asked hotly, eyeing Bristol as if the sole objective of the meeting was to drain Brimvale of its fuel supplies for the benefit of her own people on the coast. "I mean, I'm pretty sure *none* of those office towers needed their own generator for the fu… for the lights to function five years ago."

"The city was disconnected from Brimvale's electrical grid after the earthquake," Bristol explained patiently, despite how certain she was that Sunken City's broken and submerged infrastructure had been a little more common knowledge than what Lora was letting on.

"Vwhy can't they just plug it all back in?" Abhilash asked, feigning interest with his eyes closed and his eyebrows raised. Apparently the meeting was a little too early in the morning for him.

"Even if by some miracle," Rhonda began in a measured tone as Bristol hid her face behind her coffee mug, "The rest of the city's cables were still intact after the earthquake, which is extremely unlikely, we'd be running the risk of overtaxing the solar farm and subjecting ourselves to blackouts, unless we burnt more of our own diesel just to keep up with the extra demand. And that's during the day. Night would be far worse."

"Abhilash might be onto something there," Bristol realised, and his eyes popped open in surprise. "We could line up the spotlights along the shore and hook them up on their own dedicated line to Brimvale's grid. We wouldn't need to power the entire city. We only need to give them enough electricity to continue watching the coast."

"Yes, that's exactly vwhat I meant!" Abhilash was quick to support the idea, especially if there was a chance that he might receive some of the praise.

Uncle Quentin nodded his approval, seeing that Bristol's loyalty was to Brimvale rather than to Sunken City, whose modern conveniences were not a priority when faced with the threat of the pirates attacking.

"Alright! Good thinking, guys!" Teddie's bushy grey-streaked beard parted with a toothy grin. "Bristol, let's get you to head this up for us. I think Dwight might have a list of all the people who worked on the solar farm project back when the Army Reserves were running the show. Those workers will be your best bet for *switching on the lights*," his fingers animated air quotes before clapping his hands together, ready to move on to the next topic. "Now, I'm gonna tease myself here and leave the best for last. Does anyone have anything else to raise before we talk about the Rookson deal?"

"Pass along our condolences to the people of Sunken City," said Rhonda, eyeing Teddie with her eyebrows raised before turning towards Bristol, the senior officer's hardened gaze slightly softening with sympathy.

"I've got one, Ted," Uncle Quentin offered as Bristol nodded at Rhonda's request, and Lora's eyes went wide across the table. "Farm belt's getting unstable. We're not trading diesel for fish. We need a new food source."

Lora breathed a subtle sigh of relief as she returned to scribbling the meeting's minutes into her notebook.

"That's true," Teddie nodded, brushing his beard in contemplation. "Our orchards alone won't be able to feed us for the long term either. What are you thinking?"

"Plenty of land south of Stillborough Pines," Uncle Quentin replied, having already prepared his proposal. "Some over by The Ravine too. We could hire farmers, plant some crops, and avoid history repeating itself."

"I vwas just about to say this," Abhilash claimed, slouching even lower in his chair. It wouldn't be long before he was parallel to the floor. "In fact, I vwas vwondering vwhy vwe hadn't set aside some land for agriculture sooner."

"Maybe you should have raised the issue sooner," Rhonda shot back, her tolerance for his seemingly stolen suggestions running thin.

"Yeah, we probably should've done this years ago," Teddie acknowledged before Abhilash could muster a reply. "But maybe waiting was the best thing we could've done, because now we've got people with years of farming experience, and they're all in the same place right now. I'm gonna leave this one in your hands, Quentin. Head on over to Rubicross when you're ready and bring us home a win!"

Teddie looked around the room expectantly, waiting for anyone else to raise a concern. His toothy grin widened with each passing moment of silence.

"Alright, let's hear it!" the Mayor bounced up and down in his chair excitedly as he looked towards Lora.

"Well, Teddie already knows the result," Lora smiled as she closed her notebook. "But the Rookson deal… was a success!"

The room erupted in applause, with Mayor Paxton clapping the loudest before shaking Uncle Quentin's hand. Rhonda allowed herself to smile for the briefest of moments as she offered her congratulations, and Abhilash sat up slightly in his chair to join the ovation before reaching back and clasping his hands behind his head again.

A wave of warmth washed over Bristol as she clapped her hands along with the others. Restocking Brimvale's supplies of ammunition meant that the people of Sunken City could call on their neighbour's garrison of guards whenever they were in trouble. And after the attack last night, this news couldn't have come at a better time.

Uncle Quentin cleared his throat as the applause died down, staring intently at Lora.

"But…" Lora began, her smile fading, "Victor added one condition: he's asked me to join them on the Rookson Council. He needs me to help advise them on how to handle the attacks from the Grismorne savages east of Rookson City. He said that the position doesn't have to be permanent, but he specifically requested *my* assistance."

Lora sat up in her chair, swelling with pride and glancing around the room to study everyone's reactions, her eyes settling on Bristol with a boastful note of condescension.

So this was the juicy gossip she's been saving, Bristol thought to herself. She was happy for her, truly, although she couldn't work out why Lora felt the need to brag. Back when Bristol had been selected to become the liaison officer between Sunken City and Brimvale, she had been filled with more apprehension than arrogance.

"And what experience do you have in handling *any* attacks?" Rhonda asked Lora sceptically. "I'm sure I don't need to remind you that we still need to deal with the pirates from Attiker Island, and we still have yet to receive any word of success from the mercenaries we hired to hunt down the Rauders. What would you advise us? How would you handle our own threats?"

"Well, he said in exchange for my time in Rookson," Lora turned away from Rhonda's relentless stare, "Victor has offered to negotiate a ceasefire with the pirates on our behalf. So that… solves that."

"I vwill miss you in the office," Abhilash cut across Rhonda before she could continue her line of questioning, to which Lora blushed.

"I knew Victor was gonna drive a hard bargain," Teddie remarked as he turned towards Uncle Quentin, the Mayor's earlier excitement over the success of the ammunition deal having evaporated after reading the fine print, "But I didn't expect him to poach someone from the team. What are your thoughts?"

"Might be beneficial," Uncle Quentin replied, having had enough time to mull over Victor's proposition on the way back from Rookson, "Someone we can trust over there. She could look after our interests and maintain our relationship."

"The ceasefire would help," Bristol spoke up in favour of the idea. She didn't know whether it was to side with her uncle or to send Lora away, but she saw value in the opportunity, and she seized it, just as any other liaison officer would. "I don't believe for a second that the pirates are going to honour a peace treaty over the long term, but it *could* serve to buy us enough time to get Sunken City's spotlights up and running again."

"Bristol has a point," Rhonda reluctantly conceded. "This whole thing seems suspicious to me, but if it gives us more time to prepare against future attacks, I'll support it."

"Well, it wouldn't be my first choice," Teddie sighed, turning back towards Lora, "But I guess it couldn't hurt to check it out. I mean, it's been working for us with Bristol so far. That's something to be said for collaboration between communities, at least... But how do you feel about staying in Rookson?"

"Whatever you say, I follow," Lora replied, her hands folded over her notebook as she stared into his black-rimmed glasses. "You was there when I needed support. It's only right that I support you now from wherever I'm needed."

Bristol couldn't believe how incredibly naive Lora was being, and from the way Rhonda was shifting in her seat, she could tell that the senior officer was turning the same thoughts over in her own mind.

Despite Lora believing that she was single-handedly putting an end to the pirate raids, all she was really achieving was leaving Brimvale and its problems in order to secure a shady ceasefire deal that could fall apart at any moment, in exchange for helping to resolve a conflict that had absolutely nothing to do with them.

But if it gave the people of Sunken City a chance of having even just one more day to prepare for another assault, Bristol was willing to pay the price.

CHAPTER 28 – JEREMY

"Are you sure that's him, Ollie?" a young man's voice swirled and eddied through Jeremy Royce's skull, weaving circles around the carcasses of his dead brain cells.

Lying on his back, he was still floating somewhere in the void between the fading silhouettes of his feverish dreams and the blurred streaks of his semi-conscious reality. An oppressive light flashed intermittently just beyond the veil of his eyelids as the figures standing over him moved back and forth.

"Probably it's him," a second voice answered, the intense light overhead eclipsing for a moment as Ollie bent down to take a closer inspection. "One of the girls said she recognised him, but she looked like she'd recognise a lot of guys."

"He looks dead!" a nervous giggle erupted from a third speaker, roughly prodding Jeremy's ribs with a shoe.

Jeremy made no reaction. He just wanted to be left alone. He knew that if he could keep his eyes shut for long enough, eventually they would get bored and wander off to find something or someone else to prod and poke.

"Good thing we're here to revive him," the first voice came again, this time with a troubling undertone.

"Maybe give him some mouth-to-mouth, Pedro," the oppressive light returned as Ollie drew back.

"Don't worry, I'll save him!" Pedro yelled with glee, leaping upon Jeremy and straddling his stomach. "Nurse, give me ten thousand volts! CLEAR!!"

A searing pain coursed throughout Jeremy's chest as a bony pair of thumbs and forefingers pinched his nipples through the fabric of his black shirt, twisting in excruciating semicircles and yanking upwards.

Jeremy's eyelids snapped open, blinded by the afternoon sun as he yowled in agony. He shoved Pedro off to the side and rolled over in the dirt, massaging his tender nipples and blinking groggily.

"I just saved his life," Pedro exclaimed mischievously as he fixed his glasses, the lanky imp shaking with laughter, "And *this* is how he thanks me?"

Jeremy vomited then, hacking stomach bile over the heaps of food scraps and empty bottles of Haydar's hooch lying in the dirt beside him. Other drunken revellers camping out at the protest party outside the walls of the Royce Estate cheered as they passed by the designated garbage area, welcoming him back to the land of the living. Jeremy retched and spluttered and spat before gazing up at the two young men standing over him, both of them holding brown bottles of Stillborough beer.

"Who…?" was all his scratchy voice managed to rasp before erupting in a series of dry coughs.

"Bronson Hopper," Jeremy recognised the first speaker's voice as the handsome broad-shouldered youth introduced himself, "From Brimvale. Former assistant to the Mayor."

"Ollie Geary," said the stockier of the two, "Former Mayor."

"And you can call me Doctor Pedro," the third sniggered, as if Jeremy needed any clarification.

Jeremy licked his cracked lips with a dry tongue. Staggering to his feet, he swayed momentarily as he found his balance before seizing one of the bottles in Bronson's hands and taking a swig, quenching his thirst and rousing his blackened liver to prepare for another long night.

"Breakfast of champions, huh?" Bronson smirked, shrugging at a scowling Pedro. Apparently it had been the lanky youth's beer.

"I don't feel like a champion," Jeremy croaked before leaning back to take a few more gulps of the nutty brew. Wiping his mouth, he asked, "Any reason for waking me up so early?"

"Probably Pedro just wanted to squeeze your tits," Ollie chuckled before taking a pull of his own beer.

"Our boss wants you to come and talk," Bronson explained, nodding past the tents in the dirt lot towards the caravans and the RVs of the Velvet Convoy.

"You mean Zatar?" Jeremy stared back, frowning while flattening his unkempt brown hair. *What could that depraved dwarf want with me?* He gargled some beer in his mouth to wash away any leftover chunks of whatever food had been in his stomach.

"No, we mean one of the whores," Ollie snorted, and Bronson almost spat out his beer.

"Have some more drinks waiting for me and I'll be there," Jeremy replied absentmindedly, shading his eyes from the glare of the afternoon sun as he stared up at the Royce guards posted along the wall. "I have something to take care of first."

"Do you need to buy some nipple cream?" Pedro blurted out before Ollie ushered him away, the pair of them laughing aloud as they disappeared into the crowd.

"You got it," said Bronson, suppressing a grin of his own as he began to follow his friends, "Just don't take too long."

Jeremy rubbed his bleary eyes as he caught sight of what he was searching for; the green baseball cap of Terry Delaney, one of the estate's gardeners.

After Evelyn had caught Jeremy coming back from his night out at The Mezzanine, she had instructed all of the guards that he was under no circumstances allowed to set foot inside the walls again until further notice, and all of his complaints and pleas were to be ignored. Luckily for Jeremy though, Terry preferred to spend his leisure time patrolling the walls, pretending to be part of the garrison. The ropey gardener had been the first person in the estate to notice him drunkenly ambling among the crowd, and the first person to respond to his requests.

"Terry!" Jeremy's hoarse voice broke as he waved one of his gangly arms up at the wall. He swallowed dryly, his Adam's apple grating in his throat as it bobbed up and down. He took a thirsty gulp of the Stillborough beer and tried again, "Terry!!"

The green baseball cap shaded his face as he glanced down at the pack of protesters, fixing his gaze on Jeremy. Terry looked over his shoulder before motioning him towards their usual meeting spot; a small break in the tents pitched beside the wall.

"Jeremy!" his whispered shout floated down through the babble of the crowd, "Everything alright? Need me to drop you another stack?"

There was plenty of food and water to be enjoyed freely at the protest party, since the majority of the people gathered in the dirt lot consisted of families from the farm belt who had come to Rubicross with everything that they could carry, including fresh produce that was sure to expire unless they shared it among the crowd, and more generous settlers were arriving every day as their supplies of diesel ran dry.

Some of the finer things though, like the liquor and the women of the Velvet Convoy, came at a price, and so Terry had been tossing golden bucks taken from Jeremy's bachelor pad over the wall. Admittedly, the arrangement had initially seemed like a risky request, but Terry had wanted to show his gratitude for all of the voluntary assistance that Jeremy's son, Jordan, had given to the gardeners by helping them tend to the estate's grounds over the years.

Besides, being the brother of the richest man in Rubicross had its perks. Once Nathan came home from his business trip to Cloakwater, Jeremy was certain that he would be welcomed back inside the estate, and he would make sure that Terry was well taken care of.

"No, I'm fine," Jeremy replied, pushing his croaking voice to its limits. He glanced over his stooped shoulder, as if his next words would land him in more trouble than he was already in if anyone else overheard him. "I need you to organise a meeting with Evelyn."

"Evelyn? Why?" Terry cocked his head to the side. "She's not letting you back inside."

"I know," Jeremy confessed, looking down at his feet before meeting Terry's gaze again. "I need to see her though. It's important."

"If I set up a meeting between you two, she's gonna be watching me like a hawk," Terry warned, his head turning back to the residence for a moment, already paranoid that she was listening to their conversation all the way from her bedroom window. "I might not be able to help you again after this. I can't even guarantee she'll come. You know that, right?"

"I know," Jeremy repeated, considering the half-empty brown bottle of beer clutched in his hand. He was already beginning to get the shakes again. "She needs to hear what I have to say though."

"If you're sure," Terry nodded sympathetically before shaking his head and turning his attention back to the residence. "Be at the gates by nightfall. I'll do what I can."

"Thanks," Jeremy croaked, but Terry had already resumed his patrol.

No more alcohol. No more women. It was a sobering thought, even as Jeremy took another swig of the nutty brew to calm his nerves. It was the sort of risk his brother would take. It was also what his brother had asked of him in the first place. Except this time, he would have to completely cut himself off again without the comfort of having a roof over his head and a crew of professional chefs on-call to distract him from his thirst.

Forcefully turning the thought aside, Nathan's other request echoed in Jeremy's head; the one that he had made almost as an afterthought at Linchpin Station on the day that he, Jordan, Ryan and Zita had left for Cloakwater. Dess Sheridan was supposed to have passed through Rubicross on her way back to Stillborough, and Jeremy had been tasked with making sure that she stayed in town for a while.

He hadn't seen her though. Admittedly, he hadn't seen a great deal of anything. Each day spent outside the estate's walls had carried the same familiar blur of faces that he would forget, and the regrets that he would remember. Perhaps Dess had already arrived and was staying in one of the residence's guest bedrooms, awaiting Nathan's return just as eagerly as Jeremy. Or perhaps she had seen the protest and simply decided to avoid the crowd, heading back home and waiting for everyone else to follow suit.

Jeremy leaned back and finished off the dregs of his beer, patiently letting the last drops trickle down into his mouth before adding it to the communal collection of empty bottles in the dirt. Sighing, he looked past the motley canvases of tents and awnings pitched haphazardly across the camp towards the Velvet Convoy, where his next free drink awaited him. Although knowing Zatar, the meat-hole mongering midget, nothing was ever free.

He took his time navigating his way past the smoky barbecue grills, craft stalls and circles of people sitting cross-legged on blankets, savouring the atmosphere of sizzling sweet-smelling meats and drunken laughter mingling with mellow music. Some of the protesters had connected portable speakers to miniature solar panels, breaking up the fare of acoustic guitars and bongo drums that would inevitably make their return around the campfires as night fell.

In the corner of his eye, past an elderly man who was passionately spooning simmering smoky sauces over smouldered slices of braised beef brisket, Jeremy happened to catch sight of a small boy in an oversized black college hoodie lurking beside the shopfront of Drew & Colin's Metalware, keenly watching the Brimvale buses coming and going as if he was waiting for a particular passenger to arrive.

The image of the crouching boy in Jeremy's peripherals was soon replaced by the back of a yellow school bus as he passed through the Velvet Convoy's rectangular perimeter. Four pickup trucks occupied the centre of the field, parked back-to-back in an X formation, the convoy's guards standing in the truck trays or on top of the camper vans and RVs and repurposed ambulances lining the rectangle's edges.

"Look, it's Quentin the Unsmiling!" Bronson announced from the back of one of the pickup trucks.

Quentin Davis, a clean-shaven man with close-cropped copper red hair, glared up at the guards standing in the truck trays as he handed over a stack of chips to the smiling Zatar.

Jeremy had seen Quentin recruiting some of the protesters who had come from the farm belt for an agricultural project within the borders of Brimvale, offering payment and shelter in the suburbs to those who were willing to work for it, along with the implicit comfort of being connected to Brimvale's electrical grid. It was a generous proposal, and some had wholeheartedly accepted the offer, although others had chosen to remain at the protest, happy to finally have a holiday after years of trying to tame the prairies.

"Probably he's going to ask for a frown-job!" Ollie added as Quentin and a slim blonde dressed in a green cargo jacket – and nothing else, it seemed – passed by, the blonde trying and failing to stifle her smile.

"You just have to frown at his ginger nuts until he creams!" Pedro instructed before bursting into a high-pitched giggle.

The blonde led Quentin towards one of the caravans, where she struggled to open the door as she shook with silent laughter. Quentin turned and seethed back at the three youths while the rest of the guards quietly chuckled, their assault rifles and shotguns rattling as they hung from shoulder straps. The score of scantily-dressed prostitutes sitting in a row of camping chairs were tittering among themselves as the blonde finally managed to open the door with Quentin slamming it shut behind him.

"Maybe Krystal can put a smile on his face," Zatar shrugged with a grin as he dropped the handful of golden bucks into a tin on the timekeeper's desk. He turned back towards the line-up of his whores, speculatively eyeing other potential customers as they prowled back and forth, when he caught sight of Jeremy approaching. The hairy broad-nosed little man raised his arms high, "My friend! Welcome!"

Jeremy crossed the field warily, still unsure why he had been summoned. The women in the camping chairs averted their gaze as he approached, and he quickly became acutely aware of his shabby appearance. He had no idea how many nights it had been since Evelyn had kicked him out of the estate, but ever since then, he had been sleeping wherever he fell unconscious, usually in the dirt. He had lost his threadbare coat early on, and both his black shirt and moss green corduroy pants were soiled brown. As ever, his hair was messy and unkempt, his eyes were red-rimmed, and his scruffy beard completed the look; a veritable black hole of self-pity.

"Zatar," was all he managed to say before swallowing dryly. He offered his hand, and the short and shameless hussy hustler reached up to clasp it warmly.

"Come! Have some whiskey with me," Zatar's curly grey-speckled beard caught the warm breeze as he led the way towards one of the nearby motorhomes, casting a medium-length shadow in the late afternoon sun.

Lured by the promise of another drink, Jeremy's feet were moving before he could stop and ponder the reason behind the invitation. The tall dark silhouette of a guard standing in the shade of the RV struck familiar, his facial features slowly materialising as the pair approached, revealing a dark goatee and sharp brown eyes. Haydar's brawny bald guard, Omar, nodded at Zatar before turning to open the entrance.

"After you, my friend," Zatar gestured for Jeremy to step up into the motorhome.

Jeremy lingered in the doorway for a moment, sizing up what awaited him inside. A perky-breasted redheaded woman in her early twenties sat nude beside a dinette table, her eyes downcast as she poured herself a shot of whiskey. Haydar was fully-clothed – thankfully – and lying sprawled across a grey suede sofa, his big hands clasped over his portly belly, rising and falling in time with his bear-like snores, a content grin plastered across his dozing face.

Jeremy dimly remembered that the perpetually drunken potato farmer's birthday gift, a crate of his own homemade vodka, was still somewhere inside the estate's warehouse. Perhaps if Jeremy had been strong enough to pace his drinks, he could have kept Haydar's gift in his bungalow, and he never would have felt compelled to get his fix outside the walls.

"Cherry," Zatar called as he climbed up into the RV behind Jeremy, closing the door softly, "Have you been keeping our friend happy?"

"Yes," she replied sullenly, brushing her cheek and taking the shot. "Should I go now?"

"Not yet," Zatar answered, ambling towards one of the two armchairs opposite Haydar and gesturing for Jeremy to join him. "Why don't you pour us a couple of glasses?"

Jeremy's eyes crawled over her naked body as she sniffled and rose to her feet. Her supple pale ass flexed as she reached up to open an overhead cabinet, fishing out a pair of crystal tumblers. He couldn't decide whether he was slavering at the sight of her stiff pink nipples or the smoky single malt whiskey as she served their drinks, bending over to place the glasses on the counter between the two armchairs.

Pouring another shot for herself and downing it at the dinette table, Cherry returned with the bottle to refill Haydar's empty glass. The potato farmer's snoring ceased as she passed by, smelling the whiskey's wooden aroma floating on the air. Just as she finished topping up the glass, Zatar leaned forward to give her bare ass a hard smack, and she closed her eyes, taking a deep breath before standing upright again.

Haydar beamed up at Cherry with a wide grin as he blinked himself awake. Tearing his gaze from her firm conical breasts as she sat down at the dinette table again, he looked around for his glass of whiskey. Jeremy was reminded of a turtle trying to flip back onto its stomach as the potato farmer rocked himself from side to side, finally planting his feet on the floor and holding his glass out to Zatar.

"My friends," Zatar began as they clinked their glasses together, turning to Jeremy to repeat the gesture, "Thank you both for coming. Over the past many years, I've been both amazed and humbled by your generosity. Haydar, even now, you're sharing your food and drinks with the people outside, supporting them while they make pleas for their livelihoods. And Jeremy, even though the people are begging for your family's diesel now, your brother, Nathan, has always been open-handed to strangers in need. As a token of my admiration, I've decided that I want to share my gifts with both of you."

Jeremy took a grateful swallow of whiskey, determined to finish his drink before Zatar realised that he had nothing to do with his brother's overwhelming charity.

"I confess, part of my offer is for my own selfish gain," Zatar continued, smiling at the pair of them while Cherry poured herself another shot. "I'm getting restless here. I want to see the world! But, I cannot deprive these good people of their companions, especially now, while tensions are so high. I wish I could stay and go, but I cannot be in two places at once!"

Haydar sloshed his whiskey as he slurred his agreement, his indecipherable words enthusiastic if nothing else. Having said his unintelligible piece, he settled back into the sofa, humming an off-key tune to himself that only he alone could find rhythm in.

"So what can we do?" asked Jeremy, quickly finishing the rest of his whiskey and motioning to Cherry for another.

"It's not what you can do," Zatar replied with a smile as the naked redhead approached with the bottle, "It's who you can be! And I want both of you to be my business partners. I will split the Velvet Convoy in two. You will remain here in Rubicross, while I resume my tour of the countryside. Haydar will feed our workers, and Jeremy, when your brother returns, you will fuel our engines. What do you say?"

Haydar harrumphed with a dazed grin, raising his glass again for Zatar to clink. Jeremy, on the other hand, knew that his role in the partnership would be short-lived if he couldn't deliver his end of the deal. And judging from Zatar's reputation for how he handled unpaid debts, Jeremy didn't want to gamble on the possibility of being unable to pay the tab.

"*Relax*," Zatar soothed, catching hold of Cherry's arm before she could retreat again. He guided her down to her knees, and she swept her hair over one shoulder, glancing sidelong at Jeremy before dutifully unzipping the depraved dwarf's fly. "I know Nathan is in Cloakwater. It will take time for his return. We have plenty of diesel for now, and we will only be driving half the vehicles."

Haydar set his glass upon the floor and lay back on the grey suede sofa, unzipping his own fly as he watched Cherry's head bobbing up and down in Zatar's lap. Devoted to the proposal of sharing his gifts with the two men, the hussy hustler rose to his feet and steered the perky redhead backwards towards the sofa. Detaching herself from Zatar's hairy cock with a wet *pop*, Cherry took a swig straight from the bottle of whiskey before clumsily climbing on top of Haydar, straddling him as Zatar pushed his armchair to the other side of the RV, having to stand on the seat for Cherry to take him in her mouth again.

"Join us," Zatar urged Jeremy as Cherry began rocking back and forth, moaning meekly with her mouth full. "Drink and fuck as much as you want, and you'll have one third of the profits from your half of the Velvet

Convoy."

Jeremy was certain that Haydar didn't even understand the terms of the partnership, but the potato farmer happily picked up his glass of whiskey again and sipped all the same, pleasantly hypnotised by the pair of perky tits in his face.

Studying the submissive redhead's supple ass as she bounced up and down in Haydar's lap, Jeremy took a gulp of his own glass. He knew that it was a dangerous gamble, but what other choices did he have? Sleeping alone in the dirt and cutting himself off alcohol again while waiting for Nathan to come back; or accepting the partnership and enjoying everything it had to offer while waiting for Nathan to come back.

Without a second thought, Jeremy rose to his feet and stumbled towards the grey suede sofa, sliding down his soiled corduroy pants and putting one knee over Haydar's thighs, taking up position behind Cherry as she reached back to pull one of her seat-cheeks to the side. He spat whiskey-laced saliva at her tight ass, making her flinch, but she paused her rocking and waited in anticipation all the same.

Zatar grinned back at him as Jeremy steered his cock towards her ass, thumbing the tip inside as Cherry groaned. The accommodating redhead clamped down on Haydar's cock with her pussy to take her mind off the pain. Jeremy pushed himself deeper inside, and she coughed and spluttered as she extricated herself from Zatar, taking another mouthful of whiskey from the bottle and gritting her teeth before sucking and riding again.

"Okay, I'm in," Jeremy breathed as Cherry's ass clenched around his cock, the three men sighing with pleasure while the redhead grunted and churned, her three holes stretching as she worked to satisfy the unlikely new business partners.

"Many thanks, my friend," Zatar beamed back at him, raising his crystal tumbler in victory.

Jeremy hopped closer on one foot to bridge the distance, clinking his glass together with Zatar's. Haydar reached around the multitasking woman with his drink to join the other two, and Cherry raised the bottle of whiskey overhead, knocking it against the three glasses.

* * *

Eventually, Jeremy was able to extract himself from the unsightly foursome. Zatar had invited him to try out her other holes as they switched positions, but Jeremy had made sure to blow his load. Zatar had simply laughed and told him to come back later, as he was paying Cherry generously by the hour, solely to service the three of them, and she was determined to make as much money as she could.

As tempting as it had been to stay, night had already fallen outside, and Jeremy didn't want to reek of sex and booze any more than he already did. He leaned against the concrete wall for support as he made his way towards the big wooden gates of the estate, dazedly knocking on the timber with his numb fist.

"It's about time he showed up," Evelyn snapped on the other side.

Jeremy couldn't help but snort in response. He was definitely drunk.

One of the gigantic double doors creaked open just a crack to reveal Marv standing on the other side, wearing one of his trademark Hawaiian shirts. He looked back at Jeremy through the gap with a contradictory mix of apprehension and nonchalance, almost as if he knew that he was about to witness something that he didn't want to care about.

"How are the food supplies holding up?" Jeremy asked, if only to break the uncomfortable silence.

"Why do you think that's any of your business?" Evelyn answered with a question of her own, standing out of sight behind the closed door.

"I guess I don't, really," Jeremy admitted with a shrug.

"Just say what you came to say," Marv urged him, eager to get back inside.

"Well, regardless of how your food situation is," Jeremy began, leaning his back against the closed door and staring at The Oxhouse bar across the street, lively with all of the new customers in town, "You might wanna think about how you're gonna get more water."

"But the water's on tap…?" Evelyn replied, and Jeremy could tell that even as she said it, she was exchanging glances with Marv, searching each other's faces for a clue to his riddle.

"For now, it might be," Jeremy mused, recalling the epiphany he'd had during one of his more dehydrated recovery sessions. "But all that water's getting pumped through the pipes with electricity from Brimvale. And sure, they've got their solar grid to keep everything running during the day, but they're still burning diesel at night. What happens when Brimvale decides to take care of Brimvale, and they start cutting off everyone else?"

There was a long silence from the other side of the gates, and Jeremy wished that he could see the look on Evelyn's face. That was probably the reason why she had chosen to hide behind the door. As much as she had wanted to oversee the planning of the estate's resources, she had overlooked the most important one of all.

A couple of days without water, and they would be forced to open the gates.

CHAPTER 29 – LIAM

In all honesty, they could have walked the distance from the town hall to Sunken City. It was a nice enough day, and a leisurely stroll through Brimvale's apple orchards would have been a welcome way to spend the afternoon. Mayor Paxton certainly could have used the exercise, and it would have served as a compelling demonstration of just how concerned they actually were about conserving fuel during the diesel shortage.

At least the pair of Brimvale officials had chosen to carpool for once, although sitting in the back seat and being sandwiched in between two of the Mayor's bodyguards, Wilson and Harriet, Liam found himself grateful for Rhonda's lead foot stomping the accelerator.

Everyone in the SUV lurched forward as the senior officer hit the brakes just before they reached the intersection at Broadbeach Road, warily gazing left and right on the off-chance that there were trucks cruising up and down the coastal highway, delivering loads of construction materials to the labour crew tasked with running lengths of electrical cables along Brimvale's shoreline.

The midday sun gleamed off the calm ocean waters stretching across the expanse of Bellevue Bay like a great cerulean canvas, the lazy tide coursing between the columns of the broken Wickford Swing Bridge on the right and swirling through the shattered windows of Sunken City's submerged office towers away on the left. Across the bay was a distant ribbon of white sand, set against the backdrop of Rookson City's defunct commercial district, while the Sovereign Rapture cruise ship sat anchored in the centre of the bay, like some rusty hulking mediator overseeing the peace between the two seaside cities, despite the hobbyist fisherfolk aboard the ship having little to no bargaining power over either of them.

Rhonda floored the accelerator across the intersection and took a sharp right turn as they entered a beachside parking lot, sending Wilson's bony elbow driving into Liam's ribs.

They were both the same age, in their early twenties, although Wilson had chosen a different career in life, having enlisted in the Army Reserves just before the top had been lopped off the chain of command. It seemed that the slim soldier had never gotten the chance to grow accustomed to the regulation haircut though, with his thick jheri curls hanging over his protruding ears.

Liam was tempted to shove the guard back over to his end of the seat, but he knew better than to piss off the people who were paid to protect them. He had to admit that even though he had been squashed in between Harriet's sturdy arm and Wilson's bony elbow for the entire ride while they vigilantly stared out the tinted side windows, it was still a better deal than having to accompany Quentin to Rubicross.

Quentin the Unsmiling had managed to convince Mayor Paxton that it was probably for the best that Liam skipped the trip to the trading town due to his inherent issue with boozed-up birdbrains, all of Brimvale having heard the rumours of drunken revellers running rampant outside the walls of Royce Manor during their prolonged protest.

Liam however, knew that the senior officer's supposedly sympathetic suggestion was far from some deep-seated sense of compassion or under-standing. The more likely scenario was that Quentin had simply wanted to spend the government's time and money on some of the local women in Rubicross without having to suffer Liam's judgement or the cost of situating him in the finest accommodation that the trading town had to offer, as per their arrangement.

Liam certainly wasn't complaining though.

Rhonda reversed into a parking space and they stepped out of the vehicle, the salty sea breeze pervading their senses, along with the soothing sound of gentle waves breaking along the shore on the other side of the low concrete wall that separated the asphalt from the sand. It was difficult to believe that only a few nights ago, the peaceful beach had borne witness to the blood and bodies washing up on the shore from the gun battle that had been waged between the rooftops and the canals of Sunken City.

"How do you think Lora's doing over there in Rookson?" Mayor Paxton asked as he stretched and gazed across the bay's shimmering surface.

"In over her head," Rhonda replied over the noise of the labour crew's drills and hammers buzzing and banging as they riveted metal frames into the sidewalk. She checked the pistol on her waist before slamming the driver's side door, "Without a doubt."

Lora had bragged to all of the junior staff in the office – which currently consisted of Liam, Dwight and Shelton – about how excited she was to be taking up the Rookson Council's offer of employment, not realising that Liam and Dwight had been just as excited for her to leave, even going so far as to throw their own farewell party, to which she hadn't been invited.

Words couldn't express how hopeful Liam was that her temporary role in Rookson would become permanent. Truth be told, he wouldn't have cared if she had never even made it past the mercenary blockade in the seemingly abandoned bayside town of Bellevue, as long as she stayed far away from Brimvale.

He hadn't heard one snarky comment in the office ever since the day she had left, although he did pity Sergeant Butch Gorman and the thirteen-year-old orphan guard Bulldov for having to move cities with her, serving as her personal security until further notice. Bulldov hadn't exactly been thrilled about the prospect of having to leave Brimvale, but he figured that if Butch was going, then he didn't have much left to hold on to in Brimvale anyway.

"Well, that's probably true," the Mayor's bushy beard bristles stirred in the gentle breeze as he surveyed the spotlights being mounted along the highway behind them. "I really didn't wanna let her go either, but just like you and Bristol said, if Lora's what it takes for Rookson to work out a ceasefire with the pirates for us, it might give us enough time to organise our security along the coast."

Admittedly, Liam hadn't spent much time puzzling over why the seniors would have agreed to send Lora of all people to Rookson City to help Victor MacDougall and his council of yes-men to handle their own problems, but now it became clear. She was a pawn, plain and simple; an expendable sacrifice to distract the other pieces scattered across the chessboard while they focused on building up their defence.

He began to fidget with the top button of his business shirt, knowing just how highly Lora was held in the Mayor's esteem; and if she was expendable, what did that make Liam?

They followed Mayor Paxton as he decided to take a walk along the beach, passing through a gap in the low concrete barrier and distancing themselves from the noise of the construction.

The purpose of the spotlights being built along the highway was to illuminate the waters of the bay at night, the labour crew of electricians, mechanics and welders working to prevent another unseen pirate raid on Sunken City.

Granted, it wasn't the most ideal solution, given the amount of ground that they needed to cover, but by bathing the mouth of the bay in a pool of light along with the waters surrounding the city, it would at least give the coastal community enough time to prepare their defences against the next attack.

"Ceasefire with the pirates," Rhonda scoffed as they hit the sandy beach, Liam hanging back between the two guards, "I'm not holding my breath on how long *that's* gonna last."

"Relax, I'm sure everything's gonna be fine," Mayor Paxton reassured her as he stooped to roll up the cuffs of his black slacks and take off his shoes and socks. "And if it isn't, then we pull Lora out of Rookson *the moment* the pirates hit the coast again. Negotiating for the ceasefire was Victor's part of the deal. Right, Liam?"

"Pretty much," he answered. It was the first time he had spoken since leaving the office.

As usual, Liam found himself wondering what the fuck he was even doing there. He had nothing to do other than stand around and observe, just like Wilson and Harriet, but without the dignity of having an actual purpose. Despite having received his promotion weeks ago, he still felt that the position was utterly useless and unnecessary. It was no surprise that Lora had fit the role so perfectly.

He would have much preferred to be back in the office doing his old duties, as humdrum as dispatching mail and managing the bus routes had been. It would have saved Dwight the juggling act of having to complete his own work while using every spare second to teach Shelton how to handle Liam's previous responsibilities, since Liam himself was always being pulled away on some pointless road trip.

Technically, Liam shouldn't have even been on the beach in the first place. Earlier, he had overheard the Mayor asking Abhilash to accompany him for their afternoon meeting with the officials of Sunken City, but Abhilash had simply clucked his tongue at the invitation, reasoning that he would be busy with interviewing new office assistants to replace Ollie, Bronson and Pedro, instead nominating both Rhonda and Liam as stand-ins.

Bristol, the liaison officer between the two communities, was supposed to be meeting them in the beachside parking lot, along with Perry Wisniewski and his advisors, but it seemed that Mayor Paxton had wanted to arrive early enough to dip his feet into the ocean.

"Don't you think this can wait until after the meeting, Ted?" Rhonda asked as the jolly stout man waded out into the shallow depths.

"Absolutely not!" he called back over his shoulder, his mop of thick dark brown hair falling over his black-rimmed glasses as he shot the four of them a toothy grin. "Who knows how long they plan on talking for?"

"Briefly, if you intend on meeting them barefoot," Rhonda replied impatiently before taking a measured breath. "Wilson, head up to the highway and let us know if you see them coming. Maybe it'll give our Mayor enough time to dry his feet and put his shoes back on."

The slim guard nodded and tramped back up towards the parking lot, leaving the other three to monitor the municipal man-child. Liam sat down on the low concrete wall while Harriet adjusted the strap on her M4, looking up and down the shoreline.

"You know, Rhonda," Mayor Paxton began, bending down to pick up a pebble and skipping it across the water, "I'm surprised you don't have more grey hairs with all the worrying you do!"

Rhonda bit back her response, reluctantly allowing him to enjoy his chuckle at her expense as she glanced over her shoulder at the highway, restlessly pacing back and forth while waiting for Bristol and the Sunken City officials to show up.

"I remember back in the early days when we dropped anchor out there," the Mayor reflected, gazing out at the cruise ship and retelling the story of how he and scores of others had arrived in South Tekota aboard The Rapture. "Man, I'm glad we ended up on this side of the bay. Who knows what would've happened to us if we landed in Rookson or Bellevue. None of us knew how to steer the lifeboat though, so we just let the currents take us. Got pretty nervous when we started drifting out to sea, but…"

The buzz of electrical drills began to drown out the Mayor's voice, and Liam looked over his shoulder at the labour crew milling about the row of spotlights. The noise of the construction somehow seemed to be growing louder. Wilson was standing with the rest of the guard patrol assigned to protect the workers while one of the labourers was calling for an extra pair of hands to help them carry a spotlight over to the next metal frame.

"Ted, get back to the fucking parking lot right now!!" Rhonda's voice cracked like a whip above the intensifying whirrs.

Liam raised his eyebrows and turned back to the beach with a faint smile tugging at his lips. Perhaps this wouldn't be such an uneventful day outside the office after all. He moved to scoot off the edge of the concrete barrier to get a better vantage point for the argument that was sure to follow when he noticed something that poured ice over every muscle fibre in his body.

Rhonda was pointing her pistol at Mayor Paxton.

The Mayor simply gaped back at her, dropping a pebble into the water as he raised his hands in the air, the dissonant chorus of drills heightening and deepening at the same time, as if the snapped synapse inside Rhonda's brain was twanging for them all to hear.

At the same instant, Harriet was unslinging her M4 and setting it down softly on the sand while edging towards the senior officer just outside the range of her peripheral vision. Crouching like a spring, the former Army Reserves soldier launched forward, grabbing the pistol with both hands and ramming her shoulder into Rhonda's side, making her shout and squeeze off a round into the air as the two women fell to the ground.

"STAY DOWN!!" Harriet yelled as she wrestled the gun from the senior officer's grasp and backpedalled towards the M4. "Wilson! Get down here, now!!"

"Look! Just *look!!*" Rhonda shouted from the sand over the noise of the blaring uproar reverberating across the bay.

That's when Liam saw them. Just glints on the water at first, flashes of metal winking at them on the shimmering tide as they sped past the broken section of the Wickford Swing Bridge. It was the pirates from Attiker Island. They were fanning out in speedboats and jet skis, dozens of them, hurtling straight towards the shore.

Cracks of gunfire echoed over the waves as the pirates began shooting. Mayor Paxton gave up a garbled cry, clutching at his chest and folding over face down in the shallows.

"Ted!?" Rhonda yelled as Harriet crouched to return fire with the pistol. "Ted!!"

She began crawling on her belly towards the Mayor's motionless body when spurts of sand erupted in her path. Quickly changing her mind, Rhonda spun around, scrambling back up the beach.

Liam's frozen muscles thawed the instant a stray bullet crunched against the concrete barrier. He flung himself backwards and swung his feet up over the wall, landing in a heap upon the asphalt on the other side.

"You fucking bastards!" Wilson yelled as he ran towards the shore, the slim guard jumping up onto the wall and spraying wildly at the pirates. "I'll kill you all!!"

The rest of the guard patrol posted along the highway weren't far behind, their assault rifles rattling as they rushed across the parking lot. Liam watched as one caught a slug to the hip, the man dropping to his knees mid-run and thwacking his chin hard on a kerb. One guard stopped to help him and took a bullet to the neck, her gun involuntarily firing into the fallen man's torso as she collapsed beside him, their blood pooling together on the asphalt.

Liam's wide eyes settled on the bloody pair of M4s only a short distance away. There was no way he was joining the fight – he had neither the training nor the desire to die today – but he knew that he had to get back up to the highway somehow, preferably before the pirates reached the shore.

A spray of blood splashed across Liam's cheek while he watched the labour crew scatter in their search for cover, and a man fell to the ground beside him. Liam stared back at the dead gaze in his eyes, the guard's face drawn with the belated realisation that he probably should have been wearing a helmet.

"Fucking die, you bastards!!" Wilson yelled overhead, miraculously surviving the barrage of bullets. His M4 began clicking impotently, and he turned his gun up, looking down the smoking barrel before tossing it aside, "What the *fuck!?*"

Rhonda crawled through the gap in the concrete barrier with Harriet on her heels. Both the pistol and the M4 were gone, and the two women had their eyes set on the black SUV across the parking lot. Liam abandoned the rapidly-thinning row of guards returning fire, scrambling after the soldier and the senior officer even as an explosion sounded in the distance and the retaliating guards sent up a cheer.

Rhonda was the first to reach the vehicle, throwing the passenger side door open and climbing over the handbrake into the driver's seat. Liam laid flat on the floor in the backseat, not even daring to reach back and close the door behind him.

"Wilson!" Harriet yelled over the roar of the engine as she ducked down in the front passenger seat, "Let's go!!"

Liam rolled to the side, looking over his hip as the slim guard wrestled a replacement M4 off a fresh corpse, yelling more profanities and adding to the barks of gunfire in the air, not even pausing to aim.

"We've gotta go," Rhonda said through gritted teeth, clenching and unclenching her grip on the steering wheel as she stared sidelong at Wilson. It wasn't until the back window shattered before she decided, "Fuck it."

She gunned the engine, the tyres screeching and smoking as they fishtailed out of the parking lot, a volley of hot lead puncturing the SUV's rear quarter panel. Explosions of glass shards sprayed on either side of the intersection as the newly-installed spotlights erupted in their wake.

"Bristol was right," Rhonda fumed as she stomped the accelerator, flying down the highway back towards the heart of Brimvale, "We need more guards along the coast."

"Experienced ones," Harriet added from underneath the dashboard.

"So much for that fucking peace treaty," Liam muttered, his bloodstained cheek pressed against the floor mat.

CHAPTER 30 – ODESSA

Dess knew that they were travelling the long way back to Rubicross, but nobody seemed to mind. Or the more likely scenario, none of them were particularly in a rush to reach their destination. The four riders galloped across the wild yellow grass of the prairies with the waning orange hues of the late afternoon sun at their backs, searching for a suitable camping spot before nightfall.

They had been riding off-road ever since the night they had left Coyote's Rest when a gunshot had echoed in their wake, perhaps one of the drunken cowboys bidding them good riddance. Erring on the side of caution however, they veered off the track to canter cross-country, wanting to put as much distance between themselves and the town for fear of being followed. They hadn't even been lighting a campfire or setting up their tents at night, wary of giving away their position, choosing instead to cover themselves and the horses with canvas and huddling together for warmth.

The first time they had stopped to rest in the early hours of the morning had been the most difficult, but only for the other three. Dess had learned from Emmett how to camp in the open plains without waking up to find that their horses had wandered off. They would feed and water their mounts before laying them down in a rough square and loosely tying their lead ropes together, criss-crossing the knots beneath a blanket, with the four riders lying side by side in the centre.

Between watches, Nael Fletcher, the rugged bald Englishman, would take the end behind Alix Carter, the slender brunette, followed by Dess, with her back to Carter. Monroe, the dour dark blonde deputy who had volunteered to escort them in the absence of the other four Royce guards, refused to be spooned, and so she and Dess slept in each other's arms instead.

As exposed as they were to the elements, attacks from their potential pursuers and the roving Rauders, along with the occasional distant barking from the packs of stray dogs roaming the prairies, Dess had to admit that she'd been having the most comfortable nights of sleep she'd had in years. And judging from the gradual softening of Monroe's hardened facial expression; she could tell that the deputy must have felt the same way too.

Monroe, a woman in her early thirties, was the widow of a police officer who had been killed in the violent protests during The Long Summer Night; the same night that Byron Ashby had avoided his duty to keep the peace. Resenting the people of Brimvale for what they had done to her husband, Monroe moved out west the moment that the residual radiation had cleared from the prairies, using the self-defence techniques her husband had taught her in a role that didn't involve making a living off her back. Based on her competency and skill alone, she should have been elected the Sheriff of Coyote's Rest, but just like in the old world, no job was ever given to the most capable of candidates. In any case, Dess was glad to have Monroe as an ally along for the ride.

The other four of the original six armed escorts, Blair Frost, Kirk Boaz, Merrick Werner and Lloyd Price, had decided to linger in Coyote's Rest, under the guise of maintaining Garrett's protection, although Dess suspected that they had simply fallen for the allure of the prairies lifestyle.

The setting sun kissed the horizon behind the four riders as they passed by rocky outcrops, clusters of giant anthills and across dried riverbeds, familiar landmarks from a lifetime ago when Dess and the other railroad workers had chased Wallace Pelletier across the prairies. The former foreman had driven his dual-cab pickup truck cross-country with the intention of evading pursuit, although he had failed to realise that his getaway car wasn't made for off-road driving, leaving a trail of punctured tyres and twisted metal in his wake.

Garrett had led the manhunt to a spot just outside where Linchpin Station now stood, where they had found the truck idling on two broken axles, the engine still revving impotently. Wallace had been inside, clutching his flabby chest with fear and agony frozen upon his face, his overworked heart having seized up the moment the dust cloud of underpaid railroad workers had appeared in his rearview mirror.

Dess wondered how different her life would have been if Wallace had chosen to flee along the pothole-pockmarked road that snaked its way through the farm belt instead. It was likely that they would never have caught up to him, or if they eventually had, by then he would have bought sufficient security to keep himself and his stolen golden bucks safe. Emmett, Harlan and Garrett might have moved back to Stillborough with her, probably all going into business together instead of going their separate ways.

But even Dess herself had decided not to steer her mount back towards the road, even as they heard the tell-tale sound of Archie Callahan's bus slowly navigating its way through the farm belt the morning after they had left Coyote's Rest. She hadn't been in the best of moods after having accused Harlan of killing Emmett, and she couldn't imagine a reason why Archie wanted her to wave him down, other than for him to try and coax her into boarding the bus back to Rubicross again.

They had purposely taken the long route, keeping the cliff behind the fenced-off railroad in their sights as they rode east, so that Dess could spend some time with her thoughts. For her, the ride had been a cathartic journey, allowing her to deal with her emotions and reminisce on happier times, a necessary healing process to prepare her for what she planned on doing next.

She had considered confronting Bruce Mallory over whether he had arranged for Emmett to be killed, if only to reopen the possibility that Harlan was indeed innocent, but she had found that if she gave any more thought to the curious nature of Emmett's death, it only served to make her withdraw into herself again, and she felt that after two years of not even hearing from the man she had once loved, she was finally ready to move on with her life.

Dess had decided to take up Nathan Royce on the offer of becoming his business partner in establishing trade relations with the inhabitants of Woodrow College. It was imperative that she no longer thought of them as mutants, but as an unfortunate group of people who had been deformed by the North Tekota missile blast. If she could convince herself, then she could convince others, and maybe then, they would have a fighting chance of ensuring that the college's wealth of medical and scientific knowledge and equipment wouldn't be lost forever.

She knew that her older neighbour, Errol Chandler, would look after Fritz until her eventual return to Stillborough. Although she would be working predominantly on the other side of the Shield Mountains, only a half-day's ride away, her homecoming would have to wait until their diplomatic relationship was firmly rooted, and the ongoing trading activities were capable of running independently. She would be sure to write as much to Errol once they reached Rubicross.

"Oi," Fletcher's voice came as the point man's horse crested a rise, his stark figure framed by the impending twilight, "Something up ahead."

Dess and Carter laid hands on their thigh-holstered pistols while Monroe reached over her shoulder for the rifle slung across her back as they joined him on the hillock. Away in the distance, in the centre of a sprawling field of golden wheat, was a modest farmhouse, which was a dwarf in comparison to the unpainted wooden barn and slowly-turning windmill on either side.

They spurred their horses into a friendly trot, approaching as amicably as possible while keeping a wary eye on their shadowy surroundings. The feel of a mattress after long nights of sleeping on hard ground would be a welcome luxury, but even one night under the barn's roof was a tempting comfort; although if they were indeed being pursued, this would also be the perfect place to set a trap.

With the whispering wheat stalks surrounding the property, any number of assailants could creep up on them in the dead of night and take them unaware. And even if they survived a midnight raid, the threat could still be lurking out there in the morning. If it came to that, their only hope of escape would be to set the field ablaze and use the smoke to break away, or perish in the flames along with their foes.

In spite of the potential death trap that they were walking into, Dess kept her mount to a steady trot, determined to have at least a few hours of rest behind closed doors.

"Anyone home?" Carter called out cautiously as they neared the homestead.

No answer.

The pair of Royce guards dismounted and tied their horses to the veranda's wooden balustrade before knocking on the door.

Again, no answer.

Fletcher tested the doorknob. It was unlocked.

"We're coming in!" he announced, pulling out his pistol and flipping the safety off.

Carter followed him inside the dark doorway as Dess and Monroe drew their weapons, still on horseback, circling the farmhouse in opposing circuits while keeping an eye on their surroundings, meeting up again at the rear of the homestead.

Both women aimed at the back door when it swung open, only to lower their sidearms at the sight of Fletcher emerging.

"Place is empty," he reported with a shrug.

"No food in the fridge either," Carter shared her observations as she joined him. "No signs of struggle or scavengers. Looks like they just packed up and left."

"Fletcher, check the generator for any diesel," Monroe instructed before turning to Dess. "Bring Carter with you to clear the barn. I'll take the mill. Meet back out front."

The generator was completely empty, as was the barn and windmill. Monroe told them about the purported protest in Rubicross. People of the farm belt had supposedly been gathering outside the walls of the Royce Family's estate, demanding new supplies of diesel. She concluded that the settlers who had been living on the wheat farm might have abandoned the house to join the protest.

Dess was inclined to agree, especially since there weren't any spare fuel cans or barrels to be found, but at least there was still some clean water in the big tank on the side of the house. Not enough for a much-needed shower, but more than plenty to refill their canteens and scrub their grimy faces and necks.

Carter and Fletcher were busy securing their horses in the barn when Monroe called Dess over, the deputy's expression as hard as the day they had met.

"Keep your eyes on the house," Monroe began as she casually walked towards the front porch. "Somebody's been watching us from the cliff."

The deputy sat down on one of the weathered wooden rocking chairs in the corner of the veranda, allowing Dess to look past her towards the rock face above the railroad. Sure enough, she could see the faint flash of field glasses reflecting the last rays of the sunset. Her first thought was that Harlan had been following them from Coyote's Rest, although that couldn't be right, as she would have expected Garrett to stop him.

Unless he already tried, she thought to herself. *He's already killed Emmett, what's Garrett's life in comparison?*

"I know what you're thinking," said Monroe, creaking back and forth in her chair as Fletcher and Carter eagerly headed inside to enjoy the amenities. "But if we make a move now, they'll know we know. And if they try to rush us, I'd prefer to have a defendable position over being caught out in the open."

She was right. They needed cover, and it was too late to find somewhere else to stay for the night. It was dusk now, the purple twilight surrendering to a closing black curtain that would soon blanket the star-studded sky. At least the night was clear and the moon was full, because they would have no other way of illuminating their perimeter without diesel for the generator.

"So what, then?" asked Dess, keeping her voice low. "We just wait until they attack?"

"No," Monroe replied, keeping her eyes on the rippling crops. "We bide our time here. Make it look like we're settling in for the night. And then we launch a pre-emptive strike."

The two women circled the farmhouse together, eating strips of beef jerky and smiling wistfully at the sound of the headboard hitting the wall as the two Royce guards "rested" inside, Carter's gasps and moans mingling with Fletcher's groans of exertion. The man had been backed up for days now, Dess having warned him that if he tried anything while they were all under the same canvas, he would be left out in the cold every night until they reached Rubicross.

"Feels wrong to think about it without him, right?" Monroe ventured, her dour facade having vanished completely. She eyed Dess with a combination of forlorn nostalgia and probing curiosity.

"It's strange," Dess admitted, her breath catching as she met the woman's gaze, "It's like the urge isn't even there anymore. I guess I just got caught up in so many other things after we split up, I stopped taking care of myself."

"I hear you," the deputy replied, breaking eye contact and looking back at the field under the moonlight. "Just doesn't feel the same. When I'm alone, I mean."

Fletcher roared his pleasure as he climaxed inside the homestead's master bedroom, the guards' sighs of ecstasy-filled exhaustion subsiding as they collapsed into a series of wet smooches.

The deputy and the lumberjack had barely cleared the water tank before Monroe turned on Dess, catching her by the hips and pushing her up against the wall, kissing her passionately. Surprised, but magnetically drawn to the woman's lips, Dess took control, seizing Monroe by her neck and toned midsection before spinning her around and pressing her up against the wall in turn, snaking her tongue into the deputy's yielding mouth.

Savouring the lingering flavour of spicy beef jerky on her breath, Dess broke their lip lock, turning away to survey the field again before resuming their patrol, her heart pounding.

"Fletcher!" Monroe called, wiping her mouth. "Get the fuck out here now!!"

By the time they reached the front porch again, Fletcher was outside, buckling up his belt with his gun drawn, his rugged gaze scrutinising their surroundings. Monroe had Dess by the waist, urging her up the veranda's stairs and into the house, where Carter was still pulling on her shirt in the hallway. They pushed past her and laid claim to an unsoiled bedroom; not that it mattered, even the linoleum kitchen floor would have sufficed.

They pulled each others' riding clothes off, almost tearing at each other's buttons and zips, clutching firm yet soft and willing flesh, kissing, biting and sucking every new patch of skin as it presented itself. They hadn't even stopped to kick off their boots, collapsing onto the single bed with their sweat-stained pants and panties pooled around their dirt-encrusted boots, spreading their supple thighs wide as they rubbed each other with impatient circular motions, warming themselves up before plunging their callused fingers into one another, both women having yearned the indelicate touch of a man's hands for years.

Dess squeezed one of Monroe's gooseflesh-covered breasts while she sucked and slurped on the other, giving teeth to the stiff pink nipple until the deputy yelped and pushed her away before pulling her back for more.

Monroe shrieked with delight as she sprayed her juices across the neatly-tucked sheets, hungrily pushing Dess down and finger-blasting the lumberjack until she squirted in turn. Their shuddering bliss-filled gasps and screams of intense pleasure resonated throughout the abandoned homestead, certain that Carter and Fletcher were smirking in the same way that the two women had been only minutes prior.

* * *

They snuck out through the back door with their weapons drawn as the full moon climbed higher into the clear night sky, letting their eyes adjust to the darkness before weaving their way through the wheat. Despite still reeling in the euphoric after-effects of each other's ecstasy and embrace, the four were ready to kill their pursuers.

Clearing the crops, they came upon the railroad's barbed wire fence, where they found that a hole had been cut into the chain-linked mesh. It was large enough to walk through without stooping as they crossed the rail tracks to the other side, where well-worn grooves in the cliff wall created a natural ladder in the rock face.

"Rauders," Dess whispered as the other three gathered behind her. "This is how they've been raiding."

Flexing the slender muscles in her jaw, Dess holstered her sidearm, silently volunteering herself as the first to make the climb. The night wind of the prairies tugged at her riding clothes as she scaled the dirt rungs. She had climbed roughly two storeys before succumbing to the urge to glance down, where the others were intermittently checking their surroundings and looking back up at Dess. A fall from this height was sure to snap bones. Pulling herself closer to the wall, she looked back up at the top, readjusted her footing and kept on climbing.

The faint twinkle of a campfire glowed in the distance as Monroe, Carter and Fletcher formed up behind Dess. She didn't even need to motion towards it as they all beheld the flame in their eyes. Slowly creeping forward from one overgrown desert shrub to the next, they closed in on the solitary figures huddled around the campfire.

One silhouette was playing a melancholy melody upon a harmonica while the others silently chewed upon skewered husks of roasted meat, each meal the size of an overgrown rat. Dess and the others fanned out behind them, staying to the shadows of the dancing flames as they picked their targets.

"Hands up!" Dess warned once they were all in position, holding her pistol on the harmonica player, "Or I'll give you another hole you can blow through."

The woeful warbling stopped as the man withdrew the metal instrument from his mouth and licked his lips, swallowing before holding his arms up obligingly. The others sitting around the crackling campfire nervously followed his lead, their lanced lizard and roasted rodent dinners wavering in the air.

"We're just the lookouts," the musician mumbled, his eyes on the ground. "We don't want any trouble."

"I'm sure the folks in Torzal Arroyo said the same thing," Monroe replied through gritted teeth. "You fellas have a pretty price tag on your heads. Ten cases worth."

"Ten cases…?" the man repeated, chancing a glance over his shoulder to see the deputy crouching beside a spiky desert shrub. "I don't know what that means. We're just–"

"What's cookin', good-lookin'?" a woman's voice called out from the darkness as a group of shadows approached from behind, their boots crunching over the gravel. "SHIT!!"

Dess, Monroe and Carter whirled their weapons on the newcomers, but Fletcher was the first to fire, squeezing off two rounds before being gunned down. Carter dropped her pistol and rushed to his side, her slender fingers shaking and scrabbling as she tried to staunch the blood flow pooling from the punctures in his torso.

Outnumbered, Dess and Monroe slowly laid their weapons at their feet and stood as the ambushers drew closer to the light. The armed men and women were all wearing hoods, obscuring their faces. Seeing that the threat was neutralised, a few of them began to usher a band of ashen-faced prairie settlers closer to the campfire, their eyes glued to Fletcher as he lay shuddering on the ground with Carter kneeling over him.

"I told you to keep *watch*, Cecil," the same woman's voice growled as she holstered her pistol.

"I thought it was you, Ruth!" the harmonica player exclaimed, still holding his hands up in surrender. "Nobody comes up here but us. How was I supposed to know?"

"Fuckin' useless…" Ruth replied. She turned her attention towards Dess and Monroe, "And you, do you have *any idea* what we're tryin' to do here?"

Standing with her hands in the air, Dess eyed the nervous faces of the women among the unarmed civilians from the prairies. She had a fair idea of why Fletcher was the only one bleeding on the ground, knowing the reputation of the Rauders. It didn't take a genius to figure out why she, Monroe and Carter had been spared.

"Maybe I can talk to them," Cecil offered, putting one hand on his chest.

Dess and Monroe locked eyes for a brief moment before the deputy looked pointedly at Dess's discarded pistol. One of the hooded men caught the gesture.

"Ruth," he murmured out of the side of his mouth, keeping his gun trained on the pair of women, "I don't think they deserve to come with us."

"Stay with me," Carter sobbed, smearing blood across Fletcher's cheek as she tried to keep him from passing out. "Somebody help me, please!"

Seizing opportunity in the distraction, Monroe crouched to pick up her rifle, blasting at the Rauders, bodies falling to the dirt as they scattered in disarray. Dess dropped to the ground as bullets zinged by overhead. She snatched up her sidearm, ready to rain hot metal, but before she could take aim at anyone, a searing slug sunk into her breastbone.

The gun fell from her hand, and she rolled onto her back in the dirt, the wind knocked out of her, spluttering as she clutched her chest in confusion. Mere moments later, Monroe keeled over beside her with a dribble of blood oozing from between the strands of blonde hair strewn across her forehead as she stared lifelessly into the campfire.

"There are worse ways to die, sister," Ruth's voice floated down to Dess as the stars in the night sky began to blur together. "These days especially," the woman added as she kicked the gun aside before glancing back over her shoulder to address one of the Rauders, "Make sure you burn the bodies."

The stars, the moon and the fire disappeared, and Dess's world faded to black.

CHAPTER 31 – HARLAN

The eighty-something riders from Coyote's Rest reached the ramshackle remains of Maisey Belle's Motel just in time to sit back and watch the desert sunset as it painted the sky in gold and purple hues. Harlan had never been this far west prior to the apocalypse, but he and most of the other men and women in the hunting party had stayed a spell in the highway haunt during the railroad's construction.

The abandoned motel had been a bona fide shithole back when Harlan had laid eyes on it for the first time, with drifts of sand scattered across the roadside parking lot and heaped up in piles along the two-storey L-shaped wing of rat-ridden rooms that looked out over the whale-shaped swimming pool beside the car park, the water left inside having collected enough sickly-green scum to make any thirsty mountain lion that happened to pass by keel over and die.

During their not-brief-enough stay, the railroad workers had cleaned up somewhat to make the place at least liveable, but that had been over three years ago.

Now, it was little more than a desolate ruin, with the desert having reclaimed the entire parking lot, burying the wheels of forsaken family sedans and rusty campervans in the sand. Every piece of glass on the motel's premises had been shattered, as if the very existence of windows was an affront to whoever had passed through the area. Pests and rodents had established vast colonies, their empires rising and falling to the frequent culls of desert wildlife that had used the motel as a hunting ground, evidenced by small piles of bones and big piles of shit.

The only improvement on the hideous eyesore was that the scum of the swimming pool had been filled in with sand, trash and desert debris that had blown into its depths over the years; although a gigantic garbage dumpster wasn't exactly a selling point that someone might expect to find on the motel's brochure.

The riders weren't picky though. After long days and hard nights of roughing it out in the wilderness for the past week, some were glad to have the privacy of four walls again – regardless of how thin they were – while others were satisfied with just dragging the soiled mattresses out into the dunes of the former parking lot and lying down on something soft for a change.

Olaf Kaufmann's LED lanterns had died only a few hours outside of Coyote's Rest, so they had resolved to travel by day, setting up camp with huge bonfires at night to deter the packs of feral dogs that plagued the outskirts of the prairies. Many of the cowboys and cowgirls could still remember the horrors of the first time that they had been attacked by wild dogs back when they had been building the railroad, and being dragged off in their sleep to be mauled alone in the fields wasn't particularly going to help them find the Rauders.

Garrett had been leading them on horseback over the broken asphalt of forgotten highways, his keen eyes scanning for disturbances along the roadside, occasionally venturing down old motorbike tracks, narrowed by overgrown yellow grass that had sought to reclaim the dirt paths, but to no avail. He was an excellent tracker, yet in spite of his prowess, it was impossible to follow the Rauders' trail without even knowing where to begin.

When Harlan had suggested that they could start at Torzal Arroyo, the sorry excuse for a small town where all the rumours had started, Garrett had replied that the trail would have turned cold by now, and it would only be a dead end.

And so the hunting party had been zigzagging across the hinterland for the past week without a clear direction in mind, riding past abandoned farmsteads, drained petrol stations, ravaged and burnt-out husks of roadside diners, and the occasional tiny backwater town that wasn't even worth the trouble of being put on a map.

The small scattered groups of settlers that they had encountered always seemed to rush indoors at the first sign of the riders' dust cloud rising on the horizon, fearing an attack from the Rauders, but when Harlan would announce that they were only there to help, the most common answer from each derelict cluster of hovels regarding the rumoured return of the phantom raiders was that it had been a while since they had heard any news from some other derelict cluster of hovels.

Less common answers, but equally as fruitless, were far-fetched tales that had been passed on from one settler to the next, no doubt having been embellished with each retelling. They told of mercenaries coming all the way from Rookson City with the sole purpose of attacking small towns, leaving nothing behind in their never-ending search for new resources that they could melt down and recycle in their munitions factory; hooded kidnappers descending from the cliffs in the north to abduct men, women and children, somehow managing to haul all of their captives back up the sheer cliff wall without even leaving a trace of struggle or an attempt to escape – the claim sounded plausible at first, until they remembered that the Rauders had never been known to kidnap men; and Harlan's favourite, an absurd story of some great devouring force of otherworldly creatures that were currently rampaging across the west – easily the most reasonable conclusion anyone could have ever imagined as to why the diesel had stopped flowing from Cloakwater.

These people are living out here for a reason, Harlan had supposed. They were outcasts living on the outskirts of society because there was no place within society for them to live. The same thing could have been said about some of the men and women who had ridden along with him from Coyote's Rest, but at least they had a job to do and a purpose to serve.

Although if they continued to keep coming up empty-handed, sooner or later they would be forced to give up on the hunt, and hope that they could convince the Mayor of Brimvale that the settlers were simply leaving the prairies for better prospects. The towns that had been abandoned were done so voluntarily, and the Rauders were just as dead as they had been two years ago.

Harlan would still be sure to collect on the bounty regardless of whether they finished the job though, and regardless of whether Brimvale's Mayor believed their story, for that matter.

He climbed down from his big red stallion, walking it over to an external flight of stairs and tying the lead rope in a loose slipknot around one of the railings, the other riders soon following suit, fanning out across the desolate motel's premises. Big-Stack sidled up beside him with Emmett's smooth black fox trotter, habitually hitching it next to Harlan's, the pair of horses nuzzling each other.

"Satisfied?" the brutish redhead growled as Harlan finished inspecting the beautiful black mare. Billy still held some resentment for not being allowed to attend Emmett's funeral to pay his respects. As much as he didn't like Emmett, he still respected the man, as did everyone else, and Billy had begrudgingly agreed to treat Emmett's old horse with the same level of respect.

"Still waiting for the day you fuck up," Harlan replied, once again impressed to find that there wasn't a single mark on the fox trotter.

"I'll bet y'are," Big-Stack grinned menacingly before taking a swig of his whiskey flask and handing it to Harlan.

He drank obligingly and tossed it back before searching for a decent armchair in one of the motel rooms on the ground floor.

The hunting party had made sure to stop by Haydar's potato farm on their way to Firmfield, having forgotten to pack a supply of food and drinks and hoping to purchase some provisions at a bulk-rate discount. To their surprise however, Haydar had left his farm completely unattended, serving up his stock of crops and liquor on a silver platter.

Some had objected to the blatant burglary, but Harlan had reasoned that it looked as though the place had already been picked through, and by leaving it unprotected, they were only ensuring that somebody else would make off with the merchandise. A few were still unconvinced, but the moment he had promised to give Haydar part of Brimvale's bounty as compensation after the hunting party were paid in full, the rest of the riders were all too eager to take as much as they could carry.

While the decision had increased Harlan's popularity among the other cowboys and cowgirls, who were happily handing him a share of the loot whenever an opportunity presented itself, Garrett had clenched his jaw in silence throughout the entire ambiguous acquisition, only pausing his brooding to pull Harlan aside for a brief moment, quietly reporting that he hadn't observed any signs of prior pilfering.

"I know," Harlan had admitted underneath the sounds of crates crunching open and sacks being torn and shaken empty into saddlebags. "But if we don't take it, somebody else will. Better sooner than later, right?"

It was impossible to ignore the uneasy tension building between the two men. Although Harlan had been glad when Garrett had chosen to hang around after Dess decided to ride back to Royce's bedroom, he still couldn't shake the feeling that his old hunting buddy from Stillborough was only staying behind to keep tabs on him, especially given the fact that Garrett hadn't yet declared whether he believed Dess's claim that Harlan had killed Emmett.

As much as the accusation had stung, Harlan could accept that he remained the biggest suspect in the investigation. Going from rags to riches and accepting the Brimvale shit-stain's proposition to become contract killers in the wake of Emmett's death was sure to raise some questions, but it would have been nice to know whether he could trust Garrett to have his back, especially out here among so many strangers, along with more than a few acquaintances who were equally as unreliable.

Finally coming across a cracked brown leather armchair that hadn't been completely gnawed away by vagrant vermin over the years, Harlan dusted off the cobwebs and shook out the roaches before hauling it back outside into the evening air, where many of the riders had taken to throwing furniture that was beyond salvation into the debris-filled whale-shaped swimming pool.

Harlan sank into the leather seat and watched as Werner doused the garbage dump with half a bottle of Haydar's hooch before sharing it around with the rest of the former Royce guards while Garrett stooped to strike a flint. The sparks took, and the flame roared, blazing up the bonfire. Some of the horses had reared and bucked during their first few nights camping out in the prairies, but now they had grown accustomed to the fires, occasionally welcoming the warmth with an appreciative whinny. While the blaze was a beacon to anyone glimpsing the glow for miles around, it was sure to ward off whatever else was skulking in the darkness.

Elwood and Gabe had drawn the short straws tonight, and they set about starting on dinner, first laying a squeaky wire mesh bed frame across the top of the burning whale's head before sliding cast-iron cooking pots over the fire. On tonight's menu was a bland broth of boiled potatoes and lizard guts; a sure-fire way of ensuring that they would never be asked to cook again.

Dante and Cactus Jack disappeared into some of the rooms upstairs with their latest out-of-towner flings, while Werner followed Frost into one of the rusty campervans, which soon began to creak from side to side as the promiscuous blonde moaned her pleasure through the broken windows. The rest of the riders either gathered around the bonfire to complain about saddle sores or broke off to find a private space where they could indulge their own vices.

The old and new faces of the funeral attendants had originally come to Coyote's Rest to mourn Emmett's death, but with each passing day, Harlan suspected that after having been subjected to the same humdrum routines of Stillborough and Brimvale and Rubicross and wherever else they had come from, they had all been yearning for an adventure outside of making the journey west to simply attend Emmett's funeral. One by one, they were all falling victim to the allure of life in the prairies; but for the extra eyes and guns in the field, far be it from Harlan to deny them the pleasure.

"So what's next after this, boss?" Boaz asked, lounging on the hood of a busted sedan beside Price while they waited for their turns with Frost. "We kill the Rauders, get the money, and then what?"

"That's if we find the fuckers first," said Price, hawking spit at the ground as he eyed Garrett, holding him – their best chance of tracking down the raiders – responsible for not having tracked down the raiders yet.

"Everybody's free to do as they please," Harlan replied, echoing Emmett's exact words after they had split the Wallace Pelletier payday. Garrett was listening in from his squat beside the bonfire, the flickering light dancing over his unshaven beard, eager to hear what the new leader of the cowboys had planned, but admittedly, Harlan hadn't given the idea of "what's next" much thought himself. He deflected the question with one of his own, "What about y'all? Planning on heading back to Rubicross?"

"Everythin' I own is in my saddle pack," Price declared proudly before looking around for his horse, "So I sure as shit ain't in a rush to go back and work for *the man*."

The rusty-hinged door of one of the motorhomes screeched open as Werner emerged with a satisfied grin, buckling on his belt and breathing in the potato-and-lizard broth wafting on the warm breeze. Price leapt off his perch on the sedan to double-check his horse's slipknot, under the guise of taking a piss.

"Well, I know what I plan on doing," Boaz smirked, sliding off the hood as Werner tagged him in on his way past. Marching towards Frost's open campervan, he called over his shoulder, "I'm gon' fuck, ride, drink, and fuck some more!"

Big-Stack led the chorus of cheers in his wake as the door slammed shut and the rusty motorhome began rocking from side to side again.

Harlan removed his umber brown cowboy hat and hung it upon the shoulder of his armchair when Elwood and Gabe announced that dinner was ready, with everyone standing back to allow him the first serving of soup. The potatoes were mush and the lizard guts were tough, just as the cunning cooks had intended. Garrett approached Harlan a few minutes later, sprinkling a clump of salt into his bowl until the taste of something similar to chicken overcame the soft yet chewy texture.

"You remember the stories Archie used to tell us about this place?" Harlan sat back as he spooned his soup, staring up at the unlit neon sign of Maisey

Belle's Motel. Several of the letters had fallen from the roof over the years. Even now, the big "B" was melting in the bonfire, but he could still picture the way it must have appeared according to Archie.

"The 'Maybe Motel,'" Garrett recalled, his lips curling into a thin smile.

The highway haunt's nickname had stemmed from the housekeepers cleaning the rooms inconsistently, so maybe the sheets were clean, and maybe they still had the same suspicious stains from the week before, but travellers who had been on the road for long enough were always willing to take the chance.

One night, a bunch of drunk college students passing through from Woodrow had climbed up onto the roof, selectively cutting off the juice to the neon letters so that the sign read precisely what people were calling the place. The owner had never bothered to fix it up after having heard the many jokes surrounding her business, even spreading around a few of them herself.

Maybe you don't get food poisoning from the vending machine, Archie's dark-humoured drawl echoed as they stared into the bonfire. *Maybe you can make it to the next stop before you need to drop a deuce. Maybe that hitchhiker you picked up really is a woman.*

They chuckled together, before Harlan set his empty dish down in the sand, smacking his lips. As simple as it was, the salt had made the difference.

"You think I killed him?" he asked, eyeing Garrett.

"Emmett?" the tracker stroked his scruffy beard before taking a knee beside the chair, still staring into the fire. He took a long moment before he finally faced Harlan, his discerning blue-grey eyes cutting into Harlan's gaze as he answered, "I know you better than that, brother."

* * *

Many of the riders had already begun to dismiss the rumoured return of the Rauders as worthless gossip among bored folks who liked to exaggerate whatever hearsay they came across, but just because the settlers were telling outlandish tales, it didn't make the possible threats that could have been prowling the badlands – whatever they might have been – any less dangerous, and so the hunting party posted a rotating roster of sentries each night, with everyone ensuring that their guns were never too far away.

Harlan was slumped in his cracked brown leather armchair, dozing off as he basked in the warmth of the crackling bonfire, occasionally stirring at the sound of a woman's delighted mewl of pleasure or a cowboy's customary retch of Haydar's hooch, when a shout rang out from the motel's rooftop.

"Heads up!" Garrett's voice shook Harlan from his snooze, "We got company!!"

Blinking groggily against the blaze of the bonfire, Harlan reached for his pistol and lurched to his feet.

CRACK!!

The sound of a gunshot bullwhipped across the desolate motel's sand-covered parking lot, bouncing off the walls of the two-storey L-shaped wing of rooms, smacking everyone awake like an unpaid whore. Harlan ducked behind the leather armchair, one hand holding the seat to steady himself with the other holding his gun aloft while he tried to discern which direction their attackers were coming from.

Price was yowling on the hood of the busted sedan, holding his bleeding foot as the end of his gun's holster smoked. Werner was lying on his stomach beside him, reaching over the broken windshield to return fire, taking pot-shots into the night. Soon, the entire car park was blaring with gunfire, half-clothed and half-drunk shooters flashing muzzles from every nook and cranny of the motel.

"Eat lead, you fuckin' cocksuckers!!" Big-Stack yelled as he fired Byron's repeater from the open door of Frost's rusty motorhome, the blonde's long braids hanging over her breasts as her rifle's barrel poked through a broken window.

"West side, you dumb shits, west!!" Cactus Jack shouted over the gunfire from a second-storey window as he paused to reload, with Dante, Elwood and Gabe crouching among a crowd behind the balcony's balustrade, slinging slugs in the same direction.

Harlan left the cover of his armchair and hurtled towards the other end of the parking lot, ducking low as he scrambled through the debris while the cowboys and cowgirls blasted bullets at shadows of cacti and boulders and every other vague silhouette looming in the distance.

He narrowly avoided head-butting an out-of-towner who had the bright idea of using one of the rearing horses for cover. The wide-eyed stallion kicked out with its hind legs, sending the rider into a somersault before landing on his ass in the sand to cry over his crushed collarbone.

Harlan's heart hammered in time with the barrage of bullets as he crouched behind the rear end of a black RV, craning his head forward and sizing up the open stretch to a rusty red pickup truck on the west end of the car park.

He stood with his back against the RV, closing his eyes for a moment to steady his breathing before breaking into a run, keeping his head down as he covered the distance and leapt into the pickup truck's tray, only to come face to face with a gun barrel.

"Fuck me," Boaz breathed as he jammed a new clip into his pistol, "You're lucky I'm reloading."

"How many are there?" Harlan asked, poking his head up over the side of the big bucket before Boaz could answer.

"Less than there were a minute ago," Boaz chuckled, cocking back the slide and propping himself up again.

Ghostly flashes of silver materialised over a dune in the middle-distance, a handful of dark figures half-running, half-staggering towards the motel despite the hail of hot lead pockmarking the sand around them.

Otherworldly creatures, Harlan remembered the settlers' not-so-far-fetched tale as he took aim at the closest one and fired, a guttural groan greeting his gun's bark. A second fell to a stray slug, and a third folded the moment Boaz squeezed off the first shot of his fresh clip. The last of the four attackers froze in place, only to career backwards with a warped wail as a rifle round ripped through its chest.

Whatever they were, they weren't running anymore.

"Hold your fire!!" Harlan bellowed as he lay back down in the tray beside Boaz.

The pair of men had to repeat the order half a dozen times before the salvo stopped, and even then, some were still shooting out at the dark contours of the desert, nowhere near where the attack had actually come from.

"Put your fucking dicks away!" Harlan yelled, waiting for the gunfire to die down into deafening silence before jumping out of the pickup truck.

He approached the fallen bodies in the sand with his gun raised, Boaz by his side. Dark patches of soiled and blood-soaked orange cloth began to materialise between the strips of silver as they drew near, soon taking on the form of hi-vis overalls; uniforms of Cloakwater's miners. None of them were carrying weapons.

Harlan grimly surveyed the four grimy-faced miners; one man and three women, either dead or dying. They had been riddled with bullet holes the moment they had stopped moving. He knew that he was directly responsible for at least one of their deaths, but after being accused of murdering Emmett by people he had once called his closest friends, what was the life of an innocent stranger?

"Should've gone... other group," one of their so-called attackers wheezed, blood seeping from the mouth of her weather-worn face.

"Looked like Rauders," a man managed to mumble before gurgling and choking to death on his own blood.

"Rauders?" Harlan asked, lowering his gun, "Where?"

"North... hour back," the old woman answered feebly, "Saw your fire... came here." She glanced back at her dead companions before she began to splutter. Boaz knelt beside her, examining the wound in her chest before shaking his head at Harlan. Her eyes went wide, remembering something. She moaned in pain as she tried and failed to sit up. "Rubicross...! Have to... warn..."

"They already know about the raids," Harlan reassured her, taking his umber brown hat off and holding it to his chest as he bowed his head in respect. "We'll take care of it."

The alarm in the old woman's face didn't fade as she mouthed silently, her last words lost in her death rattle.

A pair of boots crunched across the car park's gravel.

"You said!" Garrett yelled, shoving Harlan from the side. "You said we'd be hunting Rauders!! They look like raiders to you!?"

Harlan dusted his hat off and placed it back on his head, casting a moonlit shadow over his face as dozens more came to gather around the bodies, investigating their kills. Some gasped in horror as they realised that the miners were unarmed. A few of the shooters muttered curses, swigging ruefully from hip flasks before spilling some sauce onto the sand. Others weren't as generous with their drinks as they had been with their bullets.

"Who the fuck fired first?" Cactus Jack asked, pushing his way to the front of the crowd.

"Blame this asshole," Werner's voice answered from the back, supporting Price as the former Royce guard hopped along on one foot. "Dumb son of a bitch left his safety off."

"You said we had company," Price scowled at Garrett before hawking spit at the ground. "Sure as shit that means we're under attack!"

"You're the one who called it," Boaz stood, stepping over the dead woman to stare down Garrett. "How the fuck we s'posed to know they was friendly?"

"I ain't say start killing," Garrett growled, clenching his jaw as others began taking sides.

"I didn't sign up for this shit!" one of the out-of-towners cried.

"Nobody signed up for half the shit we see out here," Dante said dryly, taking another pull of his hip flask as he stared out into the night.

"They were innocent people," another complained.

"Everybody's guilty of somethin'!" Big-Stack yelled, one burly arm around the now fully-clothed Frost, "If y'all can't handle killin', what the fuck y'all doin' out here!?"

"Enough," Harlan warned, stepping in between the lines forming behind Garrett and Boaz. "We all made the same mistake. Maybe Garrett should've said something else. Maybe Price should've checked his safety. Maybe the rest of you trigger-happy fucks should watch where you're shooting. Maybe… maybe we shouldn't have checked in at the Maybe Motel." He stifled his dark-humoured smirk, pausing to stare around at all of them before looking down at the dead miners. "But I'll tell y'all now. If we weren't out here in the first place, they would've died anyway. If not from exposure, then the Rauders would've killed them, or they'd have wished they had. Their deaths are on us, sure, but we just put them out of their misery."

"Ain't seen no raiders yet," Garrett reminded him, still staring down Boaz.

"No, we haven't," Harlan agreed before nodding at the miners. "But they have."

"It's true," Boaz backed him up, breaking his staring contest with Garrett as he turned to the riders gathered, "West one hour, then north."

"Y'all got a choice," Harlan continued, craning his head forward as he began pacing through the crowd gathered. "You can head back to wherever you call home. Tell everybody we killed some folks who didn't announce themselves on hostile territory. While you're at it, don't forget to tell them how many shots you fired… Or, we can hunt down these motherfuckers who killed so many of our own, put an end to the raids, and split the reward money after!"

The cowboys and cowgirls sent up a cheer, turning on their heels and running towards their horses. Nobody in their right mind was about to let the past week spent searching the prairies go to waste, let alone confess to multiple counts of manslaughter. Like anyone else would have, they chose to take the money and the vengeance over a criminal sentence.

"If you ain't there, you ain't gettin' shit!" Big-Stack hollered as he led the crowd.

"Hope you boys and girls got a few more rounds left!" Frost shouted wickedly.

"YEEHAW Y'ALL!!" Price whooped as he attempted to hop along on one foot before giving up. "Somebody bring me my fuckin' horse!"

"Guess we got ourselves a hunt," Garrett sniffed, loping off towards his brown mustang without a backwards glance at Harlan.

* * *

They bore blazing torches from the bonfire to light their way during the midnight ride, their whoops and hollers drowning out the long howls and low growls of desert wolves, mountain lions and packs of stray dogs. It was impossible to move in stealth with eighty riders, so they were going to strike on the other end of the spectrum; hard, fast and loud enough to make half the Rauders run while the other half shit themselves.

After years of enduring raids in the prairies, losing friends and family members during each and every savage attack, it was time for the victims to unleash their rage and anger on the Rauders. The missile that had wiped out North Tekota couldn't hold a candle in comparison to the scorched earth the cowboys were about to leave behind. All bets were off if the raiders had families of their own. Not one person participating in the midnight massacre would feel an ounce of sympathy or shame if a Rauder had his entire bloodline permanently purged from what was left of the human gene pool.

A handful of pitiful campfires gleamed in the distance, dispersed between dozens of tents. The eighty-something riders fanned out across the dark terrain, firing on horseback before they were even within firing range.

Cries of alarm went up as the Rauders scrambled to retaliate.

Blood mist sprayed across Harlan's left cheek, with Gabe keeling over in his saddle and falling from his horse, trampled by the riders bringing up the rear. The man's only consolation was that he would never be asked to cook again. For every rider that ate the ground however, ten unprepared Rauders paid the price, and that was only the beginning.

Big-Stack ran out of bullets long before they reached the camp, so when Emmett's black fox trotter vaulted over the pathetic defensive line, the towering brute held his repeater by its smoking barrel and swung the wooden stock like a golf club, shattering some poor cocksucker's skull like an overripe pumpkin and snapping the gun in half.

Throwing what was left of the barrel end over end at another hooded raider who thought he could escape, Billy leapt to the ground, bellowing as he rolled, jumped up and chased the coward down, beating him to death with his bare hands.

"YOU! KILLED! MY! PA!" Big-Stack roared, his huge fists crunching through bone with every syllable before he turned his fury on the next Rauder. "YOU! KILLED! MY! PA! YOU! KILLED! MY! PA!"

"This one's for you, Gabe!" Elwood shouted, unfurling a burning motel curtain from its pole and draping it over a man he had caught reloading.

The screaming wretch fired wild shots into the night as he struggled to take off the flaming curtain, killing his own companions who had come to his aid before turning the gun on himself.

The defensive line broke as more riders breached the camp, setting fire to tents and shooting at anyone they caught attempting to escape. Emmett's riderless black mare circled back and hoofed at the ground next to Harlan's red stallion as he halted by one of the campfires, letting the chaos wash over him.

Cowboys, cowgirls and out-of-towners alike were dedicating kills to their lost loved ones before brutalising another victim. For some, it wasn't enough to just shoot at the Rauders, and several of the riders had leapt from their horses.

"You killed my husband, you whore!" Blair Frost yelled as she kicked a screaming woman backwards into a burning tent, taking a swig of her hip flask before dousing the canvas.

"Fuck them up on the other side, Emmett," Harlan muttered as he lined up half a dozen youths fleeing into the night, gunning them down one by one.

"For Flem," Garrett declared as he shot a man who had thought to seek refuge in one of the tents, frightened squeals erupting from inside as his corpse hit the canvas.

"For Flem's family," Cactus Jack added as he set fire to the end of a rag stuffed into a half-empty bottle of Haydar's hooch. With a nasty grin, he hurled the bottle and set the screaming tent ablaze.

"You killed my sister!!" Dante yelled with tears in his eyes, tripping up an unarmed Rauder and unloading a full clip of bullets into his face. Dante's sister was worth the lives of five more men before he began blaming the women and children too.

Scowling in his saddle, Price squeezed off rounds at people's feet, letting them stagger around first before Boaz delivered the kill shots.

"Please! I have a wife!" one sorry excuse for a man begged on his knees before Big-Stack accused him of killing his Pa.

"She's mine now," Billy replied menacingly, wiping his blood-stained hands on the fresh corpse's shirt.

As if on cue, the man's wife emerged from one of the tents wielding a butcher's knife. Harlan shot the blade out of her hand, and she floundered for a moment before resolving to attack Billy anyway, pounding on his back with her small fists. Laughing boisterously, Big-Stack swept her up over one burly shoulder and carried her kicking and screaming back towards her tent.

"Put her down, Billy," Garrett warned, his brown mustang holding steady as he aimed his pistol at the redheaded brute.

"What are you gonna fuckin' do?" Big-Stack chuckled, turning back to the tent.

Garrett shot at the ground in front of Billy, drawing everyone's attention, the brief and bloody battle already over. Elwood and Werner, who had taken to tossing the bodies of dead and dying raiders into one of the campfires, followed Big-Stack's lead instead, catching the nearest women they could lay hands on and dragging them towards the few remaining tents that weren't burning yet. A score more riders leapt off their horses to do the same thing, but many of the cowgirls and out-of-towners took Garrett's side. One by one, they all looked to Harlan, waiting for his decision.

"You ain't gonna let this happen," Garrett said in his ear, although it was more of a request than a statement.

"Be a drop in the bucket for all the shit they did," Harlan shrugged, his indifference written plainly across his face, although he couldn't meet the gaze of any of the captured women as they hung on his next words.

"Please!" Elwood's captive screamed, attempting to fight off his grip in futility. "We're not raiders, we're settlers! They're trying to save us from what's coming!"

"They'll say anythin' to get 'emselves outta trouble," Elwood declared before clocking her across the jaw, rendering the woman unconscious.

Harlan studied his men's smiles dancing in the fiery glow of the burning camp at the hint of his consent. He hated the idea, but he knew that if he denied them their catharsis while they were still drunk on blood, he would lose control over them completely, and there was no telling what would happen after that.

Besides, they had already killed those unarmed miners from Cloakwater. The lives of the Rauders meant nothing in comparison to the lives of the innocent, and if anyone was still confused about the difference between the two, it was time for them to learn.

He swallowed the lump building in his throat, hardening his resolve.

"This is revenge!" Harlan announced, loud enough for everyone to hear as he walked his red stallion forward. He reached into his saddlebag, cracking open a bottle of whiskey before addressing the grinning cowboys. "You take yours however you see fit."

"Guess I ain't know you as well as I thought," Garrett growled at Harlan, anger and disappointment etched upon his face, the conflict between loyalty and morality once again ageing him beyond his years.

"They're all gonna die anyway," Harlan replied, eyeing Garrett's trembling pistol.

"Better sooner than later," Garrett sniffed, his brown mustang trotting towards Billy. "This one's for my friend. My brother. Harlan Reid."

Garrett swung his gun up and took aim at the captive woman draped over Big-Stack's shoulder, putting a bullet in her temple before kicking his spurs and riding off into the night.

Emmett's black fox trotter nuzzled up against Harlan's stallion as screams sounded and hooves pounded all around him. He had the bottle of whiskey raised halfway up to his lips when a familiar voice spoke softly into his ear.

"What'd you think was gonna happen?" the man asked, his breath hot against Harlan's cheek – as hot as the desert breeze blowing through the burning tents.

Harlan stared sidelong at the cowboy straddling the black mare's saddle. His rugged gaze was hidden beneath the darkness of his coal black cowboy hat, but there was no mistaking the man's stony jaw and broad cheekbones.

Feeling a cold shiver run down his spine, Harlan took a long pull of his whiskey, his eyes dilating as he stared into the shadowy face of Emmett Pearce.

TO BE CONTINUED

Enjoyed Treading On Ashes?

I'd love to hear your thoughts!
www.facebook.com/SteveHeuzinkveld

Find out what happens next in the series!
www.amazon.com/dp/B09G5WD4VM

Join my semi-occasional newsletter to receive an email when my
next book gets published.
https://steve-heuzinkveld.ck.page/newsletter

Can't wait that long?

Follow me on Patreon for **exclusive sneak peeks** of my next book!
www.patreon.com/SteveHeuzinkveld

ACKNOWLEDGEMENTS

First and foremost, I have to thank my beautiful wife, Hariezoy, for supporting and encouraging me every single day, and for giving me the freedom to burn the midnight oil to hit the keyboard every night until the sun comes up.

A big thanks also goes to my Patreon followers, Greg Hyndman, Rupert Lugo, J Sekula and Martin Georgiev. Your support really helped soften the impact when I was hiring professional artists for the book cover and maps, who have both done an incredible job!

But more than that, having you guys in my corner was a reminder that there are passionate people out there who really appreciate my work, and it encouraged me to continue focusing on what I love doing – creating compelling characters and stories and sharing them with the world. The world is a better place with people like you!

My heartfelt thanks goes to Ana Schaeffer and Erick Flieger for your feedback on the early chapters. You helped me set the bar for the rest of the book, and I feel blessed that you've both been part of the journey from the start!

Thanks to Les from German Creative for the stunning book cover. I only had a vague idea of what I wanted to see and she captured the exact theme I was aiming for. Thiago did an amazing job on the maps too, bringing my imaginary landscape to life.

I suppose I have to thank Emperor Dan for the countless lockdowns we've been subjected to in Melbourne Australia throughout 2020 and 2021. Without being trapped inside the house for months on end, I doubt I would have found enough time to hammer out this book.

And last but not least, thank you. As an independently-published author, this is very often a one-man show, and after the hours upon hours I've invested into this project, it means the world to me that you've taken the time to meet the characters living in my head.

I'd love to put your name here in my future books, right alongside Greg, Rupert, J-man and Martin. Join us on Patreon to speculate on the plot, share fan art and connect with me while I work on the rest of the series!

www.patreon.com/SteveHeuzinkveld

Also by Steve Heuzinkveld

When somebody goes missing, nobody ever suspects the Lizardmen.

For thousands of years, the Kirzakai have avoided all human contact.

Until now.

While their estranged father investigates a reported Lizardman sighting, Raymond and Benjamin Rauder are kidnapped and forced to work in a harsh prison on the other side of the world.

Having lost his memories during the abduction, Ray only knows one thing for certain: he doesn't belong there.

Knowing even less about their father, Ben slowly unravels the mysteries surrounding the prison and the forgotten reptilian race.

Plagued with internal strife, the Kirzakai fight against a shadow organisation, The Faction, who are intent on eliminating their species once and for all.

Embroiled in the beginnings of an all-out war, *The Rauder Brothers* struggle to escape *The Lizardmen's Pit*, but with each attempt, they are pulled further in.

Follow the link below for your next adventure!
www.amazon.com/dp/B09FZDNFRT